For Linda,

Dancing with Jou Jou

A Novel

Keep on dancing!

By

BARBARA LOUISE LEIDING

I deeply appreciate your interest in my writing. While this book may not be my best, it won't be my last.

With much love,

iUniverse, Inc.
New York   Bloomington

Barbara Louise Leiding

Dancing with Jou Jou
A Novel

Copyright © 2008 Somerset Communications LLC

All rights reserved. No part of this book may be used or reproduced by any means, graphic, electronic, or mechanical, including photocopying, recording, taping or by any information storage retrieval system without the written permission of the publisher except in the case of brief quotations embodied in critical articles and reviews.

The events depicted in this book are pure fiction. They have never occurred in real life or in any other story as far as the author knows. Names, characters, places, actions, and dialogue are either products of the author's own imagination or have been fictionalized to fit the story. No one alive or dead, two-legged, four-legged, hoofed, winged, or finned needs to be concerned about being represented in a factual or realistic manner. Just relax. Enjoy the book.

iUniverse books may be ordered through booksellers or by contacting:

iUniverse
1663 Liberty Drive
Bloomington, IN 47403
www.iuniverse.com
1-800-Authors (1-800-288-4677)

Because of the dynamic nature of the Internet, any Web addresses or links contained in this book may have changed since publication and may no longer be valid. The views expressed in this work are solely those of the author and do not necessarily reflect the views of the publisher, and the publisher hereby disclaims any responsibility for them.

ISBN: 978-0-595-52755-7 (pbk)
ISBN: 978-0-595-62807-0 (ebook)

Printed in the United States of America

iUniverse rev. date: 08/24/2009

This book is humbly dedicated to Lucy, Ricky, Ethel, and Fred. Thanks for the laughs. And the inspiration. I still watch your reruns now.

"The purpose of life is not to get to heaven, but to seek happiness on earth. And the best way to do that is to have a warm, kind heart."
—The Dalai Lama

"… Or by dancing with the ladies and picking a few pockets clean."
—Mason Samuels Otterman Figg

"Oh, quit your jabbering. Go buy a lottery ticket. I did. And look at me! I'm rich! I'm rich! I'm rich!"
—Dagmar Twist

"To tell you the truth, I just want to find my forever home."
—Valentina

"Playing tennis and drinking beer at the same time
—that would be happiness to me.
Just need to figure out where put the coaster."
—Jafford Ames

"Happiness. Hmm. I'll meditate on that, and get back to you."
—Laughing Sun

"I'd be happy if I could just find my hose."
—Vanilla John

Contents

PART ONE: GRAND MASTER PLAN 1
    Prologue: The Duck 3
    Chapter 1:   The Ladder 5
    Chapter 2:   The Deal 21
    Chapter 3:   The Gong 30
    Chapter 4:   The Conga 36
    Chapter 5:   The Cottage 39
    Chapter 6:   The Gown 58

PART TWO: MASQUERADE BALL 69
    Chapter 7:   The Haircut 71
    Chapter 8:   The Staircase 80
    Chapter 9:   The Truth 87
    Chapter 10: The Wall 93

PART THREE: NEW YORK OR BUST 105
    Chapter 11: The Beetle 107
    Chapter 12: The Tunnel 116
    Chapter 13: The Shoot 125
    Chapter 14: The Buggy 137
    Chapter 15: The Shiner 146
    Chapter 16: The Guacamole 156
    Chapter 17: The Door 166
    Chapter 18: The Headlines 176

PART FOUR: FRIENDS IN DEED 187
    Chapter 19: The OxiClean 189
    Chapter 20: The Mouthful 195
    Chapter 21: The Balls 202
    Chapter 22: The Horse 213
    Chapter 23: The Privilege 223
    Chapter 24: The Fireplace 241
    Chapter 25: The Key 247

PART FIVE: HOME IS WHERE THE TV IS 257
    Chapter 26: The Helicopter 259
    Chapter 27: The Housewives 266

Chapter 28: The Remote 272
Chapter 29: The Snobs 283
Chapter 30: The Gang..298
Epilogue: The Kids...305

PART ONE: GRAND MASTER PLAN

Prologue

The Duck

Sometimes the universe sends out a sign that's impossible to ignore—like a large, white duck named Peepers. He charged out of his private little pool behind the waterfall at Tannery Pond, flapping his wings in a rage. His quacking was loud and harsh. I thought it would never end. By the sound of it, you'd think Mason and I were poking him with a pitchfork, but neither of us had gone anywhere near the little brat, nor had we done the slightest thing that could possibly be construed as offensive—I swear it. That fussy duck was working himself into a tizzy all on his own the minute we arrived at the cottage with our luggage. Clearly, he did not want us moving in. He was probably brazen enough to believe he ruled all one hundred acres of the grand country estate known by the name of Swan Crest Farms.

I never want to see his feathered butt again.

The bitterness between us arose out of nowhere. He hated me at first sight on that fateful summer's day. I'm still trembling now, recalling how he zipped across the Great Lawn and headed directly toward us, where we were standing with a pile of boxes and bags by the cottage's front door. His head was snaking out low to the ground, his shoulders were hunched, his wings were outstretched, and his goofy, orange feet were kicking up clouds of buckwheat mulch in the rose bed as petals dropped in his wake. A hissing sound replaced his quacking as his bill flapped open and shut. I was convinced he intended to bite me.

Before I could comprehend the terror unfolding in front of us, Peepers hopped on the old millstone that served as the first step of the cottage's porch. He was strutting back and forth with a swagger in his waddle, blocking the entrance to our new, humble home. He looked up to my eyes with one of his, as if challenging me to a staring contest, and started quacking all over again.

I covered my ears. I turned to run. I wanted no part of a duck's turf war. But while I was determined to head back home to the city, Mason reached down to pet that officious beast on his puny, velvet head. And Peepers finally shut up.

Instantly, that private paradise on River Bend Road with its lush summer greens and a waterfall spilling joyfully out of Tannery Pond, returned to its natural tranquility. Sunshine was sparkling on the surface of the water where a bevy of swans floated like angels. The clouds blew away. The sky became clear. A warm breeze wafted through the air with the intoxicating aromas of apple blossoms, roses, and pine.

It couldn't possibly last. Everything changes, and rarely for the better. But I do know one thing for certain. Peepers was my sign. He had been quacking me away from danger. I just didn't realize it at the time. I wish now that I had heeded his benevolent warning and never moved into that crumbling, little house surrounded for miles by lavish country manors and officially dubbed by Dagmar and Duncan Twist as *The Cottage at Swan Crest Farms*. But moving to the country was my second mistake. Falling in love was my first.

God help me. I did love him—Mason, that is. Not Peepers.

Chapter 1

The Ladder

The perfect serenity on River Bend Road, the kind of pastoral bliss only the rich have the means to afford, was shattered by the sounds of a boogie-woogie band. Horns were wailing, drums were pounding, but none of the neighbors would complain. Regardless of the crude music invading their Ralph Lauren world, everyone within twelve square miles was arriving for Dagmar and Duncan Twist's masquerade ball.

Everyone, that is, except for Mason and me. To be blunt, we were snubbed.

I always knew in my heart that Burberry Hills wasn't our kind of place. Neither one of us was Ralph Lauren type. We were more inclined to hunt for bargains on flea market sale racks than pay top dollar at fancy boutiques. For that reason alone, in the pecking order of the social elite, we were *not* at the bottom; we simply didn't exist. Yet, despite that we were hardly welcomed at the Twists' swanky party, we could still feel the vibrations of the music echoing off the Far Hill and across the Great Lawn. As the live band was jumping and jiving, the two of us were hiding in the rhododendrons on the side of that giant house. I was holding a ladder beneath the master bedroom window. Mason was cuddling me from behind.

"Three minutes, Lucy my love," he whispered in my ear. He even dared me to time him. "Up the ladder, diamonds in my pocket, then back down the ladder I'll come."

I braced myself for his ascent, leaning into the ladder with all my body weight. It was a position that required my full concentration as if I was in yoga class doing the downward dog. My hips were hiked up, my head was poking through the bars. But Mason was taking far too long to go up, in, and back out.

"I'm ready," I whispered. "Let's go!"

I thought he would race up to the bedroom window while Dagmar and Duncan were busy greeting their guests. That was the Grand Master Plan. Instead, he started sucking the sweet spot on my neck with extra slurping noise, the sort of playful move that never failed to set my toes to wiggling. I needed to resist him; we had a schedule to keep. With all the discipline I could muster, I held my position steady, forcing myself to be stoic and still, until he finally launched.

"Pssst!" I hissed over my shoulder. "Come on!"

His hands were gliding around my thighs. They were moving to my waist. I wanted to turn around to kiss him as I felt my toes inside my boots begin a quirky dance all their own. I shivered as his hands slipped under my sweater and onto my skin, but it wasn't because they were cold. Whenever Mason touched me, I couldn't help but tingle and coo.

"Oh, Mason! Oh!"

Time stopped. For a few minutes—or was it hours—I was close to the ground. It was covered with moist leaves. I was feeling quite moist myself. My heart was thumping. Mason was, too, as flaming torches cast flickering shadows through the leaves of our camouflage. A steady stream of cars was rolling up the cobblestone driveway, while parking valets hired for the affair opened and closed heavy doors of Hummers, Range Rovers, Jaguars, and even a Rolls Royce. And Mason kept time with the band.

"Oh! Oh! Oh!"

My toes had wiggled themselves into a frenzy. Had I not been wearing boots, they would have flown off my feet, while costumed guests were swarming to Swan Crest Farms in droves—exactly the time Mason was to swipe the *ice*, as he called it. Instead, he was giving me one more kiss before breaking free from our embrace, and then he jumped to his feet, refastening his trousers. Right there in the rhododendrons, he began rocking to the music blaring from the party. He couldn't help himself. My man was born with natural rhythm. Unlike myself, dancing was in his genes, not his toes.

"That's my favorite tune," he said. "I hired those guys myself. I directed their arrangements!"

By then, I no longer wanted him to leave me for a pocketful of diamonds in the Twists' master bedroom safe. I was hoping he'd cuddle me some more, wrapping his arms around my trembling body, keeping me close and warm, and telling me that he'd love me forever. But while I was catching my breath and leaning against the ladder by myself, Mason was all keyed up.

"Listen to this!" he said.

He started singing loud and strong using his flashlight as a microphone as if he were in Swan Crest's ballroom, instead of outside by the rhododendrons—and me. I should've grabbed him by the single lock of hair that always looped out of his pompadour and reminded him that he wasn't Brian Setzer. But rather than following my instincts, I hollered at him in a whisper.

"Mason!"

I couldn't exactly shout, despite that I certainly wouldn't be heard over the band's loud music. Even if I had shouted and Mason had heard me, I knew he wouldn't stop. He was always charmed by the sound of his own voice and was singing stronger with each note.

"Hey!" I mouthed, waving my hands frantically in the air. But hand gestures were just as futile in getting Mason to simmer down.

I knew my role. We had reviewed it together every single night after dinner for weeks on end. I had taken a solemn oath to follow his directions to the letter, holding my designated position while counting out the promised three minutes, and then assure he had a stable means of escape after he got the goods. But he seemed to have forgotten his part in our little caper, because as I fumbled with my clothing, he kept on serenading me along with the squirrels and snakes that undoubtedly lurked in those rhododendrons. It took a drum solo for him to finally stop singing, but then he started thundering around the bushes with lightning-fast feet.

"Hey!" I tried again. "We're running out of time!"

Mason paused long enough to bend over backwards, dipping his head to face mine while I stayed nested in the leaves and scratchy branches along with the squirrels and snakes. I wasn't sure which spooked me more: rodents, reptiles, or Halloween. How I despise that senseless holiday.

"We'll be back home at the cottage quicker than you can say bobbing for apples," he said, looking at me upside-down. "Trust me, Lucy my love. I give you my word as a gentleman."

He uncurled himself from his backbend and grabbed the ladder, then swung it around as his wooden dance partner. I certainly wasn't jealous. Nor was I really a thief. I knew stealing is wrong. I guess I figured that the sooner we completed our mission, the sooner we could lounge in front of an open fire back at the cottage, stretching out on the bearskin rug, lingering with a shared snifter of Benedictine, while Mason would resume sucking the sweet spot on my …

But at the time, more practical matters required my attention. For starters, I could've used one of Dagmar's tennis rackets to protect me from those squirrels and snakes. To tell you the truth, perspiration was dripping from my temples despite that a chilly October wind was blowing dead leaves through the air. The thought of being caught by Dagmar Twist herself gave me the heebie-jeebies. She was one scary broad, not to mention surprisingly ill-groomed. She could've easily afforded regular trips to a day spa or had a day spa make house calls to Swan Crest Farms. But Dagmar had other priorities, none of which involved sprucing up her looks.

I wouldn't say she was exactly fat, although her short, muscular body gave the impression that she was on the plump side of thin. She actually had a regal looking face, which was appropriate considering she and her husband, Duncan, lived like royalty after becoming the biggest winners in the history of the SuperDuper Lottery. But it was her forearms, hairy enough for a gorilla, that really gave me the creeps. I cringed at her casual disregard for keeping on top of her personal grooming. Call it a hazard of my profession as a waxing salon technician, but the vision of being captured by those unsightly limbs was enough to give me second thoughts about our diamond heist that evening. Couldn't she have worn long sleeves or elbow-length gloves?

"They're just lottery winners," Mason had said when he was trying to convince me to go along with his Grand Master Plan. It was as if that fact alone justified our intended crime. He could tell that the entire concept wasn't sitting right with me from the start. He knew me intimately and well just as I knew him. Or so I had thought.

"Relax, Lucy my love," he had assured me. "You worry too much. The Twists will never suspect a thing. They'll be too busy dancing the night away with their new rich friends."

I wished I could be as confident as Mason and half as jolly. While I was kicking the leaves of my camouflage checking for squirrels and snakes, he kept dipping and gyrating with the ladder, making it come alive as it dipped and gyrated along with him.

"Besides, think of it this way," I remember him saying. "We helped finance the Twists' fortune ourselves with all the lottery tickets we've bought. The way I figure it, they owe us. It's payback time. I want my cut."

How could I have fought logic like that? Mason was not only more confident and happier than I ever was, he was smarter than me, too. He even had better taste. He was the one who selected the clothes he thought I should wear and instructed me to put them on. I have to admit, his styling was impeccable. He was blessed with a keen artist's eye and always knew the perfect outfit to wear no matter the occasion, despite that neither one of us could afford Ralph Lauren.

On the evening of the Grand Master Plan, Mason had me dress up in all black from head to toe and wrap my long hair tight around my head so it would fit underneath my big, black hat. Then he had me flip the brim: one side up, the other down. When I turned around for him to give me the once-over, I knew he was pleased with his creation. He was nodding with approval. But it was more than that. He paid me the highest compliment an artist, master craftsman, and accomplished forger ever offers.

"You look authentic, Lucy my love."

Authentic. That was Mason's favorite word. He told me he fully intended to trademark it someday, for it was a fitting description not only of his artistic masterpieces, of which there were many, but also of our love. He did love me and I loved him. Our romance wasn't a fling. It was real. Just twelve hours earlier, before we had even eaten breakfast, he had pulled me back to bed—twice. Then that tingly sensation you feel, the kind that sends waves of warmth all over your body and lasts the entire day, is what gave me courage to follow through with our mission.

"The meadow stompers are the perfect touch!" Mason had said.

I'll confess. I had grown accustomed to wearing my mud boots, which Mason liked to call meadow stompers. A bit clunky perhaps, but they were actually quite practical whenever I fed the animals on the Twists' land or poked around the chicken coop searching for eggs. Those boots came in handy, too, whenever we—Dagmar, Duncan, Mason, and myself—waded into the shallow waters of Tannery Pond for our weekly snapping turtle battle.

I had no choice in the matter. We always did whatever the Twists asked—Dagmar more than Duncan. When you live in a cottage on the lower grounds of their estate, the lines of power are clearly drawn. If Dagmar Twist barked out orders, Mason and I carried them out or there'd be hell to pay. I'd do just about anything to keep the peace; it was far better than listening to her squawk. Besides, the Twists were our employers now, ones with a passion for raising all kinds of animals. I didn't get it. I never saw any reason for collecting so many of those creatures that, if you ask me, belonged behind bars in a zoo. But then I wasn't the one who had been blessed with so much loot. It wasn't my choice as to how to spend it.

I wished the Twists had been the kind of millionaires who were satisfied sipping tea from dainty china cups whenever they weren't throwing lavish parties, because I certainly never enjoyed our foursome's peculiar pond ritual that Peepers always watched. It wasn't my idea, nor did I ever fathom that a genteel animal farm posed daily struggles of life and death. Foxes lunched on chickens. Blue heron dove for fish. And Dagmar Twist went to combat with snappers in the pond. She said we needed to assure the safety of her twenty-two swans and assigned each of us a paddle. Armed with long planks of well buffed wood, we'd step through the water like a playtime army of G.I. Joes and Janes. Our orders were to maintain the grace and beauty of Tannery Pond and keep Swan Crest Farms pristine. No snapping turtles allowed.

As soon as one of us eyed a giant reptile swimming past our knees, we'd signal with our paddles charging the air. Then Dagmar would give the official command and blow her whistle, shouting, "Hit 'em! Hit 'em!" and the four of us would attack. We'd start slapping the water silly, aiming directly for the enemy's head, not just its shell. We needed to make certain the intruder was completely knocked out, no longer capable of gobbling up a precious swan.

Dagmar herself assumed the distinct honor of hauling the poor, defeated snapper out of the pond, hoisting it over her shoulder, holding onto its hind feet, and letting its limp head dangle. Then she'd entrust the spoils to Mason, ordering him to whip up another batch of what he called Victory Stew. Peepers would second the motion with a few loud quacks.

The difference between the rest of the group and me wasn't only that I alone passed on eating the stew; nor was it that I alone deliberately missed slapping a turtle directly on its scaly head. It was also that while they all wore meadow stompers that were solid black, mine had yellow stripes on the rims. That's the problem with having big feet. The only pair of boots that fit me were secondhand. Mason had discovered the right-foot boot in a dumpster behind the abandoned firehouse in town; he fished out the left-foot boot with a stick from the crevice between that same dumpster and the rotting picket fence surrounding it. Go figure. They fit.

"Yes, indeed!" Mason had said as we were dressing for our mission. He held out my mud boots at arm's length and motioned for me to put them on. "It's important to appear normal. We need to blend into Swan Crest as if this were just an ordinary night."

But nothing at Swan Crest Farms—that last chunk of prized land carved out of the elitist Village of Burberry Hills, that seemingly enchanted haven where humming birds drew nectar from honeysuckles all the long day and butterflies fluttered through the sky without a care in the world that they'd ever be net, that rare country enclave sought after by Wall Street bankers, world leaders, rock stars, supermodels, an Internet mogul, exiled royalty from an exotic, foreign land, defrocked CEOs sprung from prison, assorted television personalities, a couple of trendsetting heiresses, a famous tennis player with more product endorsements than Tiger Woods, and exactly two lottery winners named Dagmar and Duncan Twist——none of it seemed the least bit ordinary or normal to me.

Maybe it was all too pretty. It lacked a certain, well, *authenticity* to be real. All around me hinted at Disneyland handiwork, where everything was bigger and more dazzling than necessary, and everyone—two-legged, four-legged, hoofed, winged, or finned—was not merely a hog's breath off-center; I'd say that the entire neighborhood on River Bend Road was a masterful illusion erected with mirrors, paper-mâché, and spray paint. It was all too beautiful to be real. I never fit in. I knew it early on. I simply didn't belong, not when all the housekeepers in the neighborhood rode golf carts down cobblestone driveways to collect the mail, and the *Battle of the Snapping Turtles* at Swan Crest was the sport of the week.

But if I looked beyond the well trimmed hedges rising and falling along the gentle curves of River Bend Road, if I ignored the infuriating whir of electric golf carts, if I managed to stop wondering if a professional tree inspector had been hired to assure that rows of poplars were perfectly uniform in having exactly the same number of leaves, if I could hold back the persistent tickle in my nose to stop sneezing from a mix of pollen and animal dander that infiltrated the grounds of Swan Crest, if I were being totally honest—and usually I am whenever I'm not leaning a ladder against the side of a country mansion—I know in my heart that, save for turtles who bite, Dagmar, Duncan, and certainly Mason genuinely adored all the creatures that howled, whinnied, growled, mooed, grunted, and clucked on the Twists' land—or as they took pride in calling it, the *farm*. By whatever name they wanted to call it, if you ask me, those useless beasts trampling the grounds would still stink.

Their love of animals eluded me with the one and only exception of our cat, Cuban Pete, but even I had to admit that the Twists' lavish pile of bricks was an architectural wonder. Strangers who'd pass by always stopped in their tracks and gawked at the sight of the manor house sitting majestically on the highest peak of Swan Crest. They might've overlooked the little cottage on the edge of River Bend Road that Mason and I called home with our cat, but they unfailingly gazed beyond the waterfall where a bevy of twenty-two swans were often seen floating in formation on the pond, and up to Dagmar and Duncan's digs in the distance, staring at that fanciful dwelling far longer than at any of the other mega-mansions on our street.

Swan Crest was the kind of place you simply cannot get out of your mind's movie screen. Flocks of onlookers stepping out of minivans with children in tow every Sunday afternoon, paused long enough to pull out cell phones and cameras. You'd think they had just stumbled into Egypt and were seeing the pyramids the way they'd keep shooting the Twists' palace from all angles. But I couldn't really blame them. When I first saw Swan Crest my mouth stopped rambling the way it always did whenever Mason and I were together, which was nearly all the time. I simply could no longer speak. I thought the massive structure was a resort hotel, not a home for two people. The windows alone would require a team of full-time window washers. But that's the difference between the Twists and me. I was the sort of person who'd prefer living in small quarters if it meant doing less housework.

Mason never worried about such things. He said that he could easily picture us living in a castle like that someday. He said that he fully intended for us to do so. He told me that we'd hire help to wash all the windows while we'd be free to sit by the pool counting the butterflies in the sky and sipping fruity concoctions in large crystal glasses with tiny umbrellas speared into shaved ice, and that our personal wait staff would serve them to us on shiny silver trays.

I laughed. I thought Mason was joking. It never occurred to me to have such dreams. When you grow up as an orphan shuffled from one foster home to another, the only wealth you long for is the kind that arises from hearing "Happy Birthday" sung by people who actually remember your name. Besides, I was close to broke much of the time. I never imagined myself living any other way. Waxing legs, upper lips, bikini lines, and an occasional back—I always managed to make a living before Mason moved us to the boondocks. I never worried about money. I knew I could depend on another hirsute client waiting in line for my services. I had a stellar reputation in my chosen field. Counting up tips and pocket change was my daily habit. I never went hungry. I always collected enough at least to buy soup. Campbell's was good, but Progresso was better. With a coupon, six cans sell for five dollars. As long as it didn't include snapping turtle body parts, I was quite fond of soup.

I suppose I wasn't like most people, at least not those who showed up to gawk at the Twist estate or the ones who R.S.V.P.'d for the big Halloween bash. For starters, I never felt the urge to dress up in a costume. I didn't see the point in setting up torch lights on the cobblestone driveway when they'd only need to be taken down the next day. But Dagmar had insisted. They had been one of Mason's brilliant creative concepts. Dagmar pounced. Mason set to work. He installed the torch lights at carefully measured intervals beginning at River Bend Road by the gatehouse where a security guard was stationed for the evening, past the humble cottage where Mason and I lived with Cuban Pete, and extending all the way up to the portico at the Twists' manor house perched at Swan Crest's crown.

Those sticks of fire weren't intended to light the way for trick-or-treaters, for there wouldn't be any in a village like Burberry Hills. I never knew that fifty miles outside of Manhattan, houses were formidable enough to be named instead of numbered. Free candy or not, twenty minute hikes to ring doorbells while wearing costumes and plastic masks were hardly worth a sack of Tootsie Rolls®. Instead, the torches Mason strategically positioned on the driveway were intended to create the proper atmosphere for what had been engraved on formal invitations as *Swan Crest Farms' First Annual Masquerade Ball.*

Strictly adults. No kids invited. And certainly not Peepers. But if you ask me, the only difference between children yearning for free candy and grownups jammed into Swan Crest's ballroom that regrettable evening wasn't a need for a sugar high. My best guess is that the reason so many people showed up for the Twists' party was a mass craving to see the inside of Dagmar and Duncan's great big house.

Lottery winners can be extravagant. Easy money is quickly spent. New friends seem to emerge out of nowhere when one is well heeled. Dagmar herself would openly admit that no matter the source, money commands respect. After all, $469 million from the SuperDuper Lottery is hardly on par with winning a free Coke® from a bottle cap sweepstakes. Free money or a free soda, for a single buck, the investment is the same. One dollar paid off handsomely for the Twists. Common sense would tell you that the rest of their lives would run amazingly well. Dagmar claimed she deserved it.

Thanks to their lucky numbers, the Twists had ample resources to build a country palace in Burberry Hills and give their new digs a name. To assure Swan Crest's rightful place in *Architectural Digest* and solidify the Twists' newly-found position in what Dagmar called the "upper crust crowd," the couple hired Mason to be the estate's official artist-in-residence in charge of procuring show-off treasures from all over the world. They even offered him the old cottage to live in, an odd relic of a place left intact on the grounds. I was just part of the deal, like a free toy that you don't really need or like when your mouth is hungering for a Whopper. Compared to Mason, I was the plastic, he was the beef.

We could hear the band concluding its first number. Mason took a bow alongside the ladder. Before climbing up as he had planned, he reminded me about the best reason to go along with the heist. He probably sensed that his dawdling had given me time to have cold feet. He was right in more ways than one.

"If you really want us to afford a baby, we'll haul in enough loot in three minutes to have ten," he said. "You still want a big family, Lucy my love. *Dunchu?*"

How could I possibly say no to that? I patted by belly, hoping to feel a tiny kick, an echo of a burp, a sensation of warmth, a vibration that hadn't been inside me before—anything to assure me that a new life had begun. Instead, I felt only hope.

I don't mean to make excuses for myself. What's wrong is wrong. Baby or not, I should never have allowed Mason to rope me into one of his screwball plans. He had plenty of them, believe me. He was forever kissing up to Dagmar and even Duncan. Then when the couple was out of sight, he was scribbling new ideas into a clothbound notebook, pleased with himself for being clever and original. That much I'll give him credit for. No one more than my Mason had the rare combination of brains-plus-guts to dream up a Grand Master Plan as wacky as the one he called Project Peepers.

Yup. Mason named our diamond heist for that stupid duck, for out of all the animals the Twists possessed, it was Peepers who was the prince of Swan Crest. He had even told Dagmar and Duncan that their most recent acquisition, a rare pair of blue diamonds, was known as *Blue Diamond Peepers,* and educated the couple about how diamonds of that color were only found in certain parts of the world, such as Australia, Brazil, and some of the western and southern countries of Africa. He claimed that the ones he purchased on their behalf had originated in the Congo, and that he had negotiated the record-setting price of $17 million at the diamond dealers' annual, four-day trade show in Switzerland.

"Where you bought that chocolate? When are you going back?"

"Lucy my love," Mason had said, inhaling and exhaling and stretching his arms out as if he was bored. "When you have the wherewithal to buy a rare, blue, six karat, round diamond for $6.5 million—and another one for $6.5 million—and they're as identical as twins, adding a premium of $4 million to the total purchase price—you can bathe in enough Swiss chocolate to keep you sweet for life."

We never did fill up a bathtub with Swiss chocolate. We had other priorities on the night of the masquerade ball. I was peering at Mason through the leaves of the rhododendrons as he was telling me for the millionth time about the intricate details of the scheme. I think he was giving me the hard sell for following through with my promise to be his accomplice in swiping the Blue Diamond Peepers from Dagmar's dressing room safe—switching them with copies, which Mason called *Authentic Baubles.*

"Genius! Pure bloody genius," Mason was saying as I shivered in the shrubbery. "Even if anything goes awry, the insurance company will pay out big time," he said. "The Twists will recoup the losses and still cause Donald Trump to flex his furry eyebrows. But the best part about it all, Lucy my love, is that you and I will be rich, too!"

I must've looked at him kind of funny. My brain was working overtime. I wasn't the one who was good with figures. I had no clue as to why a pair of shiny rocks was worth so much, even if they were round, blue, and twin.

"Put your mind at ease, Lucy my love," Mason said as a small spider jumped out of the bushes. It shot up my nose. I snorted fiercely out of one nostril, while using two fingers to clamp the other nostril shut. Without skipping a beat, Mason pulled a linen handkerchief from his pocket, and then led me out of my camouflage as I kept snorting to clear out that eight-legged pest.

"I drew up the appraisal papers myself," Mason said, gently squeezing my nose and instructing me to blow. "We'll all win!" he shouted as he folded the newly-moistened cloth into a neat square then stuffed it into *my* pocket. "Nobody loses! Trust me!"

The band was revving up with a brand-new number. Mason seemed to be revving up, too, stepping in place and jerking his head, gearing up for a jitterbug. He clasped my hand in his and tried twirling me around, but I got all tangled up and landed in the bushes on my rump. Mason effortlessly lifted me back to my toes, then spun me around once more—this time guiding my hips with his free hand and picking dead leaves from my hair and off my clothes.

"You've got to trust me, Lucy my love," he said. "Follow my lead."

He placed my fallen hat back on top of my head, and fiddled with the brim until the angles pleased him. As I regained my footing, he was smiling. His arms were outstretched like an eagle's wings. I couldn't help but give in. There was something about his joyful eyes he'd occasionally pop out that reassured me that everything would be alright. But as he covered my face with tiny kisses and drew me close, I was still percolating over how he had gone through the monumental lengths to plan Project Peepers and how I had promised to play a role. Before I had a fleeting moment to consider backing out of the caper, he embraced me so tight, I thought he wanted to make love right there in the rhododendrons. Again.

"Lucy," he whispered in my ear. "You'll finally have your forever home. And a whole lot of kids! They'll be yours—and mine. We'll have a family of our own," he said. "Together. You and me. That *is* what you truly want, *dunchu?*"

Before I could respond in a breathless, *"You know I do!"* he started kissing me so deeply, he was practically lapping my tonsils. It was far too late to renege on my promise, because he no sooner pulled his tongue back into his own mouth than he zipped up the ladder—and without my steadying the base.

In an instant, he was gone.

I was left all alone.

Mason's saliva was wet on my lips.

I stepped back through the rhododendrons and resumed my designated position. We were in this scheme together. I wasn't going to break my promise. I vowed to play my role. Besides, I liked being needed. I liked being loved. I liked how Mason lapped my, uh, tonsils.

The promised three minutes rolled into twenty until an entire hour had passed. I didn't get it. Mason had masterminded what would be the means for us to begin a family and start a new life. Together. So what the heck was going on? Why wasn't Mason following his own script? He had assured me that he had chased away all the squirrels and snakes. He had rehearsed me on how to kneel down and lean into the ladder. At long last, the Grand Master Plan was in motion.

What was the hold up *now*?

I needed to recall every word he had uttered that led to my unfortunate predicament. Had I listened closely enough? Didn't he tell me three minutes? What had I missed?

"Up the ladder, diamonds in my pocket, then back down the ladder …"

I started muttering the phrase he had given me over and over: *"Bobbing for apples, bobbing for apples, bobbing for…"* Hadn't he told me that we'd high tail it out of there and head back to the cottage faster than I could say that? I tried to be patient. I even tried humming along with the Brian Setzer tunes that were blasting from the party. I needed to settle my nerves. I could feel the vibrations of that band through the bars of my ladder. My protruding hips seemed to be moving to the beat all on their own.

It wasn't until Peepers started quacking and I turned my head, nearly decapitating myself in the ladder's rungs, that I realized I had been discovered. That duck was flapping his wings and quacking so loud, he caused me to let out a yelp that to this very day is echoing in my ear drums like a primal wound. The sight of his two blue eyes alone, flashing in my face up close and personal as he fluttered his wings and sprang up to me on the ladder, was enough to spook me for life.

"Mason!"

I couldn't hang around much longer. Grand Master Plan or not, I desperately needed quick cover. That nasty beast Peepers was hovering in the air like a feathered helicopter trying to make a landing on my nose.

"Quack! Quack! Quack!"

I know now that I should have had more respect for the little noisemaker. He spotted trouble in places where I was blind.

"Quack! Quack! Quack!"

But instead of paying attention to his instinctual alarm, I pulled my big, black hat tighter on my head and retracted my face into the folds of my turtle neck sweater. I tore up the ladder to where the bedroom window was wide open. But when I reached the top, I didn't know which was worse: the threat of being attacked by a raging duck or seeing what Mason was doing inside Dagmar and Duncan's master bedroom suite while facing a tri-fold mirror.

I couldn't believe my eyes ...

In an instant, all of hell was emptying out, when mere minutes earlier I had the safety of the rhododendrons. Had I paid more attention in high school English class, I would've known that Shakespeare had declared centuries ago that hell was already empty. The devils are here. I suppose, in this century, one of them took the form of a quacking duck—at least on a night like Halloween. As I watched Mason through the window, I was hoping that he, too, wasn't ...

Dare I say it? Was Mason really the man who loved me? The one who wanted to be the father of my children? Was Mason, along with Peepers—not to mention Dagmar and Duncan—and all of Swan Crest—actually possessed on that night of the Twists' ball?

Take it from me. I may not know anything about diamonds or large-eyed ducks. I couldn't begin to explain all the ins and outs of insurance claims or calculate the odds for winning a lottery. Don't quiz me on my knowledge of the delicate balance between snapping turtles and a bevy of mute swans that floated like an angel dance troupe hovering over the waterfall tumbling out of Tannery Pond. But I do know that yoga class pays off well. I was holding onto the top of the ladder with more endurance than I ever had for a sun salutation. I could hardly go back down to the ground where Peepers was eager to bite me. But I wasn't sure I had the nerve to enter the Twists' bedroom either. I was simply at a loss as to what to do.

I was frozen by indecision as the nippy country wind was kicking up again. Dead leaves were shaking off their branches and showering over my head as I held on tight to the ladder. I could see leaves chasing each other in the twilight while I cowered under the brim of my hat. They were colliding in mid-air and scattering aimlessly through the darkening sky. I couldn't help thinking how lucky they were to abandon their posts when I needed to hold fast to my own.

I know now that I was a dope. I stayed true to Mason. I believed in him. I believed we had an *us*. And I longed for a baby. When you grow up without real parents or blood siblings, the prospect of having a family that would last for a lifetime is far more valuable than a rare set of twin blue diamonds. I know now that I'm not like other people, because as far as I was concerned, Project Peepers was never about the money. I really didn't care about how much of it a couple of lottery champions like Dagmar and Duncan Twist had won. All I cared about was my love for Mason. I just wanted the two of us to have a kid. Or ten.

I was in a pickle. I winced as if brine were stinging my eyes. I debated whether to go in through the window or back down to the rhododendrons. Some sights are too absurd to process in an instant.

My feet were trembling …

The music was blaring …

The wind was blowing …

Leaves were flying …

Peepers was quacking …

And Mason was …

I couldn't help myself. I could hardly comprehend what my eyes saw Mason doing in the Twists' private quarters. I stood at the top of that ladder with one hand on my hat and the other on the windowsill. Some sounds are organic. I called out with the loudest scream I never knew I had in me, and this time it was *not* in a whisper.

"Maaaaa-sssson!"

"Quack! Quack! Quack!"

CHAPTER 2

The Deal

I never intended to move to the country. I was a city girl. I never realized before how monotonous it was to see so much green instead of concrete. Trees, lawns, and one slimy swan-and-turtle pond—I never should have allowed Mason to pull me away from New York City. It was our native habitat. Maybe a studio apartment over a frame gallery wasn't paradise to other people, but I'm *not* convinced that true happiness can be accompanied by fleas and ticks.

"Another tick bite, Lucy my love?" Mason asked me one night after dinner at the cottage. "You must have tasty blood. Hang on! I'll fetch the smoker."

I was in the middle of reading an article in the latest issue of *Waxing World Journal* when Mason heard me slapping my thigh. He dropped his notebook and the pencil he was using to put the final touches on his Grand Master Plan, then he raced to the furnace room for an appliance he said was used by professional beekeepers. If smoke could paralyze bees long enough to collect honey from hives, he proclaimed, it could work miracles on tasty legs like mine. All I needed to do later was remove the tiny pests out of my pores with a pair of tweezers. Or with a slathering of hot wax that was cooled, then yanked off with linen strips.

I never minded all the smoke that poured out of Mason's beekeeper's device; Cuban Pete seemed to enjoy getting lost in the haze, too, as he wandered out of the furnace room. For me, that billowing cloud always made me feel like Barbara Eden from *I Dream of Genie* as Mason primed and pumped his tin lamp long enough to fill up the cottage's tiny living room.

Cuban Pete watched, mesmerized by the sight of magical smoke swirling in front of his red pupils. I can't speak for our cat, whose primary job was to keep an eye on Mason's growing collection of *Authentic Baubles* stored in glass bins in the furnace room, but I know I always felt soothed. Maybe I was never on the receiving end of loving hands when I was still an orphaned kid and now couldn't get my fill as a grown-up; maybe I liked how determined Mason was to come to my rescue and keep my legs unmarred by tick bites. As an added measure, Mason smoked Cuban Pete, too, before sending him back to guard the furnace room.

Whatever the reason that I tolerated Mason's magic lamp maneuver, getting smoked while spinning around on my toes, navigating the fluff of the bearskin rug by the fireplace, stretching my arms up high and touching the beams in the low ceiling as Mason kept pumping his smoker and puffed-puffed-puffed, I knew that when I consented to move to Swan Crest Farms, I was doing my part to help Mason just as he always did his part to help me. I wanted his career to flourish. While it is true that there are more art galleries and museums in the Big Apple than you can flick wet paint at from an artist's camel hair brush, funding from private patrons like the Twists with deep pockets and praise for Mason's artistic expressions, was a rare find. There was simply no choice in the matter. I supported my man. We bid for a Kitty-Karry bag on eBay for Cuban Pete, locked up our city apartment, and made the cottage our home.

Trouble was, Dagmar hadn't been keen on the idea of me moving into the cottage, too. She had fidgeted for a few minutes and looked me up and down.

"You two married?"

"No," Mason said.

"Don't tell me she's pregnant."

Cuban Pete let out a loud meow and scratched on the walls of his portable home. It wasn't exactly the sturdiest valise; just paisley vinyl with a lot of air holes.

"You don't want to be tricked into becoming a father before your time, now do you, Mason? There's a lot of that going around these days. You really need to be careful."

Hissing sounds were now emanating from Cuban Pete's direction—and mine. He was clawing the heck out of the paisley vinyl. But neither of us had any choice. We had to stand by Mason. We had to endure Dagmar's poor manners. The future of his art career depended upon our cooperation and tolerance for Dagmar's outrageous remarks. I just wished she was equipped with volume control. That voice! So loud! So screechy! Strap Dagmar to the hood of a fire truck and she'd scare off squirrels for miles.

"You have nothing to worry about," Mason said as if my intended motherhood was any of Dagmar's business.

"Good thing I nipped *that* one in the bud, right here and right now," Dagmar said. "You did read about those seventeen girls in Massachusetts who made a pact to get pregnant at the same time, didn't you? It was all over the news. How old is *she*, anyway?" Dagmar said pointing at me as I squatted down to pet Cuban Pete through the Kitty-Karry.

"Don't worry. She's legal."

I never heard our meek cat growling before. I never encountered anyone like Dagmar who would talk about me as if I weren't in the room, not since I was a foster care child listening to social workers speculating on my next home. It seems we all have our own karma. History was repeating itself in the Twists' main living room in the mansion. I had seen a lot of living rooms in my journey through the system, some spiffy and some shabby, but I had never seen one with as many sofas as there are displayed at Ikea, only none of the Twists' sofas were covered in cotton and none of them were solid white or block stamped with large, orange flowers.

Instead, fine tapestries, silks, and even suede were upholstered on pairs of sofas that sat back to back, forming enough seating areas to accommodate a party of more than a hundred guests. Leather side chairs in colors of midnight, blood, and hunter were studded with gold nails and strewn into the mix, while a concert grand Steinway piano anchored it all in the center. Royal palm trees standing in porcelain planters soared up to the top of a three story atrium. A solid wall of glass was the only thing separating us and a panoramic view of twenty-two majestic swans all dressed up in formal white feathers and daintily gliding in procession across the luminous waters of Tannery Pond. Even Cuban Pete would've been impressed, had he not been stuffed and zipped inside paisley vinyl.

"You should be playing the field, Mason! A good looking guy like you should be sowing your seeds. I could divorce old Duncan here, then you and I could see what comes up."

Was Duncan deaf? He didn't move or say a single word. He looked much older than the rest of us and seemed lonely, forlorn, wistful. Put that poor man on a street bench in New York City, he'd be one of the nameless waiting for a bus.

I chomped furiously on my bubble gum. It was either that or take up smoking. I needed to keep my mouth busy. I feared what might shoot out of it that would surely blow Mason's chances for career advancement. I knelt down to calm Cuban Pete in his valise as he was still rumbling and the paisley vinyl was puffing in and out. I unzipped the bag. He shot out in a flash, finding a safe haven beneath my waist-length hair and draping his long, furry body around my neck like a stole. I rose slowly to my feet again, careful to keep my balance, as he twitched his tail around to my face.

But I didn't miss the sight of Dagmar smiling at Mason. She was bobbing around in her leather chair as if she were clenching the cheeks of her bottom in an attempt to prevent an embarrassing sound from escaping. She might've had a genetic tendency for flatulence, but I really wouldn't know. I wasn't part of her family. Being an orphan, I always wondered about other people's gene pools. I was envious of those who could note clear signs of a common heritage and take comfort in actually knowing their family members. To me, family knowledge was a blessing. Some people are born lucky to be sewn together on the same quilt, while some of us are misplaced patches.

Whatever the reason Dagmar kept flipping and flopping in that slippery leather chair, at first, it didn't occur to me that her jerky movements were her way of flirting. Could it be possible that Dagmar was actually trying to seduce Mason while *posing*? Was she brash enough to believe she would be attractive to my man? She was holding her hands behind her head, fluttering her eyelashes, and heaving out her massive chest, displaying her large, droopy bosoms. She should've tightened up her bra straps.

I couldn't help noticing that despite all their money, both Dagmar and Duncan were dressed in ratty farm clothes appropriate for feeding their hundreds of animals, yet Dagmar had on an eye-popping blue diamond broach in the shape of a small duck that resembled Peepers adorning her tattered sweatshirt. The sleeves were pushed up to her raw elbows, revealing a Rolex watch along with a flashy set of gold and bejeweled bangles clanging around her hairy forearms. I thought I'd be doing her a favor if I offered to give them a wax—her arms, that is. Not the watch and bangles.

"Quit chewing that gum! It's so low class!"

Dagmar abruptly snapped out of her posing mode as I chewed my wad with increasing furry. Perhaps I should only put one piece in my mouth at a time from now on, not three. I had once earned the title of Bubble Champ in a foster home. But a jealous kid had popped the winning bubble with a pencil. I couldn't see who it was; it was hard to see with gum in my eyes.

"No bubble-popping allowed! This is a respectable neighborhood. I'll have none of that gum-chewing here at Swan Crest. What would people think?"

People? Like who? I hadn't noticed a single soul when the Twists' car service drove us through town—or as the driver corrected me, the *Village,* for that was the official moniker of Burberry Hills. We had turned left onto River Bend Road just past the third tree stump from the main district of a *village* that only consisted of a small church, a general store, a train depot and a fire station that was apparently brand new. The banner across the single garage door announced as much. It wasn't until we veered onto our new street that we saw houses—all mansions with high iron fences and small, tasteful signs that announced their names. But no people were in sight. What war was Dagmar fighting? She needed to mellow out. Gum would help.

"I'm only financing *one* person to live at the cottage, not *two*. When I'm the one doling out the big bucks, I call the shots. Don't forget it!"

Ah. I finally got it. Money. That—along with her obvious attraction to my man—was the *it* Dagmar was so worked up about. But it seemed to me that money didn't buy her manners. She seemed to be talking to me as if I were a naughty child, but it took no time at all for her to be hot on Mason.

I was accustomed to women lighting up the moment they'd see my handsome boyfriend. He was always offering to help our female neighbors back home in the city. He'd carry packages up to their apartments and even stay long enough to fix a leaky faucet, he'd tell me, or tighten up the screws of a crooked curtain rod. Then he'd stay longer to accept their gracious hospitality. He'd gobble up their homemade goodies whether they were good or not, and always thanked them appropriately, he'd say. He even gave dancing lessons to a shy teenage girl—and her mother. They were so grateful, Mason told me, that each had insisted on posing with him for a picture, just like all the other ladies on our block had. Mason had an entire collection. He pasted them into a series of photo albums he kept on a shelf.

No doubt about it: Mason's reputation for being the most thoughtful—not to mention handsome—man was well deserved. It never surprised me that women swooned. Dagmar was not the first one to be dazzled by Mason. He had polished manners. His mother did an excellent job raising her son to be a true gentleman. But he told me that his gift for dancing was in the genes.

"Yeah, sure, okay," Dagmar finally said, nodding her head as if she had been spellbound by Mason's palpitating rhythm. He was tapping his foot and slightly rocking his hips to the music playing softly in that great big house. It was Mason's movements that persuaded Dagmar to grant the *tagalong*, as she called me, permission to move into the cottage, too.

Oh, joy. I was approved.

Cuban Pete's rumbling was settling down, but I could still feel his vibrations around my neck. He wasn't exactly purring. He sounded more like a buzz saw that was charging up before chopping down a tree. I didn't want to disturb him any more than he already had been, so I swallowed my wad of gum instead of spitting it out, while Dagmar ticked off a list of stipulations for living at the cottage, all of which involved me.

How much experience did I have, Dagmar asked Mason as if I weren't standing alongside him, in feeding goats baby bottles filled with fresh, warmed milk? Did I know how to efficiently collect eggs without breaking their shells or infuriating a Bolivian rooster? How much knowledge did I have in the proper care of a koi pond? And one pedigreed duck named Peepers? Did I possess sufficient agility to balance myself on slippery, algae-covered pond boulders? And did Mason believe that a skinny twig like me had the muscle to wield a heavy paddle? Was my eyesight sharp enough to spot snapping turtles swimming underwater before one attacked her swans?

I thought Dagmar was joking. But this time, the only one laughing in the room was me as Mason held his eye contact steady, assuring Dagmar none of that would pose a problem.

"None of what?" I blurted out.

I was stunned by the sudden shift of subjects. Cuban Pete must've been, too, since his motor was revving up all over again. But Mason was swift and slick. Without so much as a hiccup, he expertly redirected the topic of discussion from the farm work Dagmar expected me to do, to the subject of the cottage where we were to live. He was saying that he had no objection whatsoever to us moving in and was glad that the Twists hadn't knocked down the little house when they purchased the property to build Swan Crest. The puny size of the dwelling didn't bother him; when you're accustomed to living in a walk-up studio in New York City, he told Dagmar, it'd be a luxury to have two floors and windows on all four sides of an actual house.

I didn't mind the size of the cottage either, not that anyone seemed interested in asking for my opinion. And I liked that we would have lots of natural light. But the architectural style of the cottage—*that* did bug me. I don't know what it was officially labeled, but I'm sure Tinker Bell would feel right at home there shacking up with one of Santa's elves.

Mason wasn't displeased by the architecture of that humble abode, nor was he bothered by the cottage's age. He said that *prewar*, a term used to describe a building constructed prior to World War II in Manhattan, would mean *before the American Revolution* when applied to the cottage. He wasn't too far off base. But his hesitation to accept Dagmar's offer to be the artist-in-residence wasn't the age, size, or style of what would be our new home. The trouble was, Mason wasn't satisfied with the modest stipend Dagmar initially proposed for the job. In fact, he didn't care for the job title, at least not all by itself.

Mason suggested adding *Global Curator for the Advancement of Fine Taste* to his business card. He told Dagmar that if she expected him to contribute not only to the artistic value of Swan Crest, but also travel the world in search of the finest treasures to do so, he should be granted an appropriate designation, which naturally justified raising his base salary, he said. Commissions and quarterly bonuses, he told her, would be charged as his artistic enhancements progressed. No need, he assured her, to worry about paying them up front.

"Trust," Mason declared, "is a crucial ingredient when important artistic goals are at stake. It's a two-way channel," he said still rocking his hips and penetrating Dagmar with his eyes. "Collaboration is unquestionably essential when one considers the long-term impact of building a legacy, such as the one you envision for Swan Crest."

Then Mason went in for a grand pause, which raised his compensation even more. He said later that pausing allowed his words to sink into Dagmar's thick, yet pliable head. He told me that with Dagmar, shifting the power over to his side was as easy as swiping a banana from a little, hairy ape. I guess he, too, had noticed her unsightly arms.

"Make no mistake," Mason asserted. "Swan Crest Farms deserves only the finest appointments salvaged, auctioned, and purchased from a treasure trove of sources around the world. We must pay attention—and this is crucial—to quality, taste, and authenticity. If you intend to compromise on my three-pronged selection criteria for Swan Crest's artistic acquisitions, then I'm not your man. I shall leave at once." Then Mason fell silent again.

Dagmar would've saved herself a chunk of money had she broken Mason's silence sooner, for just as I thought she was about to bounce out of her chair and latch onto my boyfriend with some sort of unspeakable gorilla foreplay, Mason walked out of the living room and kept on going. He didn't look back. He never said good-bye, not even to me and Cuban Pete.

I noticed Dagmar's eyes widening. I could see red rising in her face as Duncan's face grew paler. Then that bossy dame, Dagmar, proved she was powerful, alright. She ran as fast and yelled as loud as an ape hungering after a banana.

"Stop! Mason! Wait!"

Mason's power play worked. He hedged his bet well. The Twists consented. They signed the papers. Mason already had them drawn up. They met his sky high price while I was designated as a farmhand who was required to earn her keep by selling eggs at a roadside stand and working the grounds of Swan Crest Farms. But there was no question about it in my heart or my mind: my Mason was a rare talent. He'd sized up Dagmar in an instant. Cheapskate or spendthrift. She could've gone to either extreme, Mason said, for Dagmar had no center.

Unfortunately, Dagmar must've been covered with farm animal dander that did not agree with Cuban Pete. It was a good thing the ink was already dry on Mason's contract, because as soon as we were leaving with Cuban Pete still rumbling and still draped around my shoulders, Dagmar, true to form, insisted on having the last word.

"You have a lot of eggs to collect, missy," she said to me. "You must not be a slacker. You'll need to pay your rent in full and on time. And make sure you remember to take the pill. Don't you dare miss a single day. The cottage wasn't built to accommodate a baby. I'm not going to stand by and see you starting a litter of unwanted kids."

It all happened so fast. A near-fatal accident unfolded in front of our eyes. One minute Dagmar was shaking her finger at me as her glistening bangles clanged around her Rolex watch and her blue diamond broach sparkled at her beastly breast. And then the next minute ...

"Ahhhhhhhgha!"

... she was on the shiny black marble floor of the foyer by the double front doors with her hands covering her face as she rolled around on her back, her stubby legs flailing just like a snapping turtle's after a sound beating with a paddle.

"Ahhhhhhhgha!"

I lunged across the slippery black marble and grabbed Cuban Pete—bloody paws and all. I stuffed him back into his paisley vinyl bag and pulled the zipper so fast, the pull broke off.

"Ahhhhhhhgha!"
"Meow!"
"Hello, 911?"

Chapter 3

The Gong

The reported number of stitches on Dagmar's face climbed higher and higher each time she reminded me of the costs for her emergency medical treatment and how many eggs I needed to sell to not only pay my rent, but also to reimburse her for the unfortunate calamity with Cuban Pete's claws. After Mason hastily constructed a brand new, pagoda-style egg stand alongside the cottage on River Bend Road, I set to work in my new job. Then Mason was off and racing to execute his grand master art projects throughout Swan Crest. Dagmar picked him up on her horse and had him ride with her bareback. I wasn't jealous. I just felt sorry for the horse.

Mason's first recommendation as artist-in-residence was to create a fresco on the ceiling of Swan Crest's ballroom. He labored tirelessly on his back while suspended in air just like Michelangelo had done for the Sistine Chapel, he said. Only he told me later when I took a break and trudged up the hill to the mansion to bring him soup for his lunch, he never needed to set up scaffolding.

"It's a miracle what you can accomplish these days with stencils from Home Depot and an overhead projector," he said. "Angels, clouds—magnificent!"

"Huh?"

Mason broke up. When he stopped laughing at my perplexed expression, he explained he was only joking.

"I should have a camera, Lucy my love. Your face is priceless right now. I should capture you on film, for doing your portrait in oils may prove to be a challenge, even for me. Don't worry. The fresco's authentic. The plaster's still wet. Did you expect anything less from your precious artist? You should never doubt me, Lucy my love."

It wasn't only angelic figures dancing through the heavens that Mason was applauding. In between mouthfuls of leftover soup he'd made himself the night before, he was admiring his masterpiece ceiling with his keen artists' eyes.

"I'd defy any expert to figure out I used laser beam paints. They'd never know. Not in a million years. They're my own invention. Genius! Pure bloody genius! Michelangelo had nothing on me."

He scarfed down the last of his soup and stood up. Then he grabbed me from behind cupping his two big hands under my gumball-sized breasts, and squeezed ever so lovingly.

"Do you see *us*, Lucy my love? Look. We're everywhere!"

He pointed to the ceiling while I squinted, but I only saw divine figures dancing throughout the ballroom's newly painted sky. I probably needed a stronger prescription for my contact lenses. But Mason was prepared. He let go of one of my breasts long enough to rotate the binoculars he had mounted on a tripod, then pointed up to the ceiling again.

"Look around! All over! You see them, *dunchu*, Lucy my love?"

And I did. Gracing the heavens inside that fancy ballroom as I examined it close-up, were faces of Ricky and Lucy Ricardo from *I Love Lucy*. He had immortalized our favorite alter egos, painting the likeness of Lucille Ball and Desi Arnaz onto the faces of angels. He had even painted one of the Ricky figures banging a conga drum in front of a Latin bandstand filled with cherub-like musicians donning black mustaches and ruffled sleeves. They were fanciful enough as I gazed through the binoculars for me to imagine I was hearing the throbbing beat of *our song*—Mason's and mine. While there wasn't an actual band, speaker, or even iPod in sight, I was listening to "BaBaBaLu" playing inside my head.

"You believe me now, *dunchu*?" Mason's fingers were now fiddling with my nipples, popping them out playfully as if he could coax them to grow on the spot; he could and they did. "That proves it. That seals the deal. You'll forever be my Lucy."

As an extra benefit in the ballroom, Mason installed a circular tray ceiling with recessed lighting to give off that awesome Sistine Chapel vibe, he said. Then he told Dagmar that he himself would attend to all the nitty-gritty details of planning elaborate affairs and put that grand ballroom to proper use. It would be a travesty to leave it in the dark without anyone to see his creation.

"We shall begin by establishing Swan Crest Farms' First Annual Masquerade Ball," he announced. "I already have torch lights stockpiled. No extra charge."

Mason's second project at Swan Crest was replacing the boulders at Tannery Pond with slabs of marble, claiming that natural boulders were too commonplace for an estate as distinctive as Swan Crest. Marble, he said, and only the finest, was more befitting Dagmar's cherished duck, Peepers, who by-the-by deserved not only a towering marble waterscape, but also a respectable flock of assorted ducks to boss around.

Dagmar and Duncan were animal fanatics; so was Mason. But if you ask me, with so many animals already running around loose on the grounds when we first moved into the cottage—whether they were feathered, furry, or scaly—Swan Crest was like a zoo without cages.

"Think of Swan Crest as the East Coast version of Hearst Castle," Mason told me.

But I didn't know what he meant. He explained that an infamous tourist attraction halfway between Santa Barbara and Monterey, California, had been originally built as a private residence by newspaper mogul William Randolph Hearst. Just like San Simeon, as Hearst had named his legendary estate, Swan Crest sat high atop a mountain with rolling hills leading up to a sprawling mansion, complimented by a collection of outbuildings and pools. But before you reached the safety of the compound, wild animals were roaming freely on the grounds. Panthers leaped, elephants ran, giraffes galloped all over Enchantment Hill. Just like Hearst, the Twists took pride in having their very own wildlife reserve on what they called the Far Hill.

Mason could tell I wasn't impressed. In fact, I was scared.

"Don't worry, Lucy my love," he had said as he nuzzled my neck.

"If those animals bother you that much, I'll rent out the grounds to big game hunters. We'll make a killing—in more ways than one. Do you have any idea how much a leopard's pelt is worth on the black market?"

For his third project, Mason thrilled Dagmar to no end when he recommended that the Twists finance his trip to Thailand. He had his eye on an ancient gong from an abandoned monastery, he said, and claimed that if she placed it in the Bamboo Garden, installing it in just the right spot by the Monkey House, its ancient powers would assure that her tall pile of money from her lottery winnings would multiply each year. He said that its mystical properties were more reliable than any high-priced financial advisor she could find. Then he showed her a picture of the gong, pointing out the one feature that Dagmar, along with Duncan, couldn't resist: an intricately carved ring of animals leaping, flying, and slithering through symbols for water, air, earth, and fire.

Animals! Such useless creatures to me. I never considered Cuban Pete to be one. He was more like a roommate and pal. But to the three of them—Mason, Dagmar, and Duncan—animals, the kind not restricted now to the confines of our furnace room, held the power that ancient monks had bestowed on the gong over five thousand years ago. At least that's what Mason said. He told me later that it was actually only five *hundred* years, but that Dagmar wouldn't know the difference and that she'd buy anything he recommended. He called her a "pigeon" and said that one thing he could be sure of about rich people was that no matter how much money they had in the bank, they were in constant fear of losing it and always wanted more. Rich people, he said, are superstitious. And they always keep a tight grip. That is, unless they're spending it on showpieces to knock the cashmere socks off their newly found rich friends.

Then Mason grinned so wide, his ears started puffing in and out.

My grip was never on a wad of money. I couldn't care less about how much loot Dagmar and Duncan had in the bank or how an ancient gong could assure them of having more. Matters of money always eluded me, so I let Mason handle such things and was glad I always managed to pay the landlord back in New York my share of the rent each month.

Unfortunately, although I was unaware of it at the time, Mason and I didn't actually have a landlord in New York. I didn't realize that Mason owned our apartment outright along with the framer's gallery below it. Had I known the truth back then, I would've left Mason all by himself. I should've gone back home to the city where I belonged. The country was no place for me. But as the landscape at Swan Crest had turned from green to brilliant autumn colors, then to black, gray, and brown, and Mason had installed the gong, I was still all alone in my ignorance.

"Bong!"

We—Mason and I—had planted seeds for our new life together and I intended to see them grow. We might've had a few kinks in our new rural beginnings, namely the pitifully scarred Dagmar, a pesky duck called Peepers, and a pond filled with hungry snappers. But my love with Mason was powerful enough, I believed, to forge on. True love is simply that way. How could I change the picture when my heart masked me to its flaws?

"Bong!"

But sometimes I'll admit that the haunting call of the ancient gong stirred up my conscience. I'd hear it reverberating in the wind, traveling all the way down the Far Hill to my egg stand alongside the cottage on River Bend Road. I had no idea why Mason thought it was necessary to have it calibrated so that it measured wind speed and direction. Weather vanes were senseless inventions, if you asked me. But to the Twists and Mason, one was expected on a properly outfitted farm.

"Bong!"

Sometimes the gong sounded serene. I sensed an enduring moment of peace wafting through the fresh, country breeze while I rang up the cash register for my egg sales. Other times the gong made me start feeling guilty all over again, wondering if I had been right in leaving my last boyfriend, Craig, trading him for Mason.

"Bong!"

Craig liked gongs. It was about the only sort of music that drew his attention. He was hardly a dancer like Mason. He could sit all day long in his meditation, all folded up in the lotus position. He'd never once move except for the breath, as he described it, that he was to "count" as it flowed in and out of his nose. But I really shouldn't say much more about my former boyfriend than that. I won't utter a word about how he liked embracing me in his arms for hours at night and the two of us became one. Or about him entering what he called the jade doors, then staying there in quiet stillness when we both should've been moaning while he moved in and out and ...

"Bong!"

We were on different life paths, Craig assured me after I confessed I had fallen in love with Mason. He understood, he told me, that I faced a fork in my road, that I had seen the sign, and I was choosing the best direction for myself to finally discover my true life's mission, not to mention find my forever home, as my social workers always told me to pray for. He said he knew Mason would make an outstanding father to the children I longed for and that he himself never wanted a traditional family life. He said he could never give me the one thing I most wanted, not when he considered himself to already have children, ones that came in the form of his students to whom he taught meditation in Washington Square Park. For Craig, that was enough. That was his path. But it was hardly mine.

"Bong!"

Wisdom arrives in its own precious time. Tears do, too. By the way Craig had been drying mine—"I'm sorry! I'm sorry!"—you'd think that he had been the one who had broken up with me—"I'm sorry! I'm sorry!"— I was grateful to the man who put me through beauty school and supported my decision to major in hair—superfluous, not coiffed—with a minor in cosmetics. And I really did like him. He was wise, he was kind. I know in my heart that he was quite fond of me, too. But I simply had no interest in his interests. I didn't want to learn about the symbolism of the lotus flower or acquire the discipline necessary to fold my legs into a pretzel—"I'm sorry! I'm sorry!"

I wanted to be with Mason. I wanted to learn how to dance.

CHAPTER 4

The Conga

Pet names are reserved for those we love or hate the most. For the longest time, I thought of Dagmar and Duncan as the Goon and the Buffoon. The names were interchangeable. But the love of my life, Mason, had only one: *Ricky*. It was the counter-part to what he called me: *Lucy*. They were the same names of our favorite TV characters, the Ricardos, from the 1950s black and white rerun on the Nickelodeon channel. We even named the stray cat we adopted, "Cuban Pete," a name from that famous Latin band hit, "Chick-Chick-a-Boom." Mason said that our big kitty had been born too late and that he could've been a sitcom star more famous than Mr. Ed or Lassie. He was a natural, Mason boasted, considering that Cuban Pete was a tiger stripe, only he wasn't orange, but black and white.

In times of trouble—and we did have our quarrels—I resorted to Mason's given name. Whether he was actually christened Mason Samuels Otterman Figg by his mother or himself, I really don't know. But one thing was for certain, he wasn't born an ordinary Tommy, Timmy or Johnny. That characteristic alone—not his name, but his vibrancy, dapper good looks and, most of all, the way he made me laugh and swoon at exactly the same time— dangerously playful as it turned out to be—was enough for me to fall in love with him during an *I Love Lucy* marathon.

I know, I know. Don't call me a dope. You can chalk up my

indiscretion to being naïve, which I suppose I was when I had suddenly fallen in love. Even when I look back on it now, I can still picture me imagining Cupid above us, thinking that he'd matched up the perfect couple—only now, I question whether it was some kind of demon that had hovered over our heads, for I really should've exercised more restraint on the night Mason and I first met. It was a hard lesson in the wisdom of self-control. While it may be too late now to reverse my behavior, I know now that I never should have allowed Mason to hold my hand while Craig was seated on my other side. Now I know I should've been more discrete, or at least slowed down.

It wasn't only holding hands that ignited my love affair with Mason, for holding hands was his final move, the subtle gesture that sealed the deal for me, a deal that started with a mere glance, a longing in his big, blue eyes, ones that he'd occasionally pop out just like Ricky Ricardo.

Quirky? Yes. But somehow those popping eyes of his made me woozy with lust rising up through my middle. I could feel warmth emanating from deep, deep inside. And, I'll admit, those bulging eyes made my lips part, and I started breathing heavily, the sort of heaving of your chest that feels so good, as if all of the sun and moon's magical energy is filling your whole body and you kind of become light-headed and the world seems clearer than it ever seemed before.

Then, just as I thought my feet would lift off the ground, Mason was blowing kisses to the sweet spots on my upper arm and neck, knowing exactly how to caress a woman without actually making contact.

My feet were floating. My toes were wiggling. I needed more.

A single, silent sigh, a stolen glance in my direction, and it was as if Mason had stripped me naked right there on the sofa. Just when I thought I could no longer restrain myself from kissing him in front of Craig, he sprang to his feet, dancing along with Ricky Ricardo on the TV, banging his conga drum—a real one he used as a side table in his living room—while belting out "BaBaBaLu." He slipped the strap of the drum over his shoulder at the exact time that Ricky Ricardo did, and then he played it in precisely the same rhythm that was pounding out of the TV speakers. It was as if Ricky Ricardo himself had just leaped out of the small screen and into the room with us, his head jerking, his hair coming loose from its pompadour, and both of his eyes bugging out of his head. Just like the real Ricky, Mason did a few rumba side-steps back and forth in front of Craig and me on the sofa, until he concluded his performance with a big bow, then posed, standing squarely in one place, his drum still strapped around his shoulder, arms stiffly at his side, his face looking up to the spotlight, proud and satisfied with his performance, while the audience—both live and in black and white—erupted with applause.

Only, for Mason, standing by the television set, looking up to the ceiling, the light shining on him was not from a night club spotlight. It was coming from two bright beams of light from one pair of eyes: *mine*.

I know, I know. Don't tell me: *sucker*. It was the first, but wouldn't be the last time, for iHt really is true what they say about bad boys being more intriguing than the good, and therefore, more desirable. Trouble is, some are badder than bad, others better than good. As much as Mason was diabolical, Craig was spiritual, sitting each morning in meditation, then sharing the wisdom he'd gleaned from the Universe of Spirits. He'd share his insights and knowledge of the metaphysical with his growing flock of followers, too. He held tea ceremonies in the park, and had his students interpret koans. But I have to be honest, I never understood how one hand clapping could ever make a sound and wanted to tell them all it was useless to discuss it. Besides, I wanted to confess to Craig that although he always fixed us a nice pot of tea each morning, I actually preferred coffee.

That night of the *I Love Lucy* marathon, I had more important confessions to make to Craig than my preference for a hot morning beverage. As I sat on the sofa between the two boys, I looked to my right and then my left, then back again. It was an easy decision. Why should I worry about being reincarnated into a cockroach with Craig in the next life, when I could dip with Mason in the present?

Hey, we all have our callings. But I wish now that I never got tangled up with the likes of him or moved into that miserable shack known as The Cottage at Swan Crest Farms.

Chapter 5

The Cottage

According to the Historical Society of the Village of Burberry Hills, New Jersey, *The Cottage at Swan Crest Farms*, the official and legal name as of November 2007, was originally built as a chicken coop, then expanded to be a trading post where Indians came to buy and sell livestock, dry goods, and guns with the local settlers. Alongside it, Tannery Pond was used to cool animal skins in the tanning process, while the falls that spilled over the rocks twenty feet into Tannery Brook, were harnessed with a wheel structure for milling flour from wheat. By 1875, the trading post was refurbished as a residence and originally dubbed *Moonglow Cottage*, one of the three outbuildings, along with a barn and icehouse, owned by Virgil and Amanda Pearson who lived in the main farmhouse. When the mill was destroyed by a fire after a mishap with the tanning chemicals, the three-ton millstone survived, and was hauled away by a horse and plow. To this day, that same millstone serves as the front step of the cottage's porch.

Over the decades, a long line of residents used that millstone as a welcome mat. Among them were a new bride and groom by the name of Wyatt, during their first year of marriage. Eventually, the couple had a daughter named Jane, who grew up to be an actress best known from the television series, *Father Knows Best,* as well as having been the first wife of Ronald Reagan, an actor himself, who ultimately became president of the United States.

At least that was the rumor.

While there really was a man named Reagan who was an actor and then president, no one can be sure if the Wyatts who had lived in the cottage and had a daughter named Jane were really his in-laws, or if they merely had the same name. That's how rumors get started, I suppose. Then one thing leads to another, and someone from the local historical society decides to write it all down.

That's a good trick, I thought, for elevating a rumor to the status of a legend. Eventually, with sufficient time, that document tucked away in the archives seemed authentic and made that anonymous scribe from the historical society seem like an official historian who'd put a quill pen to parchment and created historical truth.

Whatever the real story might have been, a half century after the family named Wyatt moved out, Duncan and Dagmar Twist purchased the property with their lottery winnings. While they retained the three outer structures—the ice house, the barn and the cottage—they erected a brand new, farmhouse-style mansion the size of Buckingham Palace atop the Far Hill. But first they bulldozed the original house—furniture and all. A couple of months after that, Mason and I locked up our apartment over the framer's gallery in New York City, and made the cottage—rechristened by the Twists as *The Cottage at Swan Crest Farms*—home.

Stranger things have occurred in life than a chicken coop morphing to a cottage with a name, such as an actor being elected as a nation's president. But politics aside, no event I've ever read about could compare to the life the four of us—Dagmar and Duncan, Mason and myself—led on the farm. I knew that Dagmar was a nut about her animals; Duncan was proud of them, too. Their passion and pride of all non-human creatures was directly and inversely proportional to the havoc they spun in my life. They tested my resolve and promise to Mason that I'd go along with his deal to be the artist-in-residence, like the time the Twists decided to campout by the pond. We were to have a pig roast on an open fire and sleep in tee-pees, which Mason naturally designed and set up. Only, instead of a hog being selected from Swan Crest's pig pen, Mason roasted a fox.

I'll never again believe such gamey meat is pork.

The three of them dressed up like Indians—or rather, Native

Americans—and designated me to be a cowgirl who got tied up with rope to a tree. They left me there for an hour before allowing me to join them for a moonlight performance of *Hiawatha* with Dagmar playing the lead role. Mason, in loincloth, body paint, and a head full of feathers, beat his drum while chanting, hollering, and punctuating his rhythms with an occasional yelp and a scream. He worked himself up into a frenetic dance, hopping and hooting and calling like some kind of crazed bird, the kind you might find in a prehistoric African jungle, not on an estate farm in New Jersey.

"Ooooo! Awwww! Hee-huck! Hee-huck! Hee-hee-hee!" Mason twittered his tongue on his hard pallet, then let out a long, loud, "Twaaaaaah!"

Endorphins must've been launching like fireworks in Mason's brain. He might've lived in New York City, but out in the woods, he was in his favorite habitat. He persuaded our primitive foursome to follow him in a line while waddling in a squatting position and leading us in what he called an authentic ritual for *quacking the moon*—the very same sequence of movements and sounds, he told us, that had been performed by the original natives of that exact geographical region for assuring prosperity. His research, he told us, was quite thorough.

"Be a good sport," he coached me later back at the cottage when he rubbed suave from an aloe plant on my rope burns. "Just play along, would you? Where's your sense of humor, not to mention sense of purpose?" he asked. "Can't you at least pretend to be one of the gang? You did promise you'd go along with the Grand Master Plan. All of it. Every *Article*, every *Section*, every *Addendum*. You promised me you would play your role. Remember?"

Living in a cottage the size of a kid's milk carton in a neighborhood where houses are mansions and each has a name, I had thought that Mason and I were glued together, a force of two soldered together to form one. I assumed we had an *us* and a plan; but at times, I wondered if there was only a *them* and a *me*.

"An attitude adjustment on your part would do wonders for the status of my career here," he continued. "After all, the Twists are my art patrons. Think about that. You've got to be patient. I've got them in my claws now. We're so close. Just trust me, Lucy my love. You do, *dunchu?*"

And so I did. I trusted Mason. His words were always something to gnaw on; anyone would have faith in the opinions and thoughts of one's cherished lover, wouldn't they? As best as I could, I tried to follow his advice and played along, surviving tree-tying and fox-eating and turtle-slapping and egg-collecting and monkey-feeding. But whenever I was with the Twists, I was beginning to feel as though Mason and I were a mismatch, two flavors that didn't quite meld well together, like peanut butter and tuna.

He had his freedom from them during the day up at the Ice House whipping up another one of his projects commissioned by Dagmar and Duncan. He often worked late into the evening, sometimes past midnight. Whenever I wandered up to coax him into coming home to the cottage, I could hear him playing his favorite drum music and see lights flickering through the milk glass of the old windows. But I never dared disturb him. He always told me that his artistic spirit was working at its peak whenever he heard the sound of drums beating and hundreds of candles were burning bright. I certainly could not interrupt his muse. I'd just trudge back home and grab Cuban Pete from out of the furnace room and carry my big kitty up to the sleeping loft to keep me company until Mason finally snuggled in. I'd think about how different our lives were—Mason's and mine—despite that we lived together. While he worked up in his studio in the Ice House on most nights, I labored side-by-side with Dagmar, Duncan, and their housekeeper, Bertha, tackling the tedious chores of the farm by day. On top of that, I had to sell eggs.

Call me lazy, say that I was a party-pooper, but if I had won $467 million from the SuperDuper Lottery, believe me, my idea of bliss would *not* be mucking out elephant stalls with a miniature bulldozer and scrubbing giraffes with a broom. Feeding a baby bottle to Buckwheat, Dagmar's treasured kid goat that had been born premature in a pile of buckwheat shells, was an annoyance each morning. I didn't have a single day off. I had to prepare the bottle with goat chow mush and fresh spring water I'd hoist up from the well. Then I'd warm the bottle on my stove at the cottage at the break of dawn. Dagmar didn't tell me for the longest time that her prized goat, as revered as he was, slept the same way all goats do: up high on boulders and in his own poop. No wonder I was always sneezing whenever I fed that white, four-legged creature a branch for dessert; I had never heard of anyone being allergic to rocks.

It seemed I had traded my city life in Manhattan for Hooterville as if I were playing Lisa to Mason's Oliver. Please, I sometimes prayed. I want to be *Lucy*. How, when, dear God, can I hop on the next train and get back to where life is normal in New York? I swore I'd never again complain about the noise of a subway or the rush of the crowds.

I might've complained a lot, if only to myself, about life on a farm. But I do have to admit that not all of our days at Swan Crest were perpetually dreary. On our own, without the Twists hanging over us, Mason and I carved out a nice routine together as homespun as living on a real life set for one of those feel-good shows from the 1950s, only without a kindly Aunt Bea to feed us or any kids running around, smacking a baseball through Mr. Wilson's window or playing pranks on Barney Fife. But Mason and I were working on that—the cooking part and the little ones, that is. I believed whole-heartedly that we shared the same dream.

Each night we'd try out yet another recipe for dinner, using a cookbook we borrowed from the Twists, one of the few antique treasures they salvaged before demolishing the original main house. We might've swapped chicken breasts for rabbit loins, and shrimp for squirrel meat, but the stews, soups and pot pies turned out to be delicious. Even I got to be a fairly decent cook. We always enjoyed a hardy country meal, except for the times Mason brewed up what he called an authentic Native American corn chowder—husks included—with a broth made from earthworms, rabbit paws, and a woodpecker he'd killed with a sling-shot.

"It's an ancient recipe for enhancing fertility," he told me. "I did the research myself. *Not* eating it was their method of birth control."

After dinner, I'd fetch our crystal decanter of Benedictine on a silver tray, which we kept in the built-in cabinets by the dining room's love seat. But instead of an apple pie made from the fruit of the tree outside our little house, we'd occasionally opt to make s'mores in the fireplace instead. I'd count out graham crackers, chocolate squares, and marshmallows to stack on the tray, while Mason would run around clicking an automatic match wand to light the living room candles. He'd tend the fire, poking it with an iron rod, then he'd retie the silk belt that'd slip loose on his smoking jacket (of which he had an impressive collection thanks to eBay) and wait for me to bring out the tray with the liqueur and dessert fixings. I'd find him sitting on the bearskin rug, gazing up at the portrait of himself with his arms around his beloved mother.

But one night, instead of finding him in his usual, solitary moment, lost in his own thoughts, I saw Mason standing on the bearskin rug greeting me with his arms wide open. His eyes were popping out in the way they did whenever he was feeling one of those special, intimate sensations way down low below the equator, while his eyebrows were arching into two sharp points up on his forehead.

He didn't need to say a word for me to know—to feel—what he was thinking. Instead of the two of us sipping Benedictine and threading marshmallows on two long sticks, Mason grabbed my hand and kissed it. Then he walked his lips up to my neck and lingered there forever. Marshmallows burned. Clocks stopped. Coyotes howled. Our private little world in that cottage glowed in orange and red hues while crackling logs scented the air with the pungent aroma of hickory and pine. He held me close as he softly, slowly buffed his cheek with mine and our hearts beat together as one.

Well, at least one of us had a real heart.

We danced by the fire, dipping and twirling as best as a good dancer and bad dancer could, with lots of kisses in between. Mason made me think that our movements were in synch as if in a mirror, while the Benedictine heated up on the silver tray I'd placed on the slate ledge by the fire. I couldn't have put it on top of the mantel; as formidable as it was and far more sizable for a fireplace in a tiny, one-bedroom cottage, it was already adorned with a row of candles and pairs of ducks whose eyes sporadically lit up. Their heads turned on occasion, too, but I never bothered asking Mason about why, how, or when. They obviously were on a timer or motion sensor of some kind, but I never cared to inquire about which one. He crafted so many wooden decoys, wiring them up with lights hidden inside, I just accepted their inner electronics as Mason's artistic touch.

As I always said, Mason was a mason, only in a fine arts way. He was always so busy with his hands, hammering and chiseling and engineering so many decoys along with his metal stampings, tapestry weavings, statues, and assortment of master pottery and vases, that Dagmar permitted him to take over the Ice House as his studio. Only a few select objects d'art made their way to our little abode sitting on the edge of River Bend Road. I never gave a second thought as to why Mason would choose to display so many pairs of ducks with eyes that flashed and necks that turned throughout each humble room of the cottage. Just like the cottage itself, I had thought that the pairs of ducks with lights shining from their beady eyes were one of a kind and exclusively for us.

Ha!

Dagmar let it slip that Mason had given her a pair of duck decoys for her dressing table, another pair for Duncan's high boy dresser, and one pair that had been split up for each of the nightstands. He had even rigged up a line of four of them perching on a long branch high on a tree outside their bedroom window.

I should've known then that something was askew. Mason wasn't carving out gifts just for me. Why would I doubt him when we had *trust*? I'm sure he did his best to hook me into believing that we were connected at the heart as well as the hip, revealing only the "Articles" and "Sections" of his Grand Master Plan that he wanted me to know. To make sure he had his way, he'd remind me that Dagmar hated my guts, that she hungered for power over me. But I never was one to be vengeful. Orphans always fear what may happen to them next if they ever dared to question authority, and considering that I lived in a humble cottage while the Twists reigned supreme at Swan Crest Farms, Dagmar was my ruler. Mason needed to try another angle to persuade me to go along with his screwball scheme to steal the Blue Diamond Peepers: he put in extra schmaltz as he romanced me at the cottage, assuring he'd have his way.

"*Lucy,*" he crooned in his best Ricky Ricardo voice when our dancing concluded by the fire with my back arched and one leg kicked up high on his shoulder. It was about then that he began roping me into the crux of what Project Peepers was really all about. The gist of it all was that the theft wasn't really a true theft when he'd merely be repossessing his own creation and that Dagmar and Duncan would benefit by the insurance payout. Besides, he added, he needed a lot of money to make his mother proud. And me. He told me that he had overstated the true value of the diamonds, though the value was high as it was, then created appraisal papers that looked authentic.

"We'll all win," he said. "Dagmar will still have her money in the bank. And she'll have no idea that the Authentic Baubles are actually copies, not the original Blue Diamond Peepers. Genius! Pure bloody genius!"

I was convinced. Why would I doubt him? After all, he was a man who loved his mother. Besides, we were in love. He was determined that Project Peepers would come off without a hitch. To make sure I was convinced, he had perfected a Cuban accent thick as syrup from freshly thatched sugar cane, sweetening any words that oozed out of his mouth. Whether he spoke, hummed, kissed, or cooed, Mason—my personal Ricky, my faux-Latin lover—was impossible to resist.

"Just this once, then never again. Don't you trust me?"

Back then, I had a sweet tooth and needed a regular fix, but I didn't immediately answer. Not a yes, not a no. So he clamped a pair of strong, wet lips on the sweet spot of my neck and softly, slowly, with all the eroticism he could summon in his deeply rich voice, hummed the theme song for *I Love Lucy* until I erupted with a mixture of chills and giggles.

"Trust me," he whispered.

Then he said the magic word again, the one little thing that would assure him of getting his way. With all the passion of a Latin band leader whose Little Ricky was bulging beneath the sheen of tuxedo pants, poised to pound out the repeated refrain of "BaBaBaLu," he uttered that single incantation:

"*Lucy…*"

I was a goner. High on another hit from my sugar-tongued, "BaBaBaLu"-humming, conga-banging lover, I hadn't yet figured out that I was also a chump, one who'd grown accustomed to the taste of woodpecker soup.

Candles were flickering throughout our little cottage lighting it up like our own private Tropicana supper club, only instead of doing another samba on a dance floor, we retreated to the bear skin rug and kangaroo blanket—pouch in tact—where Ricky—or, uh *Mason*—regularly replenished our supply of condoms that we went through by the dozens. But we were working on making a baby now. Finally, we could be not just a couple of cottage rodents in heat like the kind that squealed in the eaves, under the sink, and inside the staircase, making the kind of sounds that scared me so much, I'd hide while biting my fingers up to the knuckles until Mason—not Cuban Pete—had exterminated each one. That night by the fire, when he was preparing to reveal his big plan for stealing the Blue Diamond Peepers, the only sounds I was hearing were echoes of a conga drum, the crackling of logs, and Mason humming in my ear. Finally, we could be real grownups now, with no reason for protection.

At least *I* thought that wanting a baby was the reason for skipping the latex.

The first bundle of firewood for the season was blazing as a scratchy recording of *Desi Arnaz and His Orchestra* blared from the speakers that Mason had mounted throughout our little house as expertly as a technical crew on a Deslilu set. The conga drum he'd brought from the city as a testament to our love held a large vase of freshly cut holly branches from the bushes outside the cottage's back door. Our bodies were moving to the syncopated rhythm of a fifty-piece band of horns, drums, and backup singers, wailing "BaBaBaLu" as our clothes shed into a private tango of their own on the floor.

"Just once," Mason had promised again. "There's only one set of Blue Diamond Peepers in the world. I brokered that deal in Switzerland for Duncan and Dagmar myself. And I know where they keep them. I was the one who installed the safe in the master suite dressing room and memorized the combination for them—for their protection, of course."

"Those dopes," I said, breaking his uncharacteristically serious mood, but in keeping with our playtime standards. "Such pigeons," I said. But I was the one merely playing a game. I gave him a mischievous wink. But Mason wasn't cracking his usual grin. He seemed—dare I say it? Mason was serious, as stern-faced as I'd ever seen him.

"The Twists trust Ricky," he said twirling the "R" in his name and referring to himself in the third person. "Don't you?"

"Say that five times fast and I might," I dared him, wanting to test the boundaries of his oral talents. But most of all, his love. With accent intact, he immediately came about and jumped into the game: "The Twists trust Ricky. The Twists trust Ricky. The Twists trust …"

Before he uttered the line for the fourth and fifth time, he planted a wet one on my mouth and thrust a warm, sweet, and familiar tongue deep inside. He was serious about that tongue, moving it first in, then taking it on a long, luscious trip a-way down south to a hot little island in the Caribbean. He lingered there for awhile until an earthquake rumbled and a monsoon gave way. Then, as he made his way back north, he proved to be equally as intent on revealing his criminal plan as he had been a rain forest tourist.

"I can swipe it in an instant. Three minutes. You can time me," he said. "Up the ladder, diamonds in my pocket, then back down the ladder I'll come," he promised. "Do it for me, Lucy my love. For us. For the baby. You do still want one, *dunchu?*"

He studied my face with those big eyes bugging out in a way that was curiously both funny and seductive. Had they been brown, not blue, and his hair wavy black, not auburn curls, he'd pass for that famous Cuban band leader himself. His hips were starting to rock, gently at first, but in a quick turn of roles that would've jolted any other lover off that bearskin rug, perhaps sending her running from that little cottage forever, never to look back, Mason was suddenly sitting up on his knees, swinging his arms in the air, alternating his hands under his elbows and cocking his head from side to side like Carmen Miranda.

Ricky well knew that the best foreplay was making Lucy laugh, dispelling the myth and proving once and for all that it is absolutely possible, anatomically and biologically, to laugh and orgasm at exactly the same time.

"Ay-ay-ay-ay-ay!"

Believe me, his Little Ricky was ill-named. That throbbing love appendage extending far from his pelvis was doing a mambo freely in the air, teasing me with a mating ritual, a bobbing dance on top of that bearskin rug. Then he tossed aside the kangaroo throw, a pelt that had been illegally acquired on one of his buying trips to Australia and was, naturally, authentic. I suppose that he would do his best to unleash the answer he wanted from me. Call it *kangaroo interuptus*, I guess.

I couldn't hold out any longer.

"Yes!" I squealed. "Yes, yes, a thousand times, yes!"

I spontaneously shed tears like the waterfall spilling outside our little cottage window from Tannery Pond. Geese were honking, the fire was crackling, and my voice was catching in a ball at the top of my throat. But what I was agreeing to—the only thought foremost in my mind and heart—was not plotting a jewel heist using a ladder propped up to the Twists' bedroom window; I was saying *yes* to willingly, enthusiastically, with all the life force careening through my five-foot-eleven frame, having Mason's baby.

Yes, yes. I know: *chump*.

He calmed my trembling body, soothing my hormonal whimpers with a million tiny kisses on my face and telling me those three words that added up to one big fat lie: "I love you." Then he popped that Big Little Ricky in until he mamboed himself silly—and spewed a cascade of baby making seed …

As we cuddled together in the afterglow, all wrapped up again in that Australian fur while sipping a shared snifter of Benedictine, Mason skipped the graham crackers and chocolate, licked a marshmallow stick clean, then outlined his reasoning for the theft of the Blue Diamond Peepers that seemed to make perfect sense. At least it did at the time.

"It could take years for me to sell enough of my real art to afford a baby. I'm sick of knocking out one sculpture and bejeweled doo-dad after another to suit the Twists' schlocky tastes. I need to concentrate on *my* art, the real stuff. I never get a chance to anymore—even though it's my paintings that originally drew Dagmar's eye. Now she's spoiled. She keeps getting the bug for one hunk of high-priced goods or another—and she expects me to put down my paint brush and jump at her command to broker the deal and hop on the next plane."

For the first time in I think ever, I felt sorry for the man I hopelessly loved.

"I'm an artist," he said. "Not a gofer."

If I'm going to be completely truthful, I'll admit, despite all that's happened, I still feel sorry for him even now, to this day. I mean, could I blame Mason for longing to fully utilize his true gifts? He had world class artistic talent, only the world didn't know it yet. Come to think of it, Hitler failed in his art, too. Would history now tell a different story had Eva encouraged Adolf to go back to his paints?

"I know you said you didn't want any part of climbing a ladder and breaking into their house. I know you're not the type to seek revenge for the way Dagmar talks to you. She really can be degrading. But just think of Project Peepers as a shortcut to starting a family. It's the Crown Jewel of the Grand Master Plan."

I knew he was serious and perhaps desperate whenever his voice broke up.

"You, me, and a baby. That'll be our forever family. Yours and mine," he had told me. "That's what you always wanted, right?"

Mason knew all my stories of how growing up as an orphan was not only lonely, but scary. Being shuffled from one foster care family to another was always frightening. And the worst part about the experience wasn't having a different bedroom every six months, it was the food. Awful! No wonder I never finish my plate even now. But I'd learn to be the best cook ever. I'd eat well myself and make sure our children were properly nourished, if only we could have a family of our own—a forever home!

"Besides," Mason continued, "the Twists are just a couple of lottery winners. It's not like they earned all that money with the sweat of their brow, the pluck of their business savvy, or any authentic talent."

I thought Project Peepers was going too far with the original idea. I thought that Mason would merely be doubling or tripling his prices for one artful project or purchase. It was a whole other kettle of fish to become thieves in the night. But it's hard to disagree with the brilliance of one's cherished lover, especially one who prides himself on being "authentic." Ironic, I know, for a forgery painter, sculptor, and master craftsman to yearn for what's real. I suppose he was trapped in an illusionary world for too long, yearning to break out.

"Maybe we never should've left the city," he whined. "I wasn't always a thief. In the beginning, I had thought the Twists would be my art patrons who'd hook me up with their rich friends. But the only people those lottery winners know are not from the art world; they're just poor relatives who have their hands out for money."

I did remember seeing an old jalopy of a car parked out by the front gate once. It turned out to be owned by a second-cousin-thrice-removed on Duncan's side. The poor woman was ringing the bell incessantly while a pile of kids were hollering in the back seat. They never came back after Bertha appeared on the driveway and blasted them away. The only people who made it past that fortress of a housekeeper were delivery men with regular shipments of animal chow or a new swan, monkey, pig, or goat.

Still, the Twists' parties always drew crowds, though the guests weren't really close friends. Probably just neighbors who wanted to know what kind of people would build such a grand estate with animals roaming the grounds. Naturally, they'd also want to calculate if Dagmar and Duncan were wealthier than they were based on the prized possessions they'd showcase all over the house. Even the doggie bowls were plated in real gold for a bunch of well-manicured mutts that wore matching collars studded with real rubies, diamonds, and emeralds.

"Early on, before we even moved in, I was beginning to realize that I wasn't going to get anywhere with my career *here*," Mason groaned. "My father never had to move back to the country. And he was written up in *Art News*. He was even featured on the cover. And my brother was proclaimed to have inherited his art gene when he was still in art school. And my sister's music career is really taking off, according to *Rolling Stone*. She's fronting a white trash band that hit platinum with its first ..."

Mason's naturally melodic voice was beginning to break up like a teenager's. I wanted to cuddle him and dry the tears that threatened to pour out—the same as he would comfort me. It's the kind of care I'd come to expect from a lover who was also my closest ally, confident, and best friend.

"Nothing is going according to my life's plan. Even my mother is gone now."

"Your mother? Mason! You never told me she ... Did your mother ... pass away? When?"

I never heard such a long pause from Mason. I glanced up to the portrait of mother and son hanging over the fireplace, imagining how happy they seemed to be together. I wondered how long it had been since the two of them had seen each other. I was afraid to ask. I didn't want to say the wrong thing. While I might've been an orphan myself and never knew my own mother, I felt awkward asking about his. I simply was not accustomed to happily chatting about family matters and always felt tongue-tied whenever I felt the urge to know more about Mason's background. When you've been raised in foster homes meeting other orphans, the subject of birth parents is a bit squirrely. I didn't have a clue as to how to address it, at least with those who actually knew their natural mothers and fathers. Would I be choosing the wrong words if I pried?

"She's tied up in … Africa," he said. "She's in … jail."

Mason's voice was less emotional now and more matter-of-fact. But that's not what gave me pause. 'Jail,' I thought. I've heard that one before. Whenever a social worker mentioned jail in connection with an orphan's parents, I knew that nothing more needed to be said. No one ever dared to ask about the specific crimes that had been committed. Some are more horrendous than others, I suppose. Being a foster child shuffled from one house to another was sufficient enough to bring on nightmares. None of us ever wanted to add to our nighttime struggles. So I didn't prompt Mason to tell me more.

"Just a customs snafu. Incomplete exporting papers," he said. He rattled out a few more brief facts surrounding the unfortunate circumstances of his mother. "It's complicated," he said, ending his laundry list. "But I do write to her often. She writes to me—to us—too. I just never had the nerve to show you all her postcards. She can't wait to meet the true love of my life. She even puts your name on the address," he said.

Now that's proof, I thought to myself. When your man's mother actually includes your name alongside her own son's on a postcard from jail all the way in Africa, I'd say that seals the deal. Mason really did love me. I was feeling all warm inside again. My toes were wiggling, too. But as my heart was opening wide enough to believe anything he'd say next, he retreated back to his whining. At the time, I didn't think much about it. I just figured he wasn't ready to tell me more about his jail bird mother. Looking back on that night at the cottage, I suppose it was a tad odd how easily he could switch from one mood to another, but Mason was a master at mood switching. I chalked it up to his artistic temperament. As I think about him now, I guess his mood depended more on whom he was manipulating and for what purpose, than it did on his creative spirit. But at the time, with my toes wiggling and after emptying an entire half bottle of Benedictine together, more than double our usual limit—I felt only love.

"Even my dumb cousin Arnold found fame," Mason was

complaining. "He only wrote a couple of cheap thrill paperback novels. But *now*," Mason sounded utterly frustrated. "Arnold's making *movies*."

Mason was starting to hiccup. It was a sign that tears wouldn't be far off.

"Arnold-Schmarnold!" he said as if he were swearing. "The whole world sees his movies now, but not my artistic masterpieces. But Arnold never would have graduated from high school if I hadn't changed his grades."

"Changed his grades? How'd you do that?"

Magically, Mason's face brightened. Tears that had been promising to break loose from the floodgates suddenly dried up. He looked up at me as he took a swig of a newly opened bottle of Benedictine, his eyes bugging out with mischief, his lips pursed together, not saying a word. I should've known better; his best tricks were never shared, not even with me. I knew that if I pushed him to reveal his secrets, he'd start humming and change the subject. But I tried anyway.

"Tell, me," I urged him. "How did you change his grades? Did you break into the principal's office? Or hack into the computer system?"

Mason clammed up. That should've been my tip off that he was putting on an act—for me—only I was too much in love and, yes, too loopy from the Benedictine to call him on it at the time. His mischievous grin dissolved into a pucker of his lips, but instead of planting a few more kisses on my face, he started to whistle the *Leave It to Beaver* tune.

"Have it your way, *amigo*. Don't tell me. Let me guess," I ventured. "You humped the teacher?"

"Of course not!"

Mason pretended to be disgusted by the mere suggestion.

"I merely danced with her," he said innocently. "The whole school was watching."

He had been in charge of the decorations committee for the junior cotillion and selected a colonial theme, only instead of overseeing a bunch of teenagers attempt to construct an indoor historic village from scratch, he persuaded local craftsman to do the job as a donation to the school in the form of free labor. Then he held Cotillion Preparation Dance Classes to make sure that the students knew how to do the minuet, waltz and Virginia reel, and he commandeered the sewing machines in home economics rooms for volunteer seamstresses to whip up costumes for every student, teacher, and chaperone from the PTA. The results were spectacular, he told me, with photos splashed all over the pages of the yearbook.

"You'd think that Colonial Williamsburg had been built right there in the Cyrus Pepper High School gymnasium," Mason crowed. "The history teacher told me it was very authentic. That infamous cotillion is now considered to be a local legend. But trust me," he said with a wink. "It was real. It was authentic."

He reached for another stick of roasted marshmallows and downed another hit of Benedictine as he stretched out on the bearskin rug and wiggled his toes by the fire.

"I thanked the teacher, of course, for her compliment. I was very grateful to hear praise for my art. She was grateful, too. You'd be surprised how long you can hide under a hoop skirt without anyone being the wiser."

I sprayed out a mouthful of my Benedictine.

"I did all the work, but by golly, old Arnold got his A."

"You didn't really …"

But Mason retreated once again to his devilish silence. Then he raised one eyebrow over a bulging eye, looking at me, of all people, who knew first-hand that his talents were numerous and real.

"The math teacher required an entirely different approach. And don't get me started about the science teacher. It's no small feat to lure die-hard Trekkie fans to East Bobtail for their annual convention. Do you have any idea how hard it is to fit Spock ears on an entire rafter of turkeys?"

Sometimes I forgot that Mason was a genuine country boy. I had only known him as a New Yorker and, as I've said, only for a short time. It was hard to imagine that he was raised on a turkey farm with the knowledge that they are collectively referred to as a *rafter* not a *flock*, let alone the knowledge of how to kill them in an assembly line procedure. He told me how he'd invert the birds one by one to snap their heads off in a turkey guillotine before tossing them into a vat of water. After the feathers were softened, the headless carcasses were rolled onto a conveyer belt leading to a feather-trimming machine.

When their skins were plucked clean, he'd inspect each one himself, he said, before allowing the slaughtered birds to be encased in plastic and mesh, then piled up in a walk-in freezer, awaiting the next Pathmark pick-up.

"It was our family's Thanksgiving tradition," he said with a shrug. "Made the cows happy."

I'll confess, had I known about Mason handling decapitated turkeys, I would've made a stronger case for having been a picky eater; more than that, I might've thought twice before dumping a self-styled spiritual leader like Craig who now goes by the name of Laughing Sun back in Washington Square Park. Maybe I never would've experience a mystical, spiritual conversion myself, but maybe I would've finally become a devout vegetarian.

"It wasn't until we fled the farm and moved north to Manhattan that my father's art career took off. While he had show after show all over the world, we—my mother and I—ran the framer's gallery when my brother and sister moved on with their lives; they're older than me. I had no choice but to leave my best artwork back home. It's probably still there rotting on the side of the barn."

I suppose the Twists' offer to commission Mason's art wasn't the only incentive for him wanting to move with me to the country. He might've been a master of many talents, livestock farming included, and meeting Duncan and Dagmar, it seemed, was fortuitous in more ways than one, enabling Mason to reconnect with his rural roots. Still, I pushed aside the vision of him working levers and switches of turkey-beheading equipment and chose to see him through my eyes only, as the artist he truly was, not to mention a savvy New Yorker, one who knew the subway system like the palm of his own hand. I didn't want to picture him driving a tractor or hauling hay to a barn. I cringed thinking how he'd been splattered in turkey blood when his smock should have been covered in paint. The man I loved should be working diligently on expressing his artistic talents with brushes dipped in oils and turpentine and applied to canvass, then showing at the finest galleries and selling his masterpieces to authentic art patrons, not the Twists.

And who cared about Mason's adolescent pranks in the past when I had him close to me in the present? It was easy to toss aside the stories of his youth, tales of dazzling high school teachers into altering their grade books. I cared not a lick about a bunch of old crows who were probably still boring their bridge partners silly, retelling the stories about the time they danced with a devilishly handsome and talented student named Mason Figg, and the fire he incited deep inside them. I had the real thing right there on the bearskin rug at the cottage. We were planning our future—together. I was his only dance partner now. It took a shared half bottle of liquor and a few swigs of another to be convinced that my personal Ricky Ricardo had the power to do anything he dared dream. Heck, he sometimes made me believe I was a good dancer. I could dip. I could twirl. I could rumba, tango, or salsa.

After all, I was Lucy.

Mason tossed a new log on the fire, and memories of his adventurous youth evaporated in the smoke while our own private little world retracted once again to the confines of the cottage's living room. The Latin rhythms of *Desi Arnaz and His Orchestra* were still pounding away through the speakers, and I sighed with contentment, full of love for the man who was to become the father of my children, snuggling close to him again as he returned to our baby-making nest.

"The Twists have no real talent between them," Mason said, knowing that I was fertile for his plot to swipe the Blue Diamond Peepers. "Save for taking turns picking lint out of each other's navels. But I suppose I shouldn't overlook Dagmar and Duncan's picking skills. After all, they did pick lottery numbers that turned out lucky."

How could I fight logic like that? Or question the depth of Mason's love? More importantly, how could I prevent him from financing his true artistic talent—and, at the same time, be the only one who could enable him to have it? Irony along with common sense tumbled out of my mind in the wave of warmth emanating from my hopefully pregnant belly, still feeling the impression of Mason's Big Fat Little Ricky doing a lambda with my Cuba as tears started welling up in my eyes. I wanted my man to be successful. He—and our baby—deserved that. It was my heart that posed the one question I didn't need time to answer: *What other man would be willing to stoop to burglary for the sake of affording a baby?* Surely, my Mason, my Ricky, my man, must've truly loved me.

I could puke just thinking about that now. Then again, unlike the stomach that has an appropriate and immediate negative reaction to too much booze or fowl food that it inadvertently ingests, the heart requires ample time to realize there's trouble in its system. It doesn't know when it's time for true love to end.

"It's not like they'll notice if anything's missing. They've accumulated more gems, art, overpriced gee-gaws, status toys and elite trinkets than they can keep track of. They don't even realize the value of what they've bought. And it'll only take me three minutes. Up the ladder, diamonds in my pocket, then back down the ladder I'll come. And … Oh, I love you so much! I even love how you snore!"

"Snore? I don't snore."

Mason suddenly stopped gushing. He paused long enough to grin. Before I could figure out what he was smiling about, he was back on a roll. A new tear was forming in his eye.

"You are my Lucy now and until the end of time."

I looked up to him as he passed me the snifter of Benedictine. I was still glowing from the warmth of the fire, still feeling the rhythm of that internal mambo echoing throughout my body, imagining it was the start of a baby's pitter-patter feet, as a familiar tune played over and over in my head with my own version of the lyrics: *"I love Ricky and he loves me…"*

Yes, yes. I know: *chump*. Pity. Visits to that Caribbean island are more frequent and romantic when one is still naïve.

Chapter 6

The Gown

Blue eggs made my stomach turn, but they were the only kind Dagmar's chickens laid. I'm not sure if they were blue because of the sperm from the Bolivian rooster known as The CEO or if the chickens were the ones with the gene that made the shells blue. But I am certain that the color of the eggs at my roadside pagoda were never dyed. The color was authentic. I know this for certain, because I collected those blue eggs myself. Right out of the shoot, they're warm. A little gooey, too. You need to pick off the hay that sticks to the shells as soon as possible or you'll never get it off. And then there goes your sales quota for the day.

    I used to like eating eggs. Mason would make them scrambled; he knew I wasn't one for experimentation. I never tired of eggs. I could eat them for breakfast, lunch, and dinner. But on the night we were to finally implement the Grand Master Plan, I hadn't eaten anything all day long. I was too busy trying to commit to memory the many directions Mason had recorded in his journal. I was in a tizzy until the moment actually arrived and we were standing by the ladder in the shadows. Swan Crest Farms' First Annual Masquerade Ball was starting to heat up.

    "Leave the dirty work to me," Mason kept repeating on that fateful evening "Wear your meadow stompers. And keep your hat on. Hold your head up, but maintain your posture in a relaxed, but upright slouch. Follow my lead. Remember to hold your designated position when leaning into the ladder at the appropriate time. Wait until I come back down with the ice. You want Project Peepers to come off without a hitch, *dunchu*, Lucy my love?"

Mason rattled through a final verbal rehearsal, ticking off each of his one hundred directions with a single breath.

"Let's summarize now, Lucy my love. It's vitally important to appear normal and blend into our everyday surroundings and, at the same time, look the part for Project Peepers," he said. "Doing so will help you maintain a seriousness of purpose."

I shouldn't have expected anything less from a forger like Mason than striving for authenticity. He was very successful in selling a lot of art with such an approach, although I didn't know at the time about that either. I only knew as much as Mason chose to tell me. Like a bunny munching on a trail of pellets leading to a trap, I followed his directions and wondered, who was I to risk being sloppy after he'd labored so long?

"Don't worry about the nitty-gritty. All you need to do is trust me no matter what happens at the Twists' mansion. And always know—deep, *deep* in your heart—that I only love *you*," Mason had said. "You'll remember that, won't you, Lucy my love?"

Lucy. That magical name chimed in my heart, melting away any residual doubt and frustration. It was the name *Lucy* that gave me the courage to play my part. And I knew it well. We had reviewed each line, each action, each move of the caper as if we had been rehearsing roles for a theatrical production. We knew every single scene and twist of the plot before anything actually happened.

"Three minutes. That'll be that," Mason said.

What we weren't counting on was that crazy duck Peepers quacking at me as I counted the seconds and knelt down by my ladder. Only that rare specimen himself, that freak of Mother Nature, could spook me from my designated position. He quacked at me as if he wanted to eat me for dinner. Then he hovered in the air while nipping at my big, black hat and staring me down with those bizarre blue eyes that sparkled and shined like diamonds. In a flash, I finally made a decision. I was peering into Dagmar's bedroom window. I was screaming Mason's name.

"Mason!"

But I suppose I was merely whispering on that chilly Halloween night, perched at the top as leaves were shaking and the wind picked up. Mason didn't seem to hear me.

"Hey!" I shouted as I leaned on the windowsill, hanging on for dear life. "What the heck are you doing? Come on! Let's go!"

I could see Mason standing on a platform in front of a tri-fold mirror …

He was wearing a Princess Diana gown …

He was checking the hem!

"The ice!" I barked, using the word he had taught me.

I was feeling more of an urge to escape than to find out the reason for his get-up. It was quite spectacular, really. A copy of a Princess Diana original worn by the world's most beloved princess. It was regal. Midnight blue. Strapless. A dropped waist. Silver stars embroidered in diamante on the bodice. Four or five layers of toile for the skirt, each trimmed with more diamante.

It might've been Halloween, but why would Mason be wearing that dress? He could've at least let me wax the hair off his chest. I never knew his parents, but I wouldn't be surprised if one of them was a bear. I just hope that the one who carried the gene for excessive body hair was his father, not his mother.

"Grab the ice!" I screamed through the window.

When my pleas failed to capture his attention, when he never for a second peeled his eyes away from his apparently dazzling reflection in the mirror, I used my own language.

"The diamonds, Mason! Take them *now*. And let's get out of here!"

My eyes were bugging out so far from their sockets, one of my contacts popped out, causing me to become nearly half blind, but I knew what I was seeing. My long fingernails cut into my face. And my hat was no longer on my head. It had flown into the room with the invisible wings of the strong country wind, landing at Mason's feet in front of the mirror. As I pushed back my hair that was flying loose from its hairpins, *Mason was still checking his hem.* For all I knew, he was planning on crashing the Twists' masquerade ball. Had we ever received a formal invitation?

Dancing with Jou Jou

"What is the matter with you? Let's scram!"

Scram. Just like "ice," the word wasn't part of my everyday vocabulary, but with my newly found identity as a jewel thief on the look-out, it seemed appropriate enough. I was proud of myself for thinking it up on my own. Or maybe I heard it from an old black and white movie, the kind with cops and robbers. Those were the ones that were among our favorites. We liked being retro. We liked playing roles. Sometimes Mason would even call me a dame when he wasn't nuzzling my neck and whispering the one name he knew had the power to make me swoon: *Lucy*. But that night, as Dagmar and Duncan Twist's party was just beginning to rev up, my *Ricky*—or, uh, Mason—seemed to be dressing up for the affair himself. But he hadn't told me about that part of the plan. Would he dare deviate from the instructions he himself had so carefully etched into his cloth notebook? Would he improvise? On the night of Project Peepers? Would he go to a party? Without me? On his own?

"Mason! Where's the ice? The jewels, the gems? Did you get them?"

Was he going deaf? While I was blinded in one eye? As far as I was concerned, our mission could be scrubbed. I had enough of his tomfoolery. If he intended for me to dress as a thief for the party, well, he could keep the hat that was still lying at his feet; I no longer intended to act the part in real life. I was starting to feel I was playing the fool. I suppose that was an easy matter. Unlike Mason, I could be molded like Play-Doh®. But he always remained strong within himself no matter the circumstances. He could wear a gown of a dead princess and still be secure in his masculinity, not a shred of self-doubt or worries about other peoples' perceptions. Besides, I thought, Mason was always making people laugh.

Or maybe he'd just watched an old rerun of Milton Berle wearing a dress. He just couldn't help embodying the saying that imitation is the sincerest form of flattery. I suppose it could've been worse: he might've taken up the violin after listening to Jack Benny. But I don't think either Milton Berle or Jack Benny would do what Mason did next: he raised the back of his flowing, blue gown, exposing his bare bottom. Then he raised that, too—and mooned me.

"Why, Lucy my love," he crooned in his best Ricky Ricardo voice. "You should never doubt your Ricky. I've got them right here."

"Where?"

"*Here*," he said more emphatically, wiggling that butt of his in the air, the rear end I'd cup with two palms when we made love. "Care to go spelunking?"

For the first time since we had been together—after perhaps a thousand matings—I was seeing his hind quarters from a brand new perspective. Until that moment when he told me the secret hiding place for the Blue Diamond Peepers, I don't think I fully realized that my hairy boyfriend had a little bum that was smooth and silky enough beneath errant strands of hair to reflect the glow of the moon that was shining in from my perch at the window. Aside from the bottoms of his feet and the palms of his hands, it was about the only place on him not covered in human fur.

"Best hiding place in the world," he said. "You'd need a miner's helmet to find them. But first, you'd have to know where to look. And who'd ever think to look here," he said as he pointed to his booty. "How else do you think diamond dealers get past customs duty-free? Diamond dealers are the world's richest and cheapest bastards. The Twists have nothing on those greedy thugs. They'd hold pieces of coal up their bums if they could live long enough for them to transform to diamonds. Bodily orifices are their treasure troves. Sacred human ground! It's their tradition! Who am I to go and break it?"

Then he started dancing with a smile on his face and a pulsing action in his hips as if he were doing the mojito.

"Quit clowning around," I shouted, forgetting to whisper. "We have a Grand Master Plan to follow! Project Peepers? Remember?"

But Mason was still shaking his cute booty in the air. It *was* magnificent. I think I could've watched him shake it all night just as long as he'd eventually …

There was no time to ponder such dermatological wonders as the luminescent qualities of my boyfriend's tushy. I might've finally appreciated why some people install mirrors on ceilings, but we had to get out of there. And in a hurry. There was just no telling when or if the Twists would pop in, perhaps to adjust their costumes or, who knows? Perhaps Dagmar would decide at the last minute to retrieve the

Blue Diamond Peepers from the safe and wear them for the party. No matter what persona she had chosen to assume for her First Annual Masquerade Ball, there was one thing about Dagmar that was certain: she never tired of showing off the spoils of her lottery riches, especially her newly acquired pair of gems.

"Drop the dress and grab your clothes," I hollered in a husky voice strong enough to strain my vocal chords. "And let's *va-moose* out of here!"

But Mason appeared disgusted with my command. Seemingly oblivious to the dangers of being discovered, he finally peeled himself away from the sight of himself and his gown in the mirror and turned to me with a scowl.

"This is *couture*," he declared as if I were some kind of an ignoramus. He swished the gown at its skirt, then smoothed it down to cover his bum. "It's quite valuable," he said.

He was fingering the bodice as if pointing out how the hand-sewn diamante stars glistened against the midnight blue to prospective bidders at a Princess Diana gown auction. Then he kicked my hat across the room that was obstructing the view of his hem in the mirror. But it didn't go far, so he tossed the hat toward me at the window. I missed it and it dropped to the floor.

"Only one hundred, thirty-two designers are designated by the great state of France as being authentically couture," he continued. "They're actually *licensed* by the government to produce such goods."

"You're not one of them," I said. Mason was always making up statistics, but I think he was right about those. "Besides," I told him. "That gown was made by an Englishman. The original one, that is. I suppose he had a license, too?"

What was I doing? I might've flipped through a book of Diana gowns Mason had studied when he was sewing one for Dagmar. But it was hardly the time or place to debate fashion or a couture license to create it. Not in the Twists' master bedroom suite. Not on the night of Project Peepers.

"I don't need a license. I made this myself."

"I know," I countered, utterly perplexed by why he'd be modeling the fake Princess Diana gown while the gems were presumably lodged somewhere up his derriere. "I watched you make it. I modeled it for you. I was your human mannequin, your dress form with legs. Remember? I do! I was *there*."

"And a more stunning dress form there never was, my little living doll," he said. "Dagmar and Duncan paid me royally for my efforts—and yours. Who ever doubted that lottery winners were generous? It was quite a haul for us, Lucy. A cool $200,000 pay out with a mere $368.73 investment of fabric, trim, and thread. That's a grand profit of $199,631.27.

Mason never joked about his art and handiwork. Nor about money. He'd calculate to the last cent. Money and art he was dead serious about. But I never knew all the details about the selling of the gown. He had only confessed to me that he palmed it off to Dagmar as an original from an *authentic* Princess Diana collection. He recorded it all, he said, in his notebook.

"Genius! Pure bloody genius!" Mason said, quite pleased with himself. "Those couture twits in France have nothing on me. They would need a battalion of seamstresses working for months to achieve what I created in a matter of days—and alone. Who needs a license when as a knock-off gown, my work is perfection. Even better than the original, don't you think, Lucy? Genius! Pure bloody genius!"

It may have been Halloween, but I wasn't liking that he was wearing the gown now as his costume. And I knew I was in over my head, for this was not his first crime. How could I have been such a schnook? I had watched him cutting and sewing as thread and scraps of fabric were flying in the air, his hands a blur of artful craftsmanship, applying the same exacting standards as he did to any of his arts, of which there were many. Mason was forever busy with his hands and an endless variety of tools and brushes as he carved and pounded and meticulously arranged stone and wood, clay and glass. He created all kinds of artistic treasures for the Twists in the three months that we'd lived in the cottage on the grounds of their estate—statues, jewelry, and even the wooden duck decoys. The only works of art he was proud of, the ones he considered to have any originality at all and his personal stamp of approval, were his paintings of animals large enough to hang on a wall of a castle. It was that talent alone that had inspired the Twists to commission him as their artist-in-residence and transplant him from New York. But one of Mason's paintings was the only masterpiece he had yet to whip up. I knew from the day we moved to the cottage after the Twists had foisted the invitation, that something was askew. I despised collecting eggs. Dodging the rooster known as The CEO required a shield and a saber. Dagmar got a free farmhand along with Mason's high-priced art.

I felt my ladder at the window starting to rock, but I think it was from the uncertainty of my wanting to stay or leave. The thoughts were ping-ponging from my heart to my brain:

Do I stick around at the window until the man I love decides to *adios*?

Or do I slip down that ladder and skedaddle alone?

Logic told me to get lost, but my heart still belonged with Mason and clearly feared no danger. That is, until Dagmar popped in. She burst through her own bedroom door and the wind blew billows of pink dupiani silk at the window. I held on tight to those draperies for quick cover. Short of scampering back down that ladder like a squirrel seeking shelter from a sudden roll of heavy thunder, or worse, being discovered by Dagmar herself outside her own bedroom window on a ladder—well, it was the best I could do at the time.

"*Jou Jou!*"

Jou Jou? I echoed like one of the parrots in the Swan Crest's Aviary, but only silently to myself. Who's Dagmar calling *Jou Jou?*

"Why are you wearing my new Princess Di gown?" she asked. "That cost me three hundred grand."

Three hundred? I thought Mason had told me he'd only charged *two* hundred.

"And why didn't you do as I asked you to do? I told you, Valentina is supposed to model it for my party. I gave you written permission for your *tagalong* to enter the mansion and with instructions clearly spelled out. Didn't you tell her?"

Valentina. Hearing my real name for a change jolted me back to reality. I might've been smothered with dupiani silk, but I wasn't really a thief. This was not a game. No longer was I *Lucy*.

"Don't tell me you finally ditched that girlfriend of yours, that bean stalk with two beans for breasts?"

Maybe my breasts were the size of two beans; that would make hers watermelons, perhaps accounting for her choice of color for curtains as well as her inability to model the Di gown herself.

"Valentina's so lanky and tall, we should make her live in the Giraffe Park."

I heard her laugh at her own joke. It was bad enough to be the butt of her humor, but then she overstepped the boundaries of even my tolerance for snide remarks with what she said next.

"Come here, my *Jou Jou*, my personal plaything, my toy," she commanded in an affected French accent. "Out of all of my animals, you are my favorite pet. How you do make me laugh!"

Then she let out a riveted squeal like one of her monkeys up in the Bamboo Garden singing for a banana supper. I just wished that she'd go up there and let a monkey bang her head on the gong.

"I suppose it *would* be funnier if you were the one to model the dress instead of Valentina. You do always tell me, *mon paramour*: 'Anything for humor,' *n'est-ce pas, mon Jou Jou?* Ah, how you do exist exclusively for *mon pleaure, mon amusement*. Come, *mon cher*. Take my hand *now*! I want to dance with my *Jou Jou* ..."

"Ah, *oui, oui*," I heard Mason stutter. After what seemed to be a couple of half-hearted attempts to spit out a few strings of high school French, he called Dagmar, *"Ma petite Chou Chou."*

Huh? Was I to understand that she was his *Chou Chou*—a little cabbage of all things—while he was her *Jou Jou*—a toy? How tacky! At least *our* love charade had more meaning behind it and the good taste to be based on real people, like a rumba band leader and his redheaded wife. But the dupiani silk plugged up further thoughts of a romantic games competition when Dagmar started humming and I could just picture Mason dancing with her on the other side of the drapes. Then I heard a moment of silence, followed by panting and sighs.

"Oooo-la-la"

That did it. Instead of feeling a baby kick from the inside-out from what I was hoping would be our first child by then, I felt as though I had just been kicked from the outside-in by Dagmar. But instead of hollering and letting my pain be known, a sudden wave of nausea made me cold and flush. Could morning sickness occur in the evening? Suddenly, I was feeling not angry, but sick; it's hard to be both at the same time. So I covered my mouth and folded over like a rag doll, holding it all in. With all the strength I had left in me, I was imploding like a volcano in reverse, burning up with one, single question I wanted Mason to answer—and pronto:

When did my personal Ricky Ricardo start speaking French?

PART TWO: MASQUERADE BALL

CHAPTER 7

The Haircut

The Brian Setzer Orchestra couldn't make it to Dagmar and Duncan's party, Mason had said, but the famous band leader sent a handwritten note of apology, explaining that he and his musicians were already booked for Halloween Eve at the Rainbow Room on the top of NBC at Rockefeller Center in New York City. Mason held out a bouquet the bandleader had also sent over as a gift to Dagmar and Duncan, one that was arranged in autumn colors with African orchids, Tiger's Eye, and Birds of Paradise. But despite not having a celebrity musical group lined up for her party, Dagmar still paid Mason handsomely for having made the connection as well as for designing an entire line of leopard skin jackets that he suggested the band should wear. After all, he already had the jackets made, he told her, after the last trip to Thailand where he purchased a rare pair of monkeys. According to Mason, when you've journeyed across the globe to Asia, finding exquisite fabric and a cheap tailor in Hong Kong was just a hop away.

With a substitute band dressed up in the new jackets on the night of the big bash, you'd never know another boogie-woogie band was taking Brian Setzer's place, for it sounded quite good. It was also quite loud. Vibrations could be felt in the Twists' master bedroom, despite that Duncan had specified steal-enforced floor beams when he and Dagmar had designed their new house. Drums were beating, horns were blaring, and the party seemed to be already rocking, sending dear

Dagmar out of the bedroom to go greet her guests. Had she left just one doo-whop later, I feared that the volcano imploding inside me behind the watermelon dupiani silk, would reverse itself and explode, spewing fire onto those new drapes.

"Hey, you!" I said to Mason when the coast was clear, curling my index finger and gesturing for him to come to me at my perch in the window. But he wasn't budging. He just stared at me with those eyes of his, both of them bulging out, and looked me squarely without flinching. "Yeah, you," I said, as if there could be any doubt, as if anyone else were in that room. I felt we were in a movie and I was the jilted moll whom Mason would start calling *doll face*. But I had already played that part when he'd transformed me into a human mannequin while he was sewing the gown. "Yes, you, *amigo*," I said, seething. "Or should I say *Jou Jou?*"

I stepped off my ladder and through the window into the bedroom, away from the draperies one measured step toward Mason at a time. No longer was I Lucy. I was a panther zeroing in on its prey, half blind, perhaps, with only one contact in. But a thirst for *Jou Jou's* blood couldn't stop me from pouncing. It's lucky that *Chou Chou* had already rolled out the door like the roly-poly cabbage that she was.

"Now, Lucy ..."

"Don't you Lucy me!"

For the first time in our little romance, my hand was balled up into a tight fist that scared even me. Still, Mason wasn't budging. At least not at first.

"What's with the dame? You cheating on me?"

The transformation from good girl to bad was starting to take hold, a process that began when I climbed up the ladder.

"And you told me *two* hundred thousand smackers for that gown, not *three*. You holding out on me, too?"

And the transformation was complete. It was official: I was an accomplice, a criminal, a moll. Mason's shady underworld life had not only seeped into my vocabulary, it had transcended into my life, too, eclipsing my entire being. He stood there observing me with those luscious eyes that always had the power to seduce me, capable of popping out of his sweet face whenever he commanded. I searched that face I dearly loved for some kind of sign that he wasn't really the man I knew him to be. I wanted to witness for myself at least a clue that he was someone else other than my Mason, my Ricky, my one true love. But as I studied his face, I just couldn't find one. *God help me*, I thought. I loved him.

"What are you talking about, Lucy? I wouldn't hold out on you. We're partners. Fused at the hip. We're not just in this little caper fifty-fifty, but one hundred percent. If you ask me, what's yours is mine, what's mine is yours. It's not eighty-twenty or sixty-forty or fifty-five-forty-five. It's a hundred percent. See?"

I've got to admit, Mason always managed to make me feel stupid when he talked numbers. He knew it, too. But I did warm up to his declaration of being partners. That much I could understand. I liked being a couple. He was part of me. I believed I was part of him, too. We were nearly one in the same. At least I wanted to think so at the time.

"You told me you sold that gown for $200,000. And she said $300,000. What gives?"

"Lucy," he said shaking his head in disbelief. "You've got to account for research, labor, and materials. Not to mention import tax and travel expenses and shipping and bribing the border patrol and ..."

He went into a dissertation that only a seasoned world traveler could, one who had countless dealings with importation snafus. He well knew how I detested such legal entanglements and kept rattling off whole passages of import laws until I waved my hands to get him to stop.

"Why did Dagmar call you *Jou Jou*? And more importantly, what are you doing calling her *Chou Chou*? How long has this been going on? I heard you smooching with her. And dancing, too! What else are you doing with that ... that bossy dame? 'Fess up!"

I stood firmly, my hands on my hips, and my toes tapping inside my big mud boots, as Mason started coming toward me one step at a time. And then he took yet another, all the while kissing me in the air.

"Don't you dare!" I warned him.

When he finally held out both of his arms, revealing the hair of his underarms, I couldn't help thinking, *couldn't he have made a gown with sleeves?* After what I had just witnessed and heard from Chou Chou and Jou Jou, did he *still* really have the power, the magic, to make me laugh? Even when I was a panther about to pounce? Whatever reflex for laughing that I might've held within me, I suppressed it as best I could. I held out hope that he did have a logical explanation. When you intend to enter motherhood, you hope for the best.

"Not one step more," I shouted, forgetting for the moment that we weren't in our own home. But Mason knew me well. All it took was just one little wiggle, his right elbow in his left palm, then left elbow in his right, then back again, while those bug eyes of his popped with each thrust of his hips. Goofy. But I wasn't going to crack, despite that those whacky movements drew me to him and gave me such joy. Call it blind love.

"Stop that," I shouted.

I vowed silently to myself that not one single corner of my mouth would dare to crinkle, not if I could help it. I watched him starting to wiggle and dance, but was determined to stay firm until he gave me an answer.

"What were you doing kissing Dagmar? How could you …"

But Mason came closer and closer. Seeing him clowning around in that ridiculous dress—royal as it might have once been—my panther-like roar that had threatened to be unleashed from the depths of my soul, was starting to convert to a giggle. I just couldn't help myself. He looked so silly in that flowing blue dress. Without heels, it was at least six inches too long. And his underarms desperately needed a good waxing.

Then he gave me a reason to finally release all the laughter I was holding back: he picked up my black hat from the floor and tossed it in my direction.

"Evidence," he said, starting to shimmy and twirling around in a circle. He was dancing with himself, shaking imaginary maracas and celebrating his brilliance for kissing his pigeon named Dagmar—or rather, *Chou Chou*. Then he did a back bend in that dress and picked up the big, black hat from the carpet with his teeth.

"I had to either get rid of the evidence that you were here with me or prevent Dagmar from seeing it," he mumbled with the hat in his mouth. "Quick thinking on my part. Don't you think, Lucy?"

Then he grabbed the hat by the brim and tossed it out the window where the wind swept it far away.

"Kissing Dagmar is enough to make my curly hair straight."

Then he shimmied some more like a human vibrator on high speed.

"Do you see the sacrifices I make for you? For us? For the baby?"

I didn't know at that moment if I should be grateful or mad. He certainly proved himself to be resourceful. I was recalling how hard he had toiled at his work table at the cottage, before moving his paraphernalia up to his new Ice House studio. Such drive! Such fortitude! He wasn't distracted, not for an instant, until his hands finished moving like two Ferris wheels with synchronized precision and sending thread, fabric scraps, and paper pattern pieces onto the hardwood floor, until the knock-off Diana gown was, at last, complete.

But my thoughts were snipped short when Dagmar—that is, Chou Chou—came back into the bedroom. Stripped from my cover under the silk at the window, she could see me in plain sight. And I could see her, too, in her costume for the evening: a Parisian can-can dancer right out of the Moulin Rouge. And, sure enough, she had the Blue Diamond Peepers on a gold chain around her neck. But I thought that Mason had stuffed the diamonds up his …

There was no time to question Mason now. I had to think fast, which didn't always come as naturally to me as it did to Mason. Should I smile and greet Dagmar in the usual way? Or stand in horror that she probably wanted to steal my man? Would Duncan be shocked by the news as he stood right behind her wearing a striped shirt, beret, penciled mustache curled at both ends—the works—or was he part of a three-way tryst?

It was as if I were looking into a mirror as I searched Dagmar's face for a signal for the most appropriate expression to present, for it appeared that she was trying to figure out exactly the same thing. Smile? Shout? Silence? What was the proper etiquette for greeting your man's art patrons, our employers, in their very own bedroom, just after sneaking into that master boudoir through the window by way of a ladder?

"When did you pop in, missy?" Dagmar said. "Fly in on a broomstick?"

Then she laughed in that monkey way she had, throwing her head back, and shaking and bouncing all over. But perhaps she was right.

Without my hat on, my hair by that time must've looked like it'd be appropriate for a witch.

"I had her sneak up through the service staircase," Mason jumped in. He might've been sneaky himself, but this time I was grateful. "I didn't want your guests to see her before her entrance in the Princess Diana gown."

"Yes," Dagmar agreed. "That would be a *royal* blunder."

The three of them laughed, but I didn't get it. What was so funny about the word *royal*? Oh, yes. The dress. Mason's dress. I could never concentrate too well in the presence of the Twists, especially Duncan. Clearly, in that marriage it was the wife who did all the jabbering, while we rarely heard the husband utter a word. We—or at least I—barely knew Duncan. He never even commented on Mason wearing a dress.

"Thank goodness your architect thought to include service stairs in his master plans," Mason snuck in. "Brilliant!"

"Yes," Dagmar said again.

I suppose she was uncharacteristically struggling for words. But I guess when one's French-speaking lover is discovered in one's master bedroom—and wearing a dress—while his girlfriend suddenly appears there, too—while one's husband is costumed up in an Apache dancer's outfit—and a hundred guests are awaiting your arrival—I guess that words would be in short supply.

"Let's toast to that architect! Let's toast to the service stairs," Dagmar continued. "And what the heck. Let's toast to the lottery, too! I just love being rich. It's so much fun!"

She squealed again in that monkey laugh of hers, shamelessly bragging about her good fortune. Anyone else might've been thinking the exact same thoughts about having struck it rich. But the difference between other people and Dagmar was that she'd come right out and say aloud:

"I'm rich! I'm rich! I'm rich!"

A real toast would have to wait until our little foursome made its way to the bar and the bar tenders shook up appropriate cocktails. By the sound of the wind outside the window, perhaps hurricanes would be about right. With a thunderous rattle at the opened window, Dagmar darted to close it, but Mason beat her to the quick.

"Allow me," he told her like a gentleman, then dashed three steps ahead. Quite a feat considering the voluminous nature of his gown.

"I've got to get a picture of you in that dress," Dagmar cackled. "You look like a runt compared to your girlfriend here. Or like a princess who'd be turned away from the palace and never be crowned queen. You could've at least dabbed some Nair on those pits," she said. "I never realized you were so fluffy."

Ah, good, I thought. They never formed the monster with two backs or she would have known that Mason's body hair was similar to one of her monkey's—that is, if the monkey had a perm. Then again, knowing Mason's penchant for being authentic, perhaps he wooed Dagmar inside Swan Crest's pig pen. Or perhaps he'd think it'd be more romantic on top of the goats' rocks at night; Dagmar did explain to me how goat droppings provide warmth and comfort. Either place would be fitting to heat up a bitter smelling cabbage like Chou Chou. I was beginning to like her name.

As I was considering the possible locations on the farm for a moonlit rendezvous between two faux-French lovers, Mason was pulling the latch on the hinged windows. Then he turned on his bare heels.

"Please," he began, holding up his hand like a constable directing traffic. With that single gesture and a new serious tone in his voice, he took command of the room. "We need to show some respect for the original owner of this magnificent ball gown. And Princess Diana, as we all know too well, never ever would live long enough to be crowned queen."

Then Mason bowed his head in respect for the late princess who'd been killed in her prime along with her fiancé when their drunken driver careened through a tunnel—a French one at that—while being savagely chased by a throng of camera-snapping paparazzi.

"She knew it, too," I piped up, breaking Mason's moment of silence. "When Princess Diana was still alive, she said in that television interview that she'd never be Queen of England, but she wanted to be 'Queen of the People's Hearts.' Remember?"

I surprised myself by inserting that fact, seeming to join Mason's side. Up until that night, being his partner came naturally enough. Why was it that whenever the four of us were together, I always felt demoted to his sidekick?

"I don't know if I want *her* to wear this gown," Dagmar said directly to Mason as if I didn't have two ears to hear. She was speaking about me in the third person, but she was clearly cooling down. I didn't think she ever liked it when I put in my two cents. In this case, pointing out how she had been disrespectful to a royal—a real one who probably never *once* bought a ticket from New Jersey's SuperDuper Lottery.

"Why don't you wear it after all," she said to Mason. "I think the gang downstairs would get a hoot out of you."

As long as Dagmar wasn't getting a *hoot* out my Ricky, I'd be just fine with that arrangement. I was beginning to calm down, too. I think it was her husband's presence that offered such an effect. Wordless and often motionless as Duncan was—unless he was smacking snapping turtles in the pond—hanging around that silent man often felt like being a visitor at his wake. It wasn't so much that Duncan out-aged Dagmar and the two of us by about twenty-five years, as much as it was the way I'd never see him blink or turn his head. Could he be soused before the party even began? Whatever the reason for Duncan's eerie silence, I still loved Mason and didn't want Dagmar to have him. I hoped for the best. At least for the sake of our baby. That is, if that last mating ritual sent Little Ricky sperms swimming in the right direction.

After seesawing back and forth over which one of us, Mason or myself, would wear the gown, Mason managed to work his magic again. He weaved his words into the debate until he emerged the winner. And it was decided that I would be the one to wear the Princess Diana gown.

"Just make sure she's authentic," Dagmar said as she yanked Duncan out the door by his arm. "That's your specialty after all, Mason. Isn't that right?"

Mason stood at attention in his gown, facing Dagmar straight-on. "Authentic. Of course."

"I want her really to play the part. And I'm not kidding. She's got the height and figure of Princess Diana."

"She's a perfect fit. No worries."

"Good," Dagmar said before she finally slipped out the door and dissolved into the boogie-woogie music rising up through the floor. "But just one last detail."

"Detail?" Mason questioned. He liked those.

"Yes. I want her hair to look authentic, too. Just like Princess Diana's."

"Authentic, of course. But …"

"No wig."

"Huh?"

"Just make sure you …"

"Yes?"

"Cut her hair."

Dagmar slammed the door behind her. Then she thundered back into the room.

"And bleach it!" she hollered, turning on her heel.

Before banging the door closed for the third and final time, Dagmar lifted the back of her can-can skirt, revealing her red lace slip, garters, and stockings. Then she mooned us. Not even a g-string. Only it was me, trapped into modeling the gown at the party after being Mason's lookout on the ladder, who was the ass.

Chapter 8

The Staircase

The grand staircase in the Twists' farmhouse mansion—not the one intended for service that was hidden somewhere in the wall linking the master bedroom directly to the housekeeper's quarters—but the main one leading to the foyer by the front door, was a flier. That is, it didn't exactly follow a straight path, nor was it curved. Instead, it sort of jutted out in a way that was vaguely reminiscent of the waterfall spilling from Tannery Falls, following a series of black marble landings before merging with the same polished marble on the floor, which was where the party guests were bouncing to the beat of the stand-in Brian Setzer band.

Trouble was, until the night of the party, I had never gone up or down that staircase. I wasn't familiar with the unconventional pattern of landings and steps and, considering my obstructed vision from having just cried my eyes out, I must've misjudged how far down or out to put my feet as I made my entrance to show off Dagmar's newest acquisition. I felt a bit wobbly as it was with all the excitement thus far into the evening. An itchy neck from my new short haircut didn't help my disposition, nor did the high heels I wasn't accustomed to wearing after mucking around the farm all the time in mud boots. And the blue tint of my new contacts was coloring my world in a new light; Mason, of course, had already prepared for such an ocular detail, assuring I was a fitting faux-Diana.

Before I continue, I wish to extend my sincerest apologies to every Brit in England or wherever they happen to be on the face of the globe. I am sorry for having portrayed the beloved royal, Princess Diana, as anything less than regal. But you see, I simply felt I had little choice under the circumstances. I just couldn't help myself when I slipped on those stairs. Sure, I could've made good on my threat to leave Mason in a huff and scampered back down that ladder; maybe I should never have allowed him to take a scissors to my hair. But I do blame myself—and only myself—now for my poor judgment. You see, making promises and keeping them have always been a sacred matter to me. I had always become unnerved as a foster child whenever promises to me were broken. I swore I would never break one to anyone else. Perhaps I should've chosen to forgo the one I made to Mason about swiping the Blue Diamond Peepers. But it seemed too late to renege on that one by the time Dagmar and Duncan were all costumed up and their guests had arrived and had already started to boogie. I was trapped like a fox in one of Mason's hand-rigged crates. I know now I wasn't as agile. I guess you could call me a dumb bunny, one with a brain the same size as one of my bean-sized breasts. At least that's how I was feeling. I'm just glad that no one seemed to notice when I tripped on the stairs.

I'll be forever grateful to that substitute swing band for the volume of their amplifiers. The music was so loud that the guests, bobbing around to the beat of the drums, were too busy with each other—and themselves—to notice me at all. They were admiring their costumes and greeting each other with the same question: "Is that you?" They must've needed to work hard to hear the answers, bending and shouting to speak and be heard.

Besides, who would know to watch my entrance when it had never been formally announced? Without Mason pulling the strings, Dagmar and Duncan were lost in the crowd. The only announcement she made, if you could call it that, was blurting out:

"I bought a Diana gown! I bought a Diana gown!"

She was jumping up from the crowd, pointing toward the staircase for her "gang" to all look at that gown, hoping, no doubt, that they'd cheer. But they just didn't get the message. Here, Mason—and I—had gone through somersaults and back flips to assure that the Twists' latest acquisition would have an authentic first showing, and there was

Dagmar drowning in the crowd with Duncan at her side keeping her anchored.

Not one of the hundred party guests noticed me up there on the stairs making a royal entrance. Nor did any of them see that I had slipped. With music blaring, the joint was a-rockin' with each couple wearing his-and-her costume sets, except for the single mother dressed as a mouse who clung to her stroller at the party with her triplets dressed as kittens and a Maltese pup tied to the handle and wearing a small black mask. Aside from that pitiful group, there was a cheesy playboy with his arms around a hot dish who boasted more cleavage than there was satin holding it all up. A god and goddess from Greek mythology were wearing togas and crowns, while a couple wearing Viking hats held a live goat on a gold leash. Standing apart from the pack were three sets of Anthony and Cleopatra's gussied up with tasteful touches of gold, feathers, jewels, and asps, while a pair of flappers in fringe and feathers shimmied next to their escorts wearing white bucks, narrow ties, and straw fedoras. And then there were three couples who arrived in bear fur get-ups—one of them in white, another in brown, and the third in black and white.

None of the invited masqueraders noticed I had fallen on the stairs, except for The Jaff who came dressed as himself, the tennis star that he was in real life. He was known for only wearing tennis clothes wherever he went. Only when watching a Yankee game in box seats when a camera would zoom in on his face, would he be seen donning a baseball cap as a sign of respect from one world class athlete to others out on the playing field. Baseball caps were his trademark style, along with a braided ponytail. Sometimes he'd be seen wearing two of them like Willie Nelson, but he always had an earring on one of his rather large ears that slightly jutted out. But no one ever mentioned that trait. It was part of what made him uniquely handsome, like a prominent nose on a princess; such a feature simply was never discussed, in private or in the media.

But what I couldn't stop gawking at as I paraded down the staircase in my pathetic attempt to model Dagmar's newly acquired Princess Diana gown, was my big, black hat sitting on top of The Jaff's head— one side still flipped up, the other down. The sight of what Mason had called *evidence* was as alarming as if I had seen a sheriff's badge in my face—or a pair of blue eyes belonging to that freaky duck named Peepers. When I saw the hat on The Jaff's head that matched his black athletic gear bearing the Nike logo on his shirt, jacket, pants, and footwear, I gingerly took another step down. But I was still on one of those ridiculous landings, the kind that had been built strictly for show. Believe me, when you think a landing is another step on a staircase just after your man presumably stuffed two diamonds up his crack and a *Chou Chou* just ordered him to snip off your long locks, well, I wasn't exactly having a pleasant evening. Nothing was going according to plan. My world seemed to be spinning on a new axis causing my balance to be off.

But no one noticed that I had fallen. Only The Jaff.

"Who—or what—was that?" The Jaff asked as he crouched down to help me.

Mason had shot down the railing right past us, now donning a Prince Charming costume complete with a full set of shiny armor. And the crowd was going wild.

"Look! Look! That's got to be Mason!" one of the women cried out. Then one housewife after the next called out Mason's name, too.

"Mason! Oh, Mason!"

"I'd know his moves anywhere! Mason!"

"Mason! Oh, it's him. I just know it's him!"

The women were following his streak of silver into the ballroom *en masse* as their husbands followed. Then we heard Mason break out of his royal metal suit as it clanged to the marble floor, followed by gasps filling the ballroom.

"I knew it! It's Mason!"

"Oh, Mason!"

My party-stopping boyfriend hit the piano keys with a dazzling rendition of "Let's Live It Up" as Dagmar sounded like she was attempting the counter chorus. Duncan, no doubt, was standing alongside her, stiff as a possum, all while The Jaff stayed with me on the landing. But I wanted to get back up on my feet. I wanted to get the heck out of there.

"The party's just starting. What's your hurry?" The Jaff asked while testing the limits of flex in my ankle. "That squirt is banging out some great tunes."

Squirt? Why was he—as well as Dagmar—suggesting that Mason was small? Say what you will about Mason, but my man wasn't lacking in height. I suppose what The Jaff was actually pointing out without coming right out and saying it was that Mason and I were a mismatch based on our appearance alone. Perhaps his shiny armor had overwhelmed his frame and he seemed smaller than he actually was by comparison when he unleashed himself from his tin can costume. But Mason wasn't really short as much as I was unusually tall. Perhaps Dagmar was right. Maybe I did belong in the Giraffe Park. But my new friend on the staircase interrupted further self-deprecating thoughts.

"The Twists are a hoot!" The Jaff continued. "You've got to see them for yourself. I never knew I had such funny neighbors. Someone ought to put them on *Saturday Night Live*. Although the *Live* part might pose a problem for Duncan."

Huh? Did I hear him correctly? Was someone finally talking real sense to me? And seeing a circus of people who claimed to have class, through my eyes? Instead of playing retro make-believe love games? Or feeding me woodpecker soup? Or shooting me with insults about my bra size or height? Or barking out orders for my hair to be cut short and bleached blond? Or tying me up to a tree? Or shoving a paddle in my hands and commanding me to strike a snapping turtle, interrupting the natural order of Tannery Pond? Or leading me to believe that a roasted fox was a small pig on a campfire skewer?

As this new perspective on our little world called Swan Crest Farms started seeping into my little bean-sized brain, until I had fallen on the staircase, up until that very moment when The Jaff described Duncan in the same way that I viewed him, too, I don't think I realized that I hadn't heard *anyone* speak the truth since moving into the cottage.

So much for being humble. No more being naïve.

In that exact moment, I think I had passed the puberty mark and started wriggling out of my orphan shell, and I wanted to wriggle out of the little house called the cottage, too. I was starting to feel like a grownup. I liked how The Jaff was looking at me with a twinkle in his eye and the type of grin that seemed to be acknowledging that we had the same point of view. Then he laughed, sort of like Woody Woodpecker. It was a funny kind of sound, but endearing in a joyful, cartoonish way.

"If that shrimp at the piano was supposed to be made up like Prince Charming, then that must make you Princess Diana. That's what she always searched for, you know. That is, when she was still alive."

Chalk up another one for The Jaff. Out of all the animals, four-legged and two-legged at Swan Crest Farms, it seemed only one was capable of putting two together with two, then come up with the right sum. The Jaff might've been talented on the tennis court as the world knew. But I never followed tennis. Still, I was sure that he wasn't just athletic, rich, and handsome, not to mention idolized throughout the world. The Jaff was observant and smart. With a mere glance, he figured out Mason's costume was intended to compliment Princess Diana. No one else in the crowd of one hundred party guests seemed to notice the connection. But naturally, they did notice Mason. He knew how to draw a crowd. That is, when he wasn't being sneaky.

"Here, let me help you," The Jaff said, scooping me up gently with his free left hand as he continued to hold onto his drink with his right. "Your ankle may be weak for a while, but it's probably not broken. Just don't test it too soon."

A world class athlete must've learned about sprained muscles at some point in his career. He picked me up and placed me expertly on my two feet. His kind assistance and words were more healing than an aloe plant's sap on rope burns.

"Can't be too comfortable sitting on those steps. Can't be too comfortable walking in high heels either. How do you expect to play tennis with me wearing footwear like that?"

Was The Jaff asking me for a tennis date? Was there actually a person in that exclusive neighborhood on River Bend Road, none of whom ever extended a formal invitation to a couple of cottage dwellers, who bothered to inquire about my comfort? I was awe-struck by the thought—and ashamed of myself for having been such a dope—and for far too long. Then I looked up to his face and saw them: his magnificent tennis star eyes. Doesn't anyone in Burberry Hills—duck, tennis star, or princess—have eyes that are any other color but blue? All I could see was that same regal color that seemed to be haunting me all night, including from the Blue Diamond Peepers. But this time, with two orbs sparkling as bright as the Great White Light that one hears about shining from heaven, I was no longer seeing colors as much as

I was witnessing, well, I suppose you could call it—I don't know how else to describe it, but *truth*.

Unlike most people, mere mortals, The Jaff didn't wear a mask to play up to the cameras or merely amuse a party guest like me. He didn't need a mask, I supposed, with all the talent he possessed. With one look in my direction, he could've raised me up from my stumble with the powerful beam glowing from his magnificent eyes. I understood now what all the fuss was about on the tennis courts when the press watched his every move. I knew then on the third landing of the Twists' grand staircase that it wasn't so much the tennis balls the cameras wished to follow as much as it was to observe The Jaff himself.

As Mason's last tune concluded with the crowd applauding and cheering, I was beginning to believe that what he had said about the Twists may have been right, the part about them only having luck, not talent. I knew my man had artistic gifts and in abundance—just as I knew The Jaff had a rare air about him, too. Some people seem to be more blessed than others, but in a way that is internal and natural, something that arises from their hearts, not their wallets. But at that moment I knew two things more:

I knew I had to go home, but *not* to the cottage. And I knew I was in love, but *not* with The Jaff.

Chapter 9

The Truth

Truth **can hurt. Planning** a jewel heist was just plain stupid. Worse, it was wrong.

I realized the error of my ways when I met The Jaff on the landing, someone who seemed to speak to me with kindness and candor. But acquiring the wisdom to own up to a mistake doesn't ordinarily come in an instant, not when you trust your cherished lover and sign up for night patrol on a ladder. I guess I needed to survive danger, not to mention humiliation, before I could straighten out my pretzel logic and see that Mason and I had really goofed up. Big time.

But roses can bloom in a pile of manure after proving hardy enough to break through the hard crust of the earth. The reward for braving the rocks and boulders of life was *truth*. That heavenly gift allowed common sense and love to finally converge in my soul, enabling my spirit to flourish. Finally, I saw the light. Our path was clear to me now: it was time for Mason and I to pack up and go home—to our home. No one else's. Not the cottage, but our apartment over the framer's gallery in New York. If I led the way, I just knew Mason would follow. He just had to. He wouldn't be able to help himself. That's the way it is when two people are in love.

I floated up the stairs, hovering over them effortlessly now, as if I were flying, and found my way back from the landing to the Twists' master bedroom without a hitch. You see, the *truth* was also that Mason gave me wings. He made me feel that anything was possible—even stealing the Blue Diamond Peepers. Clearly, we went too far with that plan, but I blame Dagmar and Duncan for influencing Mason in the wrong sort of way, causing him to put aside his own artistic talents in favor of serving their needs, while bending, shaping, and corrupting him to the point where he, too, lusted after riches and was willing to lower himself to become a thief in the night—with me. But now, fortified in my newly found truth, I saw only beauty in the world, holding a vision of lasting happiness for the two of us. Together. Alone. Just us. *Los dos.* No matter what, he was still my conga-playing lover.

Who else but Mason could strip me bare of inhibitions and unleash such power within me? What could be a better expression of genuine love? Through his role-playing and love-making and soup-brewing, he gave me the courage to toss aside conventional expectations and the fears that go along with wanting to fit in. We simply didn't belong at Swan Crest. We weren't meant to live in a dollhouse that had been plopped on the edge of River Bend Road over two centuries ago. We weren't made to live our lives in servitude, catering to every whim of a pair of lottery winners like Dagmar and Duncan Twist.

Mason and I had always played by our own set of rules. We did just fine. And we belonged only to each other. We didn't need any fancy trimmings. The biggest mansion on the highest peak in all of Burberry Hills could never be formidable enough to symbolize the strength and magnitude of our love, for the best and most beautiful things in the world cannot be seen or even touched, as Helen Keller once said; they must be felt with the heart. And that's where I felt Mason, in the only place that matters. Well, as long as I'm being honest, I suppose I could think of another.

With my hand to my heart, I vowed to release Mason from the clutches of the Twists, especially Dagmar. If that human cabbage with watermelons for bosoms thought for one minute that she could wave money in my man's face and think that was enough to satisfy him, well, she had me to watch out for now. She might've thought that he was good for a toss in the hayloft while stuttering out contrived words in French, but what she didn't know was that he was capable of giving life to *truth* and that made me strong. Ironic, I know. Whether he was playing the part of a Cuban band leader with a great big drum, a rock star at the piano, a princess in faux-couture, or even a crazed bird doing a dance in a loin cloth by a campfire, Mason gave me *me*. Only genuine love can give you the gift of being yourself. In any of his many carnations, Mason would forever be my Ricky, not Dagmar's Jou Jou.

You've got to admit, despite his methods, Mason's heart was in the right place and he proved he really did have one when we were making a baby. It was his idea. He wanted to start a family—with me. How can I fault him for that? It was country life that was corrupt and just plain wrong; at least it was for us. I had my fill of mud and dirt. No longer did I care to hold my nose while braving a chicken coop before dawn and slipping my hand into straw nests while hunting for freshly laid eggs and dodging a pint-sized rooster who'd charge at me, jump up and bite my knees. I never knew before how frightening a little bird could be or that a farm was a battlefield where the owners weren't my only foes.

Enough!

Give me skyscrapers, brownstones, buses, taxis, streetlights, subways, and concrete under my feet. I needed *firma terra*. No fecal-coated goats allowed. Mason would follow me back to New York. I was certain of that. He couldn't do without the woman he loved for one single day. And that would be me, not *Chou Chou*.

My mind was clearer now. My heart was full, happily beating with love. As if I had practiced the sequence in advance, I kicked off my one shoe that had managed to stay on, wiped off my make-up, wet the edge of a towel to cleanse my sweating and scratchy neck, and fluffed up my new short hair with ten fingers. Then I whipped off the Diana gown. And finally, I was free! But then one glimpse of myself in the tri-fold mirror and I knew there was just one detail to take care of: I didn't need a push-up bra or the garters and stockings that Mason had created to match the Princess Diana gown. So I slipped those off, too, opened the hinged window, and stood in the nude.

For a moment—or was it hours—I allowed the wind to caress my body and face as moonbeams lit up the entire room. I could hear the party heating up on the floor directly below while I felt the warmth of my belly, hopeful that a baby was inside, though my abdomen didn't seem to be any plumper than usual. My hipbones still protruded close to the skin and my breasts weren't tender or any larger. I'd hoped they'd be filling up with mother's milk, but they were still just a pair of beans on a stick. Yet, I was content simply being alive, already counting the months until a little one might join us and thinking what a good father Mason would be. I could just picture him dancing with joy, and so I started dancing myself—the same dance Mason had done in that very room while wearing the Princess Diana gown.

But just as I was twirling and shimmying and shaking my maracas, the ladder outside the window was starting to shake, too. Two hands were reaching up from the rungs—and I could see the top of a wide brimmed hat ...

I leaped over the gown that was in a pile on the floor and grabbed my big mud boots Mason had placed neatly by the service door—and fled. There was no time to reach for my clothes that were hooked on one of the closet doors of Dagmar's dressing room, for I had to get out of there in a hurry. With the safe wide open—and empty—I couldn't afford to be caught in the master bedroom alone. If someone was going to be blamed for swiping the Blue Diamond Peepers, either the real ones or the copies, it wasn't going to be me. How would it look for a mother-to-be to be falsely accused of a diamond heist? After all, I never actually swiped them. I couldn't be certain that Mason had taken them either; he was probably just teasing about stuffing them inside his cute little bum. He was, after all, a perpetual joker. And I did see Dagmar wearing the shiny rocks on a gold chain around her neck. But I simply didn't really care any more about who had them or which ones were real and which were fakes. My days and nights in the underworld were officially over. I was on a new mission. I was headed back home where we belonged, in our little apartment over Mason's frame gallery, the same one his mother had once operated, to carry on his family tradition. I didn't want anything to screw up my plan, for I knew my destiny now.

But the ladder shaking at the window threatened to do exactly that.

I had no choice but to use the hidden stairway for my escape. I could hardly run back down to the party in the buff. So I clutched my big boots, slipped through the service door, and flew down one flight of stairs after the next with such speed, I reached the landing in the housekeeper's quarters in mere seconds. But the door leading to Bertha's personal rooms was closed.

Should I knock?

I assumed Bertha would be busy supervising the catering staff at the party, but considering she and Dagmar often fought over the rules for the house even though they didn't speak the same language, I couldn't exactly be sure. But I *was* sure that Bertha was one bulldozer of a broad I didn't want to face, especially when I was naked. As it was, it scared the pants off me to run into her on the farm. The sight of her bending from the waist, despite her advanced age, while pulling weeds in the garden, was bad enough, though I'd prefer seeing her lime green stretch pants more than her wrinkly face. Framed with a head full of stiff orange curls that never seemed to move, she looked like an aging Bozo in drag. Just the sight of her on the grounds of the farm was enough to cause me to have nightmares. Mason would always know when I'd run into her, as I'd snuggle closer to him when we'd sleep. Being close to him was what I needed to chase Big Bad Bertha dreams away.

But the Botox-deprived housekeeper didn't answer my knock on her door. Perhaps she was serving at the party; perhaps the band was too loud for her to hear me. So again I knocked. But again, no answer. I clutched my mud boots tighter and gathered all the courage I could muster to face the orange-haired monster—and looked up to the heavens whispering a quick prayer. But when I opened the door, I didn't see Bertha, only Duncan. He was slouched in a leather barrel chair by the TV with his eyes closed and mouth open. He wasn't watching a program. Nor was he moving.

Was Duncan dead?

A half-filled scotch glass was sitting loosely in his one hand that was resting on the arm of the chair. He had his other hand palm-up. *He was holding the Blue Diamond Peepers.* The sight of what had become highly coveted jewels that evening, caused me to gasp; but still, Duncan never budged. The only movement in that room seemed to be Bertha; her lime buttocks that could've glowed in the dark, were bobbing around Duncan in his chair.

As far as I knew, there weren't any weeds to pull inside that big house.

I figured that Bertha must've dropped something on the floor and was crawling around to find it, heaving her Spandexed bottom side to side by Duncan's knees. I didn't want her to see me when she finally did get up, so I scampered through her parlor still holding my boots and slipped out the back door to the driveway, proud of myself for finally thinking fast on my feet—and relieved to hear Duncan finally making a sound, sort of a moan with heavy breathing. At least he wasn't dead. I wouldn't want murder to be added to my list of presumed crimes. Breaking and entering was bad enough, not to mention attempted burglary. But is it a crime to impersonate a British royal when *truth* is the ultimate reward?

Chapter 10

The Wall

The ladder was gone from the side of the house. Not that I wanted to climb it again; I just worried that whoever took it must now be on the grounds. You can't trust anyone who'd be so brazen as to steal a ladder, let alone sneak around the Twists' property at night. I should know. I walked in those boots. While it may have been an easy matter to shake off my criminal history, however brief it might've been, being protective of the grounds was a reflex. I had no intention of being heroic and playing bounty hunter for Swan Crest, but I sure as heck didn't want to fall prey to a prowler in the dark, especially in the nude.

"Di!"

Die? When a city girl hears a voice shouting *die* in the night, she doesn't stick around to hear what comes next; she simply ducks or runs for quick cover. But without an alley, bar, store, or café handy as there would be in the city, I had a choice to either leap into the pen that protected the goats from foxes as well as contained the chicken coops, or I could dive into the nearest shrubs.

"Di!"

Couldn't my drama for the evening be over? I wanted to get back to New York, but it seemed a voice in the night had other ideas. I opted for my familiar rhododendrons, wanting to avoid a showdown with the rooster-in-residence known as The CEO, and wished I had time to pull on my mud boots. The way my luck had been running, I feared I'd step on a squirrel or a snake.

"Hey, princess!"

Princess?

"Over here!"

Maybe I was hearing the wind howling again, I thought. It had died down since the last time I was braving the elements while climbing up my ladder. The rain had come and gone, too, leaving Swan Crest peaceful again in a refreshing autumn mist like the proverbial calm after the storm. But then I heard it again. The voice in the night kept calling, but I still wasn't sure what it was saying.

"Hey, Di ... Hey, princess ... Hey, Princess Di ... Here ... Look up ... Look up here!"

The voice was starting to sound vaguely familiar, but it wasn't until it laughed in a Woody Woodpecker way that I recognized it as being The Jaff's. I parted the branches of my rhododendrons, cover and peered through the night, wishing that Mason had installed more torch lights on the driveway for the party. Through flames and fog, I surveyed the dark and fuzzy view, but I didn't see a soul who'd be attached to the voice.

"You lost your shoe," the voice said.

I still couldn't quite figure out exactly where The Jaff would be standing and wasn't liking that he could see me, but I couldn't see him.

"Perhaps I should call you Cinderella now," he said. "Instead of Princess Diana."

I wasn't feeling much like a princess, but I did welcome the friendly greeting. Still, I couldn't exactly explain my current lack of clothing.

"Hey! Are you still there?"

I still didn't have the nerve to answer.

"I saw you darting out the door."

But did he see that I was naked?

"And I know that you lost your shoe. I have it right here."

Being armed with truth wasn't as appealing now as being armed with clothing.

"Don't you want it?"

I didn't want it. I didn't want to see him. Nor did I want him to see me. So I kept mum.

"If you don't come here to get it, I might just have to come to you. Let's see if it fits. Perhaps you really aren't Cinderella. What *is* your real name? You never did tell me."

"It's Valentina," I blurted out. I didn't want him to come over to me as he threatened; nor did I want him to see me up close in the rhododendrons.

"Nice to meet you, Valentina."

"Where the heck are you," I shouted, worried that someone other than The Jaff would hear me—or worse: discover me hiding.

"Up here," he said. "Look up. On the wall."

There were only two walls in the world that had the distinction of being called *the* wall: The Great Wall of China and the wall that surrounded the Twists' property to keep all the animals safe. It was a massive stone structure suitable for a fortress with a gate at the front entrance that could only be opened in one of three ways: by a guard hired for special occasions, such as one of Dagmar and Duncan's elaborate balls; by one of several buttons installed throughout the mansion; or by a secret combination on a key pad. Without knowledge of the gate's code or access to a button, and with the guard nowhere in sight, short of getting a lift from a meandering elephant, I had no way to get over the wall.

"It was just a matter of time," he said to me in the night. I could see him better now as my eyes began adjusting to the dark. The ladder was leaning up against the stone wall while The Jaff sat on top of it, leaning up against the arch that framed the main entrance by the guardhouse. A cloud of smoke was billowing from his mouth, but because of a glowing ember by his head, I didn't think it was formed by the cold fog in the night air. Could it be? It looked like The Jaff, a world-class athlete, was *smoking*.

"Yup," he said. "Just a matter of time."

"Time?" I asked. "For what?"

"*You*. I knew you'd come outside sooner or later when you left me on the stairs."

That wasn't an ordinary cigarette at The Jaff's lip. I was pretty sure it wasn't a cigar, either. The way he was talking, it sounded like he was holding his breath.

"Life is all a matter of timing," he said again. "Just like tennis, I suppose."

He let out a loud, long exhale, and I sniffed the air like a bloodhound to see if I could detect a whiff. But instead of smelling marijuana, I only smelled the rhododendrons that were tickling my nose.

"I brought an extra beer. It's for you," he said. "Want it?"

Alcohol *and* pot, I thought. Who'd believe it? A renowned tennis player, a darling of the media and heartthrob to woman around the globe, actually gets buzzed? From a legal source *and* illegal? I was beginning to think that character who helped me on the landing was not the authentic sports star I had thought he was, but an imposter. After all, it was Halloween. Perhaps the man I met when I tripped on the stairs was just one of the guests all costumed up as his favorite tennis idol. This disturbing possibility caused my brain to once again shrink down to a pea and ricochet inside my skull. Could it be that what I had interpreted as seeing *truth* in The Jaff's eyes, was actually the glassy gaze of a neighborhood drunk? Who was this man, this voice on the wall? More importantly, doubting that *truth* had actually been bestowed on me on the staircase, caused me to wonder if my new mission should be scrubbed.

"Hey, Valentina! You still there?"

I wasn't sure if I wanted to answer or not. I didn't think he could see me in the shrubbery; perhaps he merely caught a quick glance of my silhouette as I darted out the back door from Bertha's private quarters.

"Valentina?"

Before I could reply or decide to remain silent, that blasted rooster started crowing again. Believe me, it's pure bunk about how those birds are only alarm clocks that sound off in the morning. When one lives on a farm, loud screeches tear up your beauty sleep at all hours of the night. The CEO crowed and cock-a-doodled about a dozen times, and then the goats chimed into the chorus. With all that crowing and now bah-bahing, the camels were hissing, the monkeys were laughing, the elephants were trumpeting, the tigers were roaring, and that crazy blue-eyed duck, Peepers, was quacking, causing my head to jerk all around, frantic as to where that feathered creature might attack me next.

"Quack! Quack! Quack!"

Like a two-foot tall cop dressed up in all white, Peepers caught me in my hideout in the bushes—and I ran screaming toward The Jaff—or faux-Jaff—at the stone wall. Still naked.

"Whoa!" The Jaff peered at me from atop the wall. He had a closer view now, but it was a bit too personal. "It usually takes me all night to get a date's clothes off."

Date?

"Or are you supposed to be Lady Godiva now? Where's your horse and long hair?"

I covered my private parts with my mud boots, but there was no time to be modest, not when Peepers was on the loose. Then I sped up the ladder for the second time that night.

"Crazy duck," The Jaff said.

He took another hit from his joint, then flicked the burning butt toward Peepers, who quacked even louder while furiously flapping his wings before taking off in a waddling run.

"Are you really The Jaff?"

"Yup," he said with a shadow of disgust in his voice. "That's what they call me, but I wish they wouldn't."

He took off his jacket and handed it to me. Then he averted his eyes as I put it on. The media was right about one thing: The Jaff was a gentleman. If he really was the real one and not a party guest dressed up for Halloween, I knew far more about him than he knew about me. I may not have followed tennis or any other sport, but The Jaff was plastered all over the media. I knew that he was known for wearing a sapphire earring, which I checked to see if he had on: he did. With celebrity minutia covered by magazines such as *People*, which I'd flip through at the dentist's office, I knew that he occasionally changed the sapphire to a dangling silver cross. Only once was he seen with a gold tennis racket charm pierced through his lobe. But that little bauble garnered far too much attention from the cameras at Wimbledon for his tastes. He might've worked diligently at his game throughout his entire life to win that particular tourney a dozen years in a row, but he wasn't known for liking the spotlight and seeing his picture splattered all over. On the sports pages was fine, he was known for saying. But when pictures of his choice of clothing or earrings or worse, when one of his romances made front page news, or a past girlfriend made a fast buck for making up stories paid for by the tabloids, his disgust simmered under a tight fitting lid.

By all accounts, The Jaff was a gentleman in the finest North Carolina tradition, his familial roots. He would never let on that a tattletale bothered him. He'd even skip the talk show circuit where he could've dispelled a rumor and told his side of one story or another. But true to The Jaff's form, he'd always opt to keep his thoughts to himself. "Neither a tattler nor a teetotaler" is how the press described him. But despite the number of romances he racked up, he was forever known as being a one-woman kind of man—that along with being a beer drinker.

The Jaff did like his cold ones as he proved to me while sitting on the wall that night. If he didn't have a Mountain Dew in his hand, he had a Corona. Whether he switched from Heineken because of an endorsement deal or he got the deal because he drank Corona, one thing's for sure: The Jaff was known for scouring Mexico in search of the perfect burrito then hiring authentic Mexican chefs for his international chain of restaurants called *Los Banditos del Jaffordo,* assuring that wherever he traveled for his tennis tournaments, he'd enjoy his favorite meal—along with a few Coronas. He was rarely photographed without one unless he was on the tennis courts, walking a red carpet for a movie premier, or munching strawberries at another Breakfast of Champions at that famous stadium in England, in which case he'd be sipping champagne.

"I guess they like to think we're buddies when they gave me that nickname. That's okay with me," he said, taking another swig from his beer bottle. He twisted off the cap of the one he'd saved for me, then offered it with the assumption that I liked beer, too; I didn't. However, after my journey to discover *truth*, I think I deserved some cheer.

"What do you prefer to be called?"

"My family and friends call me by my full name."

He was called "The Jaff" exclusively by the press. I didn't want to admit to him that I wasn't sure what his full name was. He seemed to be able to read my thoughts.

"Jafford. It's a family name. You don't hear a name like that much up north. In fact, you don't even hear it down south. I'm the last of the

Jaffords. We're a dying breed," he said. Then he laughed again. It was a funny sort of laugh, but I couldn't help think it was friendly. I was beginning to feel comfortable with him. I think he was beginning to be comfortable with me, too, as he pulled out a baseball cap from his pocket and placed it on my head. He still had my hat, the one that had flown out the window, on his head. But what I couldn't stop wondering about was why he'd climbed up the ladder when I was undressing and dancing in the Twists' bedroom? I know I saw a big hat when I peered out. But if I were being honest, and *truth* assured that I now am, I wasn't exactly certain if the hat I saw from the window was mine or someone else's. But if it wasn't mine, whose was it?

"You sure must've hated that party."

"What do you mean?" I asked.

My feelings of comfort and being friendly were suddenly starting to transform to paranoia, hoping he wasn't wise to the attempted Project Peepers. That's the catch when you share a perspective of the world and believe you can sense another person's thoughts. On the one hand, it's bonding. On the other, you need to be careful about what you think, say, and do.

"You high-tailed it out of there in a hurry. It was if you were *flying* up those stairs."

See what I mean?

"If you don't mind my asking, what happened to your clothes?"

"Couldn't find them," I lied.

Jafford thought for a moment, finishing off the last of his beer. He was looking out through the darkness as if the answer would suddenly appear in a quick flash of light. I handed him my beer that was nearly still full as I wondered how I was going to explain my series of unfortunate behavior that evening that led to my being unclothed.

"Let's see if I can figure this out," he began. "You dressed up in the Princess Diana gown at Dagmar and Duncan's, then you strutted out down the staircase to show off her latest acquisition. Then you met me. Then you flew back up the stairs. What am I missing? What happened to your clothes after that?"

He sure was a gentleman for neglecting to point out that I had also clumsily tripped. But I wasn't going to remind him of that fact.

"The lunatic guy! He stole your clothes as a joke! How did the two of you ever get together?"

"He's not a lunatic! He's an artist! He's a genius. His paintings will hang at the Met, the Guggenheim, the Frick, the …"

"Sorry, Valentina. Didn't mean anything by it. I apologize if I upset you."

Jafford looked at me, studying my face, which I wanted to hide more than I wanted clothes. I knew that Mason was unconventional. It was that very quirk in his personality that drew me to him in the first place. I also knew that I had allowed his adventuresome, mischievous spirit to land us in what could have turned out to be a peck of trouble. I longed for this shameful chapter of being a thief to end and get on with my new life's mission. I really was repentant. I could feel a tear falling from the corner of my eye down the side of my nose, and wiped it with the top of a mud boot. Then I finally pulled the boots on and looked around to see how I could climb down from the wall and head back to the cottage to pack up. We *did* belong together. We *were* truly in love. He *would* follow me back to the city. We *would* start a family together. *Los dos*. I was firm in my resolve. And I had *truth* on my side. It was The Jaff—Jafford—who'd given me such a precious gift.

"Where's the train?" I blurted out.

"Are you going on a trip?"

"I need to get back to New York," I said. "I want to go home."

"You can't go to New York like that. They'd arrest you there for being naked in public."

In the country, you can get away with displaying your flesh while sitting on a stone wall in the dark. But in New York, I'd be locked up. See? City life—*normal*. Country life—*not*.

"How do I get off this stupid wall?"

I could hear near tears in my voice. Jafford seemed to hear them, too.

"Here," he said gently. "Don't worry. I'll help you."

He chugged the last of his beer from the bottle I had given him, then pulled up the ladder with both hands and flipped it to the other side of the wall.

"He'll never miss it," Jafford said. "Probably has lots of ladders himself."

"Who?"

"Vanilla John."

"Vanilla *who*?"

"The fireman who lives in the old, abandoned firehouse where the Village of Burberry Hills stores an old fire truck—a relic that they only haul out for parades or loan out to Dagmar for her annual safari."

"Oh, don't tell me. Let me guess. She gives a tour of her private zoo?"

"Yup, only she calls it a hayride and makes Duncan drive the truck, because Vanilla John no longer drives. He's not a fireman anymore either, and the firehouse he lives in hasn't been used for years.

It seemed that Halloween in the Village of Burberry Hills wasn't just one night a year. Nothing was actually what it appeared to be.

"They built a new one. Just opened it a few months ago. The whole town …"

"Village."

"I stand corrected. The whole *village* turned out for the grand opening. Grilled shrimp on the barbeque, filet mignon—no dogs and burgers for our crowd. The new fire chief, he really knows how to throw a shindig. And he knows how to cook."

"Vanilla John must miss being the chief."

"They seem to take turns. But, you're right. Now, he's out. He hangs around the old station and sometimes helps out the neighbors on River Bend Road. In fact, he's the one who climbed up the ladder to see what was what. I helped him by steadying the ladder at its base. Don't know why a ladder would be leaning up against the Twists' house, so Vanilla John went to find out."

Now I was panicking.

"You've probably seen him around once in a while. You'd know him if you did. He always wears his fireman's uniform and rides a scooter most of the time. When there's snow on the ground, he takes out his snowmobile. But he refuses to be part of the force anymore. They say he's never been quite the same after his own house burned down to the ground, especially when it was his turn to be fire chief that night. Sad. Tragic, really. Lost his whole family."

An orphan! I never thought that a fully-grown adult could be one, too.

"I don't get it," I interrupted. "If he was the chief firefighter, why didn't he hose down his own house?"

"He was on duty that night. Seems he was on duty nearly every night. I guess it was one night too many, because the night his house burned down, nobody sounded an alarm. Nobody called in to say there was a fire. He found out later that his wife took off with a radio talk show shrink whom she'd been calling to complain about her husband never being home."

"No one likes to be ignored."

"The wife and the radio shrink fell in love over the airwaves and before you knew it, she was a regular part of the show."

"You don't strike me as someone who'd tune into a call-in shrink show."

"When you travel as much as I do, you tend to get hooked on one thing or another. Breaks up the boredom to try out new programs on an iPod. Passes the time. Beats talking to the person next to me who always wants an autograph and picture. I don't mind so much. It's flattering to have fans. But it does get monotonous."

"So what happened to the wife?"

"See? You could get hooked, too. She took the two kids with her and they all moved to Lake Tahoe and became …"

"Oh, *now* I know who you mean. That reality show couple who lived in a tree house."

"Right. They kept squirrels for pets. Then their tree house burned down and they got nabbed for arson. The two kids were sent into foster homes. Vanilla John couldn't afford to get them out, and he's so freaked out over the ordeal, he's in no shape to care for the kids."

"Makes you think …"

"Yup. Everyone thinks the couple had set fire to the house here, too, but no one was ever able to prove it."

"Tragic."

"Now Vanilla John lives in the old firehouse, the one the town no longer uses."

"Huh?"

"The guy sleeps by day and runs around all night on his scooter, always on the lookout for a fire. I guess when he was patrolling the Twists' property—they give him full permission as all the neighbors do—he saw that ladder leaning up against the window and just had to find out what was going on."

I was worried now that Jafford was putting together all the pieces of my life that unfortunately occurred over the past few hours. Some people are just smarter than others. But maybe I could suggest that a workman left it there after painting? Or fixing the roof?

"Knowing how freaked out he gets about fires these days, I thought I'd help him out by holding the ladder while I was waiting for you to come out of the house. He climbed up, but then he never came down again. I figured he got roped into joining the party, so I grabbed the ladder and moved it to the wall. For you."

I was touched by that last part. The "for you" really got to me. But my heart was still with Mason.

"Based on the antics I witnessed at that party, it wouldn't surprise me a bit if Vanilla John literally got roped. That squirt ... I mean that *fellow* who took a few turns on the piano was a big hit!"

I couldn't help but smile, picturing my Mason romping around the party. There was no doubt in my mind that he was a smashing hit.

"You should've seen him," Jafford said, breaking up in his woodpecker laugh. "He exploded out of that suit of armor, that Prince Charming get-up, when the lights were dimmed, then leaped up on the piano when a spotlight came on. He was wearing nothing but a fur loin cloth!"

The tanuki, no doubt. A Japanese raccoon. Only Mason would be authentic enough to know that knights always wore fur beneath their coats of armor. Only he preferred the more exotic tanuki, he had told me, over the more commonly worn squirrel.

"I suppose when you wear metal to protect you from the outside," Jafford mused, "you need something soft to protect you on the inside."

Mason had bought Dagmar a full-length fur coat on his last buying trip in Tokyo, which he had designed to mimic the style of a flowing robe of a geisha. But it had been too long for Dagmar's petite frame. Mason decided the back hem shouldn't drag on the ground when she walked as if it were a tail, so he cut off several inches, then made himself a tanuki loin cloth for the winter. He said that the tanuki was known in Japanese mythology for having the power for both benevolent and malevolent transformation, and in whichever direction they focused their powers, they were also known to be especially virile, which suited my man, my lover, and the father of my future children quite well.

"Under that heavy helmet of his, he had his face all painted up. Then he got everybody—and I mean everybody, including Bertha—to squat down and waddle like ducks in a long line while—get this—*quacking the moon.*"

"You know Bertha?"

"She was my housekeeper until Dagmar stole her from me when I played the Australian Open last year. It's just as well. Sort of bothered me how Bertha always kept an eye out for postal trucks. Never knew which carrier would show up. She seemed to know each one of them personally. But I can't figure out what they'd all find so fascinating to talk about with her and for so long. I'd see mail trucks by the front gate for an hour at a time. Sometimes they'd come back a second time in a single day. I don't get *that* much mail."

I couldn't imagine Bertha working for Jafford, but I could picture Dagmar bribing her away, fanning a wad of big bills in her Sharpe face.

I'm telling you," Jafford continued. "There's no one like that Mason. If there was a half-time show at a tennis match, he'd be the first one hired. Believe me, I've been all over the world, and I assure you, he's one of a kind."

That I knew for certain. There was no doubt in my mind or my heart. And that is why I scurried down the ladder, which Jafford magnanimously held for me at the top of the wall. Any other guy would've gone down first and looked up, wanting to catch a forbidden view of a faux-princess without her panties. Even my Mason would be guilty of such a voyeuristic sin. But not the gentleman known by most of the world simply as The Jaff.

PART THREE: NEW YORK OR BUST

Chapter 11

The Beetle

The best view of Swan Crest was through a rear view mirror, a view I intended to see for the very last time. Without any street lights, River Bend Road was nearly pitch black, but I knew each country castle by name when we passed them as Jafford drove me to the train station. There was *Queen Hill*, a contemporary version of a Victorian high on a hill with a wrap-around porch; a French country mansion called *Bellechants* graced by gardens befitting Versailles; *Rosecroft*, an English Tudor that could be a cousin to Balmoral; a low-laying ranch with a slightly Western motif known as *Grand Fork*; a mosque-like creation, *Umut*, with bric-a-brac trim and a stained glass dome; a jumbled pile of lumber christened *Twain Ridge* that could only be described as a Mississippi riverboat in dry dock with three stories of porthole windows; and then there was *Willow Run*, a Southern plantation with tall, white pillars and blue shutters that belonged to The Jaff.

Considering the tens of acres separating one estate from another, Burberry Hills had no use for town committees to determine acceptable color pallets or design. I suppose when you can afford to knock down an old house, one that would be eligible to be registered on the list for National Historic Preservation on enough land for a national park, you can build any kind of home you want in its place. You just need the big bucks to back it all up, perhaps by racking up wins at tennis tournaments around the globe or winning the New Jersey SuperDuper

Lottery like the Twists. Hey, we all have our talents. Some just pay out more than others. And some people are just plain lucky. But my idea of luck wasn't about acquiring riches or building a castle on a hill. It was finding the one man who made me happier than all others and going back home where we truly belonged, for that was my true life's path.

Now that my time at Swan Crest was drawing to a close, I couldn't honestly say that I entirely regretted living in a real-life Disneyland, at least for a few months. But like all vacation adventures, it felt good to be going back home. I appreciated that Jafford had waited, while I dashed over to the cottage to pack my duffle bag with a few city clothes. I was content that it was now tossed in the back seat of his car, and pleased with myself for making the decision to get the heck out of Burberry Hills. With Jafford at the wheel, I was happily strapped into the passenger seat. My toes were warm inside my mud boots—the one new acquisition to my wardrobe that I'll admit I had become accustomed to, even the bold yellow stripes. I had even tucked the legs of my jeans into the top, proud to display the unique markings. Maybe they were distinctive enough to ignite a trend in New York. If plastic Crocs could be a fashion hit, why not striped boots like mine?

Jafford was putt-putting along River Bend Road in his classic, silver 1975 Super Beetle, the same one he had bought for himself after his high school graduation. He said that only about a million of them were ever made in all of North America, and told me he'd paid all of $1,985 for it by working as the freezer boy in the stock room of the local Pathmark, then kept it all these years for sentimental reasons.

"When you've handled as many boxes of Green Giant peas as I have, you want to keep the Bug of your labor."

Besides, he added, he liked using the Bug to drive around incognito. It was a pleasure for him, he said, to putt around freely after all the planes and limousines he needed to take for his hectic globe-trotting, tennis-playing schedule. He even kept all the dents in it; they were what gave it charm and provided the camouflage he constantly sought from the media and fans. He told me how he sometimes would get it out from the garage as soon as yet another limo would drop him home from the airport. Putting around, especially at night, was his way of unwinding. He even kept a few cases of Coronas handy in a refrigerator in the garage. He'd throw a couple of cold ones in a Coleman cooler that always sat in the back seat, the same one his mother Lexi had used for family picnics when he and his brother Pete were young boys. Those were happy times, Jafford said, for the entire Ames family; it was when their father, W.G., taught them how to play tennis. But the night he picked me up at the cottage to drop me at the train station, and reached into the Coleman cooler behind him, he pulled out a thermos of coffee.

"Thought you could use a warm-up," he said as he handed me a plastic cup he'd unscrewed from the top of the thermos. "You didn't seem like the beer-drinking type up on that wall. And I suppose we both could use a pick-me-up at this hour."

It had been a long night, and my journey wasn't nearly over. Off-peak hours on a weekend for a train to New York meant infrequent runs, local stops, and a change over to a PATH train at the Hoboken station for the final leg of the trip, which would take me under the Hudson River to Greenwich Village at Christopher Street and 6th Avenue. I gladly accepted the cup of hot java and was grateful that Jafford fixed it the same way I liked it: strong with skim milk, no sugar. But just as we toasted my new life with our plastic cups, our coffee splattered onto our faces.

"What the heck was that?"

We both said it at once, only I first let out a scream—because of the hot coffee, but mostly because of the sight. Seeing a face on the windshield was frightening enough, but what made it worse was that it had two gigantic eyes and a beak.

"Peepers!"

Jafford jammed on the breaks of the Super Beetle and it spun around doing a 360. We both jumped out and hunted around in the dark for what I hoped was not a dead duck. As I was stooping and walking and looking all around the car, in the gutters, and on the pavement, Jafford was standing in one place, studying the windshield, then looking up at the sky. I supposed that with his professional expertise in estimating how far a tennis ball could travel after being hit with a racket and in which direction it would fly, he was able to accurately locate Peepers on the darkened street.

"Might've broken his neck," he said.

He went back to the Super Beetle and opened the trunk, which was in the front where most cars have a motor; in a VW Bug, it was the reverse. Then he brought out a towel, wrapped up the duck, and carried him back to the car.

"Let's go," he said.

But I had no idea where we were headed now. I had a feeling, though, that it wasn't to the train station.

I got back into the car, as directed, while Jafford flipped the driver's seat to the steering wheel and lifted off the top of the Coleman cooler, placing Peepers inside. Then, as if he knew all the steps of a new dance called the *Injured Duck Shuffle*, in one flowing movement, he flipped the driver's seat back into place, slipped in, slammed the door shut, twirled the Super Beetle around, and headed back in the direction of the cottage.

"It's possible that he's still alive. Just shaken up," Jafford said. "We just have to submerge him in the creek to see if that will revive him."

"Creek?"

Jafford laughed. I liked the sound of Woody Woodpecker.

"That's my Southern talking. I've always called a stream a creek. Or do you prefer brook?"

Whatever Jafford wanted to call it, the waterway that began in Tannery Pond at the highest peak of Swan Crest flowed into the waterfall by the cottage, then fell into a creek, which eventually became the Saddle River, and then another tributary called the Ho-Ho-Kus Brook. We could easily dunk Peepers in water without going back over the Twists' wall.

"How do you know so much about ducks?"

"I don't. I just saw a wildlife documentary on a plane."

"I never knew you could learn so much while flying."

"Maybe in my next life I'll be a flight attendant," Jafford said. "I like the idea of free beers and movies. The one I saw showed how you could revive a duck by putting it in the water. Besides, this sort of thing has happened before. There's always life and death on a farm, as Palmer and Christie always say."

"I heard about them, but we never actually met. Seems that no one on River Bend Road wants to know anyone who lives in a cottage."

"Yup. A bunch of snobs. All of them. Except I do like Palmer and Christie. They're the only ones in this town who never knocked down the original house that's been in one of their families for generations. They're both vets and have a lot of animals themselves. And I've heard about them reviving ducks before. Palmer even sewed a leg back on one of Dagmar's swans after it tumbled over the waterfall. I'm not promising I can do that for Peepers, but let's hope that we can revive the little guy. He *is* in one piece. The water technique may be all he needs. I wouldn't want Dagmar to come after me for killing her prized duck."

We pulled up to the cottage's gravel parking space, which had never seen a car, since city dwellers like Mason and me never owned one. Jafford rushed to bring Peepers in his Coleman gurney to what we hoped would be healing waters. But perhaps we were too late. Maybe Jafford's technique was off as he held Peepers in a pool in the stream, because the duck no longer seemed to be moving. His plump little body remained silent and still, while his wings hung lifelessly at his feathered side. But those eyes were still popping out as if he could still see me, holding the knowledge that I was the one on the ladder poised for a diamond heist.

"Dagmar's going to notice that *this* one's missing. That is, if he croaks. Of all her hundreds of ducks, why Peepers?" Jafford wondered. "No other duck in her flock is as conspicuous. Such a showman. He was probably a peacock in a former life."

"Or a rooster," I said with a shiver. I was beginning to develop a fear of all birds. Hitchcock must've spent time on a farm.

"Too bad we can't pick out another white duck from the bunch and pop in those blue contacts you were wearing. Think that'd fool her?"

"You knew?"

"Not at first," Jafford admitted as Peepers seemed to let out a brief gasp. "You really did make a stunning Princess Diana. You did her memory proud. But when I was looking at you close up, I could see that you had contacts in."

I had no idea that Jafford had looked at me so closely or for so long. I guess Mason could create illusions that fooled other people, but not someone as observant as The Jaff.

"I can't tell if it's working or not. It's quite dark out here. At least the moon is full."

Jafford held Peepers up to the lunar light as if the duck were an offering to the Halloween goblins. But there wasn't another peep out of the little featured creature. No quacking, just howling from the animals on the other side of the wall. I shivered, surprised at myself for wanting Mason to perform one of his rituals. When the duck that Dagmar most cherished was on the verge of croaking, I believed in Mason's magic. I believed in Mason.

"Dare I say it?" I asked hesitantly. "What do we do if …"

"We should bury Peepers if he dies. I'll explain it all to Dagmar in the morning," he said. "I'll bring her a tennis racket for the lesson she asked me to give her. That'll soften her up."

"She stole your housekeeper? Then has the nerve to ask for a tennis lesson? From a professional athlete like you?"

"Yup. I don't mind, really. She actually did me a favor. I hired Hector from one of my restaurants and he's working out well. Besides, Bertha never did what I asked. Maybe she just didn't understand enough English. And I never really figured out what language she speaks."

"She still doesn't do as Dagmar asks. Yet, they somehow manage to fight, screaming at each other with a taffy pull of words, saying, 'Yes! Yes! Yes!' or 'No! No! No!' I just get lost whenever the two of them are together or it'd be like getting caught in the crossfire of two warring countries."

"Only we don't know which country Bertha's from."

"Or planet Dagmar's on."

"I'm sure it's not Venus."

"I wouldn't really want to challenge either one of them in tennis," I said. "Putting a racket in either one of their hands would require a license for a lethal weapon."

I kept rattling on nervously. I was worried that Peepers would never come to as Jafford began dunking him in the water again.

"Dagmar does have a powerful swing. Have you ever seen those forearms?"

"I know. All that farm work," I said. "I've seen her lift up a goat while holding an eighty-pound bag of feed under each arm."

"That's one powerful woman. Maybe I should train her to be a professional tennis player. Who knows? With the right focus of all that energy she works off on the farm, perhaps she could win a few tournaments."

It was no use. Peepers was peeping no more. I didn't know which was scarier to face: a lunatic duck quacking at me up close or the wrath of Dagmar for killing him after he smashed into the windshield. I looked up at Swan Crest sitting regally on top of the hill beyond the wall, all lit up for the party. The waterfall drowned out the sounds of the substitute Brian Setzer band with a soothing whoosh over the boulders. The water music that I grew to enjoy as Mason and I drifted off to sleep each night at the cottage, was loud enough to mask the gentle humming of Vanilla John's scooter.

"Another swan fall, Jafford?" he asked.

I couldn't quite make out his face because of the dark, but I did notice that his thick mustache was curled at the ends. When he lifted up his fireman's hat to wipe his forehead, I could see that his hair was parted in the middle, the bangs pushed to either side of his wide forehead with two curls that matched the ones on his mustache. He wiped the inside of his hat, too, then put it back on as he stuffed his red handkerchief back into his pocket.

"Thought for sure the wire that Palmer and Christie strung up across the pond would keep 'em all from falling over again."

For a former fire chief who was built like Paul Bunyan, his scooter looked like a toddler's toy. But that was only fitting for a boy who presumably grew up to be the superhero that other little boys only dream about. He was the real thing, or at least he was at one time, but he was still donning a fireman's wide brimmed hat along with a black waterproof coat with yellow stripes that matched the ones on his boots.

"Nope," Jafford said. "I'm afraid this one is Peepers. He flew into my windshield. but somehow he didn't crack it. Not even a small hole where his beak hit the glass. They made the windshield extra-strong when they brought out the Super Beetle, you know. Besides, I wasn't driving too fast. Just putting by at a slow cruising speed. But still, you'd think there'd be some damage. That Peepers is one awesome bird."

Vanilla John kicked the kickstand on his scooter and knelt down by Jafford in the brook ... stream ... creek. Whatever.

"Lemme take him. I'll bring him to Palmer and Christie," Vanilla said, taking out his handkerchief from his pocket again. "They're still at the party."

"Really? I must've missed them."

"They were the bears."

"The polars? Or the grizzlies?"

"Neither. The pandas."

Geesh, I thought. Will this animal chatter ever end?

"Do me a favor, big guy?" Jafford said. "Don't let Dagmar know, not just yet. She'll go berserk. I'll explain it all to her in the morning."

"Too late for that," said the human giraffe in the fireman's hat.

"What do you mean?"

"Seems a burglar is on the loose. Stole Dagmar's new set of rare blue diamonds. Had to leave my post at the guard gate."

"You're working for the Twists now?"

"Just for tonight. Had to tell them about that ladder you helped me with. Now the police are on their way. I'm surprised they're not already here. Dagmar—you're right about her. She really knows how to freak out. Geesh!"

I was the one who was freaking out. Ladder, duck, fireman, police ... Oh, get me out of this place! New York or bust!

"But it's that funny one—the one putting on a show—that guy in the furry diaper and playing the piano—who's really going bonkers."

Despite that my knobby knees were knocking from fear of being arrested at any moment by the cops, I let out a laugh. I just couldn't help myself when picturing Mason running around a place as lavish as Swan Crest in his favorite tanuki loin cloth. Ol' Vanilla looked like he was trying to suppress a laugh, too, despite that he seemed like he hardly ever did so.

"He quit playing the piano and was lassoing up all the guests with a rope when I was leaving," Vanilla John continued. "Said he wanted to round them all up. Didn't want anyone to leave until the crook was caught."

Ah, yes. That would be my Mason.

Jafford looked like he wanted to laugh, too. Either that or he was holding back gas after having drunk too much beer. But perhaps I didn't really know him and was all wrong about interpreting his expression as he gently lifted Peepers from the water and placed him back in the Coleman cooler. Or maybe I wanted to look at anyone or anything else other than Vanilla John who certainly could've helped described the mischief that Mason and I had started earlier that evening. He could've seen me on the ladder. Naturally, the police would want to question him along with the guests, if he had been stationed at the guard's house. I didn't want him to introduce himself to me; with all the commotion, I suppose Jafford had overlooked his fine Southern manners to not have done so himself. But whatever the reason, I was grateful for once for the lack of street lighting on River Bend Road. Maybe Vanilla John wouldn't recognize me again. After all, I was the one who was now wearing a baseball cap while Jafford still had my big, black hat on. And a celebrity of the tennis world would hardly be suspect in a diamond heist.

"Don't know what happened to Duncan," Vanilla John said.

"Duncan?"

"Yeah. EMS is on its way, too. Seems he might've had a heart attack or something.

"Oh, no!"

"Could've been a bad belly ache. They say Bertha is a horrible cook."

Jafford laughed. "She once served me fish balls from a can."

"*Fiske bola?* Yum!" Vanilla said. "I buy it by the case."

Jafford stopped laughing. I think he feared he might be invited over for dinner.

"Well, anyhow," Vanilla continued. "They say Duncan's belt and pants were undone. Maybe his costume was too tight. Whatever happened before he passed out, it was Bertha who found him."

"She does seem to always have knack for keeping track of who goes where. She was always shadowing me from behind a door. I even caught her once hiding behind one of my willow trees as I went out for a run," Jafford said. "But it's hard to figure out what she's saying most of the time. She used to speak to me in her own language—whatever it is—as if I spoke it, too. Then she'd get red in the face and angry that I didn't understand her."

"The best they could get out of her," Vanilla said, "was that she didn't know why, but Duncan had left the party. Then she found him slumped over. In her parlor. In her TV chair."

CHAPTER 12

The Tunnel

The train station in the Village of Burberry Hills, New Jersey, was built in 1913, and constructed with large, rounded stones that were now covered in ivy. The parking lot was gravel and dirt, for there was little need for spaces neatly delineated by white painted stripes. Most of the residents of the area were not regular commuters. They did not need to hoard quarters for parking meters, for there were none. They never heard of purchasing a monthly parking tag and hanging it on a rear view mirror, for Burberrians were a privileged class who only traveled to New York City for an occasional Broadway show, shopping spree or perhaps dinner with a financial advisor. Compared with the neighbors on River Bend Road, a financial advisor was just another working stiff who needed to eke out a living on six-figure commissions—and probably had a colorful plastic tag hanging from his car's mirror in Westchester, Greenwich, Princeton, Long Island, or Bergen County.

Jafford turned down the volume of the speakers that had been blaring The Grateful Dead eight-track tape as the Super Beetle passed the train station.

"I'll carry you to New York," he said.

"Carry me?"

"That's Southern for driving you to your destination. I don't mind, really. After a night like this, I could use a diversion."

I had a sense that taking me all the way into the city was also a

Southern boy's way of assuring good manners—going out of his way to personally escort me, and making certain that I was safe, until I actually opened my front door. The media was right; he was a gentleman. Perhaps I could find a charm school in North Carolina for Mason; I made a mental note to put that on top of my to-do list as soon as I had time to find a pencil.

"To be honest, I was headed for the city anyway. A friend of mine is in town filming a movie and asked me to drop by."

So much for the pencil.

"He said he'll be shooting all over town to get some exterior shots. Tonight, he said, his crew will be in midtown. Wanna come?"

"I live in the Village."

"I'll take you there afterwards."

"Truthfully, I really just want to get back home. My home. The real one. I'm done with the country. And that cottage, too. Do you mind?"

"No, I don't mind at all. I'll take you to your front door. Want to make sure you're safe. But I did tell my buddy that I would probably meet up with him. He knows me well. Knows I can't stand crowds for too long."

"Crowds? What about all those tennis stadiums?"

"That's different. I meant *parties*. I can't stand them. That is, unless it's small and I know everybody. Gets sort of creepy after a while when strangers packed in a room start staring. It'd be better if they'd come up to me and introduce themselves. Usually, I just want to head out early. So I knew from the start that I'd be leaving the Twists' ball in time to catch up with my friend."

I'm glad he had a good friend to run to, because I couldn't help but feel sorry for him always needing to be on his guard. Perhaps I should have appreciated being anonymous, living in a cottage. None of the neighbors ever cared to know Mason and me. Or perhaps Mason made the rounds. He liked attention. He liked being social. They might've known Mason, but they didn't know me.

"I expect to be sized up on the street, not in someone's living room. But in New York, they generally leave me alone more than in other places. Not too much of a fuss there. Typically."

"For me, being around people for a change will be a relief after living at Swan Crest."

"Not much of a farm girl, hmm? I can understand that. It's not every farm that has herds of elephants roaming the grounds. One night I jumped out of a deep sleep, hearing them trumpeting in the distance," Jafford said. "Didn't know what country I was in for a moment. Thought someone had kidnapped me in my sleep and dropped me somewhere in Africa."

Amused by his own joke, Jafford turned to me as he was driving and let out his Woody Woodpecker laugh. As I gawked at his wide-open mouth and saw his beautiful eyes ablaze, I couldn't help wondering, did the media know about this funny little quirk? It was a friendly, endearing, uninhibited sort of sound, the kind you just couldn't help think was from the heart. But I was worried that his silly laughter was the kind induced by marijuana or beer. While Mason and I weren't normally accustomed to drinking more than an occasional snifter of Benedictine—except for that regrettable evening he seduced me to go along with the Grand Master Plan—I worried that Jafford kept laughing for the longest time without looking at the road. There wasn't as much traffic at midnight on Route 80 East on a Saturday night as there would be during commuter hours. Still, I thought to myself that he better keep his eyes in front of him.

We didn't hit any traffic until we reached the entrance for the Lincoln Tunnel that gracefully sweeps in a long curve along the Hudson River. Cars, trucks, and a few buses were starting to clog the lanes. The only thing that made being bumper-to-bumper worthwhile and helped me to stop worrying that the tennis star was high while driving, was seeing the view of the Manhattan skyline all lit up with a billion tiny lights twinkling in an urban constellation.

"Ahhh!"

It was the same spectacular view Georgia O'Keefe had painted many times from the perspective of Weehawken, New Jersey, with the river in the foreground and the moon and stars up high. I turned my head as we made our way around the curved ramp to the tunnel, wanting to take it all in as others might enjoy a view of the Alps, the Rockies, or the Pyrenees. New York was my mountain, the only one I cared to

Dancing with Jou Jou

climb. But the joy I was feeling upon finally seeing my one true home in the distance was disrupted by a pile of The Jaff fans in a passing car.

"Hey, look! It's The Jaff!"

The car was in the lane between our little VW Bug, just beneath a billboard for a Bentley Continental GTC, a convertible in a clean shade of Mediterranean blue. The Jaff's smiling face was in the picture, too, along with their motto: "Be moved by hand-craftsmanship at its finest. Book your test drive today."

"Hey, Jaff!" the fans shouted again, sticking their heads out the windows and pointing up to the larger-than-life poster in the sky. "Where's your Bentley?"

They caused such a racket, the other cars surrounding ours opened their windows, too. More and more cameras and cell phones were flashing pictures of The Jaff. But he wasn't smiling at them; he just kept putt-putting along, waiting for our turn to move another inch in the traffic. Perhaps he was accustomed to such attention and was taking it all in stride, but it was far more attention than I had ever known. I had never experienced being in the spotlight, even whenever Mason was by my side. He was always getting attention. We'd be strolling down the sidewalk in our neighborhood in the city and one, maybe even two or three people—all of them women—would pass us with big grins.

How I missed him, I thought, patting my tummy. I couldn't wait until he came back to New York. Funny how being with another man made me appreciate Mason all the more. That's the test of love. When you're apart for too long, it hurts.

I pulled the brim of my baseball cap down over my eyes, zipped up Jafford's black Nike jacket that I was still wearing, and faced straight ahead like a nonchalant passenger. Neither one of us said a word; we continued to stare blankly ahead of us now as if we were just a couple of tourists on holiday far away from home, or two commuters who'd come to the Big Apple to experience the city at night for a change. But despite our unflustered appearance—and despite that I was wearing the baseball cap and Jafford still had my wide-brimmed hat on—the fans seemed eager for a close-up.

The Super Beetle barely came to a full stop at the tollbooth as Jafford tossed over eight dollars. Then he cranked the steering wheel hard to the right and jumped into the farthest lane. He accomplished the automotive feat with such aplomb, I barely noticed that we'd cut off several lines of cars. They must not have noticed it either, as no one honked; they were probably held up at the tolls, searching their pockets for the right change or waiting patiently for an E-Z pass to be acknowledged by the sensor. Whatever the reason, Jafford's maneuver across the lanes was smooth. We darted so fast to our place in the tunnel, it was if the Super Beetle could leap in the air before landing in a slow-moving line of traffic. But being in a tunnel with two lanes divided by double solid lines, it wasn't long before the fans with their cameras seemed to be surrounding us again.

There was simple no escape route now. We could be pulverized if not careful; cameras were mounted every three hundred feet on the white tiled walls and ceiling coated in soot and the walkway that was originally built for tunnel security guards. There was nowhere for our car to scamper again out of their sight until we emerged from the other end, on the New York side of the tunnel. Horns were blowing, fans were shouting, and cameras were flashing. But still, Jafford remained steady at the wheel, never uttering a single word or even glancing at me as he had done throughout our trip. I looked at him, wanting some sort of signal as to what to do or say. When you are stuck in a silver Super Beetle, strapped in with a retro-fitted seat belt in a tunnel with fans clicking cameras, there's simply nothing to talk about. You just hope you can start breathing again instead of holding it all in.

My heart skipped a few beats as Jafford eyed an opening on the other side of the solid lines—and grabbed it. With ease, he darted past the NJ Transit bus, then one with Hasidic Jews that looked like an old school bus, only painted white and divided by a sheet separating the men in the front from the woman and children in the rear. The bus behind that one was a Mercedes with the words, "Korean World Tours" painted on the side. As we passed it, I looked up and saw that the passengers were staring down at Jafford's Bug, pushing their faces against the glass.

Did they, too, know that it was The Jaff who was driving the Super Beetle?

If lines of cars in the Lincoln Tunnel seem to be chasing yours and aiming cameras in your direction while shouting, "It's him!" you'd be frightened, too. I just didn't know how Jafford could stand the attention while seeming to remain calm, driving that little Bug as if we were in a NASCAR race. We zigzagged back in front of the bus presumably chock-full of Koreans, then back to the other side, then back in front of the Korean bus once again. We were nearly at the end of our journey when the car that had been behind us tried to scoot in front of us, and Jafford veered back and forth, swerving in front of the Koreans. Horns were honking now, but the sound no longer seemed to be joyful about seeing a celebrity known as The Jaff. One was from the Korean bus, the other from a car that let out a long, angry blast and followed us to the next lane as the Super Beetle spun around as speedily as the earth in its orbit before coming to a complete stop.

The bus squealed on its breaks ...

Horns were honking ...

A siren blared ...

"Are you alright?" Jafford asked me.

I was still in the passenger's seat, still strapped in, and still had my black baseball cap on my head. Before I could answer him, I felt his strong arms scoop me up and lift me out of the car, placing me by two policemen standing by the guardhouse at the end of the tunnel's walkway. I didn't want the third degree by a couple of coppers, and I couldn't help but feel paranoid after what seemed to have been a near-death chase through the Lincoln Tunnel. My mind was reeling back to the unfortunate events earlier in the evening.

Would the cops *check me out?* Would they know I had just left the scene of an accident with a prized duck? Or that I was the one who had climbed up the ladder? Would they *check me out?* Would they accuse me of swiping the Blue Diamond Peepers? Or blame me for Duncan's mysterious collapse? After being trapped like a couple of rats in the tunnel, nearly squished to our deaths, my recent life as a jewel thief flashed before my eyes. Anything was possible now and I feared the worst. Would they *check me out? Check me out? Check me out ...*

Drivers and passengers were tumbling out of their cars, taxis, and buses. Even a silver-haired couple opened their own door of a limousine and joined the throng of onlookers who were swarming around us where we stood on the side of the tunnel—each of them flashing their cell phone cameras. It would only be a matter of time, I thought, for our pictures to be in the newspapers and perhaps splattered around the world on every television channel. I tugged the brim of my baseball cap to cover as much of my face as possible and shivered. Had I been any closer to Jafford, I'd be inside his black Nike jacket, identical to the one I was wearing.

"Easy, there. Let's *check you out*," one of the cops said to me in an attempt to un-fuse me from Jafford. I longed to be back home; we were so close now. But mostly, I longed for Mason.

"How you feeling," Jafford asked me. "You alright?"

I was too shaken to speak or move as both of his arms were around me. A Blue Tooth was blinking on one of his prominent ears.

"*Endorsement* deal?" I heard him say. "Just have the Bug picked up. And call the insurance people ... We've got a mob scene happening here ... Gotta get out—fast ... Yes, I *do* still want to keep the Bug ... You're *still* worried about an endorsement deal? When I nearly just lost my life? ... Yes, of course. I *do* drive the Bentley. All the time, but ... Yeah, I know it's in my contract ... I *told* you, I *do* drive it ... Then ask them if they'd prefer to see a *Bentley* cracked up ..."

The tunnel cops were attempting to hold back the crowd, but it seemed to be advancing instead of retreating. I suppose that fame, the kind that comes with the territory of being The Jaff, was a more powerful magnet than a pair of six-foot-four tunnel cops were a deterrent. The crowd seemed to be thickening, the flashes brighter than before, like fire surrounding us on all sides. *hell* was heating up right there in the Lincoln Tunnel. We were all going to burn. Jafford and I would be the first to be crisped and crumble into ashes. We'd be blown away by the wind or swept up by a city maintenance crew with brooms. Not exactly my idea of a graceful ending. Besides, I wanted to die with Mason.

"It's just a couple of phone calls, Ben," Jafford was saying now to someone I assumed was one of his managers. "If it makes you feel better, I'll have Hector bring out the Bentley from Willow Run and drive it out here. He'd be happy to smash it into a wall for you, if that'll put your mind at ease. Let the media take a picture of *that*."

One of the cops was mumbling into his radio. I couldn't make out what the scratchy voice was saying in response, but I was sure an ambulance would be on its way to *check us out*. I was sure I was in one piece; even if I weren't, I was determined not to be *checked out*. Jafford seemed to be unbroken, too, without a shred of fear in his voice as there certainly would have been in mine—that is, if I dared to speak. I had no idea if anyone else in the tunnel had a need for medical attention. With paranoia setting in, I feared that someone would request it whether it was warranted or not; I was sure that celebrities attracted fortune hunters, even if that meant they sued for damages—real ones or imaginary.

Survival instincts were starting to kick in and packing a hefty punch. My own selfish needs dominated those of nameless Jaff fans with an urgency to get the heck out of that tunnel as quickly and cleanly as possible before an ambulance could arrive. Fortunately, being in New York, an ambulance could take hours. Trouble was, considering that I was accompanied by The Jaff, it could be quicker than for ordinary people. Stars do have priority even in a city as jaded as New York, and it was abundantly clear that Jafford was among the most adored, which meant the most chased.

"I'm fine," I assured Jafford when he finally concluded his phone argument that I hoped had ended in our favor. "Really," I said more emphatically. "Can we just get out of here?"

I felt bad that I was holding back on my new friend in not revealing to him that I was worried we'd be thrown in the slammer. He could be too, I supposed, for careening into a bus full of Korean tourists—not to mention for the possible slaughtering of a prized duck. If Dagmar had her way, she would assure him of that. She'd have me nabbed, too, for being the last person to see Duncan alive. Was he dead? Would Bertha pin his demise on me? Would the cops want to *check me out? Check me out? Check me out?*

"Yeah," Jafford said. "Let's go."

He handed one of the policeman a business card, presumably of his manager, along with free passes to his next tennis tournament at Madison Square Garden. Then he apologized to me for leaving for a few moments and rescued cans of tennis balls and rackets by the armload from the trunk of the war-worthy Beetle. He made the angry driver happy by giving him tournament passes along with a free racket and cans of balls. As a final gesture to make amends for his part of the accident, he stepped into the touring bus and made an appearance, handing out more free rackets, balls, and passes. I could hear the bunch of them cheering and applauding from where I waited for him by the guardhouse. He told me later that he had said a few words in Korean and bowed in the way he had been coached during his last world tennis tour. Somehow, the magic of the camera was able to morph into a sort of peace pipe, as Jafford allowed the tourists on the bus to take as many pictures of him as they desired—in both group photos and individual portraits.

"Just sign this and we'll take care of your, uh, car," one of the cops said. "Is *that* really yours?"

"Yeah. Sweet, isn't she?"

The cop shook his head. "Yes, sir," he addressed the celebrity of the tennis world. "Sweet."

I was surprised the fuzz didn't roll out a red carpet, kiss his hand, and bow.

"You'll never get a taxi from here. We'll take you wherever you want to go, Mr. Ames. But if you want a black and white, you'll have to wait around."

"Call me Jafford."

Then Jafford turned to me and whispered, *"I thought he was going to lick my face. He could've at least rolled out a red carpet. Or maybe just curtsied."*

I made a mental note to be careful about what I thought. It was hard to shake loose from tunnel paranoia, especially when my companion was a mind reader.

"All we have here are a couple of motorcycles, uh, *Jafford*."

Jafford looked at me, but I needed no time to decide. I just pointed and nodded. And the cops' spare helmets fit perfectly on my head and The Jaff's.

Chapter 13

The Shoot

Washington Square Park was hopping. Everyone, it seemed, with the exception of Jafford and me, was all costumed up. Only, compared with the guests at the Twists' party who'd selected their getups from racks of predictable stock items offered by professional costumers, the masqueraders in the park were more original and wearing costumes that were perhaps homemade.

Christopher Columbus posed with a telescope on the bow of a ship named *Nina*, which was tugged by a couple of sailors with a rope; two other ships followed, one with *Pinta*, the other with *Santa Maria* painted on the sterns, while a walking pack of Juicy Fruit contained eight sticks of gum in bright yellow wrappers, each vying to be chewed. And a pair of Siamese twins hobbled along two steps in front of a surgeon wielding a machete as a praying mantis held hands with a common housefly.

I might've preferred being back in the city on my home turf, but I still did not see the point of Halloween. I never had an urge to disguise myself, especially because, as an orphan, I never had a clear understanding of who I actually was or was supposed to become. But I did know I was feeling more like me than I ever had in my entire life and that revelation was all thanks to Mason. I smiled at how he helped me have a sense of purpose by assuring that we made a home together and planned a family to call our own. I couldn't help but feel, well, *grateful* to the man I loved. I was almost giddy as I was now merely a couple of blocks from our apartment, one we'd share forever. That's the only thing they always told us to pray for when I was in foster care: a forever home.

    I removed my borrowed motorcycle helmet and fluffed up my new short haircut with two fingers, which I could thank Mason for, too. Surprisingly, I felt liberated to be freed from waist-length hair. I must've used to look as though I were hiding. Growing up as an orphan, I was rarely treated to a haircut, at least not one by a professional. The time another foster child shaved off one side of my head when I was sleeping, certainly didn't count. But now, all grown up, I was finally on my true life's path. Fittingly, I was sporting a brand-new look.

    On any other day of the year, I would scan the crowd at the park to see if I could spot Craig—or rather, Laughing Sun, as he wished to be called—in his crimson robe, teaching a master class in meditation or holding a ceremonial tea after an interpretation of koans. But on a night like Halloween, it'd be hard to pick him out. Who else but my ex-boyfriend-turned-monk could appreciate my recent revelation of *truth*? Or impart wisdom about a near-death experience in the Lincoln Tunnel? There's no telling what Craig would say about that, but I knew he'd be thrilled for me planning to start a family—even if it was with Mason. The three of us actually remained friends after Craig and I broke up. In fact, he said he had an epiphany that a voluntarily celibate life while teaching classes in a public park was his true life's mission and his one certain path to follow on earth. He was in the early stages of setting up a foundation, a seminary for new monks, which he dubbed *The Laughing Sun Center for Right Living*. He'd probably offer some sort of wisdom to me now about the beauty of the continuity of the generations or utter a silent prayer for elevating my reincarnation destiny. But my personal self-proclaimed monk, sage, and still friend, Craig, was nowhere in sight.

    "Hee-hee-hee, Natasha. Look! Look!"

    A voice behind us was loud and clear as Jafford and I stepped off the motorcycles and handed our helmets back to the fuzz.

    "Tennis Boy has the cops eating out of his hands. Good friend to have around, yes?"

Dancing with Jou Jou

I turned to run far away from yet another fan of The Jaff. But Jafford stopped dead in his tracks.

"Only one person in the world calls me *Tennis Boy*," he said walking toward the strange voice.

It was a man's voice. Or more like the cartoon character, Boris Badinoff of *Rocky and Bullwinkle* fame. At least that's who he resembled. Jafford greeted him along with his companion, Natasha.

"Fish Boy!" Jafford said, smiling and lighting up as bright as the full moon overhead. He leaned over to kiss Natasha, but she recoiled. "You're a long way from the lake, Fish Boy. Thought for sure someone'd get wise to you by now and put a net over you."

"Hee-hee-hee," Boris wheezed. "Tennis Boy make joke."

Jafford turned back to me and explained that the man in the Boris outfit was one of his fishing buddies from the Jersey Shore, some big-time author whose paperback book he'd found dog-eared in the pouch on the seat in front of him on a plane. He was so mesmerized by the story, Jafford said, that he bought the movie rights and hired a production company to film it. The rest, he said, was Hollywood history with a string of Oscar, Sundance, and Golden Globe Awards for what apparently was a film industry legend dressed up in the Boris get-up, one of those famous people whose names are somewhat well known, but their faces are not always familiar. I supposed it made little difference if he were in a costume or not. Or if Jafford called him Fish Boy.

"Thought you told me you'd be shooting up in Midtown tonight. You trying to give me the slip?"

"Hee-hee-hee! Boris call Tennis Boy. Tennis Boy no answer."

I wasn't sure who anyone was anymore. The faux-Boris whom Jafford called Fish Boy, this author-turned-movie director, wheezed again in what I assumed was also a laugh, then he turned around to show us a stuffed squirrel that was blindfolded and dangling from a rope on a long stick.

"Hee-hee-hee! Got Squirrel. Now we find Moose. Right Natasha? Hee-hee-hee!"

It seemed that Natasha was feeling her role, too. She was as aloof as a mannequin, towering over Boris in a pair of bright red high heels and acting mysterious behind an enormous pair of Channel sunglasses with gold hinges. Her jet-black hair fell into a flip at her bare shoulders as she loosely held a black wrap around them, showing off her cinched waist as well as a briefcase that was attached to her wrist with a chain. Her lips, painted in the same bright red as her shoes, barely moved as she spoke.

"Stupid Boris," she said in a husky voice. "Boris hire cousin for movie. Boris hire wife of cousin, too."

But Boris merely wheezed. Despite Natasha swatting him with her briefcase, he was still grinning, too, and bouncing around as if his feet were attached to a pair of springs. His eyes were popping out while his painted black eyebrows arched up and down. Weird, I thought. If two people were bold enough to act out their fantasies in public, I didn't want to know what they'd do behind closed doors. At least Mason and I had the decency to keep our playtime private.

"You shooting *here* tonight?" Jafford asked him. "I see the trailers."

Long silver trucks were lining 4th Street with rows of floodlights turned on. Red folding director's chairs were set up on the pavement and police sawhorses blocked off the street. That's one of the benefits of living in the city. You just never know when or where you'll stumble onto a movie set. While they could've created a set three thousand miles away on a back lot in California, when it comes to New York, there's nothing that comes close to the real thing. But I didn't know if Boris was in costume for Halloween or for his movie.

"Hee-hee-hee," Boris snickered again. "Crew set up for new shoot now." He pointed toward my street—mine and Mason's, that is. "Big production. Hee-hee-hee! Big technical problems. Three days Boris wait. Three days rain. Not make movie. Hee-hee-hee!"

I still didn't get it. Was his accent real? Or did he really speak English? I shook my head, wanting to tune out the conversation and eyed the trailers that were blocking the view of my apartment. We had come so far, and were so close now. I just wanted to go home.

"Boris is puppet. Movie studio is master. Hee-hee-hee!"

Boris wheezed again. His congested laughter was sounding troublesome. That is, if it were real. I was beginning to wonder if he'd need oxygen soon.

"Boris not director. Boris writer. Look, look" he said, pointing this time to the bookstore on the corner.

Hundreds of books were displayed in the windows, only they were all copies of the same book. Boris's book. I was sure his name would be on the cover, but I could hardly see it from where I was standing. I had no idea who he really was and figured that Jafford was not in the habit of introducing his companions; he'd skipped such a social nicety before when we had bumped into Vanilla John. I just shrugged now and gave my new friend a silent pardon for this flaw in what I had thought were fine Southern manners. Maybe he was constantly on guard in public, fearing that the press could be within earshot or camera range at any given time. Whatever the reason, without Mason by my side, I felt alone in the crowd.

"Cousin is prop master. Never hire cousin," Boris muttered. "Big trouble. Wanted to be set designer, too. Oh, boy!"

"Stupid is Boris! Boris hire wife of cousin for movie, too," Natasha said.

This time she bopped him with a book she pulled out of her briefcase.

"Cousin give Boris apartment for movie," Boris said. "He whip up movie set in nothing flat. Artist cousin is. Genius! Pure bloody ..."

Natasha smacked him again. I didn't get it. I wanted to shout at her, *"Hey!"* I'd say. *"You've got your man. Quit hitting him with that book! Are you nuts?"*

"Genius cousin is," Boris said, enduring more pain. "Pure bloody genius!"

My head was spinning. I was putting together all the pieces and they were adding up. Either "pure bloody genius" was now the latest catch phrase, or that set designer "cousin" Boris kept referring to was someone I knew quite well and dearly loved. Suddenly, this funny little guy dressed up in a Boris outfit was familiar. Only, I had never actually met anyone from Mason's family in person. But I knew the stories well. I reached over to Natasha and took the book out of her hands. I flipped it over to see the name on the cover.

"Arnold!" I cried, holding my arms out as if he were *my* cousin. But he looked at me bewildered as Natasha snatched back the book and Boris or *Arnold* finally stopped grinning.

"You two know each other?" Jafford asked.

"Not exactly. But you," I said turning to Boris, "I know who you are. You're Mason's cousin Arnold! You're the paperback writer and movie producer he's told me so much about."

"Hardcover now," he said rubbing his head. "Should've stuck to paperback."

"And don't think he didn't tell me all about your teenage escapades," I said. "I know all about Cyrus Pepper High School, too. The cotillion, the teachers, and oh, what you did to those poor turkeys!"

But I could tell by the expression on his face he had no idea who I was.

"I'm Valentina!"

But Arnold was still blank.

Certainly, I thought, Mason must've told his dear cousin Arnold all about me and our plans. We may not have been married, but still! If the two of them had spent any time at all together on the movie set, surely Arnold would know who I was. Mason must've been working part-time helping out with the movie and keeping it as a surprise. For me! That man of mine was filled with surprises.

"I'm Valentina!" I tried again. "Mason's girlfriend!"

"Girlfriend?" Arnold and Natasha said in unison. While he looked confused, she looked angry. She started rambling in a loud voice, speaking in a language I didn't understand. Arnold was trying to calm her down, but for the life of me, I couldn't figure out what the heck ticked her off yet again. I guess she was just the high strung type. How could Arnold stand it?

"Mason let us use his apartment to shoot a few scenes," Arnold started to explain. He was speaking in English now, no longer with an accent, but I guess I didn't let him finish. "He never mentioned ..." he stammered. "That is, Mason never told me he had a ..."

"Our apartment?" I exclaimed. "For your movie?"

"*Your* apartment?" Arnold asked. But I paid little attention to what I realize now was alarm. I was too overjoyed by the thought of that man of mine being full of surprises. I never knew what he'd spring on me next. He was probably planning to take me to Arnold's movie premier and wanted to see the expression on my face when our little city home popped up on the screen. It was all so exciting!

Little did I realize back then that an engagement ring is what I should've been hoping for. That would have been the more appropriate surprise for a mother-to-be. But such traditions were never part of my history. Orphans were never exactly invited to weddings. Most of us had parents who were never hitched. Call me naïve, but I simply was not raised with any sort of cultural traditions and wasn't exactly mindful of marriage, let alone ever expected an official engagement ring from Mason. From all that I saw in my lifetime, babies just happened. Jewelry and a gown with a veil simply were not required.

But now, there in Washington Square Park, you'd think I had said something out of line, because Natasha was fussing again. And again, Arnold was calming her down. I was getting the feeling that he did so routinely.

"Natasha here thinks you're next to take a part in the movie, when she's dying to be in it herself," Arnold said, turning to calm her again.

I wanted Arnold and Natasha to shut up. The two of them were getting into a heated quarrel, so I grabbed the opportunity as an out and stepped away from our huddle under the landmark stone arches of Washington Square. I couldn't wait to see our apartment being filmed for a movie. I slipped the straps of my duffle bag from Jafford's shoulder onto my own and motioned that I was taking off. My new friend had done his job; he got me to where I wanted to go. But the time had come for us to part. I couldn't wait to get home. I thanked Jafford, of course, for driving me into the city. I managed a smile as I waved a friendly good-bye and walked at a fast clip toward my street, while dodging more masqueraders. Those costumed intruders probably traveled far to celebrate the holiday in the park, but I lived there all year long. They were visitors on my turf now. The Village was my neighborhood, my place, my home.

Jafford must've sprinted after me, because his arm was suddenly wrapped around my shoulders. I pulled away, but he caught my hand in his, and I turned around to face him.

And that's when the crowd faded away.

Time stopped.

My toes were starting to wiggle.

I heard the undeniable chorus of angels singing just above our heads as a bright shining light was beaming from his magnificent blue eyes, the same curious sort of light I had seen when I had stumbled on the Twists' staircase and Jafford eased my fall. There was no question about it. By the look in his eyes, I could tell that he was hearing those angels singing, too.

For a moment, or maybe hours, that beam of light penetrated my eyes and connected me to Jafford in a way that seemed like forever. He wasn't smiling, exactly, but I could sense he was happy just as he must've sensed I was, too. I cannot explain why I did what I did next, but I had to shake common sense back into my skull. I was thinking that in some kind of mystical, spiritual, cosmic way, Jafford had accidently slipped into the love I held for Mason and, for a moment, I was mistaking Jafford for him.

"Valentina, don't go …"

But I didn't let Jafford finish. I didn't know what he was about to say next. I had a feeling that he would tell me that he heard the angels sing, too. The way he started trembling, I thought he might either say he was sorry for holding my hand when he knew full well I belonged to another; or worse: maybe he was about to say what I was feeling, too. God help me, I do not know why, but feeling Jafford's eyes penetrating my soul, in an instant, I felt that he loved me. And that I …

I wouldn't give him the chance. It couldn't possibly be. I shook his hand as if we were concluding some sort of formal business arrangement, then turned and sped away. To make certain he didn't follow me, I snaked my way through the crowd. But I found myself wondering how I could feel Jafford tied to my heart when it belonged only to Mason. Does loving one man make your heart ripe for another?

I kept weaving through the crowd, occasionally hopping over a curb, a lost costume prop, a knee-high fence delineating landscaping from the sidewalk, until I was enmeshed in a new crowd that was gawking at the movie crew setting up a shot. A man with a megaphone was requesting the people to stay behind the police sawhorses that barricaded my street, as cameras, lights, and miles of wire were being assembled on the other side. He was polite and rather jolly about his request, though he most likely had the authority to just bark out, "Hey, you people! Back off!" He probably had the proper stack of papers in hand with all the necessary signatures from New York City's Mayor's Office of Film, Theatre, and Broadcasting. The man with the megaphone was enthralling the growing crowd with explanations about the need for them to be absolutely still and silent when the shooting was, at last, in progress.

"Valentina!" Jafford called out. "Wait!"

Not even a whisper, the megaphone man was telling the crowd. No cameras either—the flash or non-flash kind, he said. And they listened politely, proving my point that they were just visitors, not native New Yorkers. Or maybe they were to sort of people who never missed a single issue of *People*, and thought Hollywood movie makers were gods.

"Valentina!"

I could hear Jafford still calling me, but I didn't want him to follow. I sashayed past the barricade without so much as a nod to the movie crew leader while my heart was thumping. How could I possibly feel Jafford inside me when it was only Mason whom I truly loved? Why did I want to turn back, see his face, hold his hand? I had to shake off the thought. I kept my head down, looking at the sidewalk. I quickened my steps until I reached the center of the block. Finally, I was home. Movie crew or not, no one was going to prevent me from entering my own apartment. But as I looked up from the cracks in the sidewalk and reached for my front door key with my left hand, my right hand muzzled my own mouth. I couldn't believe what I was seeing.

A brand-new, yellow striped canopy had been erected over the storefront's window. Along the top was a row of bright lights, which were shining up to a brand-new sign. Instead of reading *Pearson's Fine Frames* as it had for nearly a century, the same name that belonged to the frame gallery when Mason's parents moved into the place, it proclaimed in large block letters: THE MASON FIGG FINE ARTS GALLERY.

"Miss! Miss!"

I heard the megaphone man call to me.

"Valentina! Hold up!"

I could hear Jafford, too, but I didn't look back at either of them.

"Hey! You can't go in there!"

I had no intention of following anyone else's directions but my own. I raced to the storefront window as my duffle bag slipped to my wrist. I was so surprised by what I was seeing, I let the bag drop to the sidewalk.

"I'm sorry, miss," the megaphone man tried again.

He had put down his megaphone now and was standing right by my side, trying to leap in front of me. But I rushed up to the window of what once was the frame gallery and pushed my nose against the glass.

"Valentina!"

"You'll have to get back. This area is restricted."

"Valentina!"

There, displayed in the window was one of Mason's castle-sized paintings, only it was new, one I hadn't seen before, one that depicted all of the animals at Swan Crest—with Dagmar in the foreground—posing in the nude.

"Hey, lady! Step back, will ya? No trespassing allowed! You'll have to go!"

Beneath the painting on a cloud of blue velvet—the same blue as that crazy duck's eyes—were a dozen sets of Blue Diamond Peepers along with a small sign that read: AUTHENTIC BAUBLES AS SEEN ON *OPERAH*.

"*Operah*?" I said aloud, but only to myself. Mason never could spell very well. I figured he must've meant *Oprah*. He should've stuck to art.

"Did you hear the man?" a cop asked me as he flipped open a citation book from an aluminum case. "This area's restricted. You'll have to step back."

The cop was so tall, he even towered over me. He was scribbling onto his pad with a pen, but I couldn't budge. It was if my two big mud boots had been planted in cement and my jaw was locked open.

"You are in violation of New York City Statute 135-25 ..."

The cop was scribbling into his citation book as he spoke, then stopped to shake his pen in the air. As he tried writing again, the front door of my apartment opened and shut, and I looked up to see a woman adjusting her flowered wraparound dress as she paused at the top of the stairs. She was a rather matronly woman and probably should never had worn such form-fitting attire. But from my perspective on the sidewalk, judging by her face, her long silky hair, and her shapely legs—no matter what her age—I could tell that she was the type who was a born beauty. I knew immediately that she was the same woman posing with Mason in the portrait over the fireplace back at the cottage.

"Valentina!" Jafford kept calling.

"Hey!" the cop shouted at me.

But I plied my mud boots off the sidewalk and ran up to Mason's mother on the stairs.

"I'm Valentina," I said.

Upon seeing her face up close, I suddenly felt slightly queasy. An inch of make-up was plastered on her face with a heavy dusting of powder that emphasized, rather than hid, deep wrinkles around her eyes. Her hair, while shiny, didn't look natural. With an artificial gleam to it and vague part, it must've been a wig. She was holding a stack of paper in her hand and smoothing down her skirt. Then she stuck a finger in her mouth and pulled it out, examining it to see if she had saved a rim of lipstick from mucking up her yellowing teeth. I knew then that Mason had been kind when painting the portrait.

"I've been hoping to meet you," I continued. "We've been waiting for you for so long. It's nice to finally meet you."

"Huh?" she questioned with disgust.

She snorted at my assumption and stared me down with eyes that fluttered with unnaturally long and thick lashes. Then she stuck her stack of papers in her armpit in order to pull the skinny sash that matched the jersey fabric of her dress, and tied a bow with it around her rotund waist, giving it a firm and final yank.

"I'm *Valentina*," I said again, thinking she didn't hear me the first time.

Surely, she knew my name with all the postcards she'd sent from Africa. It was a thrill to have my name along with Mason's on the address line; it wasn't every boyfriend's mother who'd acknowledge a live-in girlfriend. She knew that Mason and I had been living together at the cottage. She knew all about Mason's commissioned art. She knew about Dagmar and Duncan, all the animals and the farm. Mason told me he had written to her. She hadn't been allowed Internet access for e-mails or a single phone call. But the passport snafu that Mason described to me along with her exporting troubles that landed her in an African jail, weren't egregious enough for the authorities to prevent her from exchanging postcards and letters. At least that's what Mason had said.

"I'm so happy you finally got out! How'd you do it?"

"Huh?"

It'll be so nice to have you home. With *us*!"

I couldn't wait to tell her the news about the baby, but naturally I had to wait until Mason was there, too. But she kept staring at me as her caked-on make-up started to crack on her cheeks. She was no longer fussing with the bow on her dress or saying a word as a pair of cops now hustled up the staircase while the megaphone guy stayed behind on the sidewalk—and pointed at me. Jafford was right behind him.

"I'm *Valentina!*" I said once more. "Mason's girlfriend?"

"Girlfriend?"

"We have your portrait hanging over our fireplace back at our cottage—our little country home!"

"Your little country home?"

I didn't see Jafford, but the crowd must've spotted him for the second time that night, for they were chanting his name.

"Jaff! Jaff! Jaff! Jaff! Jaff!"

I leaned in closer to the woman on the stairs to hear what she was trying to tell me.

"Jaff! Jaff! Jaff! Jaff! Jaff!"

"I'm Valentina!" I said yet again. "And you must be Mrs. Figg, Mason's mother, right?"

"Jaff! Jaff! Jaff! Jaff! Jaff!"

"Honey, I'm Mrs. Figg, but I'm not Mason's mother," she grumbled in the raspy voice of a veteran smoker. "I'm his wife."

Chapter 14

The Buggy

For the second time in one night I found myself sprawled out on a staircase, but this time instead of marble, it was cold, hard concrete. Jafford softened the blow. He was kneeling in front of me, holding my hand and brushing my cheek. I could smell his natural scent mixed in with his cologne, Cool Water by Davidoff, I think, one of his endorsements that used to run in TV commercials. I never noticed his scent before. But I had never been knocked out before either. The pleasing fragrance was enough to stir my senses and get my juices flowing.

"This is getting monotonous," I heard Jafford say. "I may need to follow you around with a tennis net. That way when you fall, you can bounce back up."

He laughed in that way he had and I opened my eyes. I could see his face up close, but I could also see something swinging back and forth behind him.

"We're all square here, officer," Jafford said. "No need for those. I'll take full responsibility for her. She didn't mean any harm."

But the swinging object kept flying behind Jafford's head. It was making me dizzy. Until I realized it was a pair of handcuffs held by a cop, I stared at it trying to focus. And then I just felt scared. I closed my eyes again, squeezing them tight, bracing myself to be arrested and wondering how news could travel so fast from the country all the way to the city and my very own front door. I was headed for the slammer now. The Big House.

I was wrong in ever agreeing to be an accomplice in Mason's Grand Master Plan for Project Peepers. I wasn't really a thief. I wasn't a duck killer either. And I certainly had nothing whatsoever to do with Duncan's demise. It was all a series of mishaps, I'd tell the copper. But what I really needed to know was if Duncan was actually dead. And did that stupid duck survive?

No matter what their condition was at that very moment when Jafford was bantering with the police on the steps, I knew I was guilty of at least one major crime. I was the one who not only held a ladder up to the Twists' master bedroom window, I entered their house without permission. I impersonated a dead princess, too. But I was not really a diamond thief; I was only guilty of being a fool. I had no idea Mason had been pulling my strings other than those tied to my heart. Unfortunately, those were still knotted.

"Sure," Jafford was saying. "We could use an escort. But what we really need is a blanket for my friend here. She won't be trespassing again. No need for a citation."

Trespassing? Is that what they thought I had done?

"Perfect!" I heard Jafford say as he turned his head. I opened my eyes a slit and could see he was still wearing my black hat—one side flipped up, the other down. "Just a blanket, officer. Thanks!"

In a snap, I saw a big, gray blanket unfold over me then felt it wrap around my cold body as if I were a corpse.

"Yup, she'll be fine," Jafford assured the copper. "Could you just help keep the crowd back while I get her into the buggy?"

Buggy? Where the heck were we? Maybe I had been knocked out longer than I realized and traveled backwards in time, waking up in another century. But that couldn't possibly be. I could hear more chanting from the crowd as they called out Jafford's name. I could see bright lights all around me, too, as Jafford scooped me up in my blanket and carried me off.

"Jaff! Jaff! Jaff! Jaff!"

"Make sure she doesn't show her face around here again," I heard that raspy-voiced woman say.

"Jaff! Jaff! Jaff! Jaff!"

"Tell her to stay away from my husband," she bellowed. "In the city or the country!"

My head was splitting. I wanted to feel my forehead to see if it had cracked open, but my arms were tight across my chest and wrapped with the blanket and Jafford's capable arms as he placed me on a leather seat. The next thing I knew, a horse was neighing. Jafford was sitting beside me cradling my head in his lap.

"This is *my* home!" the old bag yapped again. "Not hers!"

"Jaff! Jaff! Jaff! Jaff!"

"She better keep her claws out of my man! Make sure she stays away!"

"Jaff! Jaff! Jaff! Jaff!"

I heard the clip-clop of a horse's hooves, but I couldn't see anything more than darkness when I finally felt strong enough to keep my eyes open. Jafford had pulled a cover over our heads, which I learned was the top of a horse's carriage.

"I thought there weren't livery horses in New York anymore," I muttered. "At least not outside of Central Park. Too many accidents. Too many cruel stable owners. Only the mounted police ride horses."

"I don't know about that," Jafford said. "Arnold had this one shipped in from Pennsylvania for a scene in his movie. Works cheap. Just hay and an apple."

I didn't think much of Jafford's joke, but he seemed to enjoy it as his popcorn laugh was heating up again. I can't say as I liked it, but it was beginning to be familiar to me and without knowing what was going on, I found his funny sounds comforting. I tuned into his hoots and guffaws wondering how long they would last. But what I was more curious about was where we were going. And why weren't we taking a cab, subway, or bus?

"You like Mexican food? I bet you could use a few margaritas by now," Jafford said. "Driver, take us to Los *Banditos* del Jaffordo. Know where that is?"

"Of course!" the driver said.

"... Horse?"

"What?" Jafford asked, leaning down close to my face. But I felt too weak to ask about the horse. "What did you say? Horse? Oh, that.

We're lucky. Arnold's production guys blocked off streets all around. No cabs allowed. No buses either. We're lucky to have the horse."

I never thought I'd like the sound of a horse or be grateful that we had one. I thought it was funny that the stink of manure was familiar. I had smelled enough of it at Swan Crest Farms. In the city, it seemed out of place. Somehow, I did, too.

"What is going on?" I managed to mutter. "What happened? Why can't I go into my own apartment?"

Jafford heaved an audible sigh, the kind you hear just before bad news is delivered. He started by recounting the story of how we had run into Arnold and Natasha, and how they were dressed up for Halloween to pass the time while the movie crew was delayed in setting up for the next shot.

"I remember all that, Jafford," I said. "But what …"

"Don't try to talk, Valentina," he said. "I'm not even sure you should move around too much. That was quite the fall you had. Considering the volume of your scream, the one you gave back there on the steps, I'm surprised tall buildings didn't collapse along with you. You are one heck of a screamer. Wow!"

It was all coming back to me now. My throat was sore. So were my stomach muscles. Memories were rushing through my weary mind: the old bag on the steps, the new gallery sign …

"The Mason Figg Fine Arts Gallery! What has Mason been up to?" I asked, suddenly sitting up in Jafford's arms as the horse trotted along. "Where is Mason? I want to see him *now*!"

"Easy there, Valentina. Let's take this one trot at a time. You must be in quite a shock considering the circumstances. I had no idea that Mason was married or that he was Arnold's cousin. I didn't put two-and-two together until you, all on your own, figured out who Arnold was. Then it hit me."

"Hit *you*?"

"Yeah, I knew that Arnold had a crazy cousin. I also knew that the cousin rented out his frame gallery and apartment to Arnold, and that his wife …"

"Wife? Mason's married?"

"Anything's possible with that guy, Valentina. You just can't be too sure about …"

"I am absolutely, positively sure about my Mason, and ..."

"Hold on, Valentina. You've got to face the truth."

Truth was always my territory. I never wanted anything more than that. I wanted to know the truth about my real parents when I was growing up. I hounded my social workers to tell me. I even demanded to see the papers they supposedly had signed when I was in foster care. I was convinced that the state of New York was keeping me from them, but not with their consent. I knew my parents must've loved me, but somehow they needed to leave me in the care of orphan homes. I knew that ...

But what was I thinking? I was as wrong about my real parents as I was about Mason. It was all coming back to me now. That woman on the stairs whom I had thought was Mason's long lost mother finally sprung from an African jail, told me the truth herself.

"Oh, no!" I said out loud to Jafford. "It just can't be."

"Seems like it can, Valentina," Jafford said. "I'm really, really sorry, but that guy must have been stringing you along."

"But she's old enough to be his mother. And she looked like she could be his father in drag."

"Yup, that woman had the face of a bull and the body of a cow. I'm afraid it could be true, but we don't have all the facts."

I never heard Jafford speak unkindly of anyone before—except for maybe Duncan. He'd never really made fun of a woman's appearance either— except for maybe Dagmar. I had a feeling that Jafford was just trying to show loyalty to me. I needed someone on my side.

"I remember Arnold telling me about her," Jafford went on. "Said she was one of Mason's high school teachers. The two of them have been tied at the hip for years, only she travels a lot. So does he. They have some kind of import-export racket going on. And Arnold did also tell me that they actually are married. After the wedding ceremony, they held the reception at the Cyrus Pepper High School gymnasium where they first met."

I was numb. And it wasn't because I was cold.

"Those papers she was holding were for Arnold. She had to sign them along with Mason to allow the movie studio access to their apartment, and ..."

"Their apartment!" I screamed. "That's my apartment. Mason's and mine!"

"I guess the wife was traveling when you were living there. Didn't you say it was only a short time before you two moved out to The Cottage at Swan Crest Farms?"

"She was in jail! In Africa! Mason told me it was an exporting snafu! And that she was his mother. They took away her passport. We have her portrait. Mason painted it himself. It's hanging over the fireplace back at the cottage, and …"

"Valentina! Valentina! The facts! We don't know all of them yet. Please try to calm down. You don't want to get all upset."

"Upset!" I was really yelling now. I guess I was loud enough to scare the horse, because our buggy driver turned around and gave us a dirty look. "Upset!" I said again, only more softly. "I lived in that apartment! I helped out in the gallery when I came home from work at the waxing salon! We worked there together! Ate together! We slept upstairs! We made love! Two, even three …"

I stopped myself from saying much more. Perhaps I was revealing too much information for Jafford's polite ears. I breathed deeply in and out, two or maybe three times until I collected my composure.

"That apartment was our home," I said calmly. "So was the cottage."

Jafford said nothing more. He wrapped his arms around me so many times, I thought they must be miles long. I thought that was a good thing, because to tell you the truth, I felt broken. But it wasn't exactly my body that needed to be sewn together or bandaged up. It was my soul. I snuggled closer to Jafford, fearing that if I didn't, I'd slip through the crack in the back of the horse buggy seat and spew onto the street like manure.

My future had just shifted. So did my present. More images from the gallery kept spinning through my mind's eye: Dagmar's nude painting, the Authentic Baubles on display, the sign announcing they had been seen on *Oprah* or *Operah*. And then there was that woman in the flowered wraparound dress. Had she actually said that she was Mrs. Figg?

"I suppose she, too, had a part in Arnold's movie," I suggested.

"Did you see her up close? Did you get a load of that make-up? That wig!"

"Arnold's the type to care more about friendship and loyalty to his cousin, than he is to cast for good looks," Jafford said. "Besides, he always writes horror/comedies. Seems to me that bull-faced lady was the right fit."

Jafford was sputtering out his popcorn laugh again, but I didn't think anything was funny. If I weren't so deeply wounded, I'd be mad. I had no strength left in me to shout, but there was one name that was on my lips. I opened and closed them, but no sound came out. I knew, though, what my heart wanted to scream. But before I could mouth Mason's name, my eyes were opening wide enough to pop out of my head.

"Authentic Baubles!" I managed to shout in my strained voice. "Look!"

A bus was rumbling through the intersection where our buggy was stopped at a red light. It was plastered all over with a single advertising message on the front, back, and sides. It was a moving billboard for Mason's knock-offs of the Blue Diamond Peepers.

"Authentic *what*?" Jafford asked.

"Baubles!" I squeaked. "Mason's …"

But I couldn't say anymore. Our carriage had been weaving through side streets to bypass Arnold's barricades. We needed to head north before circling back down to the Village to reach the Mexican restaurant Jafford wanted to go to. We were nearly all the way up to Union Square when the bus caught my eye. I could hardly miss it. The words and pictures were big enough to see from the moon.

"Look!" I said again. "There!"

Jafford was doing a double-take to see where I was pointing, then back to me for a clue. But I was fresh out. I just kept motioning toward the flashy bus, then waving my hand back and forth through the chilly night air as if we were playing charades. I don't know if Jafford knew of the connection between Mason's handiwork and the Authentic Baubles bus at that point, but there's no question that he recognized the driver as being Mason's bull-faced wife. I think we must've noticed her at the very same time, because we both gasped and looked at each other then back at that woman driving the billboard bus.

"Follow that bull!" Jafford shouted to our driver. "I mean that *billboard bus!*"

But the buggy was still stuck in traffic. Bull Face and her bus were lumbering away, heading uptown on Broadway. It was one of those everyday situations in the city where your destination is within view, but a jumble of hurdles separate you from reaching it like crowds, traffic, and lights.

"Go back down to the Village," Jafford commanded. "Go to *Los Banditos*."

He pulled out a bill from his wallet and handed it to the driver. From where I was sitting, it looked like a fifty.

"Keep the change," Jafford told him before turning to me. "I'll catch up with you later," he said. "Go!"

Was Jafford dumping me, too?

"I want to know what those two Looney Tunes have cooked up together," Jafford hastily added. "Something stinks. And I don't mean the horse's manure. I'm going to find out what Mason and Bull Face are up to."

I didn't want Jafford to leave me alone, but he wasn't giving me a choice.

"Don't worry, Valentina," he said. "We'll sort this out."

And then it happened again.

His eyes were beaming.

I had a feeling mine were, too.

He was smiling at me as he leaned into the carriage. While his toes might've been touching the sidewalk, mine were wiggling. I was floating above that little horse buggy as Jafford's face was close to mine. I could smell his cologne. I could practically taste his sweet breath as his lips were close to my lips, all while he balanced himself with one hand on the side of the carriage and brushed my cold cheek with his other hand.

I blushed.

Waves of warmth were starting to radiate all over my body. My eyes opened into his. He leaned in even closer. Then he kissed me. On the lips. Just a peck—yet sweet.

In a flash, Jafford was gone.

I watched him zigzagging around cars stalled in traffic and running down the sidewalk chasing that bus with the speed and agility that only a professional athlete possessed. I leaned out of the horse buggy, opened my mouth, and heard myself crying out in a longing voice—this time it was one only I could hear. I wanted to run after him. I wanted to know what Bull Face, that *wife* of Mason's, was up to. But most of all, I feared I was being abandoned. Again. It seemed to be a long-standing pattern in my pathetic life's path. Grown up or not, I was an orphan to the bone. *'Please,'* I thought. *'Come back!'*

"Jaaaaaaf-ford!"

Chapter 15

The Shiner

Umbrellas were popping. Rain was starting to sprinkle. The line waiting to get into the Mexican restaurant where the buggy driver pulled over seemed to be growing longer with each drop. Considering the number of people willing to stand in the rain, the food in that place must've been scrumptious, but I wouldn't know. Mason and I only dined out at hot dog pushcarts when we didn't make dinner at home.

"This is it, miss," the driver said. "*Los Banditos.*"

I kicked off my blanket and was folding it neatly to leave on the seat when it occurred to me that Mason was a cheapskate. He never spent money for a night out on the town. Perhaps he didn't want to be seen out in public with me. Not in the city. Not when he had a *wife*.

"Gotta get back to the movie set, miss," the driver said. "Arnold, he'll be hopping mad."

I was certain that the driver was shooting me a hateful stare, impatient for me to leave. He was clearing his throat and leaning back. His long arm was reaching to open the door. I pawed the leather seat and checked the floor of the carriage for my duffle bag. But it was gone.

"I can't find my duffle bag!"

"Ya never brung no duffle, miss," he said. "Not when I picked chew up with The Jaff."

I must've dropped it at the frame gallery when I fell on the steps.

The only item I wanted from it was my umbrella. Rain was beginning to pound the hood of the carriage and cascade down the sides. I could barely see the people lining up on the sidewalk.

"You okay, miss?"

I wasn't okay. Without my duffle bag stuffed with the only evidence of my meager existence on this planet, I was as naked as I was on the sorrowful day that I was born. What I needed even more than a change of clothes, toothbrush, or protection from the rain was a friend. I was fresh out. I wanted to say, *"Please, Mr. Buggy Driver, can't I stay here with you? I don't want to be left all alone!"* But instead, I simply thanked him for the ride.

I had no choice. The driver had a job to get back to. I wouldn't want him to be fired on my account. I slid out of the buggy and landed in a puddle. The horse carriage clip-clopped away, splashing me with dirty water from the brown river flowing down the gutter. I let the cold rain wash it off as I shuddered by myself on the curb. I wanted the rain to wash away my miserable circumstances, too, for the only place in the entire world I had to go was the end of the long line of people, none of whom were mine.

I hung my head in shame. I couldn't look anyone in the eye. All my dreams were vanishing as I slowly accepted that Mason was married. My life, as pathetic as it had been, had come to a halt. It had always been a revolving door of people flying in and flying out. I remember seeing other foster kids forever parading to and from foster homes, always toting their few, tattered belongings, and wearing ill-fitting clothes. My first bra was so big that I needed to stuff the cups with fresh kitty litter. Stray cats followed me for blocks.

I had no family. My social workers had told me that my mother disappeared after I was born and was never seen again. I didn't want to believe it, or that my father had left town to track her down. I never knew my grandparents. No one ever mentioned if I had any aunts, uncles, or cousins. The only brothers and sisters I ever knew were other foster children, but no one stayed around long enough to be more than a blur. I can't even remember their names. One home I stayed in numbered us as we filed through the door. Even back then, I was odd. They called me *Three*.

I had to face the truth: I was an orphan all over again. I might've been well over the legal age of eighteen when orphans no longer are welcomed into foster care. But despite that I was an adult in the eyes of the law, I knew I was a born loser. Being on my own with no place to go—*that* was my true life's path.

I sloshed past clusters of families and friends and couple after couple until I found my place at the end of that expanding line. But I was quickly in the middle as more parties and couples, all holding umbrellas, lined up behind me. It was as if I were the filling for an orphan sandwich, the sole person in that line without an umbrella—or a companion.

Had Jafford dumped me, too? Would he come back? Was he good for his word?

Amidst laughter and banter, I was drowning in spirit with tears of the soul. I folded my arms over my baseball cap as the rain started hammering down harder. My meadow stompers were filled up to the brim with water. I was a walking puddle. People were laughing. I figured it was at me. While they hooted and chuckled, tears were blinding my eyes. At least I didn't have to see if they were wearing costumes. How I hated Halloween.

Just as I was wondering if it was possible to drown while standing up, a million clouds finished emptying out leaving a fog between me and the laughing strangers. I swore I could hear the sound of horses' hooves clumping on the pavement, and it seemed to be getting louder. As I peered through the hazy light, I could see a fluorescent orange poncho flying toward us down the center of the street. The ghoulish vision was swooping in for a landing when I realized that it wasn't some joker dressed up as a ghost.

It was Jafford.

I could tell by the hat he was wearing. The brim was still flipped up on one side, the other down, only now that hat was covered in plastic, the kind policemen wear in the rain.

"Jafford!" I cried with outstretched arms, as if he had just come back from the dead.

He was running down the center of the street, flanked on both sides by two New York City mounted police. As soon as he spotted me in the line, he saluted them, and the pair of cops on horses took off. Then he turned around facing the crowd still lining up on the rain-washed sidewalk. But not a single person chanted his name. I guess they didn't recognize him as being The Jaff, not when he was wearing a knee-length, glow-in-the-dark poncho stamped with POLICE on the back and holding an ice pack over one eye.

"Your eye!" I screamed. "What happened?"

"She punched me!"

"Who?"

"Bull Face."

"Mason's ... *wife?*"

"Yup!" Jafford said. "Pow! It's going to be a shiner."

"But why?" I asked.

I might've been dripping wet, but my throat was still dry and scratchy from my screaming episode on the frame gallery steps. I should've opened my mouth and let the rain flood in. It was flowing out of the sky once more as if the East River had ripped itself out of the earth, changed course, and poured over our heads.

"Come on in," Jafford said. "And I'll tell you."

He was lifting up the edge of his poncho. I slipped under it. I could tell he was fiddling with the neck hole until he ripped the seam enough to allow my head to poke through the opening along with his. Like it or not, I was finally dressed up for Halloween. Together, we were a two-headed monster with our arms around each others' waists. I was still soaked, but at least I had a companion, only better: I had *Jafford!* He was back at my side!

"Old Bull Face was selling Authentic Baubles up at Union Square right out of that billboard bus," Jafford said out of breath. "She parked it where the farmers' market usually sets up on Saturdays. She hooked up flood lights powered by a generator on her bus. She had an enormous tent set up, too, along with a giant sign. The crowd—all women—was lining up. So I lined up with them."

Now *that* was low. Even Bull Face attracted more people into her life than I ever did. She even had my Mason. I should've given up right there and then. I was hopeless. Had it not been for Jafford anchoring me inside that poncho, I might've been sucked up by the water rushing into the sewer.

"I don't know how to explain it," Jafford continued. "I still don't understand what, exactly, was going on. One of those Peruvian pan flute bands was playing …"

He was giving his rendition of pan flutes with an eerie nasal hum, and still holding the ice pack over one eye while he fluttered the other to keep time with his song. As the rain let up again, we moved along with the line.

"All those women around me—they loved it! They looked like they were drugged as they swayed to the music, waving their hands in their air. But what was really a tad peculiar, if you ask me …"

He hesitated. He seemed perplexed. He was actually stammering.

"Jafford," I cried. "What was so peculiar?"

"I never saw anything like it before," he said. "Kind of gave me the creeps. I was looking all around me in utter amazement, because the ladies who weren't lining up to buy Bull Face's Authentic Baubles were clustered in circles. It was like a witch convention, only instead of wearing all black and tall, pointy hats, they were dressed up in bright colors—blue, red, green …"

"Huh?"

"Must've been casting love spells for themselves. What else would so many single women be doing out on a night like this?" he said, pointing to the rain. "And it *is* Halloween."

I shuddered at the thought, and not because I was cold. I was spooked.

"How'd you know they were single?" I asked.

I feared that was my destiny, too. I doubted I'd ever find my forever home, let alone become a mother; I wanted to be the one in my murky gene pool to get parenthood right. But I was beginning to believe there was a park bench somewhere in that city waiting for me to find it. I made a mental note to keep my eyes peeled for one inscribed with the number three.

"They must've been single," Jafford said. "The sign by the billboard bus spelled out how Authentic Baubles can attract a particular sort of soul mate. Blue is for one who'll be faithful, it said. And the zaniest thing was that the sign displayed a picture of what looked to be an exact replica of Dagmar's new diamonds. You know the ones? They're mounted on the face of a duck that resembles Peepers. And you know how proud Dagmar is of him."

I did. But I wished I didn't.

"She's forever wearing that pricy little broach even around her farm. Whenever she sees me, she makes certain that she flashes it in my face and dares me to guess how much those rare blue diamonds are worth. Can you believe it?"

I wanted to confess right there on the sidewalk as the heavens were emptying over our two heads once more, how Mason and I had schemed and plotted to steal them from the Twists' master bedroom safe. I opened my mouth, but the words were not coming out. Instead, rain was showering in.

"See? I told you," Jafford said. "You're shocked, too."

My jaw was stuck open. Jafford touched my chin with two fingers. I closed my gaping mouth. I wondered what he'd do if he found out about my part in attempting to steal Dagmar's Blue Diamond Peepers. No doubt he'd leave me in an instant. Any normal, law-abiding person would.

"You look like a fish," Jafford said. "Where're your fins?"

Should I confess? Would Jafford believe I was an attempted diamond thief? If I told him, would I lose my only friend? I knew I was lying to him by omission. Deceit was chewing me up from the inside-out.

"Jafford ..." I started, but I couldn't get the words out, nor could I bear the thought of his long arms unwrapping themselves from around my waist as he checked me for fins.

"There were more—more Authentic Baubles. Looked exactly alike, but in different colors. Each had a different power, I guess."

"Jafford, I need to tell you that I ..."

"The sign said that the red ones attract a soul mate who has passion in the bedroom, green is for attracting the rich or famous, purple is for spiritual connections, yellow is for laughter and joy, orange is for belonging to a plural marriage where one woman has many husbands, and ..."

"How'd you remember all that?"

Jafford pulled out a flyer from his pocket. He tried showing it to me, but the ink had gotten wet, smearing the words and pictures.

"I memorized it," Jafford said. "That was a long line. Didn't have my iPod on me."

Jafford was challenging me to test his memory, but I couldn't make out any of the words on the flier, let alone speak. I was woozy thinking about how only Mason could cook up a merchandizing scheme as goofy as the one for Authentic Baubles. I was suddenly feeling dizzy. I remembered how he had stored up so many fake gems in glass bins in the furnace room, Cuban Pete was getting squeezed out. It wasn't until Mason packed them all up in crates that our cat had his private quarters all to himself. I guess Bull Face was on the receiving end of the shipments. At least their business seemed to be on the up-and-up.

"There were silver ones, too," Jafford said. "The sign said that they were intended for older women who must've been ordering them by the caseload, because the sign also said they were blockbuster sellers in Florida and Arizona where the marriage rate among senior citizens was skyrocketing to an all-time high. The sign further claimed that Authentic Baubles were seen on—get this—*Operah*!"

So much for going legit. I guess Mason didn't have it in him to be anything more than a con artist. Apparently, I was one, too, since I seemed incapable of spitting out a confession about my recent criminal past. Even that turned out to be pathetic. I wanted the rain to shrink me until I disappeared inside the poncho. Would Jafford notice if I went missing?

"Get it?" Jafford asked, still laughing. "The sign actually said *Operah*!"

I got it, I got it. I wasn't sure I wanted to hear anymore. I was wishing that Mason had stuck to oil paintings. I was proud of him back then. I didn't care if he could spell or not, but this screwball *Operah* scam was setting my nerves on edge. Jafford seemed to be enjoying it though as he howled along with the wind.

"*Operah*! Ha! See, Valentina? It's a con. Her name is really spelled O-p-r-a-h."

"I know, Jafford. I know," I said. "But you still haven't told me why Bull Face punched you in the eye."

"Well, one of the women from the green tribe recognized me and started screaming my name. Before I knew it, a whole pack of green-clad ladies all dolled up with green Authentic Baubles, was circling around me. That's when old Bull Face stuck her head out of the bus and started yelling, '*Not him! He's not your soul mate! Stay away!*' Then she came barreling out of her bus and pulled the green ladies off me one at a time. '*He's bad news,*' she snorted just like a bull. '*He'll give you bad karma!*'"

"You?" I squeaked.

"Sorry, Valentina, but I guess she associated *me* with *you*. And you do recall how angry she was when she found out you were tangled up with Mason."

"I can't say she's slipped my mind."

"Well, she started picking up the ladies by the scruffs of their necks until she plowed her way to me. And then she grabbed me by the scruff of my neck and *pow*! Punched me in the eye."

I was speechless.

"I could hear horses trotting around in a circle around us," Jafford said.

I was cursed by animals. Country or city—I couldn't seem to escape them.

"Turned out to be New York City mounted police. They're the ones who pried her off me after she tripped me ..."

"She *tripped* you?"

"Yup. Didn't see it coming. I was holding my sore eye. Before I knew it, I was down on all fours. Bull Face hopped on my back."

"*What!*"

"I could've taken her, but I'm not about to fight a lady, even one with the face of a bull. Instead, I did a few push-ups with one hand and held my eye with the other. Remind me to give my trainer a bonus."

Bonus? I guess he meant a tip. That's what we'd call it at the waxing salon. I had no idea what a professional athlete like Jafford paid his trainer, but he must have gotten his money's worth. He sure was strong to have Bull face ride on his back.

"Bull Face wouldn't budge. She kept holding on."

I couldn't help thinking that compared to her, I was clay. No wonder Mason liked me. He probably could never stand up to Bull Face, but he sure could mold me.

"Before they hauled old Bull Face off to jail for disturbing the peace ..."

"How about assault?" I piped up. "She did hit you."

"Nah," Jafford said. "I'd never press charges. How'd it look for a professional athlete to be beat up by an old lady? I'd be a laughing stock on the tennis courts."

"I didn't think of that," I said.

"Besides, I'm in the paper enough as it is. I wouldn't want my picture in there along with Bull Face's mug shot. All I wanted was an ice pack for my eye, so the cops gave me one from their Official Incident First Aid Kit. You know, the kind they started stocking around town after 9/11. *That* was a *real* incident. What happened to me with Mason's wife was a mere game. Then the cops gave me this nifty poncho, too. And a shower cap for my hat. Like it?"

He was laughing at his get up and posing with his plastic-clad hat while I, hearing the word *wife* again, hid my face in shame. Not only was I a diamond thief, I was a mistress without knowing it. Altogether, that made me a dope, not to mention homeless. Perhaps jail was the logical place for me to go. At least it would be dry—I hoped. As long as I didn't have to bunk with Bull Face, I'd be fine.

"You're a fun date, Valentina," Jafford said. He was kissing the top of my head. And I let him. "But next time, let's just go to dinner and a movie. I'll call the cops for an escort. Which do you prefer: motorcycles, horses, or a plain, old black and white?"

"I don't get it, Jafford," I said, finally facing him again as he cuddled me inside the poncho and we braced ourselves for another downpour, inching closer to the restaurant's front door. "Do you always get an escort wherever you go?"

"Yup. Guess I do," he said with a shrug. *"I always depend on the kindness of strangers..."*

He was reciting lines from *A Streetcar Named Desire* by Tennessee Williams, speaking with an exaggerated Southern accent in a high, feminine voice, but I wasn't catching on as to why the police favored him with so many escorts around town. With my head securely popping through the freshly widened neck of the poncho, Jafford's play-acting turned to laughter and I gave up. He was still covering one eye with the ice pack.

"What makes you so special?" I asked.

I didn't mean to sound sarcastic, but I guess I just thought of him as *Jafford*, an ordinary person who was quickly becoming my loyal companion. I never really considered how well known he actually was.

His celebrity was global. His fame was not confined to New York. He was popular among legions of fans around the world. He also proved popular with the bouncers at the front door of the restaurant. They seemed quite chummy when we finally reached the top of that slow-moving line.

"You must've been here before," I said. "Are you a regular?"

Jafford pointed up to the sign: *Los Banditos del Jaffordo.*

I did a double-take reading the name of that place for the first time. With all the upheaval during the evening, I must've forgotten that Jafford owned a chain of Mexican restaurants.

"That's you?" I squeaked in my still-strained voice. "You own this restaurant? The entire place?"

He was smiling at me. We weren't quite face-to-face. I looked up to him. His mouth was at my eye-level. He was laughing. At me.

"Jafford," I said. "If you own this restaurant, then why didn't we go inside sooner?"

"I was having too much fun in the rain," he said. "How else could I have gotten you into this poncho with me?"

We were standing hip-to-tummy. My toes were wiggling. No longer was I cold. I was thinking about how I didn't have a soul in the world, while there wasn't a soul in the world who didn't know—and love—*The Jaff*. He could parachute onto an iceberg in the middle of the North Pole, and penguins would jump up and chant his name. But being in the heart of New York City, there wasn't a single penguin around. The only sound I could hear was my heart, thumping:

"Jaff! Jaff! Jaff! Jaff!"

CHAPTER 16

The Guacamole

I licked the salt off the rim of my margarita glass, feeling like a deer in the woods: scared and in need of nourishment. While a real deer probably would have no trouble seeing through the dimly lit restaurant known as *Los Banditos del Jaffordo*, I certainly did. Colorful lanterns strung all over the ceiling simply didn't shine brightly enough to reveal if I had just been served an enchilada or a burrito. But I wasn't hungry as much as I was thirsty, and Jafford promised me that there was no alcohol in my drink. I sipped the frozen liquid through a long straw as if I had no teeth and the margarita was all I could manage as my final meal. It should've been. After joining Arnold and Natasha at their table, I just wanted to hide.

"Maaaaaa-sooooooooon!"

Arnold was reenacting my impromptu scene as I stumbled onto his movie set, only instead of using the same volume as I had before passing out cold, he mouthed Mason's name while squeezing his eyes together and whispering loud enough for the four of us to hear him.

"Maaaaaa-sooooooooon!"

Couldn't he chomp on a few more chips? He barely had two of them with all the raves he was giving me for my unwitting performance on the gallery's side staircase.

"Maaaaaa-sooooooooon! Ah yes, that was quite good," Arnold said to me for the millionth time. "Are you sure you don't belong to the

Screen Actors Guild? We'll have to take care of that. Never done voice over work before? Astonishing! Brilliant! Masterful work! 'Maaaaaa-soooooooooon!' With talent like that, m'darling, you don't need a director."

He had finally removed most of his Boris costume and no longer hee-hee-heed. But in costume or not, I never would've recognized him as the cousin Mason claimed to have pushed through high school with retrofitted grades.

"You wouldn't believe what Mason taught the students to do in what he called his *Cotillion Preparation Dance Classes*," Arnold Otterman said. "Believe me, it wasn't just the Virginia reel. When a reporter dropped by from the local newspaper, the entire junior class—all forty-four of us—turned around with our backs to the cameras and dropped trou. I'm telling you," Arnold said, breaking up in laughter and hoots. "Ol' Cyrus Pepper would have his name changed on his tombstone had he known that his namesake high school would make the newspapers with a front page photo of bare-bottomed students under the headline, 'Moons Over Cyrus Pepper!'"

I didn't want to hear any more stories of Mason's past when I was trying to figure out what to do about him in the present. I wished Arnold would knock it off with the yarn spinning as well as the reenactment of my screaming scene that he told us was now "in the can" for his movie. At the very least, I wanted him to rub off his painted black eyebrows. I swore that the next time I packed a duffle bag, I'd remember to put in a box of Kleenex and jar of Pond's Cold Cream. Now that I could see him up close, I'd also pack my waxing supplies and take care of his unibrow. Mason's family, it seemed, was loaded with the hairy gene. Both he and Arnold were quite hirsute. So was Mason's wife. Opposites don't always attract.

"Maaaaaa-sooooooooon!" Arnold started up again, only this time he added a few more bends to the vowels. "Hitchcock had Janet Leigh to scream for his shower scene in *Psycho*. And, by golly, I have *you*!"

I sucked the last of my non-alcoholic margarita and motioned to the waiter for another. Jafford leaned close to me and asked if I wanted something else other than the *El Burrito Supremo del Jaffordo* that he'd ordered for me for dinner, but I shook my head no. He handed his empty plate to the waiter, then took my dish for himself. Good thing he pounds out tennis balls all day, I thought. Without all that exercise, between drinks and *Los Buritos Supremos*, he might have to consider switching from tennis to sumo wrestling.

"Ah, yes," Arnold continued with a lilt to his now-natural voice. "Be ready for Cannes this year, my dear. I'm going to have you recreate your performance on stage. That's one powerful pair of lungs you have, young lady."

Natasha, still wearing her big sunglasses despite that Jafford's restaurant was nearly pitch black, groaned. She didn't need to remove her glasses for me to know she was burning up, looking at me with radar. I could feel her sizing me up, probably wondering if she had enough rope left over from tying Moose to the tracks or another swatch of cloth to blindfold me like Squirrel. At least she could be happy that her cleavage outdistanced mine by a mile. I guess it wasn't enough to win her a part, not even in her boyfriend's movie. If I had my way, I'd offer to be a transplant donor and give her a lung so that *she* could be the movie's official screamer—*anything* to keep her eyes from burning me through her Channels. As it was, I had been burned enough.

"To barf Natasha now going," Natasha said.

'Hope you choke on it,' I thought to myself as Arnold's companion left for *Las Senoritas* room.

"Her name really *is* Natasha," Arnold told us. "Her accent is real, too. Only she plays it up whenever we dress up as our favorite characters. That's part of her charm. How could I resist a real-life Natasha? Could've watched *Rocky and Bullwinkle* cartoons all day long when Mason and I were kids. We'd sit in front of the TV set for hours at a time, munching on Cocoa Puffs® right out of the box."

Genetic researchers would have a field day studying the Figg and Otterman families to prove whether it's nature or nurture that accounts for Mason and Arnold's predilection for dressing up as their favorite television characters and infusing them into their real lives. Or maybe the universe had some mystical reason for reincarnating the two cousins in a similar way. I made a mental note to consult with Craig for spiritual insight, or an astrologer to interpret their charts. Perhaps Aquarius was in both the cousins' stars.

"But her English—or lack thereof—is *not* why I wouldn't give her a part in the movie," Arnold was saying. "Just too many Xs by her list of credits."

"Huh?" I grunted, as Jafford chuckled.

"Maybe they would've drawn a lot of free publicity to this movie, but honestly, it's not the kind of attention I'm after."

"I had no idea you could do such things with a swan," Jafford said. "Now I know why some of them are mute."

"You saw the Internet clip?"

"Could I help it? I had at least fifty e-mails forwarded to my in-box," Jafford said. Then he added just to me, "Don't go telling Dagmar about it, or she'll let those snapping turtles gobble up her naughty swans until they're extinct. Nasty birds," he said with a shiver.

I couldn't imagine what Natasha could do with a swan. I had a feeling I was better off not knowing. And I was certain I would never breathe a word of Natasha's nature flick to Dagmar. In fact, I had no intention of seeing either of them again. Why is it that women are wont to hate each other instead of being friends? Good thing I wasn't a supermodel. By now, the way my luck was running, I'd probably be dead.

"See," Arnold continued, "it's not all about the money. It's about the art."

"That's because you have it," Jafford chimed in. "You didn't exactly find that new boat of yours in a box of Cocoa Puffs."

"Sure, but even if I were just starting out again, it'd have to be all about the art," Arnold said. "Or the money would never follow."

The two buddies clinked beer bottles and took long swigs. It was somehow rewarding just being in the company of people who actually enjoyed what they did to make their livings—and were paid well, too. I doubted either of them played the lottery and merely won their money like the Twists. Or cooked up wild *Operah* scams on the wrong side of the law like Mason.

"As for you, my dear Valentina," Arnold said, turning toward me. It was nice to be addressed by my true name again. "*You* have talent in that golden throat of yours. And I have the film now to prove it. Good thing the cameras were rolling and the sound master was testing his equipment."

"Yes," Jafford interrupted. "But do you still have a sound master who still has his hearing?"

But Arnold was on a roll. "See, the film crew really doesn't need me. At least not all the time. I just write the scenes and tell them what to set up and where. The rest is quite mechanical, really. I provide the vision, but the studio calls a lot of the shots upfront. I'm merely a puppet with no power to override their decisions. Why they keep hiring me to make movies is anyone's guess. I'd be happy just to write the scripts and toss them across the border to California, as William Goldman once suggested in that filmmaking book of his; reading it provided my only means of filmmaking education. What I still don't know, someone else on the crew does. It's a crazy business any way you look at it. Personally, I think they want me around because they like my cologne."

"Smells like fish to me," Jafford said.

"I *am* one happy tuna. At least I'd like to be. See, people don't realize how boring making movies can be. All that waiting around!" He shook his head and clicked his tongue. "Technical troubles! Weather changes! Divas locking themselves in their trailers! And all that waiting! Waiting! Waiting!"

Arnold was shaking his head and clicking his tongue some more, the same way Mason clicked his.

"Hitchcock was right. Actors are sheep. The art begins on paper. But even I couldn't have envisioned how your sweet little mouth would punch up that scene and unleash such a deliciously haunting—and, I might add, *loud*—scream like yours. 'Maaaa-sooon!' Oh, beautiful! Just beautiful!"

Jafford was scarfing down the last of what was supposed to be my *El Burrito Supremo*, seemingly quite content. He downed the last of his Corona from the bottle and motioned to the waiter for another. While some people comfort themselves with their favorite foods when a calamity happens, I just stop eating. Then again, some people just like burritos, I guess. And it wasn't Jafford who brought on a calamity on a movie set; it was *me*. Jafford, it seemed, was my hero.

I stared into the frozen froth at the bottom of my large glass and pined silently to myself over the reversal of roles. I had thought that Mason was my hero. But instead, it was Mason who required me to need one. I wondered when he found the time to pound out so many

Authentic Baubles, let alone paint a nude portrait of Dagmar, or build a movie set for his cousin Arnold—all while he claimed that he was flying around the world on buying trips for Dagmar. But I had to face the truth: he was most likely visiting his wife—in New York City, not Africa. I had no idea if he really had a mother or not—or if she was in jail. My head was spinning. I wanted the waiter to bring me more salt.

As I crunched on the last splinters of ice in my glass, the crowd started whooping. Why, when, who started this trend of hooting like an owl? Woofing like a dog? Howling like a coyote? Whatever happened to plain old *clapping*? Just as I mourned the loss of an era where crowds in public places didn't feel the need to call out their favorite animal sounds, the lights of the little lanterns overhead were further dimmed as a spotlight flashed on the bar. As if floating down from the heavens, a stage was being lowered on top of it as horns were blaring, drums were pounding, and maracas were making their rattlesnake sound.

"Boom-boom-boom!"

I jumped out of my seat as a drum was beaten senseless—and the crowd was whooping again. Jafford slipped his arm around me and whispered in a Spanish accent:

"It's guacamole time, *senorita*! Brace yourself for the 'Guacamole Grunt!'"

Then the drums stopped beating, and a spotlight came on, shining down on the bar-top stage where a sombrero large enough to cover all of Mexico City, was sitting on top of a pile of striped woven blankets. When the music halted, the entire crowd grunted on cue:

"Uh! Uh! Guacamole! *Ole!*"

The pile of blankets suddenly sprang to life as the giant sombrero was raised up high in the air—and a little man with a long, droopy mustache popped up, then flopped back down underneath his big hat after grunting his line along with the restaurant patrons:

"Uh! Uh! Guacamole! *Ole!*"

The crowd cheered. The horns started blaring again, tooting the same jumping refrain. The guitars were strumming, the maracas were hissing, then the big drums were beating again. Then it all stopped, signaling the crowd for another grunt:

"Uh! Uh! Guacamole! *Ole!*"

The little man disappeared again inside that stage-prop hat, but this time the stage started spinning, while red, green, and yellow lights were flashing, and the crowd was rocking and shouting out on cue:

"Uh! Uh! Guacamole! *Ole!*"

Even though the decibel level in that place was probably higher than the local noise ordinance allowed, I could still hear what had become the familiar sound of Woody Woodpecker. Jafford was laughing alongside me.

"Watch this!" Jafford shouted in my ear.

I could smell beer on his breath. Between a whiff of that alcohol and the noise in the room, I was dizzy. Thankfully, the stage stopped spinning as a girl group clad in nothing more than bikinis and sombreros took turns stepping onto the stage holding large ceramic pots and dumping the contents into a vat in front of the Guacamole Man.

"Boom-boom-boom!" The drums thumped.

"Uh! Uh! Guacamole! *Ole!*" The Guacamole Man grunted along with the crowd.

Tomatoes, onions, avocadoes, and jalapeño peppers tumbled into the vat as a girl on a swing swooped over it, squirting green juice from a giant lime. Another swing girl flew by with a sprinkling of chilies, then another with a shower of cilantro. A shaker of salt and a grind of pepper topped off the mixture, as a spoon girl mixed up the concoction with a six-foot wooden stick.

And that's when the fun really got started. At least it would seem that way judging by the voice of the crowd.

Hanging from a bungee cord from the ceiling, the masher girl plunged a pistil into the gargantuan bowl and bounced up and down until the howling from the patrons blew out my eardrums and the Guacamole Man stood up again, presumably to rap out yet another line of "Uh! Uh! Guacamole! *Ole!*" But with the stage over the bar shaking and the masher girl pumping and the vibrations in that room echoing throughout my body, the fellow on the platform, the Guacamole Man, tumbled into that vat—sombrero first.

The crowd's laughter filled the room, but it didn't seem to be as if Guacamole Man meant for his slip to be part of the show. Then again, my stint in show business was merely an hour old. Who was I to be a critic?

"Ole! Ole!" Jafford shouted as he started dancing in his seat at the table. He began bobbing around and switching one elbow for another into the palms of his hands, smiling with a wide grin. As he rose to his feet, he was beaming with the same sort of light that I had witnessed shining from him before when I had fallen on the stairs back at the Twists' party—and again on the street in Washington Square—the same brilliant light that had endowed me with *truth*. But I wasn't certain at that exact moment what the light was trying to signal to me now.

"I thought you told me you hated parties," I shouted up to Jafford as he held both my hands in his. "Didn't you say you couldn't stand crowds? What do you call *this*?"

"It's *my* party, Valentina. Big difference. We're on my turf now!"

There was no denying it: Jafford's two magnificent eyes were as clear and as blue as a summer sky. I couldn't look anywhere else, not even up to the bar-stage where the girl group had joined Guacamole Man in his vat of green mush. The spotlight was on Jafford now—and me—as my escort for the evening gently lifted me up to the tops of my toes and spun me around. While the band may have been banging out a festive Mexican beat, I felt more like a ballerina fluttering around and allowing Jafford to effortlessly lift me high into the air—except that in actuality, we were still on the wooden plank floor of *Los Banditos* and without a lick of rhythm between us. Unlike Mason who was able to glide as seductively as Ricky Ricardo, Jafford and I were thumping around the restaurant tables like a couple of tipsy giraffes. Then, just as I thought I could sit back at our table to down a few more faux-margaritas, Jafford clasped his two strong hands around my hips again and swung me up on that bar-stage under the bright red, green, and yellow lights.

My toes were wiggling inside my giant mud boots.

As the crowd was heating up again with more uproarious hooting and woofing and howling—and even *clapping* now—the spotlight followed Jafford who was stepping toward me at the bar—one white Nike sneaker at a time—while writhing his arms like two snakes and shaking his tight little tennis star butt at the audience, as the band was sounding out a melody with a heavy drumbeat.

"Go for it, Jaff!" Someone shouted from the crowd.

I may not have known him long, but I had a sense that Jafford, despite the mating ritual he was performing in front of me down on the floor by the bar, wasn't really a showman. Whether the restaurant patrons were watching or not—had they been fans at a tennis stadium or not—Jafford seemed the type to play by his own set of rules. With or without an audience, Jafford was always himself and would've been dancing with a spotlight on him as easily as he would've with me back at Swan Crest in the blackness of night with a moon shining onto The Wall.

"Jaff! Jaff! Jaff! Jaff! Jaff!"

The crowd was chanting now and clapping in rhythm. No more hooting, no more woofing. Not even a single howl as Jafford did a snake dance with his two long arms and shimmied his hips along with the sounds of the maracas. He twirled around with such aplomb, he seemed to have shaken off any uncoordinated movements that he had displayed when he was dancing *with* me. And that's when I figured out what the light and my *truth* were trying to tell me: I just couldn't dance. But Jafford could. He morphed into being the star of the restaurant's half-time show as the band followed his lead. The crowd was eating it up.

"Jaff! Jaff! Jaff! Jaff! Jaff!"

With elbows out and both hands on top of what had once been *my* black hat, Jafford was dipping and twirling and sailing around the dance floor as I watched from up on the bar-stage. He was moving so flawlessly, I couldn't help but wonder if he had a professional choreographer on his payroll as well as a business manager, houseboy, and trainer. But I knew he must have *never* worn a black hat with a wide brim like mine before, for that was an original millenary creation—Mason's.

"Jaff! Jaff! Jaff! Jaff! Jaff!"

With a brightly striped woven blanket now in his hands, Jafford morphed into a matador, twirling the blanket like a cape, swooping it in front of him, then behind him with one hand, while his other hand was posed on his hip. Head held high and proud, he He was moving towards the stage and I felt his eyes penetrating mine.

"Jaff! Jaff! Jaff! Jaff! Jaff!"

In one, smooth swoop of his long matador cape, Jafford tossed the blanket into the thick crowd. A bunch of people were diving to claim it as their own just as Jafford was evolving from a matador on the dance floor into an amorous bull with a big thumping heart. He took a few long treads in place as he held his hands by the brim of his—my—hat, as if they were a bull's horns. Then he flew up high into the air and landed on the bar-stage—right beside me. I knew then that all bulls weren't bad. I suppose it's a matter of which gene pool they're from.

The crowd was exploding now with cheers as if Jafford had just won another tennis tournament and had jumped the net. I may never have seen Jafford on a court, but I was sure that a tennis net wasn't as high as that bar. I was also certain that as he looped his long, strong arm around my waist as I stood on the bar-stage in my clunky mud boots, that he was about to bend me over backwards into an arch—and plant a wet one on my lips. He did.

"Jaff! Jaff! Jaff! Jaff! Jaff!"

My toes were wiggling. My lips were parted. And time passed without notice. We could've been smooching up there on the bar stage for an hour, for all I knew. The roar of the crowd had diminished to a soft din that lulled my heart to not thump, exactly, but pulsate in a rhythm that seemed so natural, I could've been a Siamese twin with Jafford, forever fused together at the lips, hips, shoulders, and heart. I think I would still be kissing him now if it weren't for my big feet clumsily falling off of his. But Jafford was fast. We dipped.

As I opened my eyes again and Jafford was raising me back up to my feet, I could see the Guacamole Man still standing in the vat and covered with green mush. But my view of him was upside-down. Guacamole or not, I knew what I was seeing fastened to the big sombrero fellow's shoulder: a twinkling set of Blue Diamond Peepers.

I couldn't help myself. Some sounds are organic. I opened my mouth and felt a surge of energy rising up from my center. Only this time, Arnold's movie cameras and sound master were nowhere in sight:

"Maaaaaa-sooooooooon!"

Chapter 17

The Door

A steaming hot shower was just what I needed to wash off any lingering remnants of guacamole from my hair. It felt good to be cleansed. It felt good to be back in the city. I liked Jafford's loft, which he kept above *Los Banditos*. I felt pampered by how the heat lamp in his guest bathroom dried me off without need for a towel, but I took one anyway to wrap around my head. I thought a turban would help keep my thoughts together. There were too many of them spinning around. I fought to keep my balance. I had to breathe in and out, filling up my lungs with healing steam. I needed to calm my rattled soul and hope my mind would follow. Had I really kissed Jafford on the bar-stage? I thought it was Mason whom I loved.

I must've been drugged. I know now that the poison was called love.

Tall stacks of fluffy white towels filled the linen closet. I imagined that not even the Ritz-Carlton would have stored as many or had them so perfectly folded with the logo, a pair of tennis rackets crisscrossed with Jafford's name, facing up. I pulled out a second towel to wrap around my body, but a dozen of them tumbled out onto the floor. Had I not been in such shock after seeing the Blue Diamond Peepers pinned to the Guacamole Man's robe—if I could make sense of Mason's trail of mischief—I may not have been so careless. I reached down to pick up the towels and caught a glimpse of myself in the floor-to-ceiling mirror. I was naked as a newborn babe and just as naïve. I cried like one, too.

Mason had a secret life, I whimpered to myself, when I thought we had no secrets between us. He was my lover; I had believed he was my best friend, too. He was convincing enough in both of those life roles that I still had faith that, despite all that happened, there must've been some horrible mistake. Why would he go through the trouble of planning Project Peepers when he must've known that the real blue diamonds weren't in the Twists' master bedroom safe? And could Bull Face really be his wife? What would she do to me if she got out of jail and found out about the baby?

I felt my belly, still hoping to detect a sign of Mason's love, but I wasn't sure I could sense a new life growing inside me. I didn't know whether to stand up, lie down, or keep on sobbing. It made little difference what I did in that exact moment; I didn't think I would have any more moments worth living again in my life. I wasn't sure if my tears knew what to do either, for they seemed to have dried up along with the wet tracks I had left leading away from the shower stall. Did it really have twelve spigots?

My mind was turning. Flashes of random events and faces kept blinking on and off.

Dagmar. Duncan. That stupid duck, Peepers. The Twists' party. The ladder. The Blue Diamond Peepers. The cottage. Jafford's VW Beetle. Vanilla John's scooter. The mansions on River Bend Road. The Burberry Hills train station. The billboard of the Bentley. The traffic. The Lincoln Tunnel. The motorcycles. Washington Square Park. Boris and Natasha. Arnold and Natasha. Arnold's book. The movie production crew. The crowds. The costumes. The *Operah* sign. The Authentic Baubles. The cop. The handcuffs. The margaritas, burritos, band, dancing, grunting …

And, oh! The Guacamole Man! I was stunned to see he was actually Craig. Did he have any idea how much those Blue Diamond Peepers attached to his monk's gown were worth? Were they now still covered in green mush?

But I cared less about the diamonds than I did about Mason's wife. *Wife!* His *wife!*

I couldn't help picturing Mason's face. I couldn't help but still be in love! How I wanted so much for him to magically appear right there in Jafford's guest bathroom and tell me that it all had been a nightmare. He would give me a logical explanation for the wild events of the evening. And I'd believe him. He could say just about anything as long as we could go back to our dream, the real one in our real life, the one we had shared—and would continue to share—together. Forever. Maybe we'd light a fire in the fireplace at the cottage, flip on a Desi Arnaz tune. He'd take me by the hand, hold me close, and croon into my eager ear the one sound I was longing to hear, *"Lucy..."*

"Seniorita?"

Jafford's houseboy, Hector, was calling me. He was knocking at the bathroom door.

"Seniorita? May I ask of you please. Mr. Jafford, he say you want cocoa?"

"Huh?"

"Cocoa, *seniorita*. You want?"

I guess all I needed to say was either a simple yes or polite no, but instead I started rambling as if I needed to explain my hold up in the bathroom. I was so distraught, that my old orphan knee-jerk reaction was automatically kicking in. I was rambling frantically, attempting to quickly and fully explain my hold up in the bathroom, needlessly describing my circumstances and making it abundantly clear that I was not causing any kind of mischief whatsoever in the bathroom, and I certainly was not harming …

"Take time, *seniorita*. Take time," Hector hollered through the door. "No worry, please."

I guess I must've sounded a bit paranoid to poor Hector with my long-winded explanations, but I couldn't help it. I wasn't feeling like a grownup. My inner child was showing. I was a foster kid all over again. And all alone in Jafford's guest bathroom. Now that Mason was lost from my world, I felt lonely and scared. I could've used a piece of bubble gum—or three. I had dropped that bad habit, thanks to Dagmar. But I really needed a fix. I knew I should've taken up smoking.

I must've been losing it, because I started trembling all over. Instead of putting my clothes back on, I picked up the fallen towels one at a time and wrapped them around my head. Just when I must've looked like a poor cousin of Carmen Miranda, I plucked more towels from the linen closet and started wrapping them around my body. I needed something to keep me from shaking like a wind-blown twig.

"Valentine?"

Only Laughing Sun called me that. He had told me long ago that "Valentine" was enough when he was still Craig. But now, not only was he a monk in Washington Square Park with a brand new name, he was also working for *Los Banditos* as Guacamole Man. I guess he needed the money. Monks who dole out wisdom in a park don't make enough to keep up with the rent.

"You in there, Valentine?" he called through the door and gave it a few gentle knocks. "It's me, Craig."

Craig. I guess it was alright for me to use his old name. I certainly wasn't going to start calling him Guacamole Man. As it was, I was shocked to have seen him up on that bar-stage and even more alarmed to see the Blue Diamond Peepers. Even I could tell they weren't merely copies. The way they glistened with the lights from the bar stage, there was no question about it: that pair of sparkling rocks was not fake. They couldn't possibly be Mason's phony Authentic Baubles.

"Valentine! Valentine! You're worrying me. Now, don't let me come in there!"

Craig had a way of sounding parental, but always with good cheer. He knocked again as I was making myself a pair of towel shoes.

"I'm okay, Craig. Just drying off!"

But I wasn't okay. Craig knew that. I heard something dragging on the hardwood floor outside the bathroom door. Then the narrow, transom window above it popped open.

"Your cocoa's cooling off," Craig said through the crack. I could see the silhouette of his head through the milk glass of that quirky interior window. He must've been standing on a chair. "Are you coming?"

"Yes, Craig," I lied. "I'm coming."

But I was pulling more towels out from their stacks as if I was a zombie, mindlessly making a terrycloth pile on the bathroom floor.

"You're missing the show! Jafford's on the terrace. He's moonwalking while bouncing a tennis ball on a racket. You've got to come see this!"

Tennis racket? Ball? What is it, I thought, with all the men in my life? But what was I thinking? Jafford wasn't really a man in my life. That designation was Mason's. The thought of Jafford dancing with a tennis racket made me think of the man I loved dancing with a ladder while I was hiding in the rhododendrons back at Swan Crest. Oh, what a mistake! I had ruined my life! I had been a thief-in-training! A *thief*! I may even have been a duck killer, too. And oh, Duncan! What had happened to that poor, poor man?

"I think he's got an iPod stuck in his ear."

I didn't think Jafford would need one, not when the sounds of the band downstairs were thumping through the floorboards of the loft. I could hear them in the bathroom, despite the siren blaring in my imagination from a copper's black and white. I was starting to wobble on my towel-wrapped feet. I was now six inches taller than I was before.

I didn't hear Craig's voice anymore. He must've given up trying to persuade me to get the heck out of the guest bathroom or he left to find a screwdriver to unhitch the door from its frame. I knew he must've been worried about my state of emotional upheaval. He knew how orphans have deep wounds that can be reopened whenever life paths get off track. Abandonment is a train wreck for a foster kid's soul. But Craig no longer seemed to be calling for me through the crack in the funny, little window above the bathroom door.

"Valentina? It's Jafford!"

That bathroom should've had a doorbell. It was big enough to be an apartment, at least in New York. I could've easily turned the tub into a bed for myself and settled into a new studio of my own. There was more than enough room to move in Cuban Pete, too. I missed my kitty. I'd give anything to hear him purr, hold his fluffy body close to my cheek, pet the top of his head and smooth him down all the way to …

"Valentina?"

"I'm coming!"

Maybe Jafford would let me move in. I could get my old job back at the waxing salon and make that bathroom home. I sure didn't have one of my own. Not anymore. Not in the country at the cottage, and not in the city above the frame gallery. Not now. Not when Mason had a wife. *Wife!* I never thought I'd hate that word.

"I need to see that you're alright," Jafford said softly through the door.

"I'm alright," I lied.

I looked up to the window that Craig had left ajar, but I didn't see Jafford's shadow through the white glass. I guessed that he must've been standing on the floor. I faced the door square-on, wondering if Jafford would burst through it or if Craig had managed to find a screwdriver and was right then and there about to spring me from my tiled prison. But I only heard Jafford's voice.

"There's something, Valentina, that I need to tell you," he said.

I was unwrapping my turban one towel at a time. I didn't bother folding them. I let them drop to the floor.

"Are you still there?"

He knocked gently on the door.

"Where would I go? This is a bathroom!"

"Sorry, Valentina. I didn't mean to upset you."

I guess that I must've snapped at Jafford. But it wasn't intentional. I couldn't help myself.

"I'm sorry! I'm sorry!"

The thoughts of Mason being married and leaving the "hot ice" with Craig were churning up a whole can of emotional worms all wriggling around at the same time. I was angry that Mason had fooled me. I was confused as to all the reasons why. I was convinced we didn't yet know the full story.

"I'm sorry, Jafford," I said again. "I didn't mean to snap. Not at you!"

I feared what would happen to me next, where I would live, what I would do. And was I pregnant? Oh, I still loved Mason! I longed to have him by my side, holding me, kissing me, making love to me …

"Don't worry about it, Valentina. Believe me, I've heard worse. I know it was a shock to see Laughing Sun with the Blue Diamond Peepers. Can't figure out what Mason's been up to. Sounds like no good in more ways than one."

But I still loved Mason, I wanted to cry out. Instead, I buried my face in the pile of towels.

"I can't explain why, Valentina. I know it's only been a short time that we've known each other, but I … I …"

His voice was trailing off. I needed to hear more. I lifted my head from the terrycloth heap. I faced that door and stood up. I held out my arms and leaned my palms on the doorframe, stark naked.

"You've become very, very …"

Jafford's voice was trailing again. It was somehow soothing. I needed a strong, kind voice to make sense of my worm can. But I wasn't sure what I was wanting more: to see Mason again or to hear Jafford's kind voice.

"You're special to me, Valentina. I'm as mad at Mason as I know you must be."

I didn't say a thing. No words could make their way through the tightness in my throat. I leaned into the door, wishing its paint would whitewash my pain.

"I'd punch him right in the nose if I could. But that wouldn't change matters. And I'm not really the violent type. But …"

I didn't want Jafford or anyone else to punch out my Mason. I wanted love. I wanted to feel Mason's body next to mine—his hairy chest, his hairy arms, and his hairy back, too. But all I had was a cold, wooden door that was selfish about sharing its paint.

"I figured you could use a few things now that it looks like you won't be going back to your apartment."

My apartment! I had no more home! Worse: I had no Mason. He was married. He had a wife. It still didn't all make sense. I had to keep repeating that bad word and let the harsh reality sink in: *Wife! Wife! Wife! Mason had a wife!*

"I sent Hector out to pick you up a few things while we were at *Los Banditos*."

"*Si.*"

Hector's voice startled me. I wasn't expecting to hear it again. I didn't realize he, too, was outside the bathroom door. The hallway in Jafford's loft needed a traffic light.

"*Los pantolones.*"

"Pants. We had to guess your size."

"*Si. Las camias femeninas.*"

"Shirts. I hope you like Ralph Lauren."

"*Si. Las chaquetas.*"

"Jackets. You need to stay warm in all kinds of weather. And …"

Jafford kept translating as if he were teaching me Spanish. I wondered what the word was for wife.

"*Si. Los sustantivo.*"

"Dresses?"

"*Si. Si. Si. Los zapatos et las botas femeninas.*"

"Shoes and boots, too." Jafford said. "I thought you could use a few new pairs."

"*Si. Rojo, amarillo, negro, verde...*"

"Red, yellow, black, green ... I had Hector toss out the ones you've been wearing."

"*Si. Pasado las botas a la dumpster.*"

"I hope you don't mind. Hector threw your old mud boots in the dumpster behind *Los Banditos*. Maybe they were what made you fall down. Where'd you find them, anyway? At the bottom of Tannery Pond? They looked like something the snappers would barf up after chewing up one of Dagmar's swans. But not to worry, Valentina. You have brand new ones now."

"*Si. Los zapatillas a tennis!*"

"Oh, yeah. Sneakers, too. I thought perhaps you might like playing some tennis with me. I have an indoor court downstairs."

Who was his landlord, I wondered. Madison Square Garden?

"Or we could play at Madison Square Garden. They always let me practice there in the off hours. So I got you a tennis racket, too. Here! Catch!"

A brand new tennis racket was slipping over the top of the bathroom door through the popped window. I reached up to grab it and read the inscription:

OFFICIAL TENNIS RACKET OF THE JAFF.

Jafford's signature and picture were below it. I stared at the sight of his smiling face looking up at me. His bright, blue eyes seemed to shine. I started weeping all over again, but only silently to myself.

"You still there, Valentina?" Jafford asked through the door.

But I couldn't speak. I buffed the tennis racket to my check, then held it out again to see Jafford's eyes.

"And here's a toothbrush for you and some toothpaste. Hope it's a brand you like."

It could've been generic, for all I cared. I was touched that Jafford thought of my teeth.

"Oh, and one more thing, Valentina," Jafford said. "Craig told me you really like … Well, look up. I have something else to give you. Are you there? Valentina?"

By then, I had knelt back down on the pile of towels, still silently sobbing and cuddling the tennis racket with my naked body, holding my new toothbrush and toothpaste in my hand. Colgate. I'd never use any other brand again. I was grateful to Jafford. Hector, too. And of course, Craig. They were my friends. I never needed friends around more. But as I looked up to the window, I saw a slim, cigar-like box slipping through. I had no idea what to expect next. Colgate and a tennis racket were hard to beat. I stood up to catch it.

"You got it? Valentina?"

Jafford's hand was sticking through the opening holding the box. I held it on my end and pulled it closer to me until he let go. But I started crying all over again as soon as I read the label saying what was inside it. This time I was balling out loud while tears filled my eyes.

"Gosh, Valentina! I didn't mean to make you cry! It's just that Craig told me that you really like bubble gum. He said it had made you a champ."

It had.

"He said blowing bubbles would make you happy."

It does, I thought to myself. But I couldn't speak yet. The force of my whimpering was backing up in my throat.

"I want to make you happy, Valentina."

Jafford said something else, but he seemed to be stumbling for words.

"What?" I managed to ask. My ear was pressed to the door. I took a deep breath. I wiped my eyes with a towel. "What did you say?"

I could hear Jafford clearing his throat. When he spoke again, his voice was an octave higher.

"You're already …"

"Yes?" I was sniffling. I grabbed another towel as a tissue.

"You, Valentina, are already the champion of …"

I had no idea what Jafford was trying to tell me. I was surprised to learn that Craig had told him how I was the running champion of bubble gum-blowing in the foster homes I lived in. Word spread. Everyone knew me as the kid who could blow the biggest bubble. But that was many years ago. Oh, why couldn't I grow up and be an adult? I didn't want Jafford to treat me like a child. But my hold up in the bathroom made me exactly that. Was he worried that I had taken up smoking? Would it make me seem more grownup?

"You ... You ... You," he said.

"Me. Me. Me—what?" Now *I* was the one who was beginning to be worried about *him*.

"You are the champion of my heart."

In an instant, my tears dried up. Time stopped. Even my toes were starting to wiggle all on their own. I wasn't sure what Jafford's words meant, but I felt them in my shattered soul. The pieces were beginning to sew themselves back together. I reached out to turn the doorknob, but it wouldn't budge. I jiggled it. I turned it. But it was no use. Old locks in prewar buildings can be tricky. This one was stuck.

"Hector!" I heard Jafford call. "Do we have a tool box?"

CHAPTER 18

The Headlines

Craig was sitting in the lotus position, meditating by the terrace window in the living room of Jafford's loft. I couldn't remember if he needed to face north, south, east, or west; I was just glad to see him in the morning when I stumbled out of my bedroom. After the calamity of breaking down the bathroom door the night before, it had been too late to enjoy our cocoa. It was too late to do anything, but head off for bed, each of us alone. We had all said good night to each other and left for our designated rooms. I had only a pillow to cuddle and felt strange not sharing the covers. Even when Mason had been away for what I had thought was one of his international buying trips, I always had Cuban Pete. I wanted my cat with me in Jafford's loft and wondered, did he miss me? Did he think I had abandoned him? Was Mason feeding him on time? Would Cuban Pete ignore me when I returned home?

Home. I never did quite grasp the concept. Nothing in my life ever had any lasting significance. The only pattern I could count on was that my world changed by the day, week, or month. I was accustomed to thanking strangers for their hospitality then bracing myself for when I'd need to pack up again and venture into the unknown. I never did feel settled. I always knew I wasn't like other people. I suppose you could call me a rolling stone, a prodigal cast-off from a hunk of rock that no longer needed me around to be whole.

That's the kind of thing that happens. Some kids are lucky. And some become orphans.

For the millionth time in my life, I was grateful for the kindness of a stranger, although Jafford now seemed more like a friend. He had invited both Craig and me to stay over as his guests. He had more than enough spare bedrooms, he had told us, and I deeply appreciated all the trouble Hector went through, releasing me from my accidental imprisonment in the bathroom and buying me brand new clothes. I had discovered a flannel nightgown, matching robe, and slippers waiting for me in my room and made a mental note to pay Jafford back—some day. I never exactly had a clothing budget, not when I was used to being a farm hand wearing secondhand mud boots. I wasn't exactly raised to make shopping a sport. My closets had never been walk-ins. In fact, I never had one, small or large, all to myself.

Jafford had suggested that both Craig and I stay over with the reasoning that we could head back to Swan Crest together first thing in the morning, and that Hector would drive us. Craig needed to find out if Mason had stolen his ancient gong, leaving the Blue Diamond Peepers in its place, while I needed to find out what Mason had done with my heart. But I knew that there was one more reason for Jafford to have us sleep over; he wanted to make certain I felt secure. I don't think he wanted me freaking out. Besides, I no longer had a home.

Bacon was sizzling on the stove as Hector flipped pancakes on the grill in the kitchen that opened up to the living room and terrace. As I padded over to the counter that divided the rooms and poured myself a cup of coffee, I could see that a stack of newspapers had been placed on the granite top.

THE JAFF TO MARRY FIREFIGHTER

I put my mug down at the head of the twenty-foot long, polished oak table where Hector had set out silverware, napkins, and plates, and read through the papers while still standing up by the counter. Pictured under the headline of the first paper was Jafford bending me over backwards on the bar-stage with a close-up of my mud boots in the foreground. The bright yellow stripes made me appear to be a firefighter, I guessed. I let my coffee cool off and flipped through the rest of the stack.

THE JAFF STARTS NEW HAT CRAZE

THE JAFF VOWS TO BE MONK
THE JAFF TO JOIN "DANCING WITH THE STARS"
THE JAFF CRASHES IN LINCOLN TUNNEL
THE JAFF TO BE SUED BY HISEDIC BUS GROUP
THE JAFF TO BE SUED BY KOREAN WORLD TOURS
THE JAFF TO BE SUED BY DRIVER IN CRASH
THE JAFF TO DUMP BENTLEY SPONSER
THE JAFF TO ENDORSE HARLEY-DAVIDSON MOTORCYCLES
IS THE JAFF GAY?

"Gay?" I said out loud, but no one heard me. As far as I knew, Jafford was still asleep in his room with the door still closed. Craig was still meditating at the terrace window. And Hector, after driving to the city the night before in the Bentley, was still banging around in the kitchen, whipping up breakfast.

I slid the newspaper out of the stack and sat down at the table. As I sipped my coffee, despite that it had cooled, I studied the picture of Jafford with his arms around me. The two of us were wearing identical black Nike jackets. While Jafford's face was clearly visible under the wide-brimmed hat, the brim of my baseball cap that I had worn was covering my face as well as my newly shorn and bleached hair. It was impossible to tell who I was or what gender. I supposed that my big boots inspired the headline writer to suggest the first thing that came to mind—anything to sell more papers, I guessed. People just love to question a celebrity's orientation. Whether they wrote headlines for a living or not, perhaps they questioned their own. Seemed to me it was no one's business. I kept staring at the picture, amazed by how clearly a cell phone camera could take a picture. I wondered how many pictures of Jafford and me were now being electronically passed around. I supposed that the one that ended up in the newspaper paid out handsomely for whoever had taken it. I may not have liked winding up on the front page myself, but I couldn't help but gaze at it longer, trying to see if there was anything that remotely identified me as being *me*, or at least as being a woman. It certainly wouldn't be my breasts or my hips; the Nike jacket covered all that. But it couldn't camouflage my oversized shoulders or what appeared to be fireman's feet.

Hector was squeezing some fresh oranges and grapefruits by hand at the counter. He tore open a packet of protein powder and emptied the contents into a blender, then poured in the juice along with a scoop of ice cubes. In between the roar of the blender, I asked him what kind of oranges he used. They looked red to me, as if they were bleeding. In fact, they looked rather creepy, like something a vampire would suck. And I'd thought that Halloween was over.

"Mr. Jafford, he like the blood oranges. He eat when he play tennis in Spain. Very tasty! You drink? You drink?"

I wasn't accustomed to having more than coffee for breakfast, not until all the goats at Swan Crest had been fed and the eggs collected from the hen house. So I reached for my mug after Hector gave me a refill of hot coffee and passed on the red juice. Then he revved up the blender again. Good thing I didn't have real margaritas last night, I thought, or that noise would be wreaking havoc with a hangover.

"Sleep well?" Jafford asked me as he popped by the counter wearing a pair of running shorts and a T-shirt.

But I couldn't speak.

"Sounded like you did," Jafford said with a half-smile. He glanced at me for a mere second, and I thought he was pretending to snore.

"Snore? I don't..."

Before I got the words out, in that fleeting moment in time, our eyes met.

And then it happened again.

Time stopped.

My toes were wiggling.

Hector's blender was silent to me.

Craig was a blur at the terrace window.

Hector was pouring his juice concoction into large wine glasses, but Jafford waved his hand no.

"I'll have it later," Jafford said to Hector while stretching his long legs in a warm up routine. He was using the side of the countertop for pushups while my heart was thumping like the drums the night before on the dance floor at *Los Banditos*.

"I'm going out for a run," Jafford announced to no one in particular.

I could feel the sunshine from the terrace window lighting up my soul. But Jafford kept on with his warm up, bending and flexing his strong muscular limbs.

"Just need my hot lemon water, Hector, if you please," he said, now twisting and stretching from side-to-side while pumping his feet.

Was I really the champion of his heart? Had he really kissed me on the bar-stage?

"You did sleep well, didn't you?" he asked me again, barely looking my way.

I felt like a child in my new robe and slippers, longing for him as if he were a teddy bear that had come to life. I wanted to hug him. To me, he was larger than life in that living room. But I couldn't utter a word. Had I been dreaming what I had thought he had said to me before Hector broke down the bathroom door?

I watched as Jafford untied then retied his long hair into a tight ponytail. I supposed his usual two braids might flap around too much in his face when he'd run.

"I'd also like a stack of soy cakes, Hector, with flax and sunflower seeds ..."

"I already make for you, Mr. Jafford."

Jafford rolled his eyes and whispered to me that he couldn't curb Hector from addressing him with "Mr." It was just part of his native language and culture, he said. His breath was sweet. Maybe he had brushed with Colgate. Was it one of his endorsements? I sniffed the air for his cologne. But I only smelled Jafford. His natural scent was more arousing than that bacon Hector had sizzling in the frying pan.

"Could you count out my vitamins, too, Hector? And is that *tofu-bacon*?"

"*Si*, Mr. Jafford. All ready for you. Got spinach, too. And Mountain Dew, too."

Accept for that last part, I take it all back. While Jafford may enjoy his special *El Burrito Supremo*, not to mention several Coronas, he well knew how to nurture his health. There was no denying it; the body doesn't lie. Jafford was probably the world's finest specimen of a professional athlete at his peak—finely tuned, taught, and ... well—*magnificent*! But he was more than a well-toned body to me. He was *Jafford*. He was unlike any other man I had ever known before. He was one of a kind. And *I* was the champion of his heart! I longed to hear more.

I watched as he finished his morning push-ups, now on the floor, admiring how his biceps pumped as he moved up and down. His untucked T-shirt revealed the right kind of six-pack to carry, while his running shorts cut high on his thighs displayed rippling muscles that propelled him on the courts. Up close, I could now see how he had sufficient power to leap up onto that stage as he finished off his push-ups with alternate hands. I could also see how women around the world went ga-ga for him. I knew my heart was fluttering. My toes were still wiggling. But I ordered them to keep still. I slipped the newspaper I was reading back into the stack as Jafford jumped to his feet and Craig—or rather, Laughing Sun, as Jafford exclusively called him—was completing his morning meditation with a bow.

"I smell bacon," Laughing Sun said. "Yum!"

"My man Hector's a perfect host. He gets full credit for the menu. *And* the cooking. Don't look to me for *that*," Jafford said. Before bidding us a hearty breakfast and slipping out the door, he assured us that the bacon was made of smoked tofu. Then he added, "We can take off by noon."

He was just about out the door for his run when he turned back. He was walking toward me by the counter. Just as I was beginning to swoon, he bent over close to me.

"Don't worry," he whispered.

I wanted him to kiss me again or at least touch my hand. I knew that if I gazed directly into those bright, shining eyes, I swear I would've wrapped my arms around his neck, pressed my chest into his ... But what was I thinking? Was it Jafford whom I loved?

"We'll get it all figured out, Valentina," Jafford said as if he were an accountant and I had piled him up with scraps of paper from my mixed-up, poorly-run, nearly ruined life. It was as if I had suddenly transformed into his pet project. But now my toes were wiggling. I was springing quickly back to life. I wanted more. But I didn't dare show it. I couldn't.

"Laughing Sun will get his gong, too," Jafford said, still stoic.

I had never really seen him like that before. I yearned to hear his silly popcorn laugh. I would laugh along with him. If only he'd say one of those funny little quips that I finally appreciated long after he had said them. Was I too late? Had I blown my chances? Had I been a fool? Did he think I had no sense of humor? Had he changed his mind about me being the champion of his heart? Would he ask me to return the tennis racket and all the clothes? Would he let me keep the Colgate?

Jafford slipped out the door and I felt a tear roll down the side of my nose. Another one followed, then another, until Laughing Sun was rubbing the middle of my back and Hector made himself scarce. I couldn't figure out what to think about Jafford. I surprised even myself that he seemed to cause me to forget all about Mason—and so soon.

"Valentine," Laughing Sun cooed

Just like in the old days, the sound of his voice was comforting, but I knew he'd have some sort of wisdom from the universe to share with me. He always could see right through me. Then again, I might've been wrong.

"Nice to know you got some shut eye," he said. "Even through these plaster walls, I could hear you snore."

"Snore? I don't snore."

I could see him breaking out in his usual big grin just as he turned his head. He reached out to swipe another piece of tofu-bacon from underneath the plastic warming bubble that Hector had placed atop each of the serving plates, then stuffed his mouth with a couple more. He took me by the hand so we could sit at our places at the table.

"Nothing like a hearty country breakfast," I said.

There were few substitutes to food chatter and sharing a meal for making sense of the world once again. It was the primal nature of feeding that brought comfort, as Laughing Sun had once told me when he was still Craig.

"I know how much you like tofu-bacon," I blathered in an attempt to return to normal. I was pretending that we were sharing breakfast as if it were an ordinary morning. "But you like tofu-sausage better, right?"

"You can take the boy out of Detroit Lakes, Minnesota, but you can never quite take Detroit Lakes, Minnesota, out of the boy."

"Even if you put him in a crimson robe?"

"That's right," he said with a laugh. He was well named as Laughing

Sun. His smile always shined through, especially whenever reminiscing about his hometown—or talking to students—or me.

"My father still FedExes me the grouse he shoots and trout he smokes out in his ice hut on the lake. And my mother still ships out her oatmeal cookies with walnuts and raisons. Maybe they figure that if they keep sending out real food like that, I'll give up on this spiritual business. That'd be their kind of logic anyway."

"You mean they're *still* upset about you leaving NYU?"

"Yup. They were very proud to be able to brag to their friends how their only son was a professor of physics. Only, for them, it wasn't truly bragging. Just contentment, I suppose. They didn't like admitting that you and I had broken up either. They were hoping we'd get married, you know. Lead a normal life. At least that's how they define *normal*."

"I'm sorry. You know I …"

"Don't worry about it, Valentine. It was the best move for all of us. Mason included. He got the better part of the deal, if you ask me."

Shaved head or not, Craig was still handsome even in his robe. He always did know a sweet way to make me feel special. Even after we'd broken up. But could he sense this new attraction I seemed to be having with Jafford? Considering my history with Mason, would he think I was a hussy?

"All things are meant to happen," he said.

I braced myself for a pile of *truth* to be laid out for me. It wasn't always easy to hear, especially if it was about me. I wasn't certain if I wanted to share my curious, but undeniable attraction for Jafford with him, not just yet. But Craig's focus was forever on spiritual matters, not romantic. I guess that's why we had broken up. I had left him for Mason. It had only been less than six months, but it was a distant chapter in my life and seemed a long time ago.

"There are no real coincidences," Craig was saying. "We're all just a bunch of animals who've lost our instincts and are using the five senses to find our true paths. We may separate ourselves from the animals, believing we are superior with our power to reason, not to mention that human forms are equipped with thumbs. But had we been reincarnated into a fox, say, or a goat, chicken, or elephant, we'd probably lead much healthier, productive, and *happier* lives. We'd live by our sixth sense, our intuition."

See what I mean? Was I supposed to digest the wisdom of Laughing Sun along with my tofu bacon and eggs? I knew if I were silent long enough, he'd sum it all up for me using simple words he knew I preferred.

"Bottom line, Valentine, is that you were meant to meet up with Mason, just as I was made to teach meditation in the park. I may need to supplement *The Laughing Sun Center for Right Living* by making guacamole five nights a week, but I know in my heart I'm on the right path for me. Life, as we know it, is all about lessons. I'm still learning mine as I continue trying to set up my foundation."

I tried to absorb what he was saying, but I had to face facts: I didn't know what lessons I was supposed to learn. I certainly hadn't learned how to dance well from Mason, which I had demonstrated the night before, not to mention when Mason and I were *Ricky* and *Lucy*. Perhaps that's why the two of us restricted our role-playing to the living room at the cottage and never went public. But I didn't think that dancing was the lesson that Laughing Sun was suggesting I needed to learn. I was patient. I was thinking now more of Jafford, but I didn't want to tip off Laughing Sun about my new attraction. He might say I was nuts. I was beginning to think so myself.

"You *had* to leave me, Valentine," he said, still referring to Mason. "You were bored and I knew it. You weren't worried about the next life. You needed to have fun in the here and now."

He looked at me and paused.

"You know," he began, "you are actually more spiritual than me."

Oh, no, I thought. I know that look in a man's eyes. Monk or not, Craig was still a man. I could see the light shining brightly in his friendly eyes, just as I had seen it shine in Jafford's. Even Craig had hormones. I hoped now that they weren't starting to heat up. I had more on my plate than I could handle as it was. And I don't mean fake bacon and eggs.

"Here, I'm striving to comprehend Nirvana, and you, Valentine, are already there."

"Huh?"

"You want happiness on earth! The Dalai Lama would be pleased with you!"

I kept forgetting that when Craig said something, he stuck with it.

He always called his own shots. The only kind of lust he had was for reaching Nirvana. I did have to admit, he was a wise man. The only thing he lusted for was spiritual enlightenment. Not me.

I also knew that I—along with Jafford—could claim to know something about *truth*, too. We knew when we were up on that bar-stage and saw the Blue Diamond Peepers pinned to Laughing Sun's robe as he sat in his vat of guacamole, that Mason was a thief. Who else but Mason would swipe an ancient gong to hang in Dagmar's Bamboo Garden, stealing it from the narrow strip of lawn of *The Laughing Sun Center for Right Living*? Then leave a set of Blue Diamond Peepers tied to a garbage can lid in its place?

I was ready to get going. We needed answers. I was all cried out from the night before. I watched Craig chew and swallow the last of his bacon as Jafford came back from his run. He was covered with perspiration. But sweaty or not, I longed to be near him.

Craig did a double-take, looking at me, then Jafford, and then back to me. Then he stuck his head under the table …

My legs were crossed. One of them was swinging. The slipper fell off. My toes were wiggling …

Craig sat up again. I could feel his stare.

"Uh oh," he said. Craig knew the meaning of toe-wiggling.

But it was impossible for me to take my eyes off Jafford and look at Craig while Hector was removing our plates and silverware—then I could feel Hector looking at me, too, and both he and Craig were smiling as if they could read my mind …

I just wished it was Jafford who was tuning in. Then again, perhaps not. The thoughts I was having about Jafford were making *me* blush.

PART FOUR: FRIENDS IN DEED

Chapter 19

The OxiClean

The backseat of a Bentley is far more luxurious than I had ever experienced as a passenger before. Compared to a New York City taxi, which was about the top-of-the line for my transportation, and only on a special occasion, I suppose that any private car would seem like a royal carriage. But out of the millions of cars honking around Manhattan, I'm sure less than two percent of them have gold sconces flanking each side of the rear quarters, hand-woven oriental rugs on the floor, or a built-in wet bar with a flip-down table and a small refrigerator. The one in Jafford's Bentley was stocked with bottles of his own personal brand of spring water, *Agua del Jaff*, but no booze.

Without a single bottle of Corona, maybe Jafford never really did use the Bentley, despite what he had told his business manager. I don't think he was lying to me when he said he preferred the Super Beetle and driving it himself. It seems to me that we all mark our personal territories with our favorite stuff, staking claim to our chosen places on earth. For Jafford, it was tennis rackets, cans of balls, a full Nike wardrobe, and baseball caps from his favorite team crammed into a bruised VW Bug. All that and a hand-me-down cooler from his mother, ready at a moment's notice to be filled up with ice and bottles of beer.

"Leave the roof up," Jafford called out to Hector as he slid the privacy panel open. Considering the enormity of the interior, he might've used a microphone. I'm sure the Bentley was equipped with one. "The roof can stay closed today. We're not in a parade."

I had a feeling that not being in a parade was not the reason for Jafford wanting the convertible top to stay up, even as we passed through the Lincoln Tunnel—successfully this time. Driving back to the country on a quiet Sunday morning in late fall, seemed to me to be reason enough for breathing fresh air. But Jafford clearly was no longer as jolly as I had known him to be. Had we really known each other for only twelve hours? Did he forget that I was the champion of his heart? Maybe I didn't really know what he meant. I should've asked him. But Jafford didn't seem to be much in the mood for talking. Maybe he was in a snit about Mason and all the trouble he was causing us. I felt bad about the role I played.

Jafford and I rode in the backseat, with Hector at the wheel up in the front. Laughing Sun opted to join him there, saying that he hadn't experienced being in a car for many years.

"I like finding new perspectives of the world," the perpetually curious and cheerful monk said as he folded himself into the lotus position and clicked his seat belt into place. "Zooming down a highway at 65 miles per hour will give me a vantage point I haven't known since leaving Detroit Lakes. What's old will be new again to me."

"Maybe we should strap you to the top of the roof," Jafford suggested. "You could face backwards and see where you've been."

"Craig—or rather, Laughing Sun—prefers to be in the present," I wedged in, hoping to soften what sounded to me like Jafford throwing a jab. I wouldn't call him mean, exactly. But those were the first words he'd ever uttered that were tinged with a dare. Then again, we'd only known each other for mere hours, whereas I knew Laughing Sun when he was still Craig. And who knows? Maybe we all knew each other in a previous lifetime. Maybe we had been a trio of goats. But I wondered now how the spiritual man up in the front seat was processing Jafford's sarcasm. Or maybe they were just engaging in guy talk. It doesn't matter, I thought. Professional tennis player with a racket or self-proclaimed sage in a crimson robe, men will always be boys.

"You mean, where I've been in New York City? Or in a previous life?"

Just as I was thinking that Jafford's cheerful spirit had been lost, his Woody Woodpecker laugh was back. His giggles were like popcorn exploding, the super colossal kind that's processed to be microwavable in a paper bag and have extra pop. It was the kind of vocal quality that couldn't help but incite uproarious laughter from anyone who'd hear it. And, sure enough, Laughing Sun joined in as he turned around, unwrapping himself from his lotus position. Seeing his face again made me recall what he had told me a long time ago:

"We perceive other people through a single lens. Over time, if we grow spiritually, that lens expands and we expand our acceptance of others, seeing them in their totality with both evil and good coexisting within them, but without judgment. Conversely, with judgment," he had told me, "we have a tendency to compare other people harshly or favorably against one another."

I supposed that meant I had harshly judged the sound of Jafford's laughter. It really wasn't as odd as I had perceived it to be the night before. It's just that I loved Mason's laughter more. But that love seemed to now be transferred over to Jafford. I had thought I loved Mason. No other man could compare and emerge favorably. Even another man's laugh had been less attractive to my ears all the time I had been getting to know Jafford. But wherever the truth may have been about whom I loved and who loved me, I knew that Craig would tell me that laughter in itself, no matter how it sounds, is one of the most important of life's activities. Craig always had a quote ready for just about any occasion. I could always count on him for that.

"The Dalai Lama himself said, 'The purpose of life is not to get to heaven, but to seek happiness on earth. And the best way to do that is to have a warm, kind heart,'" Craig once told me. It was one of those messages he was always trying to share with me that actually stayed with me all this time. "And you, Valentine," he told me back then, "have been endowed with precisely that quality. That's why you'll always get hurt. And that's why your name will never be changed."

Never be changed, never be changed, never be changed . . . His words, I learned over years of knowing him, taking in the wisdom he couldn't help but share, were often prolific. He had forecasted that I would live in the country; I did. He had seen that I would one day be in a movie: I was. He had a sense that I'd acquire a fondness for animals and become close to their lives. Well, that one was still a lesson I hadn't yet learned. A monk-in-training with intuitive powers, with the gift for seeing beyond the present, is allowed a few slips. Or maybe he was right. I did have a cat.

But there had been one more prediction that Craig had made that I was certain he was always wrong about, and that was that I'd never have children, at least not biologically.

"Maybe animals will serve as your offspring," he had mused.

But I didn't think so at the time. And I still thought he was wrong that day we were driving in Jafford's Bentley back to Swan Crest. I pondered the thought some more, as I was rubbing my tummy, soothing its rumble and attempting to tame the bloating. Even my breasts were swollen and tender now, but somehow I didn't think they were filling up with mother's milk. I had been waiting to feel the warmth of motherhood beginning to blossom in my body, ever-conscious of signs, knowing that the *weather of my body would change*, as I read once in a Louise Erdrich novel, beginning at the *moment of conception*. But the weather condition in my abdomen was not from a growing fetus. It was more familiar. The kind I had experienced month after month for years, ever since I entered puberty and my social worker needed to fill me on life's mysterious facts.

My face turned flush with both hot and cold. I didn't have anything to absorb what I feared was now flowing from my body, but I probably did in my old duffle bag. That was long gone. I panicked. Even if I had some type of feminine hygiene product, I wouldn't exactly be able to use it, not while we were driving. I couldn't even check to see if I actually needed one or not. The fear of leaking all over the backseat of Jafford's Bentley was causing my heart to pound.

Jafford was dozing off.

Spanish oranges weren't the only places Mother Nature designates to bleed.

"Hey, Laughing Sun," I started, wanting to get closer to him in the front seat while at the same time, wanting to prevent Jafford from viewing my butt if he woke up. "Remember that time during the koan ceremony you brought me to? At the first spiritual center you joined? Where Roshi was ordaining new nuns and monks? And it went on and on for six hours instead of just two as we had thought? And the solemn ceremony couldn't be disrupted by anyone leaving the room without disrupting the karma? And the cushion I was sitting on was thankfully covered in black fabric, but was …"

"Oh no," Laughing Sun said softly. "Hector, are there any rest stops on this road? And, by the way, do you have any OxiClean?"

Miles and miles of roads seemed to be all we had in front of us. Bridges and tunnels and tolls and signs—Route 80 West wasn't any more scenic than it had been when we had been driving it on the eastbound side the night before. There didn't seem to be any convenient place to stop. So close to the city, there was hardly a bush or a tree. I never thought I'd appreciate Swan Crest more than I did while worrying that I might've been sitting in a bloody puddle in the backseat of Jafford's rarely-used Bentley. I'd be mortified if I was. I'd offer to rip up the upholstery myself and install brand-new leather. Oh, where was a dead cow when you needed one?

"There's something I need to tell you, Jafford," I said, forcing myself to hold back tears and keeping my voice steady. He awakened from his nap and stared at me, seeming to hold his breath and not wanting me to share my secret. Under the wide brim of the black hat with his blond hair once again braided into two long tails, he looked like he could be a wooden Indian.

"Don't tell me," he started. "I already know."

But he didn't know. How could he?

"It'll be our little secret, Valentina."

I worried that he might've figured out why I so desperately needed a rest stop and why Laughing Sun had requested OxiClean.

"No," I said. "That's not it. At least it's not the full story."

Newspaper headlines flashed across my mind with their claims that Jafford was engaged to a fireman, dancing with the stars, sued by at least three parties, and even questioned if he was gay. But none of those twisted news flashes were remotely connected to what I so urgently needed to confess to my new friend. Only the one headline mentioned Jafford and a hat, but my confession to Jafford had nothing to do with fashion trends.

"The hat," I said. "That one you're wearing? It's …"

"I know, Valentina. Don't say it."

"It's …

"Don't say it. *Please* …"

For all I knew, I might've been ruining his fine leather upholstery at that very moment. I might've lost Mason, but at least I didn't have his baby to lose. Seems those sperm were smarter than I was in swimming away from my eggs. But I needed to be smart now, too. When your entire life's path takes a sudden steep, curve, *truth* is the only thing that will straighten it out. I may not have been pregnant as I had wanted to believe. But I still had *truth* on my side.

"That hat is mine."

"I know," Jafford said. "I saw you wearing it. You were charging up a ladder. And that goofy duck Peepers was chasing you at the time."

Chapter 20

The Mouthful

Smooth as a royal yacht on a calm sea, the Bentley sailed passed the railroad station in the quiet Village of Burberry Hills. There was no need for a road sign to announce the speed limit or motorcycle cops to monitor traffic, for there was rarely more than a single car at any given time in town, especially on a Sunday. Despite that we were in a hurry to return to Swan Crest, Hector was driving at a slow cruising speed.

"I can't stay too long," Laughing Sun said. "Just got to grab the gong, then it's back to the city for me. I have a tea ceremony this evening. Three new monks."

"Hey, buddy," Jafford said gently. "I'm afraid it's not going to be that easy. In fact, we need a plan. We still don't know if Valentina is suspected as a thief."

I couldn't help thinking that my identity was not as a mother-to-be, but a criminal. I shuddered at the thought. And I wondered now about what Jafford really thought of me. Was he keeping a distance in case I turned out to really be a crook?

"As for the gong, I know it's valuable to you, my friend," Jafford said. "But you don't know Dagmar. She wouldn't part with it without a fight, not to mention that she'd want a pile of money to give it up."

The Bentley rolled over the train tracks that ran across the main street without so much as a bump, and Jafford proclaimed that Hector could finally open the convertible top. I inhaled and exhaled the clean country air, feeling as though I were taking my final breaths—and half-wishing that Natasha were with us. Maybe she could yank me out of that big car and tie me to the tracks alongside Moose and Squirrel; I had a feeling that death by a charging train would be more pleasant than the wrath I was about to face from Dagmar. I couldn't yet be certain if she was now aware that I was the one who had broken into her bedroom in an attempted diamond heist—not to mention that I was an accomplice to the possible slaughtering of her cherished blue-eyed duck. But I had more strength left in me for fighting off Dagmar as I pictured her pummeling me with sixty-pound bags of goat feed, than I had courage for facing Mason. I prayed that Jafford was still at least a friend.

Without so much as a text message or call on my cell phone, I knew now that Mason didn't truly love me. Ordinarily, an hour would barely slip by after he'd take off for one of his legendary buying trips, before I would hear the *I Love Lucy* theme song—the ring tone on my phone. But I no longer had my cell phone. It was in my lost duffle bag. I wondered what had become of it. I wondered, too, how Mason could fool me. The entire time we had been together, he was actually skipping over the Hudson River and building a movie set for his cousin Arnold; apparently, he also found time to trot over to *The Laughing Sun Center for Right Living* and steal the gong, too. I knew then that Mason wasn't actually hopping the shuttle for Newark Liberty Airport to catch a flight for Asia, Australia, Europe, South America—wherever he claimed he was headed on the face of the globe—and sticking the Twists for the up-front money. Maybe he really was romancing Dagmar on the side, not to mention seeing Bull Face when he was in New York. He may not have loved either of them, but I knew he liked Dagmar's money. I couldn't give him what he apparently thirsted for, but I had thought I could give him a baby. His deceptive words looped over and over through my mind. I still couldn't quite picture him with that old bag on the steps of the gallery. Was Bull Face really his wife?

I never was actually pregnant; I found that out at the first McDonald's on the road. (And no, the backseat had no need for OxiClean.) I could still conceive a baby, I was certain of that. I was young enough. But what I couldn't have and what I thought I *did* have was the love of the man I wanted to be with forever. Mason didn't truly love me. If he had, he would've followed me back to the city the night before. Did he misplace his MetroCard for the bus?

"It hasn't even been twenty-four hours," Jafford pointed out. "Give the guy a chance. He's probably been sulking, longing for you. Maybe he has a logical explanation."

Sounded like something Ricky would've said as Lucy would tell him to "Start 'splainin." Maybe Jafford was a fan of black and white reruns on Nickelodeon, too. And maybe he secretly hoped that I'd just go away.

"These matters are not so simple, Valentina," Jafford said. "Besides, we only left here twelve hours ago, and even a missing person's report requires at least a full forty-eight."

"Did you learn that on a plane?" I asked, trying to stop my quivering body from its despair over not growing a baby.

"Hey, don't minimize my Podcast education," Jafford said. "You'd be surprised what you can learn when your butt is trapped in an airplane seat and a plug is stuck in your ear. Could be worse, I suppose, if it was the other way around."

I really had warmed up to Jafford—quirky laugh, humor, dancing, and oh, those rippling muscles! Gratitude was filling up in my heart and filling up in my eyes with more tears. Only this time, those droplets running alongside my cheeks weren't only for Mason or the loss of a baby I never actually conceived; they were for Jafford. I wasn't sure for awhile if I'd ever see my new pal smile again, let alone hear his quirky sort of laugh, not after he admitted to me that he'd known all along that the black hat he'd been wearing was mine. I had no idea that wearing it all this time—even when he was the star on the dance floor at *Los Banditos*—had been a test. *For me.*

"You were butt naked," he had exclaimed. "What kind of thief makes a getaway in the nude? You couldn't have possibly stolen anything from the Twists. That is, unless you hid something in a very private, very personal bodily orifice. Believe me, I gave you the benefit of *that* doubt. I wasn't about to examine you *there*. Besides," Jafford continued, "I might've walked over to Swan Crest by foot, but I'm not in the habit of carrying a flashlight. Even if I had, I assure you, I'd never shine it up *there*."

The media got at least one story right. The Jaff *was* a gentleman.

"I mean, what do you take me for? A gopher?" he said. "Thought perhaps you might be mixed up in drugs, so I baited you with that phony joint. Took forever to find dry leaves and a match. Had to dive into a pile that Bertha had raked up to find some that would burn. And I think I should get a trophy for pretending to smoke it. Did you really think I'd get high on marijuana?"

"I didn't know you at the time, remember?" I said. "If you recall, I did question if you were really *The Jaff*."

"I was and I am."

"I might've seen your face in magazines, newspapers, and on *Entertainment Tonight*," I added, "but I never knew that your full name was Jafford."

"I thought about changing it at one time. They wanted me to, you know. But I figure I am what I am. That's all that I'll ever be."

"Rings true to me," Laughing Sun said, springing up from the front seat. "Sounds deep."

"Sounds like Popeye," Jafford retorted. "I always did have a thing for Olive Oyl."

Jafford looked right at me, and I started feeling his gaze all over my body. I guess I never realized it before, but that's about how I was naturally built: like Olive Oyl. Maybe Mason should've played Popeye instead of …

Oh, but Mason was merely a habit in my mind. All it took was one look from Jafford as he suddenly leaned in closer to me and smiled, for me to start wondering all over again: Did Jafford love me? Was I falling in love with him? For the life of me, I still couldn't make sense of his feelings for me. And they say that women are fickle. I wished that he'd make up his mind and that we'd both be a little more consistent, for just as I was pushing Mason's sweet face from my mind and squeezed out any remnants of him from my heart, Jafford pulled back in his seat. Mason was Mason while *Ricky* was forever gone. So was *Lucy*. I had reverted to just being me. But I had no idea now what to make of Jafford. Did he want to be affectionate? Intimate? Or were we meant to be only friends?

That great feat of the soul, the test of being courageous enough to move onward without a loved one, was slowly becoming easier as I gazed into Jafford's eyes. As I saw the forgiveness in his face for my

Dancing with Jou Jou

regretful slips into the underworld, my bloated tummy was no longer cramping with my monthly curse. My face was still flush, only this time without a chill overlaying the hormonal warmth on my cheeks, forehead, and eyes. Instead, I was warm all over my body—from the tips of my toes to the chopped off locks on my head. Only I still wasn't quite certain if it was *love* I was feeling for Jafford, the *romantic* kind, or merely gratitude itself. After all, it's rare to encounter a true life hero. Few men would have been brave enough to follow a potential diamond thief climbing up a ladder under a neighbor's bedroom window at night—or protect her by wearing a big, black hat with a brim that was *still* flipped up on one side, the other down.

"Why are you still wearing the hat?" I asked.

"How quickly you forget."

"Huh?"

"The Lincoln Tunnel? The crowds? The cameras?" Jafford prompted me, but I wasn't connecting the dots. "I wanted to make sure that I was the one who'd be photographed wearing the hat, not you."

Jafford may have earned a reputation for creating his own fashion statement, and without the assistance of a personal stylist other than Nike, but I didn't think his ego was large enough to insist on being the one who ignited a new hat trend in New York, as one of the newspapers that morning had proclaimed. I was blank as to why it was so important to him to have cameras capturing images of him wearing my hat—or rather Mason's hat; Mason had been the one who actually designed and made it.

"Insurance," Jafford said.

Now I was really lost. What did the Twists' insurance for the Blue Diamond Peepers have to do with my hat? Besides, it seemed that the jewels weren't really lost. In fact, Mason apparently had created several sets. He had whipped up a slew of Authentic Baubles. I saw them myself displayed in the gallery's window along with a sign that announced they had been seen on *Oprah*—or *Operah*.

"I wanted to make sure that if anyone else had noticed you charging up that ladder wearing the hat—perhaps one of the guests of Dagmar and Duncan's party, or maybe Vanilla John making the rounds on his scooter—they would later realize that it was me, not you. The only way to do that was to be photographed wearing your hat," he explained.

"As I said, wearing your hat myself was *insurance* that you wouldn't be nabbed. I knew that I wouldn't be suspect."

I couldn't believe what I was hearing. I knew he was a gentleman, but even a man with polished manners may not be willing to take a rap for a crime he had nothing to do with. Was Jafford truly willing to trade his athletic wardrobe with baseball caps for a set of prison stripes issued by the state of New Jersey?

"I knew that if I were the one who was believed to have been climbing the ladder up to the Twists' master bedroom, no one would think that I had done so with the intention of swiping a hunk of ice. I mean, what would I do with a set of Blue Diamond Peepers? They're too large to pierce in my ear. And I wouldn't split them up; I only have one pierced ear, not two."

Anyone else would've known what to do with valuable diamonds. To the average person, a rare pair of twin blue diamonds cut round could be exchanged for a pile of money—$17 million, to be exact. But I supposed that Jafford's pile was high enough. And he certainly wasn't average.

"Why would you go to such efforts?" I asked. "And do so just for me? We didn't even know each other. But I do have to admit, I feel I know you now."

"Doesn't take long," Jaff said, grinning. "Some people just click. That's why I couldn't figure out how you got hooked up with Mason."

"How well do you know him?" I asked. "I thought you never formally met."

"We didn't have to. It wasn't hard to put all the pieces together when I saw how miserable you were wearing that Princess Diana gown. I can't think of any other woman who'd be crying all dressed up in the same clothes of the world's favorite icon. She truly was special."

"You knew Princess Diana?"

"We played tennis a few times. She requested a lesson. Then we became friends."

I wondered if they served Corona at Buckingham Palace, but I wasn't about to ask him. Nor was I going to question if he and the late princess had been more than just friends. It wasn't my business. It wasn't anyone else's either, although I did feel a pang of jealously. But I pushed such emotional pain aside, for we still needed a plan for retrieving Laughing Sun's gong. And I had to prepare myself to face Dagmar and Duncan. And Mason. I needed to hear *truth* from his lying lips. I'd force it out of him. I had to or I'd never have peace.

"When that fellow slid down the banister right past us and didn't pause to see if you had hurt yourself when you had fallen on the stairs, I was beginning to realize something was askew. I didn't know what, exactly, but I was determined to find out," Jafford said. Then he added, "Besides, except for the red in your eyes that was the tip-off that you had been crying, you looked amazing in that gown!"

I thought it was amazing that there was actually a man left on planet earth who looked beyond two beans on a stalk like mine. Didn't they all prefer to ogle a pair of plump watermelons like Dagmar's? Even if they were silicone implants? I knew that Mason wasn't the only man to believe the old saying that more than a mouthful was a waste. But you've got to admit, most guys seek out big ones. Whether they're at work, at home or driving between the two places, I'm willing to bet they spend precious hours conceiving a plan for getting an eyeful. When you know what you want, when you know what you need, a plan automatically materializes. I just think it's got to be a whole lot easier for men who favor large breasts to find ways of ogling cleavage, than it was that Sunday afternoon in Jafford's Bentley to figure out how we were going to find out if I was a suspected jewel thief, if Jafford had slaughtered a duck, and how to snatch back Laughing Sun's gong.

"Hey, do you mind?" I asked. "May I take a bottle of *Agua del Jaff?*"

Between the hot sun shining down on us in the opened convertible and a tangle of thoughts boggling my mind, I was parched. *Men*, I thought. They're all *boys*.

Chapter 21

The Balls

Hector piloted the bright blue Bentley onto River Bend Road, where we cruised by a long snaking line of black and silver Hummers, Range Rovers, Jaguars, and even that Rolls Royce again—those same pricey heaps of metal that had frightened me the night before when I was a lookout on a ladder. The mere sight of them caused me to gasp.

Why would cars still be parked by Swan Crest, I wondered. When did they move to the street? Hadn't they been lined up on the driveway, closer to the house? I had thought that the party had broken up early when a burglary had been suspected and Duncan had collapsed in Bertha's parlor chair.

Strange things, I learned, kept happening in Burberry Hills, but I couldn't' imagine that the guests at the Twists' Halloween ball would conclude their celebration with a slumber party, and have their vehicles re-parked by the valets. I'd hate to think that those same people would actually return the next day for the funeral of a dead duck.

"Good!" Jafford blurted out. "Peepers didn't croak."

"How do you know *that*?" I asked.

I didn't add that I also wanted to know how he kept reading my thoughts. I mean, it couldn't just be a coincidence that I was thinking about a duck funeral, something I never once thought, let alone ever *heard* about in my life. The country was a peculiar place to me. But one thing I knew for certain was that if Jafford ever hung up his tennis racket, his next career move could be as a mind reader on the bar-stage of *Los Banditos Del Jaffordo*. That is, if he didn't become a professional dancer.

"Simple," Jafford said. "Look,"

Jafford was pointing to a fire truck that was rounding the bend. As the Bentley rolled closer, we could see it pause by the Twists' front gate. A pile of kids were loaded in the back, all hollering and waving as parents stood in a pack along The Wall, hollering and waving, too. Maybe my imagination was working overtime, but I could've sworn I heard more than one of them calling out Mason's name, just as they had the night before at the masquerade ball. How could so many of those women have guessed that it was Mason sliding down the banister in his Prince Charming armor?

"The Twists are keeping up the tradition," Jafford said. "Driving a bunch of kids in Vanilla John's old fire truck on the grounds of Swan Crest, is their version of a hayride. Always takes place the first Sunday after Halloween. I figured they'd cancel the little safari if Peepers had died. Just wouldn't be like Dagmar to *not* hold a funeral for that crazy duck. The way she doted on Peepers, she'd nix the tour of her personal wildlife reserve. And she sure as heck wouldn't hold any kind of event at all if anything had happened to Duncan. Yup, I'm sure of it. Peepers isn't dead."

"For what purpose is this fire truck-hayride-safari?" Laughing Sun asked.

"To show off. What else?" Jafford said.

Laughing Sun considered the concept of *showing off* for a few moments. I could see his reflection in the mirror on the visor. He had closed his eyes softly, leaving only a slit of an opening, while remaining all folded up in the lotus position up in the front seat. He seemed as still as I remembered him being when we were living together, but I didn't think he was meditating while counting the breath. Silently, I watched his serene face as his thoughtful mind mulled over the concept of *showing off* on a fire truck and palming it off as an autumn hayride through a country estate zoo. It boggled my mind to string such disparate concepts together, but I was confident that Laughing Sun could make sense of them if he pondered them long enough. Turns out I was wrong.

"I don't think I understand," he said. "So I'll ask again: For what purpose would a fire truck have in hauling around a bunch of children? How does …"

"I'm surprised at you, Craig … or, um, Laughing Sun," I said. "Perhaps the children will be learning lessons about animals, experiencing a new perspective on the world. I'd think you'd appreciate *that*. Or maybe someone will shout out 'teapot!' and they can all respond with 'Ai!'"

"Huh?" Jafford grunted.

"I'm pleased you remember koans," Laughing Sun said, looking at me in the visor mirror. Then he laughed in a way that always lit up his face. Like the sun. "I suppose my ramblings weren't wasted on you. You always were a good listener."

"Koans? Tea pot?" Jafford wedged in. "I'll have to review my Podcast list to see what I'm missing."

"Koans are ancient sayings that seem to not make sense. When a new monk is asked to interpret one during Laughing Sun's initiation ceremonies, and someone shouts out the word, 'tea' or 'teapot,' then the monk has to respond by shouting out …"

"Tell me later. Over *tea*," Jafford interrupted. "You two kids may not realize it, but we could be in a peck of trouble. We need a plan. The way I see it, Dagmar should be *occupado* for the next few hours with her jaunt on the fire truck. Let's head over to my place and huddle."

"*Occupado?*" I asked. "I suppose that's something you read …"

"*Yes*, Valentina," Jafford said with friendly sarcasm. "Everything I know about the real world I learned on a plane. That's where I picked up the word *occupado*."

"I'm sure you two *kids*," Laughing Sun mocked, "know exactly what you're talking about. But I've got to confess, I'm not following."

"Laughing Sun doesn't get the *occupado* reference," I explained to Jafford. "He's never flown in a plane. He only takes buses."

"From Detroit Lakes, Minnesota, all the way to New York City?" Jafford asked.

"And clear over to Boulder, Colorado," I said. "Sedona, Arizona, too."

"Talk about *sitting!*"

"He doesn't know that a lock on a bathroom says "Occupied" in English and Spanish."

"What's this?" Laughing Sun questioned. "Bathroom locks *speak*?"

Oh, teapots! Koans! And bathroom locks on a plane! I was beginning to feel like an interpreter between two people who had so far managed to find common ground, attempting to do that male bonding thing and quickly becoming chums. But despite their guy-talk efforts and our collective banter, they didn't seem now to have anything in common except for a fondness for guacamole. They weren't communicating in the same language and that spelled trouble to me. After all, we still didn't have a plan.

We could turn around, I thought to myself. It wasn't too late to scurry back to the city. I'd be willing to wait for a train. Heck, I'd be willing to run the whole way back. I'd even take a bus as long as it didn't have a certain billboard plastered all over it. But I knew that I had no choice in the matter. Not now. It was all too late when I realized that the man whom I had believed loved me had turned my *Deslilu* life upside-down with his screwball schemes. If there was one lesson I needed to learn from Mason, cooking up a scheme of my own was it. I needed to learn to think faster on my feet. I had been a slug for too long. *That* was the lesson I needed to learn. I had to face the *truth*: I didn't dance very well either. But first things first: I had to force my brain to think hard, for we needed a plan—fast!

As the volume was lowering on the Tower of Babble in my mind, I needed to transform my *truth* into action. *Quick,* I thought. *What would Mason do?*

"Passion!" I blurted out loud. "That's how he'd start."

Jafford and Laughing Sun and even Hector at the wheel, suddenly stared at me with their mouths wide open. I guess I had never spoken as loud as that before. But when lightning strikes, thunder follows. Mason, I knew, provided the fire in my flash. More than anyone else I had ever known, Mason always knew what he wanted—and he'd get it. In a word, he had what most people lack: *passion*.

"Who?" The three of them all asked as if they were owls. "Who? Who?"

"We need a plan, but first we need to be as *passionate* as Mason!"

Now the three of them looked at each other as if they were searching for consensus that in my despair over Mason—not to mention my lack of conception—I had gone bonkers.

"Don't you get it?" I asked with a big grin, pleased by my own revelation and proud of myself for finally learning a lesson about thinking faster on my feet, then moving into action in a heartbeat. "We need to *think* and *plan* and *scheme* and *act* like Mason!"

"But we're not con artists."

"Exactly!" I said.

"We've never stolen anything in our lives!"

"Precisely my point!" I said. "And that's why we *still* don't have a plan. We don't know how to steal. We don't know how to scheme. So we need to be as passionate as Mason. We need to transform ourselves and *become* three Masons!"

Our little gang was silent now, pondering the wisdom bestowed upon me in a flash. I held out hope that no one needed a translation. But it seemed now that *I* was the one whom they didn't understand.

"I hope she doesn't mean we need to change into furry loincloths and start lassoing up the guests with rope," Jafford said. "And you sure as heck aren't going to find me waddling around *quacking the moon* as Mason called it."

"I don't get it," Laughing Sun said.

But I did. I knew that Laughing Sun needed his gong back for the sake of his foundation. Jafford could deal with Dagmar about the injured duck as well as check up on Duncan's condition and sniff around about the theft of the Blue Diamond Peepers. We needed to know if the Twists were aware that I was the one who'd climbed into their bedroom window with a ladder. And I needed to summon the courage to face Mason again. I could pose as his moll—just as he had instructed me to be. Then I'd persuade him to make a new gong, one that looked authentic, an exact replica of the original that was now hanging in the Bamboo Garden for the exclusive pleasure of the monkeys.

"*Any* old gong will do," Jafford suggested.

But it wouldn't, both Laughing Sun and I insisted. The spiritual vibrations alone were ageless, priceless, and irreplaceable. But it was the intricately carved detail of a ring of animals that leaped, crawled, swam, and flew through the elements of water, fire, air, and earth, all gracing the circumference, that Dagmar would notice was missing.

I had no idea how much Mason had charged the Twists for the gong that he told them he had purchased on a buying trip to Thailand. But I did know that it was a hefty sum and that its spiritual value to Laughing Sun far exceeded dollars and cents. Unlike Project Peepers that had mysteriously unraveled with Mason pulling all the strings—*this* heist needed to be pulled off flawlessly, for Dagmar would never part with her gong. Even if she could be convinced that it rightfully belonged to Laughing Sun's foundation and that it was the reincarnation of an ancient sage who had once walked the earth in a previous lifetime, there's no telling what the price tag would be. Whatever dollar figure Dagmar might name, it certainly would be jacked up further if Jafford offered to finance; he did. That's just the curse, Jafford said, of being in the public eye.

"Never know if someone wants to give me something free for the publicity and repeat business," the celebrated champ told us, "or if they'll inflate the price."

We were all in agreement that Dagmar would fall into the latter category. We also concurred that if Laughing Sun pleaded his case using *truth* as his saber, Dagmar's price tag for a monk would still be far above what he could ever collect in donations to his foundation or earn in tips while working as Guacamole Man. But knowing Dagmar, she'd make him pay. Then she'd make Mason pay, too, by pounding him into the ground—and me along with him—with the gong. Personally, I'd prefer to have my head hammered into the earth than become an appetizer for the snapping turtles in Tannery Pond. I could still remember how Dagmar would order me to attack those turtles as we waded into the shallow waters wearing meadow stompers and holding paddles in hand. The thought of it made me shiver.

"What's *wrong* with you," she'd say. "Hit 'em! Hit 'em! Do you want them to devour my swans?"

Then she'd bang that paddle so hard over the shell of a turtle, they'd both split in two—the snapper and the paddle.

"*That's* how you do it," she'd bragged.

I'd hate to be a turtle, but I was an attempted jewel thief who'd broken into her bedroom, which was a crime far worse than being reincarnated into a slimy reptile and hungry for one of the swans. Despite that Ricky no longer loved Lucy, it just didn't matter. The truth remained: *Mason and Valentina* were jewel thieves. Together, we had plotted and set out to steal the Blue Diamond Peepers. I might've seen a whole slew of them displayed in Mason's brand new gallery in the city; I even saw a set sitting in Duncan's open hand when he was slouching in Bertha's parlor chair; I saw them on Dagmar hanging on a gold chain around her neck; and then there was Mason's claim that he had stuffed them up his cute little bum. With so much meyham, I wasn't certain then if Laughing Sun had the real ones or the Authentic Baubles.

"I've got to be honest with you," I blurted out to Laughing Sun in the front seat and Jafford beside me in the back. "I think I'm losing my passion." I didn't want to confess that I feared Mason had lost *his* for *me*. "I mean, I know it was my idea and it came to me in a flash. But now I'm getting cold feet. I'm not sure about any of this. To tell you the plain truth, I'm frightened."

"You're on the right path, Valentine. But it's not exclusively passion that's called for at the moment; it's *compassion*. That will give you strength and confidence," Laughing Sun offered.

"That's not enough," Jafford said. "I'm sure that's not all it takes."

"Well, the Dalai Lama would be sure. That's what he teaches," Laughing Sun responded. "He also says that your enemies actually offer you the finest gifts you'll ever receive. We may all learn a few lessons from Mason. And Dagmar, too. Lessons are gifts. Let's just stay in the present now and go with whatever transpires."

"That's not a plan," Jafford said. "That's a non-plan."

I had no doubt that Laughing Sun had acquired wisdom. I had no doubt that he could paraphrase the Dalai Lama or accurately recall what has been written about His Holiness, then report his teachings to me as if I was one of his students, and encourage me to read *The Art of Happiness* by Howard Cutler. But I couldn't ignore the fact that I was feeling my heart tick as if it were a timer on a bomb. *Ka-boom!* No more Ricky and Lucy. No baby, either. No longer did I have what I had thought of as my foundation—a family of two that was supposed to grow into three. I had to face facts: I had lost my one true path.

"Being cheerful no matter the circumstances is a good approach to learning. And you can become cheerful if you push aside the *fear* that holds you back, and move past what you perceive to be the evil nature of your enemies and develop *compassion* for them instead."

I didn't want to hear any more lectures. We didn't need spiritual guidance for the sake of acquiring wisdom of the universe. We existed in the here and now while I was mourning the loss of my future. But Laughing Sun was on a roll.

"That's what I interpret, anyway, about what the Dalai Lama teaches," Laughing Sun assured me. "Dealing with adversaries effectively all stems back to learning lessons, being cheerful, and acquiring strength and confidence."

"He *is* very cheerful and caring. And he actually does smile and laugh a lot, too," Jafford added.

"You know the Dalai Lama?" I said, verbalizing what I knew Laughing Sun would be wondering, too. I was certain it wouldn't be from jealously though, just curiosity about Jafford's rubbing elbows with one of the greatest spiritual leaders in Laughing Sun's eyes.

"Anyone can meet the Dalai Lama. The Dalai Lama likes people—all people. You don't even have to address him as 'Mr. Lama.' Personally, I just call him, 'Dal.'"

Laughing Sun lapped up Jafford's humor. He proved to be a more receptive companion than I had ever been—that is, when he could understand him. But he had more awareness for being non-judgmental than I ever had. I supposed he had been right about a lot of things, my needing to learn lessons filling up my to-do list. So far, the lessons proved embarrassing and painful. But then again I had learned from Laughing Sun that no matter the mess, there was always a solution. Heck, there was even OxiClean.

"You know," Jafford mused, "could be we're all wrong about Mason. It's true, he's been deceptive; I'll give you that much. He's clearly been going to New York despite his having claimed to be traveling the world. And it also seems true that he's stolen a gong. I mean, who else but Mason would leave the real set of Blue Diamond Peepers in its place? I question his tactics, but I can't help wondering about his motives. I mean, money is one thing, but there's got to be more incentive than that for an artist. No question about it, the guy's got talent. And I do think, Valentina, that he really could love you in his own special way. I mean, how could he not?"

Laughing Sun mused over Jafford's suggestions. They certainly did put another spin on our plan—or non-plan. They also triggered another chunk of wisdom that Craig had served up a long time ago when he was styling his metaphysical career path. Call me a mind reader, but that bright Sunday afternoon as I gazed at Laughing Sun's reflection in the visor mirror from the backseat of Jafford's Bentley, I couldn't help but know what he was thinking: *Perspectives of life are as numerous as there are people on earth.*

"As we attempt to concoct our plan to reclaim my gong for the sake of the foundation," Laughing Sun began with eyes still closed as if he were offering up a prayer, "and to see if we can clear Valentina of her role in the attempted heist of the Blue Diamond Peepers …"

"*Project Peepers*," I interrupted, ready for full disclosure. "That's what Mason and I called it."

Laughing Sun breathed deeply, contemplating my confession. He counted the breath before resuming his thoughts:

"… As we try to formulate our plan, we are willing to deny our true identities and transform ourselves into what we *perceive* as being Mason—a thief, con artist, and schemer. We intend to *become* him and expect to emerge victorious, when we really should be embracing our true spirits. And that's where Valentina's wisdom comes into play; we need to be aware of our *individual passions*," Laughing Sun said opening his eyes again and looking up at me staring back at him in the visor. "Is that right?"

"Did I say all that?" I asked.

Hearing Laughing Sun's prayer made me sound smarter than I gave myself credit for being. Maybe I was as slow as a slug. Perhaps my brain sometimes shrinks down to the size of a pea. Some people just have that effect on me like Dagmar and Duncan. But I knew when I was with Laughing Sun, he could always make me feel smart, just as Jafford made me feel protected. I wasn't entirely sure what wisdom the universe had bestowed on me, but the three of us were in agreement about our brand-new plan:

We would scrap all plans.

Instead, we'd focus on the present moment, tackling whatever arises. There didn't seem to be any other way to approach the situation, not when we didn't know all the facts. We didn't know if I was suspect in the burglary. We didn't think that there would be a fire truck hayride through the Twists' private zoo, either. How could we have a plan when we didn't know what had transpired the night before? Or where Mason was now? Or what we might find beyond The Wall?

"Well, now I've heard it all," Jafford said. "Our plan isn't flawed, because it doesn't exist. We have no plan, so we cannot fail at our plan. But we can't win either. I'd hate to play tennis that way. Truthfully, I like to win."

"I think you're onto something," Laughing Sun said. "Unlike Mason, *theft* is not your personal identity, but *tennis* is. I mean, you're not holding a tennis racket at the moment and there's no tennis court or net in sight, yet you still have an innate and developed need to win, because you're *still* a professional tennis player."

"I do have balls," Jafford said.

"And Laughing Sun is still a monk," I said. "Whether he's naked or wearing a long crimson gown."

"What do you wear underneath that thing, anyway?" Jafford asked. "I mean, when it's cold? You couldn't just get by with a slip."

"A boy from Detroit Lakes, Minnesota, after a lifetime of ice fishing, knows how to keep warm," Laughing Sun said.

He flipped open the folds of his brightly colored robe. We peered closer to the front seat as he exposed his long johns pinned with a set of Blue Diamond Peepers that shined more brightly in the sunlight than they had the night before.

"I've got a pair."

Boys, I thought. They may not always understand each other, but they did have one thing in common—no, make that two.

"Gotta protect the jewels," Laughing Sun said with a smile as he closed his monk's gown.

And so it was decided. Jafford would be Jafford, Laughing Sun would be Laughing Sun, and I would be Valentina. We'd embrace the present moment, maintain our individual passions and apply compassion to those whom we perceive as being our enemies. None of us would try to be Mason and cook up a crazy, knuckle-headed scheme to accomplish our mission. We would just be our true selves—a tennis player, a monk, and me, a woman with a monthly curse in full force who needed to break up with her man and tell him there was no baby.

Trouble was, I knew in my heart that I would forever be Lucy. I was starting to think all over again that I wanted my Ricky back. I wished my heart would either make up its mind or be quiet.

Chapter 22

The Horse

Vanilla John was putting around the fire truck on his scooter, all dressed up in his fireman's gear—big boots, big hat, and all. He even had on a fireman's raincoat that covered his long legs to the knees even though the sun was shining brightly on that chilly first day of November. A shiny whistle was stuck in his mouth as he held onto his scooter with one hand; he held up his other hand in the air as if he were directing traffic. But most of the cars now were parked—all except for the Bentley.

"You made it!" Vanilla John said to Jafford as he emerged at the car window.

I could see that he was straddling his scooter, but didn't hear him put down the kickstand. I could only see his middle from my perspective in the backseat, and I didn't think he could see me.

"We're about ready to begin," he said. "Dagmar's just taking a final trot through the grounds."

"Knowing Dagmar, it's probably more of a gallop," Jafford said.

The bell on the fire truck was clanging. The kids were probably taking turns pounding out their frustration while waiting, I thought. Then all of a sudden, they started cheering and I peered over Laughing Sun's shoulder to see what the commotion was for.

"Gotta get going," Vanilla John said to Jafford. "Sounds like Dagmar's finally ready."

He stuck the whistle back into his mouth and blew it as if he were starting a parade, and then he zoomed back up to where the fire truck's engines were revving up by the front gate. Just as I was about to ask Jafford who would be driving the fire truck if Vanilla John was on his scooter, a gleaming black stallion flew past the kids and the crowd. It charged down River Bend Road with such fury, you'd think it was carrying Zorro on its back. But when horse and rider approached the Bentley, we knew it was Dagmar.

"You just *have* to be different, don't you, Jaff," Dagmar said.

I could only see the legs on that horse outside of Jafford's window, but there was no mistaking Dagmar's shrill voice.

"You're the only one here with a *blue* car," she said. "What's the matter with you? Everyone else in Burberry Hills has black or gray. Why don't you get with the program?"

"You're a fine one to talk," Jafford said. "You're the only one here on a horse. Besides, I'm a style-maker now. Or didn't you hear the latest?"

"Everyone in *this* neighborhood has seen the morning papers," Dagmar said. "We may all be Burberians and in our own exclusive little world, but we do still read the news."

Dagmar was always finding ways to announce that she included herself in an elite group, trying to convince anyone within earshot that she had a pedigree, blue blood, and entitlement to a fortune. But I never really thought of her as being a true Burberrian. She had won only money, not class.

"*The New York Times* knows how to find *us*," she said. "That's one of the perks of being rich. Don't you just love it?"

I was eyeing that flip-down table on the Bentley's car-bar, wondering if it would cover me if I crouched down on the floor. But I was afraid to move in fear she'd notice the commotion—and was grateful that she was still sitting high on her horse, squealing with laughter just like a monkey. I could see that her feet were not in stirrups and figured that she must've been riding bareback again. I was never so glad for a view of an animal's belly and hind legs before. Poor horse. Poor monkeys. Poor me.

"I guess that means that *The New York Times* knows how to find me, too," Jafford said. "They put my picture in the paper."

"That's not the only thing they put in there, babe," Dagmar said with a squeal. "You're holding out on us, Jaff. Why didn't you bring your fiancé to my party? Don't tell me he's already married and a jealous wife gave you that shiner."

"Close."

"And why'd you skip out so early without saying good-bye? That bean pole, Valentina, skipped out, too. I'm so mad at her, I'll snap that walking toothpick in two next time I see her. That is, if she has the nerve to ever show her bony ass here again."

"What'd she do?"

"I'll tell you what she did—or what she *didn't* do. She was supposed to model my Princess Diana gown. I even went to the trouble of having that long hair of hers chopped off and styled exactly like Princess Diana's. Talk about gratitude! Talk about disobedience among the rank and file! There's just no loyalty anymore from the hired help, and I, for one, am just sick of it. After what Bertha pulled last night, I have half a mind to do all my own housework and cooking on top of all my farm chores."

"You're going to have to fill me in, Dagmar. I don't know what Bertha 'pulled.' If you want neighborly support from me, you've got to come out of that shell of yours. You really shouldn't hold back so much."

As much as I could hear, Dagmar's ranting opened up flood gates, but Jafford wanted a tsunami.

"Hold back?" Dagmar exclaimed in the high-pitched squeal of a monkey whose tail was being tugged. They're going to have to hold me back if Bertha ever shows up at Swan Crest again."

"Why? What'd *she* do?"

"She was playing hide the salami with my husband, that's what! I ordered a lab test to see if the lipstick marks on him matched the ones that were smeared around her mouth. No one's going to convince me that she only wears L'Oreal if they come back to be Maybelline."

"What's salami-hiding?" Laughing Sun whispered over his shoulder to me. I motioned him to be quiet, but he was perpetually curious. "Knocking at the jade door?" he asked.

"Where's Duncan now?"

"I don't care where that man is," Dagmar said. "He and Bertha can be trampled by a herd of charging elephants, for all I care. He gave her my Blue Diamond Peepers! They found them on her when they searched her and handcuffed her and hauled her wrinkled ass off to jail. Just the phony ones, the copies of the authentic pair, but still! Stealing is stealing. Off with her head!"

I breathed a bit easier now in the backseat, picturing Bertha's head rolling, not mine.

"As for you," she said to Jafford, "don't tell me I'm not good enough for you either. Or maybe you really are gay. Are you? You're not, really. Tell me you're not gay."

What a jerk, I thought from my fetal position in the back seat. How did I tolerate such a dimwit for so long? If I had any doubts about Mason preferring Dagmar to me, well, they were just dissolved by those stupid remarks. Oh, I thought. She had so many. She really was a horse's ass. But that would be unkind to say about a horse.

"Maybe you're right, Dagmar," Jafford was saying. "Maybe you're not good enough for me. Maybe you're just not my type. Know what I mean?"

"Not *good* enough for you? Not your *type*? Tell you what, Mr. Trendsetter," Dagmar bargained, "you can make up for those little wise-cracks by giving me one of those hats. I wouldn't mind being the first to have one. Who is your hat maker, anyway? Is he in the city? You *must* give me his name. If you're going to be setting a new fashion craze, your neighbors should be the first to be in on it. You know, like sharing a stock tip."

Jafford removed his—my—Mason's—big, black hat from his head and tossed it through the car's window up to Dagmar on her horse.

"Take it," he told her. "You can have the original. I'm fresh out of stock tips."

"How's it look on me?"

"You look fabulous!"

"Really? You're not just saying that, are you?"

"No, really," Jafford assured her. "I think the milliner styled it just for you!"

"Milliner? What's that?"

She didn't win any smarts, either. Too bad she couldn't buy an enhanced vocabulary. But I supposed that was at least one thing she and I had in common: a preference for plain, simple words. I guess neither one of us was very smart. Perhaps that's why we both got mixed up with Mason.

"A milliner is a hat maker," Jafford told her. "You can pull out the straps, if you want. Just tie them under your chin."

"Is he from New York? Or from some exotic place?" Dagmar asked as she fastened the hat securely on her head. "Oh, tell me he's from Milan—or maybe Paris?"

"I'd say he's from all over. But, yeah, he's been to New York. Very recently, I'd say. Here, too."

"Really? Really? Is he your gay lover? Or do you call him your partner? Which is it, Mr. Tennis Champion-Fairy? What are you anyway? And are you really engaged? To a man or a woman?"

"I'd tell you, Dagmar, but honestly, I'm too preoccupied at the moment. Can't take my eyes off you. You really do look smashing in that hat. Just like a supermodel, I'd say."

Jafford's reputation for dating supermodels must've carried weight and dispelled any rumors that Dagmar teased him about. But fodder for newspapers paled by comparison to her vanity. Is there a makeover show for lottery winners? Or a horse's ass?

"Hand me a mirror," she ordered him. "Quick! I want to see what I look like. Doesn't that Bentley of yours have a rear view mirror that can stretch up here?"

Jafford stepped out of the car to keep Dagmar up on her high horse. I could no longer hear them talking over the kids' clanging of the bell on the fire truck. But Hector could. It seemed that Dagmar had said something about seeing Laughing Sun's crimson gown as he sat up in the front seat; it must've been clearly visible to her when she was charging on her horse down River Bend Road.

"Dalai Lama, he always visit city loft when he in New York City," Hector offered up from his place at the wheel. "Dalai Lama, he friend of Mr. Jafford."

Vanilla John's whistle was sounding off again, and the bell stopped clanging.

"Yup, I've known him a long time," Jafford was saying.

"What should I call him," Dagmar muttered. "Dalai? Or Mr. Lama?"

"He say his friends call him 'Laughing Sun,'" Hector said. "That what he tell to me this morning. I squeeze him blood oranges. He like!"

Finally, Dagmar shut up. She was probably wondering how orange juice could be bloody. But despite all her newly-found money, she'd never leave Swan Crest for a trip to Spain.

"He's starting a new foundation," Jafford told Dagmar. "But he's missing a gong."

"Gong!" Dagmar cried out. "I have a gong! Tell him! Tell him! Does he want to see my gong? It's authentic, you know. Right from Thailand. It has a ring of fire and …"

Laughing Sun untangled himself from his lotus position and slipped out the car door.

"I'd love to see your gong," he said.

I could see his long, flowing gown billowing in the country wind, just as swaths of crimson had blown like flags throughout Central Park during *The Gates* exhibition.

"That's a nice horse you have there," he said to Dagmar as he concluded his bow. "Now, don't worry about that. We can bow together later. I appreciate your efforts, but I can see you have a safari to attend to. I'd like to see it myself, if you don't mind.

"Hop on up here, Mr … That is, *Laughing Sun*. Plenty of room! You can double up with me. Mind riding bareback?"

Poor horse.

"I don't mind at all. It would be my very great honor to ride with you," Laughing Sun said. "I haven't ridden a horse since I left Detroit Lakes."

"Lakes? I thought you lived high up on top of a mountain somewhere," Dagmar said. "Where're you from, anyway?"

"We're all from the same place," Laughing Sun told her with his hands hidden inside the sleeves of his gown. "We are all merely vibrations. It's an honor to meet up with yours in this lifetime."

Jafford crouched down and laced his fingers together and Laughing Sun accepted the step up, but his scared robe was flying around Jafford's head. With one, strong heave-ho, Jafford managed to lift the smiling monk up high until, at last, Laughing Sun's leg was dangling alongside of Dagmar's on the horse with his long johns showing. His gown must've been bunched up on the back of the horse, but I couldn't see that far up from where I was sitting.

"Hey Dagmar!" Jafford shouted as the horse's hooves started clomping on the pavement. That majestic animal seemed to be dancing around in a circle. "You promised to play tennis with me, remember?"

"Bring me a racket, you fairy," Dagmar hollered before trotting back up to Swan Crest's front gate with Laughing Sun behind her. "I've already got the balls!"

The bell started clanging again as the fire truck roared up the hill through the front gate. As the parents followed on foot and disappeared from River Bend Road, Jafford was rolling in the backseat, howling.

"We never needed a plan! We just needed Dagmar! What a goof! She really thinks that Laughing Sun is the Dalai Lama," he managed as he tried catching his breath.

I never saw him play tennis, but I was sure he could breathe more easily while working up a sweat on the courts than he could while trying to contain his laughter upon seeing Dagmar and Laughing Sun ride away on a horse.

"That dizzy dame!"

And I thought I was Lucy.

"Where to now, Mr. Jafford?" Hector said.

But Jafford was now on the floor.

"He pulled it off! That monk pulled it off! He's a very good Guacamole Man, too. Remind me to give that monk a raise! I'll even give him a donation. Heck, maybe I'll become a monk myself just as those newspapers predicted. Tell me again, what's a koan?"

I didn't see why Jafford was so happy. Seemed to me Laughing Sun could *never* reclaim his gong now. We wouldn't be able to steal it for him either; I couldn't even get Mason to swipe it now, not when Dagmar was aware that her cherished possession up in the Bamboo Garden would be desirable to a monk. If it went missing—no matter who or what she perceived him to be—Laughing Sun would become suspect. I mean, what kind of a thief would swipe a gong except for Mason?

"Relax, Valentina," Jafford started as he climbed up off the Oriental rug and back onto the backseat. "She'll probably give it to him as a charitable donation and get the tax write-off. If she doesn't, I'll introduce her to my accountant. She'll talk Dagmar into it."

I never was very good with numbers, taxes being the most perplexing set. While some people are superstitious on Friday the 13th, it was April 15th that always scared me year after year.

"How do you figure?" I asked.

"Valentina, I've really gotten to know you well even though it's been less than twenty-four hours. But there's no doubt in my mind: you're not a thief. You couldn't possibly be."

He paused, still gazing through me as if I were made of glass.

"Naked or clothed, you're just not the type," he continued. "Most people kiss up to the rich and famous. Some of them would do just about *anything* to be close to them, especially celebrities. And Dagmar Twist tops that list. I should know. I've been her neighbor ever since she and Duncan bulldozed the old house—furniture and all—and built that—that—that castle of theirs in its place. She's been kissing up to me ever since, only her style is to talk to me as if we were pals. Likes to kid me a lot, especially about whatever comes up in the media's gossip. Or she talks about money. But you don't."

He was right. I always left the financial figuring to Mason. It just made sense, since he was better at numbers than I ever was.

"Why didn't you just tell her that you're not gay?"

"I don't care what she thinks. Or what anyone else thinks. I know what I am. And I am what I am."

"Then why did you get all those newspapers this morning?"

"Laughs, I guess. While some people read the comic strips, I just read about *me*. It's fun! Never know what *The Jaff* will be doing next. Didn't know I'd be on *Dancing with the Stars*. Wonder who'll be my dance partner."

He looked at me with an invitation in his eyes, but I didn't think it was just for dancing. And I knew I'd never pass an audition.

"I don't care what Dagmar thinks, or the media. I don't even care what my fans think, at least about me on a personal level. I do care if they see me win. It's tennis that makes them happy. See, tennis to me is either win or lose. And that's what I do for my fans. It's nice that they seem to like me personally, but honestly, I'd be happy if they were just cheering for how I play the game. I think they picture themselves jumping the net whenever I win. If I make them happy vicariously through my tennis, then I'm happy, too. But I keep a distance from most people when it comes to my real life. After all, tennis is only a game."

Amazing, I thought, how a tennis player could make so many people happy around the world by batting a little ball over a net and making sure it never bounced outside the white lines.

"You seem to know me as *me*," Jafford said. "Of course, I could be all wrong. But whether I am or not, it *does* matter what *you* think of me, Valentina. I don't care about strangers or people like Dagmar who seem to be after something when they kiss my butt."

That's one more thing I could've learned from Mason.

"You have no idea of the power of fame or the draw that money has on most people, do you?"

He was more serious now, and looking at me as if we'd known each other forever. As if in a trance, the two of us gazed into each others' eyes—and I knew I could look at him like that for a long, long time. Maybe we had known each other in another lifetime. Perhaps we just clicked well in this one. Whatever the reason that time suddenly felt limitless, there was no question in my heart that I had something with Jafford that I knew I never experienced fully and completely with Mason: *trust*.

"I don't know why," I began. "But I do trust you."

But trust was not love, at least the romantic kind. While it seemed that Mason had been disloyal to me, and it seemed certain that he could not be trusted, I still could not shake off my love for him. I had pledged that love countless times to him, just as he had pledged his love to me—and I believed him then. I wanted to still believe him. I needed to count on that pledge now.

"Trust is a great part of love, Valentina."

I kissed Jafford on the cheek, slipped out of the Bentley, and headed back home where I belonged—my home, the one I shared with Mason. At the cottage. I had no choice in the matter now, not when the universe had sent me in a direction I hadn't planned on following. No question about it, before I continued my life's mission, before I made a decision about which way to turn for my one, true path, I had to face Mason. Maybe we don't really make our own decisions; perhaps they're made for us and it's already written as to what decisions we make. But I had to see him now. I wanted to read what the universe had dictated about me and cast upon the stars.

Chapter 23

The Privilege

Twenty-two swans had been dancing like ballerinas on the edge of Tannery Falls the day Mason and I moved into the cottage. With duffle bags slung over our shoulders and Mason's complete collection of Emile Henry cookware in tow—fondue set included—we saw them. We were hoofing it down River Bend Road from the main gate of Swan Crest, the place where Dagmar's car service had dropped us off. Eager to see our new home and secure in the knowledge that the rest of our boxes would arrive by UPS, we were following the road in the direction that the driver had pointed, wheeling our boxes on a luggage cart.

"Can't miss the cottage," he had told us.

He seemed in a hurry to collect his fee from Dagmar up at the main house beyond The Wall, then return to the city, so he tossed us a long, black iron key that looked more ornamental than functional, and waved us along.

"It's by the waterfall," he had said. "Sits up close to the street. You'll see it. If you're lucky, you'll see the swans, too. Just look up. And keep going, keep going ..."

A gentle summer breeze was caressing the tops of tall, leafy trees as we passed by hedges trimmed by Edward Scissorhands. Rose gardens bursting with pinks, yellows, and reds were in full bloom and meticulously edged with smooth river stones. All around us, lush greenery was glistening with dew as underground sprinklers were drawing water from natural springs. Then finally, as we rounded the bend that lent the road its name, we found our ultimate destination: a two-hundred-year-old dollhouse that was officially and legally christened as *The Cottage at Swan Crest Farms*.

Mason stopped in his tracks. "That's it," he said. "We're home."

It wasn't one of those surreal moments when the sun suddenly leaps higher in the sky and birds sing love songs. It was more natural and satisfying than that, one of those rare times when kisses and hugs weren't needed, not when I could see the love in Mason's eyes—for me and that cottage. It was as if we had just entered Nirvana and were holding hands without actually making contact. We had the sort of magnetism that united us, a bond that was closer than two people can be, one that surpasses boundaries of the flesh—a connection that stays whole and complete long after a shared snifter of Benedictine has been emptied, candles blown out, and pillows re-fluffed. It was like a song that we knew would continue resonating in our hearts forever, and not just "BaBaBaLu."

Yes, I admit, I did love the cottage. At least before we met up with a charging duck `named Peepers. But my fondness for the cottage that first day wasn't about how cute the little windows were with their tiny shutters or how charming the high-pitched roof looked, the kind that you'd see in a Thomas Kinkade painting. While I realized that Mason and I were the next in a long line of curators for that little house, opening the same picket fence gate that delineated it from a tall hedge and the street, and sniffing the scent of apple blossoms, roses, and pine wafting through the clean country air, it was the feeling that we had been sent on a life mission *together* that filled me with a sense of contentment. That tiny cottage, alone in a village of grand estates, symbolized the pride and strength and magic of our love. Unfortunately, it was a perception that was merely fleeting, thanks to a certain goofy, blue-eyed duck. But at least I felt as though I had finally found my forever home.

We crossed the threshold of the new chapter in our life, knowing that the driver had been right: we were lucky. We could see the swans peering over the edge of the falls. They were fluttering their wings, dipping long, graceful necks into the water, and gliding along a wire that stretched across the edge to protect them from tumbling over and smashing their delicate heads on the boulders below. Those same massive rocks poking out from the stream that threatened danger for the swans, also formed a private fortress for Peepers. He had waddled out of his hidden pool and hopped on the bank of the stream, waiting and watching us for a moment—just as we waited and watched him. Then all of a sudden he was quacking in a rage. Then he charged across the Great Lawn in a straight line with his wings flapping, and his little white head bobbing up and out. Roses were quivering as he zoomed by, bowing in his presence and dropping petals in his wake.

"Quick!" I said to Mason as I hopped onto the millstone that served as the front step of the cottage. "Give me that key!"

I was frantically fussing with the hand-forged lock that was falling off its screws and causing the lion's head knocker to rap on the thick wooden door—just as Mason was reaching down to pat that wild beast on his white velvet head. While I knew Mason had a magic touch—his artwork no exception to that rule—I didn't know until that first day at the cottage that he had a way with ducks. I had no idea that the bliss I had so immediately felt would abruptly turn …

But that moment is forever locked in the vault of time. It seemed like a lifetime ago, not a mere three months. The roses had been heeled up in their beds with soil and buckwheat shell mulch, their long thorny branches clipped short without a single petal to add color to the browning fall landscape. The swans were no longer dancing along the waterfall's edge. And Peepers was no longer waddling or charging or quacking or aiming those fiery blue eyes at me. I could finally pause on the millstone without fear of protecting myself from a crazed duck—and longed to hear Mason quieting his threatening quacks again. It'd be a long while until Palmer and Christy would release the injured Peepers from their veterinary care, as I had overheard Dagmar tell Jafford.

The black hinges creaked as I pushed open the stubborn cottage door, but the sound was more like a moan now than a scream. No longer did I need to close it behind me in a hurry, for there was no Peepers to hide from. But what remained the same no matter how many tiny hinged windows had been left open, was a musty smell that always greeted me back home. I left the door open, safely now, to let in some air and dropped the brand-new duffle bag Jafford had given me on the rocking chair. But as soon as I plopped it on the embroidered seat and set the chair a-rocking, the entire collection of wooden ducks that Mason had carved and positioned all over the fireplace mantle were lighting up, bobbing their heads—and quacking.

I had thought that perhaps it was the breeze hurling in from the opened door that had set them off and that they'd all settle down if I closed it. Instead, the little wooden creatures seemed to be revving up, frantically sounding off as if a fox were in their midst. I plugged up my ears with my fingers and eyed the broom leaning against the hearth, tempted to sweep them off that mantle and put them out of their misery and, in turn, mine. Instead, I pulled the portrait of Mason with his arms around not his mother, but his wife off its hook over the fireplace. I studied her face to make certain I hadn't been merely imagining that she was the same woman who had been driving that bus. I was certain that face would haunt me for the rest of my life—the one I saw in the portrait, on the bus, and even in person on the frame gallery's steps.

I wanted to shove that portrait into the fireplace. I bent down, holding it by its frame with two hands, ready to heave it into the ash-filled hearth with all the anger I had in me. But in an act I can only describe as divine intervention seeping into my heart from the wisdom of the universe, I stopped myself. Logic spoke to me, too; I couldn't allow myself to reach such a level of anger. I had witnessed too many orphans punished for uncontrolled outbursts, and I never allowed myself to be like them. With all the discipline I could summon from my betrayed soul, I dropped the portrait on the bearskin rug—and fled.

I sped up the narrow staircase that had once been merely a ladder when the cottage was still a trading post with live chickens fluttering around a dirt floor. Wide wooden planks long covered the bare earth, but the stairs were still so steep that I normally would hold onto the railings and lower my head to avoid knocking it on the ceiling—but the quacking wooden ducks were growing louder. I kept my fingers in my ears, zoomed up the stairs, and swung open the little window by the landing of the bedroom loft to stick my head out. I needed air.

Peering through the bare branches of the apple tree and across the Great Lawn, I could see a fireman taking a flying leap into a high pile of leaves. For a moment, he disappeared as the breeze blew a few leaves off the top of the heap. Then as suddenly as he dove into it, he sprang up out of it again, landing on his feet, only instead of fireman's boots, he had on a pair of bright red sneakers. With a large, heavy hat in hand, Mason sauntered toward the cottage—whistling.

Smooth as the silk of one of his smoking jackets, he glided across the grass, brushing the row of hedges with an opened hand. I wondered if the real Ricky Ricardo would be as rhythmic while just walking, or look as dapper no matter what he was wearing; I knew each piece of Mason's wardrobe by heart: a sports jacket, narrow tie and tie tack, pleated trousers and a pair of bucks; white lab coats he'd wear as artist smocks, and jeans with a crease, but not a single paint splatter; multiple pairs of color-coordinated and collared shirts, each sharing a single hanger, which he'd tuck into kakis with thin handcrafted belts; and then there were the loin clothes in a variety of fabrics and weights appropriate for the season. He must've borrowed the fireman's uniform from Vanilla John. Or would he go to the trouble of whipping one up himself?

With or without feathers on his head or paint on his handsome face, watching Mason from my perch at the tiny, hinged window up in our bedroom loft, seeing him reveling in the manicured beauty of the Twists' estate as birds soared across a clear November sky, I couldn't help but admire how he possessed a gift that I did not: Mason knew how to move. You could try to convince me that opposites attract, that together the two of us comprised a whole greater than our two separate parts. But as I watched him twirling around a tall birch tree, looping his arm around its narrow trunk, I understood the wisdom of the ancient proverb: *When you put on the right dance shoes, you can never take them off.*

Unlike Mason, I was a drip. While he drew from a deep well of artistic talents, I didn't even have a puddle. He knew how to seek and find beauty in life, while I was frozen in an ice block of fear. He could charm all kinds of people; he could even sooth the wild quacking of a crazy blue-eyed duck. But I was the one who only knew how to cower behind the folds of pink silk drapes, hiding my face from Dagmar—then allowing her to steal my man. I was the one who chose to let a pair of scissors snip off my long locks. I had wept as I slipped down that magnificent staircase while party guests were reveling in celebration of Halloween. And it was me, alone, without anyone's prodding, who belted out a scream so loud and sustained for so long, it had the power to make Hollywood history.

I had to be honest; I was ashamed of myself. Gazing out a second-story window—this time from my own bedroom, not someone else's—as I watched Mason tossing his big hat high into the autumn sky, I knew that one of us had to change. That person was me.

"You don't have to steal," I said in a carefully measured voice.

Mason was so close to the cottage near the apple tree, I had no need or desire to yell. I was proud of myself for having exercised discipline and not taking out my anger on Mason's portrait. I needed my mind to be clear, not clouded by rage. I didn't want conflict; I wanted love. I knew that Jafford was right when he said that *trust* is a part of that. I had to have faith now that my love with Mason was real, not imagined. Whether it would continue to exist in the future or not, I knew that it did have a past.

"You don't have to steal," I said again. I liked the sound of conviction coming from my own mouth and proudly said it again. "You have talent, you have courage. But you have more than that. You have something everyone needs: you have an *us*."

Mason's hat landed on top of the apple tree. Maybe the wind had blown it slightly off course. But I think it was fate. He stood with both red sneakers—ones I'd never seen him wear before—planted firmly on the ground, his one hand still high in the air with anticipation for recapturing that hat. He was looking up at me in the window, waiting for the first time since we met for me to say more. But I didn't recognize my next words to be my own. I don't think Mason did either.

"No more games, no more masks, no more masquerades," I said. "Tell me the truth. I deserve a few answers. For starters, I met an old bag who claims she's your wife. She looks just like that woman in the portrait—the one you told me was your mother."

Mason seemed shocked. For once, he was at a loss for words.

"Don't try to snow me, Mason. I met her. In New York! So come clean with me. Are you married or not?"

"Only by law. *Ipso facto*. That's it," he said.

He was clicking his tongue in that way he has that told me there must be a twisted chromosome in his family's gene pool. No ordinary person could click a tongue so loud or in a way that settled an argument in a flash.

"*Ipso facto.* Click-click-click! *Ipso facto!*"

I'm not sure what Della Street would say had Perry Mason clicked his tongue like that. And I hadn't a clue what Mason meant by *ipso facto*. I'm not sure he knew either. But I was determined to get to the bottom of the truth.

"Why didn't you tell me about her? How could you possibly be married ..."

But my "golden" throat was tightening up. I still couldn't bring myself to say the word, "wife." Not again.

"Why did you tell me you were on a worldwide shopping spree for the Twists when you were going to New York? And what have you been doing with the Authentic Baubles? I saw the billboard. The one on the bus. Your wife was driving it!"

"You're missing the big picture, Valentina. *Operah's* in on it. But you're too consumed by details to see how Authentic Baubles can make us all rich. You don't think *Operah's* made all her money from that TV show of hers, do you? Just ask O herself. I'll introduce you."

I hadn't watched *Oprah* for three months. How could I when Mason had claimed that television reception simply was not possible at the cottage. I was too busy with my farm chores to watch it anyway.

"O and I—we're like that," Mason said, crossing two fingers on each hand and opening up his arms like expansive wings of an eagle. "It's a little known fact that her inner circle calls her *O* while the rest of the world knows her as *Operah*."

"It's *Oprah*!" I yelled. "Not *Operah*! You spelled her name wrong!"

Operah! Authentic Baubles! And *Bull Face* as his wife! Where was I to start shoveling out of Mason's pile of stories?

"Dump your wife. She's not for you. I am. And you don't need Dagmar either. You don't need her money. You need an *us*. The *you and me* kind."

My two feet were planted firmly up in the bedroom loft, but my heart was light as I watched Mason climb up the tree. As adept as a squirrel after a prized apple at the top, he reached the highest branch that would hold his weight without bending, and cuddled it with both arms as he lay on his stomach. He looked up at me as if waiting to hear what I'd say next—or wondering what he now wanted: me and a baby—or Dagmar and her lottery winnings—or Bull Face. He couldn't have us all.

"Lucy," he crooned in a deep, breathy voice as his hips humped up and down on the branch of the apple tree with a single heave.

"Stop," I said raising a flat palm through the opened window. "No more Lucy. No more Ricky either. From now on, it's *Valentina* and *Mason*."

I was proud of myself for putting my name first, but even happier that I finally found the courage to declare me to be the real me. The sound of my own name flowed from my lips as naturally as breathing. But Mason didn't seem to like it.

"You'll always be Lucy to me," he said.

"I want more."

"Tell me," he said. What do you want?"

"You know very well what I want!"

"I thought I did," Mason said. He un-cuddled himself from the branch and stretched out, leaning against the trunk of the tree. "But you, Valentina, need to know *yourself* what you want."

I watched as his fireman's raincoat parted open, showing off his taught tummy underneath a tight fitting, black T-shirt. With one hand, he nestled his head against the tree trunk; with the other, he reached out and snapped off a twig and popped it in his mouth. The toes of his bright red sneakers were wiggling as he stretched out comfortably on the branch.

"For starters," he said, "why don't you tell me why you snuck out early last night. The whole world knows you were with that tennis fairy."

"He's not a fairy, Mason," I said. "He's been good friend."

"How do you know he's not a fairy? Did you do it with him?"

"Nothing happened."

"So I'm right. He is a fairy. At least one of the newspapers got that much right."

"You know as well as I do that stories like that are made up. Besides," I said, "only you would know it was me in those photos. Who else wears meadow stompers with screaming yellow stripes?"

I was glad Mason couldn't see my feet. He'd not let me hear the end

Dancing with Jou Jou

of it if he knew that Jafford had bought me new boots and a closet full of Ralph Lauren clothes, along with a new duffle.

"I could think of at least one person who wears big boots with yellow stripes," Mason said. "He lives right here in this very neighborhood and rides around on a scooter. I even have him on videotape climbing up a ladder to a certain bedroom window."

Those ducks! Wooden or real, it just didn't matter. I had been cursed the moment Peepers had laid eyes on me—and I had laid eyes on him. I knew then that those ducks outside of the Twists' window were fitted with cameras.

"It's your choice, Doll Face. I could *YouTube* Vanilla John. Or I could think of one other person who wears those boots."

"You'd *YouTube* me? *Me*?" I screamed. "Who do you think I am, Paris Hilton?"

I didn't want to think about what else he might've captured on video—at the cottage or in the Twists' bedroom. I cringed just picturing Duncan's wrinkled body on top of …

"You're in this deeper than me, m'darling. Got a nice shot of your tennis fairy, too. That boyfriend you've hooked looks real good in my black hat, whether he's climbing a ladder or crashing into buses in the Lincoln Tunnel."

"I told you. Jafford's not a fairy. Even if he were, he's my friend. And he's a better man than you are. I never knew you were so sneaky," I said. "I must've lost my mind when I chose you over …"

"Who? Tennis Boy? Or do you mean Craig? Or as he's calling himself now, *Laughing Sun*?" Mason said as he flicked his twig into the air. "I always did feel bad about stealing you away from him. That's why I gave him …"

"You gave him the Blue Diamond Peepers? The real pair? You mean that set really is the genuine thing? It's *authentic*?"

"He can afford to finance that foundation of his now. Only I'm starting to wonder if he got the better part of that deal. Because of my love for you, I wanted to go legit."

I could hear the wooden ducks downstairs still quacking, but their noise couldn't compete with my thumping heart.

"Your privilege should be revoked," he said.

"Privilege?"

"Yeah. Privilege to form a forever family. Or be part of an *us*—the you and me kind."

"Ricky," I started. "You've got the wrong idea …"

"Ha! Seems to me you've got a lot of boyfriends, Doll Face. You could get quite expensive for me at the rate you're using them all up. Come to think of it, you're the one who's all used up. I'm not sure you're fit for motherhood. Privilege revoked!"

And that's when the autumn breeze stopped tickling the bare branches of the apple tree. All that fresh country air that blessed the neighborhood on River Bend Road and allowed the birds to happily sing was now streaming into my opened mouth as if a wind tunnel had taken the place of my lungs. With all the force I could summon to reverse its direction through my toothpick and now weakened body, I managed to squeak out a whisper and tell Mason:

"There is no baby! We won't be having a forever family! Or a forever home!"

I'm not exactly certain how I landed on the bed—if I stumbled over to it myself or if Mason leapt from the apple tree and squeezed through the narrow window, then carried me there. But I do remember how my shivering was quickly warmed and settled by Mason spooning me.

"It's not too late," he whispered as he caressed my tummy. "We could still have a forever family, just me, you, and …"

He was kissing me gently on my cheek and licking the tears rolling down. He was rocking me with two strong, yet caring arms. Then he started humming our favorite theme song. And I let him. I was hoping he'd start singing, too, and knew that I wouldn't protest if he called me *Lucy*. But he made up his own lyrics, added a few extra lines, and used our true names:

> "I love Valentina and she loves me.
> We're as in love as two *real* people can be.
> We're going to make a baby
> (And practice till we get it right.)
> Because I love Valentina,
> Yes, I love Valentina,
> And Valentina loves …"

"Oh, *Ricky*," I cooed, rolling over and facing him. "I was such a dope! To think that I actually thought you'd ever fool around with Dagmar! And I know you couldn't possibly live with that ... that *old bag* I ran into, could you?"

"You know you're the only woman for me!"

"Then tell me again. I want to hear it from your sweet Latin mouth."

"You mean ..?"

"Yes, my dearest," I said in my best Lucy voice. I fluttered my eyelashes and smiled up at him as he cuddled me in his arms on the bed. "I want to hear you say it again."

But I think I had him stumped. For the second time ever, Mason seemed at a loss for words. He looked up to the ceiling, then back down to me, then up again to the peak of the roof as we heard a squirrel scampering a mere four feet over our heads.

"Say it, darling," I said. I want to hear you tell me that you love me. I want to know that my Ricky wants to have a baby—and only with me. I want a forever family! And I want to be *Lucy* again."

Mason unwrapped his arms and sat up on his elbows.

"What gives, here," he said in a thick Cuban accent. "I can't seem to please you. One minute you want to be Valentina, the next you're back to Lucy. Ay-ay-ay-ay-ay!"

He did have a point; but so did I. We were two real people, but as *Lucy* and *Ricky* we declared that we were a couple in love. I guess I wanted both. It was our glue.

"When's the next boat leaving for Havana?" he said, now jumping off the bed and pacing back and forth on the narrow strip of wooden plank boards in the bedroom loft. The ceiling was so low, he had to hunch over.

"Sure, you'd take a boat back to Havana, but you didn't take a train to follow me back to New York, you—you—you *Cuban heel*."

"*Heel*, am I now? I should have married a nice, normal Cuban girl from Havana! Of all the dizzy dames I had to get mixed up with ..."

"Dizzy?" I screeched, sitting up in the bed. "Well! I never ..."

"I take you to a wonderful party, a magnificent masquerade ball, and dress you up as Princess Diana, making you a star ..."

"Star?"

"Yes, a star! How many girls do you know who can say they got to wear a Princess Diana gown and make an entrance down a magnificent staircase in a beautiful mansion like *dat* one," he said, pointing out the window toward the Twists' estate. "Huh?"

He was bouncing up and down in his red sneakers, still pointing, as a lock of his hair fell over his broad forehead and into his eyes. His fireman's coat was nowhere in sight. I couldn't help but still be attracted to the muscles rippling under his tight, black T-shirt. But I wasn't sure if he really was authentically worked up or if he was playing the game. I was quite certain he wasn't about to belt out a few rounds of "BaBaBaLu."

"Dress me up?" I said, moving closer to the edge of the bed on my knees. I looked directly into his bulging eyes—both of them popping—and pointed to the Twists' mansion myself. "You dressed me up as a jewel thief *first*," I hollered. "Then you had the nerve to cut off my hair!"

I wasn't as mad at Mason as I was at myself for that act of debauchery. I didn't blame him as much as I blamed *me*. It was my fault for not stopping it at the time. Then again, I didn't want to blow Project Peepers—or be arrested. But the consequences would've been far worse if I had admitted to Dagmar that I'd climbed up the ladder to her bedroom. I didn't think she'd see it as payback for all the times she peered into mine.

"What choice did I have at the time?" Mason said, still keeping up his Ricky accent.

I had to admire him for that; it was hard to keep from giggling as I recalled how familiar he was with Latin.

"You weren't supposed to climb up that ladder! I had it all figured out!" he said. "Dagmar had insisted that I frame you in case anything went wrong."

"Frame me? Dagmar knew about Project Peepers? You agreed to *that*? How could you?"

"I had to. But what Dagmar didn't know is that I'd protect you. I just went through the motions to please her. I merely made her *believe* I was going along with her wishes. She's quite the pigeon, you know. She believes anything I say. But I wouldn't let anything happen to my

Lucy. Besides, I've got Dagmar on tape saying that she wants to stage a jewel heist."

"I don't get it. Why would she want to do that?"

"I told you, silly. You remember, *dunchu*? Rich people are like children. They're never satisfied with what they've got. They always want more."

"More what?"

"Money!"

There must be a bottom, I thought. Or maybe I should say a top. It seemed to me that the New Jersey SuperDuper Lottery had paid out quite handsomely for the Twists. That is, when they were still together. It was a heap of money as tall as the World Trade Center's towers had been. Wasn't that enough?

"Like I said," Mason continued, "I had it all worked out. I told you to trust me no matter what happened. Remember? And do you also recall that I told you to always remember I love only you? No matter *what* happened? I wanted to protect you! That's why *I* wore the gown."

I was beginning to soften. I had longed for Mason to "protect" me. But I had no time to figure out his convoluted logic, not when there was still the matter of his wife.

"What about that woman? You're married! You never …"

"She's a business deal. *Ipso facto*. That's it!"

He was snorting. I never saw him do that.

"It's you whom I love! But you had to go and run off with that … that tennis boy, didn't you? You fouled up the Grand Master Plan! And to think how carefully I had choreographed the grand finale of Project Peepers! Of all the crazy, knuckle-headed schemes you got me mixed up into …"

"Me? Me?" I yelled. "It was *your* scheme!"

"Well, you went along with it!"

"And it's a good thing I did, too," I shouted, waving a finger at him. "Forget Project Peepers! I don't care a lick about diamonds and jewels and insurance money. I don't want money. I just wanted you. I wanted an *us*. I wanted a forever family. I thought you did, too. You're the one who screwed it all up. How long have you been mixed up with that—that—that Dagmar?" Had the ceiling not been so low, I'd be on the floor, face-to-face with him, tapping a toe and holding my hands on my hips. "Or should I say *Chou Chou*?"

"Nothing *hop-pened*," Mason said, still staying in his Ricky character.

"Well, I think something *hop-pened*. Where were you last night, hmmm? Why don't you tell me, *Jou Jou*? What, exactly, were *you* doing when I was meeting your *wife*?

"I've got a better question: where were *you* last night?"

"You know very well where I was. And you know very well nothing *hop-pened*! Oooh! You make me so mad!"

"Well, we're even, then. You make me mad, too," Mason said. "And to think I had a big surprise all ready and waiting for you."

"Surprise?" I wasn't expecting to hear that. But I supposed that was the very definition of a surprise. "Tell me! What kind of surprise?"

"Oh, I don't know. Maybe I will and maybe I won't."

"Don't play games with me, Ricky."

"Oh, I'm not playing games with you, Lucy," he said, rolling his head around and batting his big eyes. Then he popped those eyes at me as if they were the lens of a camera taking in my every move. "It's a great *beeeeg* surprise. *Beeeger* than you could ever imagine. So *beeeeg*, it can't even fit into a box. But I'm not sure I can tell you ..."

"Tell me *what*? Tell me *what*? Tell me *what*?"

"Oh, no," he said, becoming more and more Latin by the minute. "No, no, no! I'm not sure you could handle it."

"I can handle it! Oh, come on! Tell me! Tell me!"

"I'd have to blindfold you first, 'coz I can't exactly tie it up with a ribbon either."

"What are you getting at, you big Cuban tease!"

He dropped to his knees—which was probably more comfortable than standing—and started kissing my hand with a lot of schmaltz. He knew my favorite *I Love Lucy* episode was the one with Charles Boyer.

"I'm not kidding, Lucy," he cooed as his lips walked all the way up my arm.

He was nuzzling my neck in a way that gave me shivers—the good kind, this time. He kept it up until my toes were beginning to wiggle.

"Lucy," he whispered, "I'm yours forever. And so is our newly refurbished ..."

"You mean The Mason Figg Fine Arts Gallery?"

"How did you know *dat*?"

"How did I know *dat*? That's where I met your wife."

"Ay-ay-ay-ay-ay!"

"I couldn't miss it! That sign was big as life. And so, might I add, was Dagmar's portrait. Just when did she pose for you in the nude?"

"She didn't. I can paint anything. My work is genius! Pure bloody genius! That painting is *insurance*."

What *is* it with men, I thought. Whatever happened to their usual topics of sex, sports, and cars?

"Okay," I said. "I'll bite. How's a painting of Dagmar Twist *insurance*?"

"I already told you! Pay attention! I've got that art patron of mine captured on videotape! And if she doesn't cooperate, I have *insurance*. See?"

"No, I don't see. *Everyone* will see that painting you whipped up. Arnold's movie will be out in six months."

"Movie? How do you know *dat*?"

"I know that you were his set designer."

"Wha …?"

"Arnold told me."

"*Arnold*?" he hollered with the same jealous rage Ricky Ricardo would shout out the name Xavier Cougar. "When did you see *him*?"

"Saw him? I'm in his movie! Just wait until you hear me scream!"

I was rambling on, recounting how I had stumbled onto the set, as Mason's eyes bugged out more and more. I was beginning to feel quite proud of myself, too, thinking that maybe I was impressing him with my new found talent. Perhaps Arnold was right: I was a fine screamer. He told me he'd put me under contract and have me scream for him again for all of his future films. Then, just as I was beginning to realize that maybe I did have a talent and a path in life that was uniquely mine, I noticed that Mason had grown quiet and his mouth had dropped open.

"Was Natasha there?"

"You know Natasha?"

"No, not really," he stammered. "But she is Arnold's girlfriend, right? And he is my cousin."

"When did you see Arnold last? I don't remember you ever mentioning ... And why are you so interested in Natasha?"

"She likes swans," he said, slowly reverting to being Mason. "I was telling her about them ...What? Why are you staring at me like that? What do you ..."

"Did you bring her here?"

"No, of course not!"

"Tell me the truth, the *real* truth this time. No more games, remember? We're in this together. Come on, spit it out."

I threatened to bop him over his pompadour with a pillow from the bed.

"Okay! Okay! I'll tell you," he said. "Just put down that pillow, will you already? Geesh! You'd think it was a crime to help her out with her documentary," he said with a shrug. "What could I say? She likes swans."

"Swans!" I screamed, raising my pillow again. "You made that video! With Natasha! And the swans!"

"It's just a nature piece. Why you getting all excited, Lucy?"

"I'll *nature* you! How dare you make a porno flick!"

"Porno?"

I belted him with that pillow until the feathers flew out.

"Okay, okay! Quit it, will you? That little piece of masterful videography made more money than any of Arnold's movies ever could.

"You put her on video?"

"It was consensual. It's not like I was being sneaky. I've got the papers to prove it. Wanna see them?"

"Let me think about this. I need a minute."

He knew how slow I could be. He paused for a moment, watching me percolate. But he couldn't help but try to sell me.

"Not only do you have the house you always wanted in the city—and I can have my art gallery—but your children will have their college tuitions all paid for—and they'll go to private schools."

He had me for a moment. It would be nice, I thought, for our future children not to struggle. I did want them to have all the advantages in life, especially a fine education. Neither Mason nor I had attended college, let alone private schools ...

I gazed into his two luscious Ricardo eyes, picturing them on the cover of *Art News* along with photographs of his paintings. I could see myself by his side and in the gallery displaying his finest work as our children—more than one—would be able to hold their heads up high, proud of their father for being such a successful and prominent artist …

I reached out and stroked the cheek that used to press closely next to mine. I felt his rippling muscles across his chest and stomach; I fingered the buckle on his belt, and moved slowly to his strong thighs …

"Well," he said, "did you meet Natasha, too?"

It was then that I noticed them again, his brand-new pair of bright red sneakers. I knew he had never worn them before. And I knew that Natasha had worn red footwear. Naturally, it could be merely a coincidence. Lots of people wear red shoes, I reasoned, even if I didn't think it was *the* color of the season that particular year. I looked back up to Mason's eyes that seemed to be yearning now. But I didn't think it was for me.

"Why are you looking at me like that?" he asked. "I did it all for you, for us, for the baby. You do still want one, *dunchu*, Lucy?"

"Don't you Lucy me!"

"*Wha-hop-pened*?" he said in an innocent Ricky voice. He was holding up both hands, palms up. "What'd I do? Are you crazy or *somepin*?"

"First, it was Dagmar. Now it's Natasha? And you have a wife? Who else has there been?"

"I'm innocent, I tell you. Innocent!"

"Oh, no," I thought out loud. "Those ducks in the cottage's living room. They must've been rigged with cameras. And all those romantic nights we had!" The realization hit me like a pie in the face. "You filmed *us*, too. Didn't you? *Didn't you!*"

"You're talking coo-coo Lucy."

"Coo-coo? What are all those ducks doing on the mantle, huh? Why is it that they're always lighting up and turning their heads whenever we're on that bearskin rug, huh? And why is it, Ricky, that you like being in front of that fireplace so much? Tell me that, would you? I'm waiting for an answer …"

I folded my arms over my chest and gave him a stare that said I really meant business. But Mason just stared back with his eyes bugging out and his mouth dropped open. He knew I had figured it out.

"Lucy …"

"You'd actually dare using me like that? Me? Us? Of all the sneaky, underhanded, deceptive, insincere …"

"I'm sincere, Lucy. With all my heart, I sincerely love you. I love *us*!"

"Ha!"

"It's a privilege to show the world through the Internet that I do love you," he said.

"Privilege revoked!"

Sometimes blind *trust* isn't enough. Sometimes you have to go with your gut. I followed my heart for too long, and I knew from experience that my logic wasn't always reliable. I just had to have faith in my instincts now; I didn't need to know the facts, not when Mason slipped back through that opened window and slithered down the apple tree.

You went too far, I thought. *You crossed a boundary I just can't accept. I'll forgive you, of course. Doing so is the only thing I can do to assure good karma. But you broke my trust.* Cheating was one thing. Capturing it on film was yet another matter, not to mention displaying it on the Internet for all the world to see. We didn't need money *that* much, I thought. And what's worse, he exploited *us*. We both do possess *some* talents.

I knew that the heart needs time to mourn its losses in its own way. As I held onto the window sill, I poked my head out. Even though Arnold's movie cameras weren't rolling and no sound master was around to get it on tape, and even though I didn't have a paycheck in hand—maybe I was breaking some sort of Screen Actors Guild rules—I just couldn't help myself. I gripped the windowsill with all the strength I could summon and yelled at the top of my lungs:

"Maaaa-soooon!"

Chapter 24

The Fireplace

The soothing sounds of the waterfall were just what I needed to hear as I sat on the edge of the bed in a daze. For the very last time—and *this* time I was determined that it *would* be—I listened to the music of Tannery Falls as it streamed into that little sleeping loft. It slipped through the tiny, hinged windows that were swung wide open and filled up the space all the way up to the steep peak of the ceiling. As the echoes of yelling Mason's name were finally hushed, Mother Nature herself was whispering a healing prayer:

"*That's all,*" I heard her call to me from the waterfall that I had always counted on to lull me to sleep. But now I was drying my tears on the same pillow that my head used to share with Mason. I hugged that mound of fluff like the child I didn't have; I didn't have Mason either. "*It's over now. Time to move on, move on, move ...*"

I inhaled deeply, wanting the fresh, cool air to cleanse me of my guilt: Where, when did I go wrong? What could I have done differently? How did my life become such a mess? Was it *my* fault that Mason was a jewel thief, a forger, a con artist, and a potential blackmailer, too? Worse, he was a cheater. A chill ran up and down my spine at the thought of how close I had been to becoming duplicitous myself. After all, I had dumped Craig for Mason; I had to admit that I was tempted to have a romantic fling with Jafford; he seemed to be suggesting he wanted as much when he dipped me on the bar-stage for the whole world to see and gave me a great big kiss. While I hadn't exactly encouraged his subtle advances, it was clear that Mason *had* pursued not just Dagmar, but Natasha, and all along he was married to Bull Facee and living with me. Were there other women? How many? Where? When? Did he manage to sneak them up to the Ice House when he told me he was working late on a new painting?

"Oh, no," I groaned out loud to no one but myself. "*That's* where his little hideaway was with Dagmar. And probably served as Natasha's dressing room. Did she make her swan wear red shoes too?"

It never occurred to me that the thumping of drums emanating from out of the Ice House wasn't what was inspiring Mason to *paint* past midnight. I realized the truth now.

Was it all my fault? My head told me, "*Don't be stupid,*" while my heart was saying, "*Yes, it was.*"

I straightened out the bed covers and pillows, hoping my head and my heart would stop fighting, and looked around the room as if I wanted to remember it. A row of windows cut out in a random pattern on the walls had always annoyed my sense of order, but now I could see how they added charm; the cottage did have its quirks. Haphazard squiggles and lines of the plaster ceiling told a story of a workman in a hurry to get his job done; planks in the floor had been placed in a patchwork pattern, as if there hadn't been enough of one size to line up in the same direction; and wainscoting lined only two walls, not all four.

I closed the little window by the staircase for the last time, wondering how many other former residents had reached outside to pick apples from that very same tree. There, in the crux of the branches was Mason's fireman's raincoat. I wondered how long it would hang there, if a future curator of the cottage would ever notice it and ask whose it was or how it got to rest in the tree. I shrugged, thinking it would add to the lore of the place and pleased that there was at least one sign that Mason and I had lived there. Had it only been three months?

As I braved the steep staircase and went back down to the living room to get my new duffle bag from the rocking chair, the wooden ducks on the mantle started peeping and lighting up all over again. I studied them for a while, wondering if any of them had successfully recorded the wild escapades of Ricky and Lucy dancing atop that bear skin rug. I put my bag down once again and got on my knees to roll up that furry, flattened creature whose jaw was locked opened in a growl—then I plunged it into the fireplace and kicked the kangaroo pelt in there, too. I seized the broom that was leaning on the hearth and slowly, methodically, swept those ducks off their shelf, sending them quacking onto the floor. One by one, I tossed them into the fireplace. I eyed the conga drum, but stopped myself from tossing it in. Some things are just too sacrosanct to touch. Instead of the monument of love it had seemed to be during our life together, it now seemed more like a tombstone.

"No more cottage, no more ducks," I said to myself aloud. "No more Mason!"

I eyed the portrait I had tossed onto the floor. I grabbed it by its frame. I turned it over and held it up, staring at it one last time, still trying to comprehend how the two of them—Mason and Bull Face—ever got together. There's no accounting for taste—his, hers, or formerly *mine*.

"Oh, what the heck!" I said. "I'm not a chump. Not anymore."

I shoved the portrait into the fireplace along with the other junk.

It took awhile, but I was beginning to breathe more easily again, even though I had no idea where I was headed to next. I only knew that I couldn't stay there and felt certain that Jafford would help out. Maybe he'd let me be a waitress at *Los Banditos* if I couldn't get my old job back. I didn't want to use him anymore than I already had. Just wouldn't be right, I thought. I didn't want to take advantage of my new friend. I was certain now he couldn't possibly want someone as pitiful as me, not for a romance. I was hardly up to his standards. I was a nobody, still an orphan known by some as being named *Three*.

I looked around the place one final time, wanting to remember where I had been and what I was leaving. The fireplace alone was worthy of study. By the sheer size of it, there was no question that it had once been part of the original main house; it was rather out of proportion in the cottage. The beams in the ceiling were low, making the place both homey and romantic, while the built-in cabinets in the dining room held a treasure trove of antique china, silver, and crystal. The love seat alongside it had never been opened, at least to my knowledge, and I thought it best to keep some secrets. There just was no telling how many spiders one could find inside. Or worse—there could be a mouse. I might someday reflect on my days at the cottage and how I had been part of its history as one in a long line of residents, but the rodents that made the cottage their home, too, were not a feature I would ever miss. I set more traps than I care to remember and knew that I'd never again eat cheese.

I smelled something burning. Smoke started filling up the room. It was merely a faint haze at first, then quickly grew to be a black, sooty cloud as sounds of ducks quacking blended with crackling wood. I covered my nose and mouth with my one hand as smoke billowed out of the fireplace; with my other hand, I grabbed the broom. But despite my efforts to quell the fire, the ducks kept burning. Flames were starting to grow higher—then leap out, rising as high as the mantle—then up to the ceiling beams. I swatted the fire as if fighting a dragon—but I had no choice in the matter: I was running out of time. In another second, I'd be burned to a crisp —along with the cottage. I had to get out!

I bolted out of the tiny front door and leaped over the gate of the picket fence, but got caught in the bristles of the hedge. For a moment, it was as if I were drowning, not knowing which way was up—only, instead of fighting my way through water, I was doing the breast stroke through branches and leaves. By the time I finally got myself untangled and stumbled onto the street, I could see the cottage's living room ablaze. The place I had once thought of as heaven now resembled hell.

"Cuban Pete!"

I dove back through the prickly bristles of the hedge and plowed through the branches as if I knew my way back through; I did. I high-jumped the picket fence and bounded over the old millstone, up to the porch door. But I stopped short of going back in. Flames of fire were dancing all over the living room floor, reaching up to the ceiling beams. Black smoke was billowing out of a window that had been left open just a crack.

"Cuban Pete!"

I rolled into the shrubbery searching for a rock to break the glass, but all I could find was a couple of lose pebbles. I grabbed them and pelted the window—and missed the glass, hitting the wooden frame.

"Cuban Pete!"

I don't know what came over me. I've heard of people who suddenly find the strength of Hercules in a crisis situation. Unfortunately, I wasn't one of them, because the old millstone that served as the first step of the cottage refused to budge.

"Cuban Pete!"

I ran around to the kitchen window, trampling through the buckwheat shell mulch in the rose bed and hoisted myself high enough to grab hold of the top of the windowsill, then I kicked in the glass. I was in luck; the fire hadn't yet reached the kitchen.

"Cuban Pete!"

I slid onto the table in the breakfast nook, bumping my head on a shard of glass from the window as I did, then fell off the end of the table, knocking over a chair and falling to the floor. It was a good thing that I was low to the ground, because just as I was about to round the corner to pull open the furnace room, I could see black smoke billowing through the dining room, all the way to the window seat and heading toward the kitchen.

"Cuban Pete!"

I tried calling my cat again, hoping he'd round the corner in front of the smoke, but Cuban Pete was nowhere in sight. I had no choice but to scramble back over the kitchen table to get through the broken window—choking all the while as the smoke followed my path. But I still had enough oxygen left in between coughing to shout for my cat one more time.

"Cuban ..."

I was probably whispering more than yelling.

"... Pete!"

It was no use. I tumbled back out the window, landing on a pruned rose bush, desperately trying to force air back into what I was certain would be black sooty lungs. I was sure that if I died and had an autopsy, the coroner would think I had been a smoker, not a habitual chewer of bubble gum. But I had enough wind left in me to breast stroke through the buckwheat shell mulch and slither onto the cold, browning grass of the Great Lawn where I laid my head down.

I must've passed out. I remember being cold. I remember that the tip of my nose was wet. And it tickled. I could smell the spicy scent of damp grass. I could smell the foul odor of the mulch in the rose bed. Then I smelled what seemed more familiar. It was the stench of wet fur on my cat.

"How'd you get out?" I asked. But Cuban Pete was snuggling in the space between my head and shoulder until I was sufficiently revived and finally stood up. Then the two of us jumped in alarm as we heard the fire roaring inside the cottage. Those ceiling beams must've fallen as they burned. We ran away from what was quickly becoming our former home, past the waterfall where the swans were no longer dancing, past the row of cars still parked along River Bend Road, and past the tall hedges, rose gardens, and The Wall—then stopped. On one side was the Twist estate; on the other was Jafford's place. I was dizzy, looking right then left then back again, wondering which way I should go: Swan Crest or Willow Run? Oh, why was it that all the houses in Burberry Hills had names?

"Help!" I screamed. But no one was around to hear me, except for the squirrels. Maybe if I had Mason's magic touch, I could convince those bushy tailed rodents to dash over to the new firehouse and sound the alarm. "Help! Somebody!"

I might've been Arnold's new official screamer, but this wasn't a movie set. It was the real thing. He might've told me I didn't need a director, but he was wrong; I did. At the very least, I thought, I needed a new line. With all the breath left in my body—and Cuban Pete safely by my side—I let out my loudest holler yet:

"*Fire at the cottage! Fire at the cottage! Fire at the cooooottttaaaaage!*"

Chapter 25

The Key

Like a prince scanning the horizon of his royal empire, Buckwheat stood at the top of Swan Crest's cobblestone driveway, his diamond-studded collar glistening in the afternoon sun. As a cloud floated overhead dimming its regal glare, I could see that His Royal Goatness was chomping on a mouthful of leaves. I noted, too, that Vanilla John was not at the guard post or patrolling on his scooter—and that the main gate had been left wide open.

"Buckwheat!" I shouted. "How'd you get out? Go back to your pen!"

But I knew better than to expect a toddler goat to listen to my command. After months of feeding him baby bottles filled with milk and mush that had just been warmed on the cottage's stove, I knew he could tell by my scent alone, even from a distance, that I was his appointed wet nurse. Even though I had arrived at his country palace empty handed, he came prancing toward me, hopping and running and nodding his head, as if he were expecting me to feed him a tasty branch that I was perhaps hiding behind my back.

"No, Buckwheat!" I said, desperately waving him away from my legs and hoping Cuban Pete would spook him away. *Who left the front gate open?* I wondered. *And the goat pen?* "Not now! No bottle! No branch! Get back to your pen! Go!"

I tried coaxing him along as Cuban Pete made himself scarce, but

Buckwheat just stood stubbornly in one place, shaking his tail and rearing up on his hind hooves while butting my bloated tummy with his forehead; it was his way, Dagmar had told me, of showing me love. But I knew better. The only love he possessed was for food, not me. He wasn't looking for kisses as he wrapped his front legs around my hips; he was agreeing to skip one meal if I agreed to dance.

"Go!" I commanded him.

I didn't want the responsibility of herding him back to his pen, but if I didn't take it, I'd run the risk of Dagmar's wrath—and I *still* had a fire to put out. I tried prying myself lose from Buckwheat's furry-legged embrace, but he was swirling around me, leading. Just like all the other animals in that private zoo, Buckwheat paid no attention to what I told him. After all, he and the other animals were my masters while I had merely been their dedicated servant at feeding time. I might've succumbed to my role as waitress for farm animals, but I drew the line at dancing. I grabbed him by his gaudy collar and led him back to the other side of the gate, only to be greeted by a chorus of more goats singing "Bah-Bah-Bah!" and prancing around Buckwheat as if they wanted to be my next partner.

"I'm not the dancer! You've got us mixed up!" I shouted at them. "Go find Mason! But you should know it's not 'Bah-Bah-Bah! It's 'BaBaBaLu!' and the conga drum is now on fire!"

One goat, two goats, three goats, four …

"Quit it, Thomasino! You, too, Harry Potter! No more dancing for you, either, Eleanor! Nor for you, Prancer! Get back to your pen, Carmine. Let's go, Cher! Com'on! All of you! *Move!*"

Geesh! I thought. Maybe I should surrender now and tell Dagmar to feed me to the snapping turtles for letting the goats get loose. It'd be a whole lot easier. By the looks of them, it seemed all fifty had somehow found freedom from their chain links. While the rest of the animals were mostly restrained by the power of electronic fencing, they needed to be safe from predators and were kept behind a tall fence, which also surrounded the chicken coops. It wouldn't be long now, I thought, before the chickens would be meandering out of the front gate, too, and hunting around in their endless search for grain—which could only mean one thing: that demon bird that made Peepers look tame, wouldn't be far behind.

And that's when I saw him …

"Oh, no!" I cried out loud. "It's …"

I was quivering at the distinct possibility that we'd soon be joined by the walking alarm clock, just as Buckwheat insisted on butting his head into me.

"I'm not Natasha!" I warned him. "And you're not a swan!"

But I had more to worry about at that moment than yet another romantic entanglement, this time with a horny *four-legged* boy on the make. I was trying to deflect Buckwheat's advances as the devil himself—all fifteen inches of him—made his entrance on the driveway, puffing his chest out as if he had balloons for lungs and sticking his bright red comb straight up into the air.

"Oh, no!" I cried again. "It's The CEO!"

That little Bolivian barracuda dressed up in a rooster suit, flicking his little wire legs over the cobblestone pavement, was revving up to charge me. He had me trained—and he well knew it. But *this time*, I wasn't going to turn and run away. *This time*, that little fluffy alarm that had the power to shake the leaves off the trees was about to be put to good use. *This time*, I wasn't Lucy whose brain shrinks down to a pea and dissolves at the mere sound of squawking, quacking, clucking, or crowing. *This time*, I was Valentina. I was the one now who was a professional screamer. And I had a brand-new mission: I had animals to round up and a burning cottage to save.

I stepped away from my goat barricade and looked directly into the laser beams he used for eyes. The CEO managed to scare away Buckwheat as he made a flying leap for my face. But his courage was bigger than his pipe-cleaner legs could lift him, so he only made it as far as my knees. What he lacked in height, he made up for in noise. That puny ball of red and yellow feathers let out a piercing screech capable of drilling holes in teeth. Only, unlike the sound that most people think of as an ordinary rooster's crowing, it wasn't just a cute little "Cock-a-doodle-doo" that you read about in children's books. Oh, no. It was more of a heart-stopping, body-trembling, teeth-drilling, eardrum-shattering "ARUUU-ARUUU!" Oh, where's a fox when you need one?

I looked directly into The CEO's beady little eyes—on both sides of his head—as he cocked his feathers and crowed at me as if he could scare me away. But I was ready. Gritting my teeth and reaching out with both hands, lunging directly for his scrawny rooster neck, I charged *him* from ten feet away—and grabbed him around his plump belly under what he'd claim were wings. But two stubs with feathers barely lifted him off the ground. It was his arrogance and courage that gave him flight.

With my volume turned up the highest it would go, I treated him to my newly discovered talent. I let out my most powerful "Ahhhhhhhhhhhhh!" to date—and was victorious in catching him off guard. That little demon had no idea that I had grown into a formidable opponent. Even Dagmar could never match the golden throat of a professional screamer. Finally, my entire amazon frame was being put to good use.

"ARUUU-ARUUU!"

"Yeah!" I cheered him on. "Scream your poultry lungs out! Let 'em hear you!"

Then I led him in an impromptu duet as I ran, carrying him and he crowed and I shouted and ran some more.

"Fire at the cottage!"

"ARUUU-ARUUU!"

"Fire at the cottage!"

"ARUUU-ARUUU!"

"Fire at the cottage!"

"ARUUU-ARUUU!"

But no one was around to hear us. Vanilla John's fire truck was nowhere in sight. Just as I was running out of breath and about to bound up the hill to Bamboo Garden, The CEO seemed to be winding down, too.

"Hey! Let's go!" I ordered him. "We've got a fire to put out, you turkey!"

But it was just no use. The CEO had cooperated long enough as I ran breathlessly to the top of the hill. Instead of finding a bunch of kids eating lunch with Dagmar, Laughing Sun, Vanilla John, and the parents, there were only monkeys. They were away from their usual habitat, jumping through the bushes and trees and squealing with laughter. Oh, to be a monkey, I thought. Then my only concern would be for where I was getting my next banana. One after another, they seemed to be performing tricks for my approval, thinking that the winner of the performance would be awarded with a bunch of their favorite treats. Personally, I'd prefer to throw them a few coconuts—and miss. I might toss a few at some of those housewives, too, if any of them had ever dared sneaking around with Mason. After all I had learned over the past twenty-four hours, I could feel paranoia looming inside me. I don't think I could ever again see other women without sizing them up for telltale signs of secret trysts.

The CEO wriggled out of my grasp. He fell to the ground with a thump so hard, I thought I had broken him, but that sturdy little hunk of walking poultry hopped onto his clawed feet, then lunged as high as my waist.

And that's when he started crowing again. And that's when it hit me. All I had to do to get him to "ARUUU-ARUUU!" again was for me to start running. There was no need to hold him. After all, he thrived on the thrill of the chase. It was his true calling.

"Fire at the cottage!"

"ARUUU-ARUUU!"

"Fire at the cottage!"

"ARUUU-ARUUU!"

"Keep it up," I shouted over my shoulder, running for my life—from The CEO and the monkeys who were following us in a line. "I've never been so glad to hear your frightening alarm before!"

"ARUUU-ARUUU!"

"More! More! More!" I commanded him as I ran up the Far Hill to the Bamboo Garden.

"ARUUU-ARUUU!"

"That-a-boy! You're doing great, you little chicken-humper," I said running out of breath—but still running. "Let's hear some more! Louder! Louder! You can do it! No, not you monkeys! I meant the rooster!"

Maybe I should've just kept running while facing forward, but I kept turning around to egg him on, taunting him occasionally with my own brand of crowing. Had I not been so intent on shooing away the monkeys and assuring that The CEO's stick legs would carry him as far as I now needed him to run, maybe I would've noticed Mason sooner as he galloped past, followed by what was quickly becoming an animal farm parade. Goats, chickens, and monkeys were now forming a noisy procession behind us with bah-bah-bah-ing, clucking, and laughing. But instead of a horse that Mason had ridden right through our unholy walking choir, from the corner of my eye I'd swear I had just seen a set of reins strapped to the neck of a giraffe. I never knew that Mason could ride bareback, at least without Dagmar in the driver's seat.

A herd of elephant stampeded in his wake. Tigers growled after them, followed by the kings and queens of the animal world, the lions. Bears—brown ones, black ones, and a few white ones—barreled by. And what looked like a field of gray beach balls, the entire population of the Twists' kangaroos, bounced after them, while ostriches raced behind. Amidst the noise and all the running of paws, hooves, and clawed feet, clouds of dust arose from the ground, causing my eyes to water. As I wiped them dry with the sleeve of my jacket, Dagmar galloped by on her horse.

"I'll get you, Mason Figg!" she hollered. "You're gonna pay for this!"

Mason! Dagmar! I had enough. The two together spelled chaos. They were the ones who'd cooked up a Grand Master Plan. They must've turned on each other when their secret was out. Mason must've told her how I knew all about it.

The dust now mixing with the autumn pollen in the air was beginning to settle just as Vanilla John appeared on the horizon of the Far Hill on his scooter. He putted down the slope then up to where I was standing with the parading animals, when I ran up to him waving my hands.

"Stop!" I shouted at him. "Get your truck! There's a fire at the cottage!"

But Vanilla John froze. He looked like a statue as he paused on his scooter that was purring in neutral. I wasn't sure if he had heard me, so I yelled again:

"Fire at the cottage! Go get your truck! Fire! Fire! Fire!"

Was he drunk? What did they serve at that safari picnic anyway? He just kept standing astride his scooter as the monkeys started clamoring alongside him, swarming us like noisy, hairy clowns. Even Buckwheat didn't know what to make of this new figure in his kingdom, as he skipped up to Vanilla John and started nudging him in his thighs. The CEO started crowing again.

"What's wrong with you?" I asked him, wondering why he was always dressed for a fire. "Where's your hose?"

But the man who was built like the tallest tree in an oak forest seemed to be stuck. His eyes were glazed over, but I didn't think he was drunk. I sniffed him just to make sure, then snapped my fingers in front of his face. But it was no use. Vanilla John stood still as a tree trunk. His heart may have been in the right place, but his courage was nowhere to be found. Gently, I hooked my arm through his and reached over to turn off his scooter. I brushed the back of my hand softly across his cheek. It was cold to the touch. I wiped the beads of perspiration that were running from beneath the brim of his fireman's hat and then helped him step off the scooter. With one hand, I put the vehicle down to the ground; with the other hand, I led him to the nearest boulder, bench or tree—*anyplace* where he could sit still and recover from whatever it was that was scaring him. Fear can do strange things to people. Some traumas are too severe to shake off. He must've been reliving that time long ago, I guessed, when he learned that his own home had burned down to the ground—and his wife took off with their kids. Or maybe seeing so many animals running wild was freaking him out. Whatever the cause of him freezing up like a statue, and as much as I wanted to comfort him now, though he was practically a stranger to me, I still needed to tend to that fire. Without any calming place to leave him, I let him stay put on the ground, while the monkeys—miraculously or not—started forming a ring around him and sitting down, too.

I was about to take off in the direction of where I'd seen Vanilla John come from, when Laughing Sun appeared on the Far Hill. He might've been a distance away, but there was no mistaking his crimson robe. As soon as he spotted me, he smiled then bowed.

"Fire at the cottage!" I yelled as he was rising up from his bow. "Where's the fire truck?"

I veered down the slope of the hill on the scooter, then up to where he was standing—and now pointing.

"Next hill. Then go to your left," he said, as if he gave directions to picnics and fire trucks every day. But I knew I could always count on

Craig—that is, Laughing Sun—for sizing up a situation quickly, then heading into action, as needed. At least he had always been that way with me. While everyday topics sometimes eluded him, plunging him into a deep meditation, he was capable of being a quick study. He may not have had such agility when conversing with a tennis star, but he was always lucid and sharp with me.

I just couldn't help myself. I may have been in a hurry, but as I passed Laughing Sun on the crest of the Far Hill, I just had to give him a quick bow. People always made a lasting impression on me. It was as if I were a sponge and I picked up their vibrations. While Vanilla John was catatonic and in need of my help, Craig was cheerful and helpful. How could I *not* sense their vibrations?

When I reached the picnic spot, the children and their parents looked as if they were confused. They were making their way back to River Bend Road in a slow trudge, when one of them asked me, "Hey, what's going on? Where's Dagmar going? The animals are all running wild. What's happening here? The kids are petrified! They even saw Mason riding a giraffe!"

Then the entire pack of women started asking about Mason all at once.

"Where is Mason going?"

"Mason? I missed him!"

"Mason!"

"Did you see Mason?"

"Mason? Where's he going?"

"Did someone say they saw Mason? Where?"

"Everything will be fine," I said to the ladies who seemed more intent on getting an eyeful of Mason than they were about why he'd be riding a giraffe. "Nothing to worry about, I assure you."

I wanted to assure myself, too. I had a mission to accomplish and needed to peel myself away from sizing up the housewives. Why were they showing so much skin and their cleavage when they had their kids all bundled up to stay warm in the chilly weather? And how could they possible hike all the way through the Far Hill wearing designer shoes with spiked heels instead of mud boots? But instead of revealing my true thoughts that were distracting me from my mission, I swallowed any paranoid words that were creeping up from my broken heart and into my mouth.

"Why don't you all just stay put?" I said instead. "It'll be safer for you here."

I didn't want them to be alarmed by the fire or the animals that were now on the loose. I didn't want any of the children to get hurt and panic if they knew a fire was blazing on the other side of the Far Hill. None of them could do anything about it, so I waved and gave them a placating smile, determined to save the burning cottage in the only way I thought possible under the circumstances. I didn't have a phone, let alone a former fire chief with a hose.

I climbed into the driver's seat of that fire truck, reached around, and fingered the ignition. I never did learn how to drive, but the lack of a driver's license wasn't going to stop me. Unfortunately, something more crucial would. As eager as I was to find that key, as diligently as I searched, it was missing. There was no key to be found. And I had a feeling who it was who had taken it.

"Maaaaa-soooon!"

PART FIVE: HOME IS WHERE THE TV IS

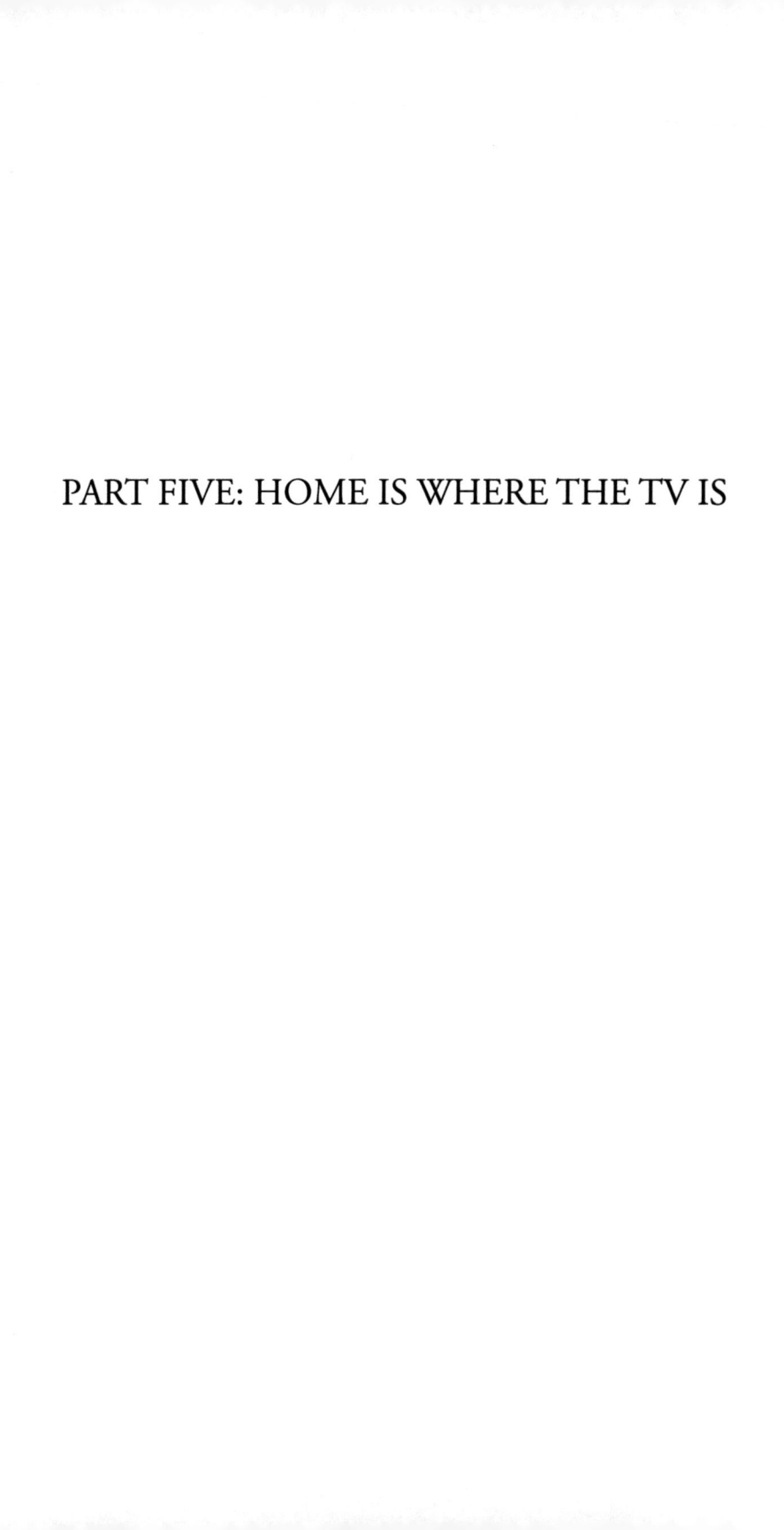

CHAPTER 26

The Helicopter

For the second time in a single day, I walked into Jafford's kitchen, freshly showered, only this time it wasn't in his city loft, but his country place. It was déjà vu all over again as I saw Hector at the stove. He was humming to himself while stirring an enormous pot.

"Corn chowder!" he said, turning toward me. "You like? You like?"

I suppose that on an early Sunday evening in autumn, a bowl of soup would be comforting to most people, but not me. As I watched Hector lift a sheet of freshly baked tortillas out of the oven and place the shells one by one on a cooling rack, I assumed that the soup was bursting with Jafford's favorite Mexican flavors. While I didn't want to be an ungrateful houseguest, the thought of slurping corn chowder made me cringe, though I was sure Hector's recipe didn't call for woodpecker broth as Mason's recipe had for his authentic fertility chowder. I'd feel extra guilty in passing it up considering the quantity Hector was fixing. I wondered why he only used pots that seemed more appropriate for a restaurant's kitchen than for home use. As far as I knew, except for Hector, Jafford lived alone.

"*Especiality* of the *hacienda*!" Hector proclaimed.

Such a happy little fellow, I thought. I didn't want to insult him, but I just couldn't eat. I couldn't help hoping for Jafford's sake as well as Hector's, that the house would soon be filled up with friends who could scarf down that soup. Or maybe he had a set of Tupperware for freezing the leftovers. But personally, after losing the cottage to a fire—as well as losing Mason—I just wanted to be left alone. It wouldn't be too hard, I reasoned to myself, considering the size of Willow Run. I thought I could stall for time to think of a good excuse to skip a place at the table if I asked Hector where Jafford was. I'd set off to find him. Was I finally learning to devise a plan?

"Mr. Jafford, he in TV den," Hector said. "He have tray just for you. I bring soup, okay?" He was smiling at me as if someone had just told a joke, then pointed me in the right direction. "That way! That way!" he said. "You find. Keep going! I come with soup. No worry!"

Hector was right. I had no need to worry, not when I had friends like Jafford who had told the new Burberry Hills fire chief that I would be staying with him after the cottage burned down to the ground. Even Vanilla John, when he was able to reclaim his voice, vouched for me, giving his word that he could not detect any signs of arson. It was *exactly* that sort of criminal mischief that Ol' Vanilla was known to be extra-sensitive to. That aspect of his reputation along with what had now been established as a close association with the infamous neighborhood tennis star, caused the big man wearing the *official* fireman's uniform to say that I was free to leave. He's the one who recommended that I go take a shower to calm myself down. A fire, after all, was quite stressful, especially when it forever obliterates your last known home. After a quick, but grateful hug with Vanilla John, Jafford had helped me into the golf cart where Hector was seated, and the three of us drove up the driveway to the house. We paused inside the gate long enough for Jafford to turn a key and open it, and then we headed home—my new one for the moment—safely behind a locked gate.

Refreshed after my shower, I set out to find Jafford in that great big house. I followed Hector's directions and meandered down a long corridor with a wall of glass on one side overlooking the indoor swimming pool, past the workout room, the sauna, and massage suite, and beyond to where the hall led to a game room. Card tables topped with green felt were set up with Tiffany chandeliers gracefully hanging over each. Three pool tables stood in a row by one wall with a rack of cues; along the other wall were ping pong, crap, and ice hockey tables. The wood floors were covered with oriental rugs so thick, I hesitated to walk over them without removing my shoes—but I did, as a moose head poking through the wall looked on. I hastened my step past the fireplace that was tall enough to stoke with trees that needn't be trimmed down to logs. Then I zigzagged through aisles of leather-upholstered chairs that were arranged theatre-style in front of a movie screen adorned by long, heavy, red velvet curtains on a stage that extended across the entire wall.

I hunted all through that giant playroom, but I still didn't find Jafford.

Then I heard it, that familiar sound that at one time had caused me great concern and even made me groan when I had wondered whether or not it was the kind of laugh induced by marijuana. Now that I knew better, it was a sound that drew me closer. But Jafford was not only hooting and guffawing, he seemed to be cheering. Could there be a tennis match on, I wondered? Had I been the one responsible for keeping Jafford from playing in it? He may have only been my friend for the past twenty-four hours, but I was already indebted to him. If my recent life as an attempted jewel thief interrupted his career, well, I'd never forgive myself. One negative thought tumbled into another. Fear, I realized, was like a house of cards. I was beginning to believe that I just wasn't fit for anyone—not Mason, not myself, not the animals. And now, I wasn't good enough for Jafford.

"Go, Dagmar, go!"

One of the panels of the game room was cracked opened, and I looked more closely at it to see that it was actually a door. Had it been closed, I thought, it would've blended into the wall without anyone knowing it was there. But Jafford's intermittent outbursts had led me in the right direction. As I opened the door wider, I saw him sitting in the den on an overstuffed chair that was draped with a red, white, and blue afghan. A folding tray was set out in front of him with a plate of celery stalks. Alternating between bites, Jafford was sipping a Corona from its bottle while his eyes were glued to the TV.

"Go, Dagmar, go!" he shouted again. Without taking his eyes off the set or turning around, he said to me, "You've got to see this!"

I sauntered closer to him and peered over to the screen of a small television set that looked like it had antennas, the kind I heard were called bunny ears that were used before cable was invented, only the ones on Jafford's TV were pushed down into stubs. Had the set been a month older, I was certain it'd be black and white, not color.

"Go, Dagmar, go!" Jafford kept shouting.

The screen was so small and kind of bulging, like a thick crystal on a cheap watch, making it hard to see what, exactly, he was watching. I squinted and strained my neck out like a turtle, but there was no sound to go along with the grainy picture and the running line of type at the bottom of the screen was too distorted to read.

"That's Dagmar!" Jafford said. "Look at her go!"

With that as a hint, we seemed to be watching an aerial view of Dagmar riding her big black horse—and wearing my black hat—while galloping along the edge of a highway. Mile after mile of trucks, buses, and cars were clogging the lanes. None seemed to be moving. Horns were honking, but they seemed to be routing her on. They certainly weren't making her stop.

Then the screen suddenly split and a news reporter appeared under the headline: *Breaking News.*

"We have just learned the identity of the rider: Dagmar Twist, resident of Burberry Hills, New Jersey … What's that? Excuse me, folks. I've been corrected. Ms. Twist resides in the *Village* of Burberry Hills. She is a recent lottery winner who owned an historic cottage that burned down this afternoon on the grounds of her country estate known as *Swan Crest Farms.*"

The announcer's picture was now replaced with a shot of the remains of the cottage. Smoke was still funneling up to the heavens as a fireman continued squirting it with a hose. As he turned around toward the camera, Jafford started cheering again, followed by a loud whistle he made with his thumb and middle finger. Then he rocked back into his chair, clapping and laughing.

"What's that?" The announcer interrupted himself again. "What kind of animals?"

"He's a movie star!" Jafford said. "Doesn't Ol' Vanilla light up the screen? We'll have to ask Arnold to give him a screen test."

I never had time to notice before, but I supposed that Vanilla John was sort of cute. But he didn't do much for me just standing there stiff as an oak tree and finally holding a hose. He still had his fireman's coat on with the wide yellow stripes across the front and the back, and I assumed he had his big boots on, too. But the camera didn't capture him in his totality. Instead, it was zooming in for a close-up of his face.

"Can you identify the fireman," the announcer was asking someone on the scene. His voice didn't seem as if it were meant for the television audience. He sounded like he was giving a request off-camera, but the microphones were picking up his voice. "What is his name? Did you get it? Ask him. *Ask him*!"

"It's Vanilla John!" Jafford shouted at the TV set. "He's the next big movie star!"

But Vanilla seemed freaked out all over again. Must've been from the television crew this time that was gathering right across the road from Willow Run. We could've run out there in no time flat, but naturally, Jafford needed to keep a distance. I did, too.

"We're just getting word now that although chickens and other farm animals are legally permitted to reside on the grounds, the property has apparently been home to … lions, tigers, bears, kangaroos, elephants, giraffes … and there has apparently been an animal stampede. Animals have been seen running through an opened gate … led by a man … riding a giraffe? … Yes … It's now been confirmed … A wild animal stampede was led by a man on a giraffe … followed by a woman chasing him on a large, black horse …"

"It's all my fault!" I cried. "Everything's my fault. The Blue Diamond Peepers, Laughing Sun's gong, the animals getting loose, and … and … and …" I was sobbing now, only instead of spilling tears out, they seemed to be turning inside me. "And the fire!" I was starting to hiccup. "I'm pathetic!"

Jafford put his Corona down and pushed his folding tray aside. Then he wrapped his arms around me and kissed me on the cheek. He stroked what was left of my chopped off hair and whispered, "Shhhhh! Shhhh!" He walked me over to the sofa, that I couldn't help notice had a few rips. Couldn't he afford to have them reupholstered?

"I've been through tougher times than this," he said. "Or didn't you catch my last match with MacKinnsey? It was an exhibition game. He had been challenging me in the media, probably in a pathetic attempt to stir up new publicity for his long lost career. What else could I do?

I had to accept. But then I blew it. Pow! Imagine what people were thinking when a crotchety old guy, that former bad boy of tennis, whipped my butt? Talk about disgraceful! Now, *that*, Valentina, is what I call *pathetic*."

It worked. Jafford's story stopped my tears from flowing inside or outside of me. Only, I couldn't be certain if he was making a joke or being serious.

"I'm dead serious," he said with a straight face. "Fires happen, Valentina. It was just an accident. But tennis is my game, it's my whole life. And I goofed up! Losing to him was not an *accident* like starting a fire. It was entirely *my fault*."

He had me thinking, but honestly, I couldn't quite figure out what he meant. I mean, tennis is about a little white ball bouncing across a net between two players swatting rackets. How could that possibly be more significant in one's life than causing a cottage to burn to the ground?

"It's *people* that matter, not *things*," Jafford said. "When I lost that match, I let my fans down. And believe me, I have more of them than that foul-mouthed joker."

I never heard or thought of Jafford as someone who'd brag, but I supposed that his fan base, just like other sports statistics, was significant in his line of work.

"Oh, sure, they might've come to see how MacKinnsey would act up. He's always been famous for insulting his opponents and the judges. Even the fans. They eat that stuff up. It's pure entertainment. But when it comes to winning the match, Valentina, they're placing their *faith* in me. They paid their money and took time out of their hectic lives to cheer me on. But I let them down."

He wiped my tears with a paper napkin. I was glad he didn't act more like Mason who'd spit on his sleeve, then offer it to me as if were a moistened towel.

"A cottage can be rebuilt. So can a fan base, I guess. Don't take all that's happened to you over the past twenty-four hours to be entirely your fault. People make mistakes. Mason alone proves that. And accidents *do* happen. But the important matter is that you not feel sorry for a *pile of lumber*. Or *yourself*."

Now that part I was beginning to understand. He was certainly right about my self-pity. I looked up at his crystal blue eyes as he was bowing his head next to mine, trying to get me to uncurl myself from the crux of his broad shoulder. And then I saw it again: *truth*. And I knew at that moment what I needed to do. Just as I had left him on the staircase at the Halloween ball, I had to run out the door. Only this time, I wasn't misguided. I knew that it wasn't Mason whom I wanted to follow me. I actually didn't expect Jafford to follow me either. But I knew I had to bust through the back door of Willow Run, head out to the driveway, and down to River Bend Road. And I needed to do so all on my own. I had no other choice in the matter. I needed to face the scene of the accident. I needed to face the crowd outside. And I needed to face *truth*.

Chapter 27

The Housewives

Night was quickly falling on the quiet neighborhood on River Bend Road. The clocks had been set back and we were losing an extra hour of daylight. I have no idea who the world's time keepers are, but they have their rules, and the rest of us are given no other choice but to follow them. Despite the early darkness, I could see that Hector had wheeled a large garbage can on a trolley out of its fenced-off area near the garage. I grabbed it and walked it down Jafford's long driveway as the full moon overhead lit my way. If I was going to be a long-term houseguest, I wanted to do my share of the chores. I'd been used to that at Swan Crest. Why not now?

In the distance, out on the main road, the bright lights set up by the television crew drew me like a moth to a flame. Only, instead of returning to a scene I had thought of as hell just after I had escaped the cottage fire, I felt I was heading for a place that symbolized peace and truth. No longer were the animals calling out in the darkness of their private wildlife reserve. No longer did I have Mason to protect me from their threatening wrath. And no longer would I hold back truth when I had been the one who had *accidentally* ignited that fire that burned the cottage down to the ground. My actions might've been deliberate in ridding myself of memories of my former life, but I assure you—just as I had assured the new fire chief who had responded to the Twists' alarm system—that the ensuing fire was entirely unintended.

With Vanilla John's endorsement when he, at last, finally managed to speak, along with Jafford's kind offer to provide shelter at Willow Run, I gave the chief my name and was told I was free to go. But my gut told me I'd be back.

Now, I was.

"That's her!" I heard a woman call out. I didn't know her personally, but I did recognize her as being one of the neighbors. "Ask *her* where Mason is now. It's all *her* fault that he left! *She's* the one who probably started that fire!"

A throng of reporters all wearing headsets and holding microphones was suddenly charging me as I stood at the edge of Willow Run's driveway where it met up with the street. I held the garbage can trolley steady, feeling confident that I'd maintain my courage to handle whatever came up. The mayhem transpiring in front of the cameras and the smoldering remains of the cottage looked vaguely familiar, but I felt more empowered now than I had been in the Lincoln Tunnel. My inner strength wasn't from being protected from the crowd by a garbage can on wheels; it was from being armed with *truth*.

"My name is Valentina," I said, proud to be the real me and grateful that I had finally shaken off my Lucy persona. "I lived in that cottage with Mason Figg."

"Who is Mason Figg?"

"Did he set the fire?"

"Is he responsible for letting the animals out?"

"Did he open the front gate?"

"Is he the one who's now riding that giraffe?"

"Did he have help mounting the giraffe?"

"Where is he headed for now?"

"Did he tell you his plans?"

"How did you meet this Mason Figg?"

"Can you describe him?"

"What does he do?"

Questions from the reporters were being tossed at me like a barrage of poisoned-tipped arrows. But instead of cowering behind my garbage can as I might've done when I was Lucy, I stepped in front of it and held up a hand.

"I'll take your questions one at a time," I said, amazed at hearing those words stream out of my mouth. It was as if I had conducted a press conference before. But I knew I wouldn't falter if I just spoke the truth. "Who's first?"

The reporters kept throwing out arrows, but they felt now to have soft rubber tips and feathers that would merely tickle. One after the other, they slung questions at me until a single voice managed to be heard above the rest.

"Who is Mason Figg?"

Suddenly, the crowd was hushed. Only Vanilla John's hose could be heard gushing in the background along with a buzzing generator that must've been giving juice to the lights. As I pondered the question, Mason's sweet face was clearly imbedded in my mind. Our antics together flashed before me, one scene at a time. We were dancing, cooking, sleeping. We were dressing up, quarreling, making up, making love …

And then the answer suddenly came to me. While Mason could no longer be defined by his place in my life as half of a couple, it occurred to me that he could be defined, not by his crimes, which merely represented misguided dalliances with the wrong side of the law, not to mention with his wife or with the heavy influence of greed that abounded at Swan Crest and throughout River Bend Road; Mason could be defined by his true identity, the one that never, ever changes, the one so enmeshed with his soul, it defined him better than any other and served as the single most driving force of his life. Unlike myself who had to search seemingly endlessly to find a true life mission, Mason well knew his.

"Mason Figg is the greatest artist the world will ever know," I said.

Judging by the silence that followed my statement to the press, I guessed that they weren't expecting me to say that. Maybe they were waiting for me to say more. But to my way of thinking, I had said it all.

A woman in the crowd, the one who lived at Queen Hill, began sobbing.

"He is a great artist!" she yelled. "He painted my portrait. He taught me to dance, too."

Then just as the cameras turned to aim at her, the woman started sobbing some more.

"I love Mason Figg! And he loves me!"

She was wailing now, unable to continue. But we all knew by the gush of tears spilling out of her like the water from Tannery Fall, she wanted to say more.

"He is my ... my ... my Jou Jou!"

"*Your* Jou Jou?" Another neighbor cried out. "Mason Figg is *my* Jou Jou!"

"He loves *me*," a third woman chimed in. "Don't call him *your* Jou Jou. I'm getting a divorce! I've already seen my attorney. Mason Figg is my Jou Jou!"

"Who do you think you all are? You're not going to steal my man—or call him *Jou Jou*! Don't think he cares a lick about you, not when I know he's all mine. We dance together every Thursday afternoon at three. Mason Figg is my Jou Jou!"

"You all better stop calling him that!" yet another woman called out.

By that time, there must've been seven neighborhood women on River Bend Road who were joining in the debate while the press conference I had thought I could handle, would be forever remembered me by my one single line—and the breath in my body started backing up again.

I looked beyond the crowd of reporters and neighbors, lights, cameras, and crew, to see Swan Crest in a shadow on top of the hill beyond the Great Wall. Down the road to my left were Queen Hill, Bellechants, and Rosecroft estates. Up the road to my right were the ones known as Grand Fork, Umut, and Twain Ridge. Had Mason given dance lessons and painted portraits at each one?

Standing now on the opposite side of River Bend Road, I was newly reborn with the blessings of a brand-new perspective. No longer did I see the world through the oppressive shadows that seemed forever cast upon me while I had submitted to being an unpaid farmhand. Working as an animal waitress was no longer the place I held in the world; I was no longer playing *Lucy* to Mason's *Ricky* either. I was Valentina with a new set of eyes.

As the reporters fought each other off in bold attempts to separate the Burberrian housewives from each other long enough to persuade them to be interviewed while the cameras were still rolling, Laughing

Sun was crossing the street. With one hand, he seemed to be pressing on his middle; with the other, he was holding a silver metal box.

"I'm proud of you, Valentina," he said, trudging along in short, sliding steps and smiling at me with a wide grin. But unlike his usual spiritual warmth, his face seemed to be ever so slightly, well, *mischievous*. I had never known such an expression from him—except for the time when we were living together and he had secretly placed long stemmed roses all over our little apartment before I had awakened from a good night's sleep—and it hadn't even been our anniversary.

"What's up?" I asked him.

"Oh, not much," he said. Then he started to whistle and roll his eyes.

I knew he wouldn't be holding a secret that he'd refuse to tell me about. I knew him well enough to figure out that he wanted me to guess.

"Should we start with the box?" I asked. "Or should I first ask what you're holding underneath your gown?"

He laughed and said, "That's just like you, Valentina. You're more observant than you sometimes give yourself credit for. You actually do have a curious mind. Not to mention a kind heart. Only you would offer me a choice as to which question I want to address first. Very considerate of you, I'd say. But this time, Valentina, I want you to devise your own rules."

And I had thought it was hard to get straight answers from Mason. Did all the men in my life have a need to play games? Jafford had launched into a lesson about tennis, and now Laughing Sun was dancing around the rules of *his* game. As I debated over which question to address first—his right hand or his left—amidst the din of the reporters and housewives, I couldn't help thinking that I was the one who was normal. The rest of the world, well, it seemed to me that *everyone*, at least in Burberry Hills, was nuts!

"Okay!" I blurted out, much to Laughing Sun's amazement. I don't think he had ever heard me sound so decisive. "The box," I began. "You found some tools and are volunteering to rebuild the cottage yourself?"

"Nope!"

"You found a treasure trove of more *Authentic Baubles?*"

"Nope!"

"The box contains ... another real set of Blue Diamond Peepers?"

"Could be, but somehow I doubt it. I do think Mason left me with the real goods," he said. Then he pointed to the box and whispered, "Evidence! Vanilla John found the strong box in the remains of the window seat in the dining room."

"Evidence?" I asked, cocking my head. "Of what?"

"I have no idea," Laughing Sun said. "But I do know if Mason went to the trouble of hiding a strong box that's locked and then concealed inside a window seat ..."

"... One he knew I'd never see, because of my fear of rodents ..."

"Exactly," Laughing Sun said, looking quite pleased with himself, along with me for figuring out the box he was holding would reveal a lot. At least we were both hopeful. One thing about Laughing Sun, he was eternally the optimist. All that meditation he does has allowed him to be cheerful. He always was that sort of person even when he was still Craig. But just like Craig, he was now ready to tease out an answer to my second question. But I wasn't sure what was underneath his long, flowing ...

"The gong!" I screamed, but only through another whisper. The television cameras set out on the street might've been capturing our every move and every sound bite of the mob scene that seemed to still be in full swing. But it wasn't the time or the place to reveal more than they needed to know about the gong. I could see the edge of the object was forming a perfect circle over his belly and chest. He must've been pressing rather hard with his hand to keep it in place, although I could see the gong's rope was looped over Laughing Sun's shoulders and neck.

"You stole it?" I asked. But he didn't need to answer. I could read "yes" in his eyes and see that despite the discipline only a monk would practice, his arm was starting to tremble holding the gong in place. While no one could miss noticing a monk in a crimson gown, I thought we'd best slip away down Jafford's driveway and dissolve into the night. For once, I was grateful that the hands of clocks were pushed back an hour. Pity, I thought. Couldn't the Time Keepers instruct us all to go back—if not twenty-four hours—then how about three months?

Chapter 28

The Remote

The theatre seats in Jafford's game room were even more comfy than they looked. I wished that we were snuggling in for a Sunday night movie, but instead, as Hector was wheeling in a cart overflowing with plates of nachos, bowls of soup, and a tall pitcher of margaritas, Jafford was testing his equipment.

"Give me the wand," Laughing Sun offered. "I know how these things work."

Some things never change, I thought to myself, as the two grown boys—a monk and a tennis champ—debated over which button to push and who should be in control of the remote.

"Not *that* one," Jafford was saying. "That just opens and closes the curtains on the stage. We need to look for the *open* button, so we can put this sucker in."

The "sucker" he was referring to was a CD we discovered in the strong box after Jafford had pried it open with a tool he normally only used on his tennis racket-stringing machine. He might've known his way around equipment for tennis, but Jafford and Laughing Sun were both fumbling with the tall block of home theatre electronics.

"Does that help, Mr. Jafford?" Hector asked, flipping on the light switch for the room.

"Thank you, Hector," Jafford said. Then he turned to me as I settled into my chair, testing out each of the buttons built into a panel on the arm, patiently waiting for the show to begin. "Where would I be without Hector?"

My seat was reclining too far back, so I pushed another button and it started vibrating. A third button lifted my feet up, while a fourth caused the seat cushions to warm. By the time I hit the one that popped a tray out by my side, Hector was serving me a margarita, but I waved away a plate of nachos and passed on the soup. I still wasn't hungry. I had a feeling that I may be in need of a few more drinks, though, with plenty of alcohol this time. After learning what Mason had kept carefully stored on a CD and locked in a strong box, for him to go through so much trouble, he had to be carefully guarding one whopper of a secret. I knew then that he didn't share all parts of his life with me. But I had to confess, I wasn't sure I wanted to know more than I already did.

As Laughing Sun and Jafford finally hit the right buttons with Hector's patient guidance, the familiar sounds of a conga drum came on, followed by trumpets blaring, then saxophones groaning to a lively Latin beat. The music stopped for a moment, and tinny dings of a cowbell sounded. Then a voice over announced the title of the production:

MASON FIGG
Presents:
THE ESTATES COLLECTION:
BURBERRY HILLS COUNTRY PALACES

Mason's deeply rich voice began narrating a documentary of paintings he had created of each grand country estate dotting River Bend Road, accept for Willow Run. That meant Queen Hill, Bellechants, Rosecroft, Grand Fork, Umut, and Twain Ridge. But the first one, naturally, was Swan Crest. He had painted the Twist estate in all its glory, masterfully depicting the Ice House, Tannery Pond, the waterfall, and all the animals and gardens in oils on canvas. It truly was a magnificent piece—followed by another painting, then another, until each of the paintings in what had been up until now a secret collection was revealed. I couldn't help but be impressed. Nor could my body escape the stirring his voice always inspired deep within me.

While Mason might've galloped away on a tall giraffe, I knew that he still occupied at least a corner of my heart.

That is, until the next segment came on. My stomach began turning.

THE HOUSEWIVES OF RIVER BEND ROAD

Mason's musical score was sounding sexier now as a montage of Burberry Hills housewives was shown, each of them, one after the next, dancing with Mason—or should I say *Jou Jou*? I guessed those women weren't kidding when they had confessed their true love for my former boyfriend. Their feelings showed on their faces and with every movement they made. They were each beaming with light shining out of their eyes. I knew, too, that they played fools in Mason's games. But they were each captured on Mason's video merely smiling and dancing. That's all. Except for the dazzling interior shots of their mansions, that was it. Just dancing. Nothing more intimate than twirling and occasional dips. Not even a kiss. At least not while Mason's camera was rolling.

The next movie that came up was a bit more intriguing:

DAGMAR'S GRAND MASTER PLAN

"Dagmar's?"

The three of us—Jafford, Laughing Sun, and myself—all said her name at once and aloud. Even Hector, I noticed, mouthed her name, but only silently to himself. We all knew that Dagmar didn't have an original thought in her head and couldn't possibly have conjured up anything remotely as complex as a *Grand Master Plan*. Such an elaborate scheme could've only come from Mason. There was no doubt in our minds that it was Mason who had managed to feed her the lines.

Mason had kept the camera on Dagmar with a close-up that was so tight, it cut off the top of her head and the bottom of her chin. Each freckle on her face was so clearly seen, they were countable, and the scars on her face from Cuban Pete's claws seemed to have healed nicely, leaving only faint lines. Occasionally, he panned down to her neck to show the Blue Diamond Peepers hanging from a gold chain. But mostly we saw Dagmar's lips all a-flutter, blathering away about how a theft of her precious gems could be staged and how she could ripoff the insurance company while keeping the original Blue Diamond Peepers safely locked up in yet another safe, one that was apparently tucked away in the Ice House behind a collection of Mason's easels, paints, machinery, and tools. We could view them all in the background of the screen as Mason's camera flashed an occasional glimpse of the room. I couldn't help but notice a glimpse of a baby's cradle propped up on top of a table in the background, just as Dagmar was revealing all the secrets of what had been Mason's Grand Master Plan. I couldn't help wondering if Mason had been constructing furniture for a nursery—and if the part of the Grand Master Plan that Dagmar was explaining, the part about hooking me into the shenanigans, was really Mason's idea or Dagmar's alone.

Oh, cradles and babies and cameras and plans! I guess I should've been glad that Mason wanted to keep me shielded from his many secrets. He wanted me to be left in the dark about the housewives on River Bend Road, too. My head was spinning with all these new truths of my former boyfriend's world and so many questions that would never be asked, let alone answered. Maybe Dagmar was the one who insisted I be used as a ... What is the word a criminal would use for *dope*? The name Mason used to use to describe Dagmar? Oh, yes: *pigeon*. I no longer wished to play that particular role.

It wasn't clear as to whom Dagmar was speaking to on camera, for Mason never said a word. But we all knew that only Mason could be the one who was holding the camera—or perhaps he had one of his carved ducks do the dirty work for him, recording every word Dagmar said. However he managed to film her, he steered clear of being recorded himself.

I closed my eyes and shuddered. Could I still be having a battle between my heart and my head? After all I was viewing in Jafford's home theatre? If I had thought that Mason couldn't have sunken any lower, I was wrong. Just as Dagmar had finally stopped talking and Mason held onto the shot of her grinning, quite pleased with herself and her proposed insurance scam, the screen faded to black.

We were all silent and still. None of us said a word as we contemplated what we'd just seen and heard. Then the screen lit up again, fading in with a shot of dawn breaking over Tannery Pond. Steam was rising from the water. The ducks were quacking. Birds soared overhead. A bevy of twenty-two swans floated in a line across the falls as the title and credits came on:

SWAN DIVING
Starring:
Natasha Micochevprokova
and
Bliss the Naughty Mute Swan

    Jafford and Laughing Sun raced each other to grab the wand, but Hector beat them to it. He hit the fast-forward button just as Mason's camera was panning down to a shot of Natasha posing on a rock at the base of the falls, looking seductively up to the swans and licking her bright red lips with an unnaturally long tongue. The spikes of her red high heels were …

    I didn't think I could've watched one more frame. I heaved a sigh of relief as the screen went dark again. But somehow that familiar tremor inside me started quaking again as soon as I saw the title of Mason's next piece on the film:

I LOVE VALENTINA

    This time it was a montage of *me*! Mason seemed to have spliced together scenes he'd filmed from some of our happiest times together. Only, unlike the video he'd shot of Dagmar, it was clear that Mason was the one holding the camera. His voice occasionally could be heard, but it was mostly only me on the screen.

    He opened with a scene in our kitchen at the cottage, the time he had placed a tall chef's cap on my head that puffed up like a popover. We were melting slabs of chocolate he'd supposedly brought back from Switzerland after returning from the annual diamond dealers' trade show, and I was stirring them in the double-boiler with a long wooden spoon. He kept stealing samples from the pot and I had thought it was funny how he kept kissing me after each taste, leaving extra wet kisses all over my face. It wasn't until he could no longer contain his laughter as he picked up his camera from its tripod and aimed it on me, that he told me that his kisses left dabs of melted chocolate on my cheeks, nose, and forehead. And I had thought he was just being affectionate! We had a good laugh after I got him back, covering his face with chocolate kisses of my own.

It was that unusually playful quality Mason always embraced that got my attention when we first met. He was as playful as one of the monkeys at Swan Crest—and just as hairy. I was dazzled by how naturally he could infuse joy into any situation—and how he knew how to dance, too. My Mason had rhythm. I might've been thrown at first by his boy-like qualities; it was as if he were still a kid, the kind who'd chew gum and carry a sling shot in his back pocket, the kind who dreamed big and viewed the world through a rosy lens. He was quite musical, too. Banging a conga drum and singing a few rounds of "BaBaBaLu" always made me smile. How many full-grown men can link humor and romance? It was a rare combination only Mason could pull off. And Ricky Ricardo, I suppose. Or perhaps I should say Desi Arnaz. Thanks to that band leader's on-screen persona, along with Lucille Ball's, Mason and I had role models to look up to. But considering the entire world knows that TV couple, our role-playing wasn't all that special. It was hardly unique. In a sense, Mason and I were more ordinary than we had liked to believe. After all, we hadn't really devised original identities; we just borrowed two that already existed, which didn't make us unusual, but … Dare I say it? If the whole world could recite lines from *I Love Lucy* episodes, would that make Mason and I actually *normal*?

I'll admit, sometimes I wasn't sure who any of us truly were, but I do know that it didn't take too long to warm up to Mason's style of humor. It was his charm, his magic, his attitude toward life that caused me to always feel happy and free to be myself. What better proof is there of true love? Laughter seemed to me to be a good start. And for a long time, our combination worked. We were inseparable, at least in the beginning. I never once felt that I needed to try too hard to impress him; I thought he liked me for my natural self. But through his playful games, he brought out another side I never knew existed. He brought out the *Lucy* in me.

From the beginning, I knew that Mason wasn't exactly the type who'd ever expect me to play a traditional role, but our love naturally grew and traditional roles seemed to be the next step in our relationship evolution. We both wanted to have children. We wanted to create a family of our own. We wanted to be together always, which meant that our roles would expand to be not only spouses for each other, but parents, too. But no matter what happened through the course of our life, we were friends first. Our love might have quickly blossomed, but Mason had always said that our friendship and romance were simultaneous events. There was no question about it, Mason did have a good side to him. Perhaps Laughing Sun was right when pointing out that qualities of good and evil can exist in one person at the same time.

My head was started to spin again as I digested the wisdom of Laughing Sun's understanding of the world and the human creatures that reside on this planet, and watched the next segments of Mason's I LOVE VALENTINA video. I couldn't help but recall how happy we had once been, seeing myself dancing in front of the fireplace at the cottage as Mason cranked up the music. For the first time since I had realized I was a bad dancer back at Jafford's restaurant in the city, I realized now that I was too hard on myself. I *did* have rhythm. And even if I didn't, as I watched myself spinning around the living room as Mason filmed each step, one truth became abundantly clear: *I was happy*. Why wouldn't I have thought we were in love?

I watched myself up on the screen reading the Sunday edition of *The New York Times* while lounging on a chair under an umbrella alongside the waterfall. I was sipping a mint iced tea that Mason had fixed for me, while two male ducks were protecting a female from the rest of the flock in Tannery Pond, following her as she waddled right up to me on my lounge. It was as if Mason had trained them to do so for a part in his movie of me. But I knew that unlike normal ducks who'd keep their distance from most humans, Swan Crest ducks were uninhibited. They were accustomed to Dagmar feeding them each morning and night, and so they must've figured that Mason and I were friendly, too.

Reading by the waterfall was one of the pleasures I had discovered while living at the cottage with Mason. I'll grudgingly admit that I liked how that particular trio of ducks would visit me on my lounge. I was hoping they were safe now after the fire. I don't think I ever fully appreciated the rare pleasures of nature while I was living at Swan Crest. It was funny how magical it all seemed as I watched the video and sipped my third margarita.

"Thank you, Hector!"

I smiled as I saw myself on screen reaching out of the tiny hinged window for an apple from the tree—then remembered that Mason's fireman's raincoat was now lying on the bare branches. Would it stay there forever? Could a strong wind ever blow it away? Would Mason ever climb up the tree again to retrieve it? Would he ...

It was no use wondering about such things. Speculation can be a waste time. I had far more practice in that particular activity than I cared to. I wanted to stop trying to figure out if love is ever genuine or merely a masquerade. If it does truly exist, is it fleeting? Or does love ever last for an entire lifetime? Didn't Mason and I at least have good intentions? I think the old saying is correct about how they lead to hell—or in my case, the Lincoln Tunnel.

Some questions in life are never fully answered, I guess—like the one Mason was posing on the video. He finally stood in front of the camera himself while I was no longer in view. He was kneeling down on the grass while wearing a tuxedo, as that female duck was poised on my chase lounge. The waterfall was in the frame. The two male ducks and swans were there, too. Other than the waterfowl, Mason was alone.

"I love you, Valentina, with all my heart," he said to the duck on the lounge. "I could never live without you. You'll always be the best part of my life. Will you marry me?"

As the three of us—Jafford, Laughing Sun, and me—sat in silence, Mason concluded his proposal and the screen lit up with a sunset over the falls. His voice was doing a fairly decent imitation of Ricky Ricardo announcing in his Cuban accent, "This has been a Mason Figg Production." As the music started revving up again with THE END flashing upon the screen, Jafford reached for my hand.

"You know, Valentina," he began, "in his own crazy, knuckle-headed way, I think Mason really did love you. Probably still does.

Maybe he just couldn't break out of his fantasy world long enough to follow through with that proposal in real life and without the camera rolling. Maybe he was going to leave Bull Face for you. You've got to admit, seemed to be going that way. I know, too, that you, Valentina, are capable of offering unconditional love. You must be. I mean, you put up with his antics, yet still have a soft spot. For him?"

Jafford was ever so slightly shaking his head, but I was shaking mine, too. Unconditional love? I couldn't figure him out—Mason or Jafford. It seemed to me that while Mason had his dance card filled, and I knew he wanted to keep the secret part of his life carefully sealed off to me, "for my own good," as I imagined he would say, Jafford was an entirely different animal. He could show me great warmth and friendship that bordered on being romantic—yet he had this way about him that respected my feelings for Mason. It was as if he could be objective about another man who had a firm grasp of my heart, while he himself tucked away any feelings he had for me—just as a fine Southern gentleman would. Jafford had honor.

Or maybe he was just shy.

"I really did mean it when I said you were the champion of my heart," Jafford said as he pulled out a diamond ring from his pocket. "When I know what I want, I go for it. And I want you."

I gasped. All this time I'd been hoping to conceive, when I should've put first things first. Then again, Mason and I always agreed on at least one thing: our romance never had rules.

"I think you're onto something," Laughing Sun chimed in. "Mason did, after all, go through a lot of trouble to assure that I received a very valuable set of Blue Diamond Peepers. He could've just swiped the gong if he wanted it that much. But he actually left quite a monetarily powerful substitute in its place. It was as if he thought he owed me something more than the cost of the gong. After all, Valentine, he took you away from me. You're far more valuable than a hunk of metal and a pair of rare gems combined. I think he does have a conscience. I think he did truly love you. And I believe that he gave me something that I could never pay for myself. Not in this lifetime. He must've really honored you over money. And in the earthly world, that's saying a mouthful."

I looked at Laughing Sun as he contemplated money. Monk or not, he knew firsthand how hard it is to make. At the rate he was going, he'd be working throughout his next ten lifetimes as a Guacamole Man before the cost of his foundation could be amassed. But Laughing Sun also knew the value of love. But I wished now he'd shut up.

"Yup," Laughing Sun rambled on some more. "I think Jafford's onto something. Mason did love you. Probably still does."

I tuned out Laughing Sun as I watched Jafford get down on one knee. I even stopped counting up all the money in my head that Mason had tossed over to Laughing Sun in the form of the authentic set of Blue Diamond Peepers. I never knew about such things—money, gongs, and animals, not to mention Laughing Sun's spiritual beliefs or unusual ways of expressing himself. *Monetarily powerful substitute?* And *earthly world?* I suppose Laughing Sun's world is *spiritual* where *love*, not money, is wealth and therefore powerful, but my brain was already on overload. I didn't want to add translation to its burden. I was drowning with too many uncertainties as it was.

But there were two things I was certain of: All those lonely housewives trapped in their grand country estates were nothing more to Mason than toys. I was the real thing. I was his true love, at least for a time. I thought to myself that deep in my heart, I always knew that I was different. After all, I used to be *Lucy*.

I was also certain of my answer to Jafford's question as Laughing Sun and Hector looked on.

"Yes, Jafford," I said as I reached out my hand. But I didn't know enough about engagement traditions and held out my right.

"Left hand! Left hand," Laughing Sun and Hector whispered while waving at me until I switched.

"There's no denying what I feel for you, Valentina," Jafford said. His voice was breaking up. His eyes were beaming. "I've been all around the world many times, and I've never met anyone who makes me feel as alive as you do. And, well, *happy*."

My heart was thumping as Jafford slipped the ring on my finger—the one on my *left* hand.

"I want to give you something you deserve. I want you to have a forever home. I've been hoping you'd want one with me, Valentina, because you are ..."

I was crying now, but I could still see Jafford through my tears. I could sense that Laughing Sun and Hector were tearing up, too, as we all waited to hear Jafford get his words out.

"You are the champion of my heart!"

CHAPTER 29

The Snobs

It's amazing how one simple word can change the course of your true life's path and transform a relationship in an instant—and I don't only mean the word "yes" after Jafford proposed. There was one more word that spun my world in a whole new direction. It was something Dagmar said. I never thought I'd ever hear such a word, especially from her.

It was about six months after I had settled in at Willow Run. Jafford and I had been enjoying our engagement bliss, spending all our time together. We were inseparable. I'd accompany him to his tennis tournaments and even his workouts with his coach then he'd shower and change, and we'd go shopping. I quickly grew quite fond of private showings at fancy boutiques, where the doors would be locked to the public, but not us. While I always knew Jafford was special, I never imagined I'd feel special, too, as shopkeepers pulled out one outfit after the next and told me which colors and styles would best compliment my eyes and tall frame. Before I could decide on which one to buy, Jafford paid for them all and had Hector load up the Bentley with the bags. When we'd get back home we'd stock our his-and-hers walk-in closets with our latest fashions, my favorite ones being from Ralph Lauren.

Then one sunny, spring afternoon, I was rolling the garbage trolley down to the street and Jafford was setting out for a quick jog, when Dagmar, long after she had been released from jail for the havoc she had caused on the New Jersey Turnpike, spotted us from across River Bend Road. In her usual way, she zoomed over to the edge of our driveway, bombarding me with insults. She actually scolded me for resuming my old habit of chewing gum, and then started bragging about how she had once popped a bubble with a pencil, leaving gum all over the face of a show-off kid. It happened, she said, in a foster home.

"That was you?" I asked.

I felt my eyes growing wider. I was instantly transported back in time. I pictured myself as a young girl, too frightened to cry, when my celebrated bubble suddenly burst. I've been haunted by the sound of an evil laugh ever since; it was hardly a friendly giggle that filled the room as I picked gum from my hair, eyes, and cheeks. It was more like a sound of wicked delight. My glory as a champ was short-lived. Humiliation set in. It was then that I knew why pride is counted as one of the seven deadly sins.

But that was many years ago. I had grown up. Dagmar had, too. I had more confidence than I ever had before. With Jafford jogging in place next to me on the driveway, I had sufficient reinforcement to look Dagmar square in the eye.

"I was that kid," I said. "I was the Bubble Blowing Champion of my foster home."

Dagmar gasped. "Foster home? You were an orphan, too?"

And then she said it, that one, simple word that changed the course of the rest of my life.

"Sister!"

Yes, that's exactly what Dagmar and I call each other now. We like telling people that we're sisters. Maybe we don't share the same gene pool, but foster kids have a special connection all their own. I guess the fact that she had been one, too, had made her paranoid about anyone giving birth to unwanted kids, and that was why when we first met, she didn't want me to move into the cottage.

The truth was that Dagmar herself would've made a devoted and kind-hearted mother. It may not have seemed that way, especially considering that she had spent time in the slammer for riding her horse on the highway, tying up traffic for miles. But believe me, she paid her debt to society. And after all I went through with her, I've had a lot of time to wade through the garbage that flies out of her mouth. Now I know that deep down, she's not shallow. She's actually quite caring. The way she cares for those dumb animals is testament to that fact. Dagmar would never stand by to see anyone—two-legged, four-legged, winged, hoofed, or finned—be cast aside and left all alone. Snapping turtles were the only exception to that rule.

"You were that bossy girl up on the top bunk," I said, wagging my finger. "And I …"

"You were that annoying little brat on the bottom! Ugh!"

"You were *One*," I said.

"That's right! I came first. Don't forget it," Dagmar warned. "You were *Three*," she remembered. "With six of us crammed into one puny bedroom, I had to get stuck with one who snores!"

"Snores?" I questioned. "I don't snore."

Jafford stopped jogging in place. His face was turning colors. He looked at me, seeming to hold something back. His lips were pressed tight together, but I could tell he was smiling. Then all of a sudden, he let out the loudest popcorn laugh I've ever heard out of him.

"Why are you laughing?" I asked him. But he didn't answer. He just put his arms around me, and gave me a big kiss. Then he and Dagmar started playfully snoring and laughing out loud all over again—at me!

I had no choice but laugh along with them. I had to face the truth: I was a natural, born snorer. I must've inherited the snoring gene. And with that honesty about myself—along with a revelation that I actually had a gene pool whether I knew my birth parents or not—all our troubles in childhood and adulthood vanished as if they had never happened at all. Bubble gum was now our glue—at least that's what I believed for a couple of minutes as the three of us were standing on the side of River Bend Road. It didn't matter that we were surrounded by mansions with names; we could've been standing by a row of cardboard boxes instead, because our joy was free. It didn't cost a dime. It simply made no difference where we lived, not when I realized I had never really laughed so freely before.

Those new sounds emanating out of my mouth were not entirely familiar. I might have been capable of sputtering out a gleeful twitter now and again, but I had never actually experienced a hardy, full-bellied laugh.

Jafford and Dagmar noticed.

"What the heck do you call that?" Dagmar asked. "You sound like an old tracker that's too cold to start up. I don't know, sister. You may need a tune up. Better see a doctor."

"Or a good mechanic," Jafford added.

In my bliss, through the tears of hilarity filling my eyes, in between my hoots and snorts, I thought that the two of them were just saying things to be funny. And so I kept on laughing and snorting louder and goofier, I guess. I had no idea it would soon cause me so much grief, the kind that could only be possible in a place like Burberry Hills.

"You keep that up, sister, and my cows may retract their utters. And the chickens may stop laying eggs!"

Cows! Chickens! It was so ridiculous how Dagmar managed to work animals into every conversation. I couldn't help but to laugh even louder than I had before.

"Would you knock it off already?" Dagmar said, waving her hairy arms. Then she pointed across the road to Tannery Pond. "Look what you're doing to my swans!"

A perfect line of twenty-two swans was peering over the crest of the falls. The long, metal wire was still strung across to prevent them from toppling over and onto the sharp, black marble below. As I shaded the sun from my eyes with my hand, I could see them turning to one side, then leaning their long necks in unison, before gliding swiftly around and retreating further back across the pond.

"See! See!" Dagmar said. "You scared them away with your pathetic, cheesy honks!"

But even Dagmar's quick temper was funny to me. One thought was colliding into another like bumper cars piling up and I apparently unleashed one too many *pathetic cheesy honks* for Dagmar's taste.

"What is the matter with you," she said. "Don't you care about my swans?"

And that's when I made my mistake, one that threatened to tear away the only sister I knew. I just wish now that I didn't have a compulsion to be so honest.

"Dagmar, I have something to confess," I started. "I never actually aimed my paddle directly for the snapping turtles' heads."

It was Dagmar's turn to have her eyes grow wide. But I guess I didn't realize what calamity would follow. As I said, I had thought we were all having such a wonderfully whacky, frivolous time.

"What? You purposely endangered my swans?" Dagmar said. Her voice was husky. Her eyes were no longer wide, but slit. She was pushing up the sleeves of her sweatshirt that had slipped down past her elbows and over her gorilla arms, causing her bangles to clang around her flashy Rolex watch. "How dare you!" she bellowed, but I still thought she was joking around.

"Slap! Slap! Slap!" I was hollering, banging imaginary pond water with an imaginary paddle. "Oops! I missed! That's one less snapping turtle for a simmering pot of Victory Stew!"

"I'm going to feed you to those turtles!" Dagmar yelled. "Let's see how you like *your* twig legs bitten off!"

Before Dagmar could tackle me to the ground, Jafford lifted me high over his shoulders. I was kicking my *twig* legs freely in the air. At least I had finally stopped laughing.

"Hand her over *now*," Dagmar demanded. "I'm going to toss her skinny butt into Tannery Pond!"

Jafford was twirling me like baton around his neck and broad shoulders. Our secluded little world on River Bend Road was spinning in front of my eyes, but I could tell that Dagmar's short legs must've been getting a workout. Her face was bobbing halfway up Jafford's back. She was growling.

"I wouldn't mind a dip myself," Jafford said. "Sun's hot. Let's all go cool off."

He swiveled me around, so that he was carrying me fireman-style. I could see the pavement under his feet change to green grass as my head dangled over his shoulder. His long, strong arms braced my thighs close to his chest, keeping me steady and preventing me from kicking. But I could still scream.

"Jaaaaaaf-foooord!"

I was bobbing around as he climbed the base of the Far Hill, until he finally came to a stop by an old, towering willow tree. I could feel his chest heaving in and out. I figured we were at the edge of the pond. I could hear water rushing over the falls.

"She deserves a ride over those black slabs of marble," Dagmar said. Then I heard her wicked delight once more.

"Nah!" Jafford said. "She'd shatter into a million pieces, Dagmar. What's the matter with you?" he asked, using her favorite expression against her. "We'd have to put her back together. Too messy. I say we just plunge her into the pond. We'll dunk her. Head first. What do you say?"

"I say we tie her to that willow tree and set fire to her—just as she did to my cottage," Dagmar said.

"Nah!" Jafford said. "You'd lose a perfectly good tree, Dagmar. That's a fine-looking willow. You couldn't buy one that size. It'd take an entire century to get one to grow so big."

"Jaaaaaaf-foooord!"

I was pounding his bottom with two fists. I didn't want to be dunked or torched. But Jafford was heaving me off his shoulder and swinging me around. He gave me a playful spank.

"Jaaaaaaf-foooord!"

He twisted me, so that I was facing the water. Then he bounced me up high in the air, while still holding me at the waist as if to get a firmer grip—and I reached out to latch onto a bunch of long branches of that thick and sturdy willow tree.

"Ahhhhhhhgha!"

My pathetic honks, goofy snorts, and silly guffaws were distant memories. Instead, I was screaming. A blue heron standing on a boulder dropped his fish, and flew away as I swung through the air. But I was dangerously close to the edge of the falls. Even Dagmar recognized the gravity of my precarious position. The wire that was strung across the pond was never intended to protect *me*.

"What's the matter with you," Dagmar shouted, no longer playing her mean games. "Just let go when you swing over the pond."

"I can't swim," I cried.

I was bluffing. I could swim. I knew how to breaststroke, sidestroke, backstroke, and crawl. Thanks to the Fresh Air Fund, I had gone to Camp Nel-K-Mar in the Catskill Mountains five summers in a row when I was a kid. But I didn't dare reveal that fact to Dagmar—or even Jafford. If I told them the real reason why I refused to get wet, they'd both laugh in my face.

"The pond's only two feet deep," Jafford shouted. "Three at best. Maybe four. Just ask the turtles."

Dancing with Jou Jou

"Ahhhhhhhgha!"

I was losing my grip on the willow vines. I could've used Tarzan to rescue me. I knew I could no longer count on Jafford or my *sister*, not when the two of them were plotting against me. They were in cahoots!

"Great," I heard Dagmar grunt. "I finally get a sister, and she thinks she's a chimpanzee."

Death by cracking my head on black marble slabs in the waterfall? Or by snapping turtles who'd eat me whole in the pond? It was one heck of a choice. Either way, I was determined to stay dry.

"What's the matter with you," Dagmar kept saying. "You've been in the water before."

"Not without my mud boots," I said, still bluffing.

"Your shoes will do," Dagmar said. "Just let go! Aim for the pond! Don't be stupid!"

"Here, I'll help you," Jafford said, racing into the water.

His long arms weren't long enough to reach me as I swung to-and-fro. And I was running out of excuses. Bluffing was as unfamiliar to me as my pathetic, cheesy honks. I had no choice. I was losing my grip on the vines. I needed to tell Dagmar and Jafford the truth.

"I'm wearing Ralph Lauren!" I shouted. My voice was so loud, a flock of sparrows showered out of the tops of the willow. "Dry clean only!"

"Great," Dagmar grunted. "You can take an orphan out of a cottage, but put her in Ralph Lauren and she's a snob for life."

"Snob?" I yelled as the vine kept swinging over the pond and the falls. I was quickly regaining my strength. Outrage has advantages. "You're the snob, Dagmar!"

Finally, I said what I had been thinking for a long time. With all that had happened, I guess I had buried my anger, absorbing the resentment I had built up for Dagmar. I suppose I overlooked it after Jafford and I fell in love, not wanting to ruin the new joy that had finally entered my life. It wasn't until I was hanging by the wiry threads of a willow tree over Tannery Falls that *truth* finally oozed out. It was a gusher.

"You treated me like a hired-hand when I lived in that cottage, Dagmar!" I said, kicking my feet in the air and twirling around.

"You *were* a hired-hand!" Dagmar shot back.

"Well, maybe I was. But you treat your animals better than you treated me!"

I was proud that my final words were honest and that the last remnants of bitterness I had held onto for Dagmar were finally being released. I was no longer scared. In fact, standing up to Dagmar made me feel grown-up—even if my feet were pumping air.

"My animals *are* better than you!" Dagmar hollered.

"See? I'm right!" I said. "You would never let any of your animals move into a cottage infested with rodents!"

I couldn't bring myself to say the words "rats" and "mice." It had been bad enough to hear them scampering up to the sleeping loft through the walls and humping in the eves. Calling them "rodents" somehow seemed more scientific and, therefore, less creepy.

"Anyone who agrees to live in an old, broken down cottage," Dagmar retorted, "deserves to live with rats and mice."

She said those dreaded words. Just hearing them aloud made me cringe. I glanced down to Jafford in the pond. I could see him scratching his head. He probably didn't know whether to laugh or break up with me for formerly being a chump. I needed to prove that I no longer was.

"You should be the one to wear Ralph Lauren, Dagmar," I said. "Maybe that way, we wouldn't notice your hairy, gorilla arms!"

"Hairy, gorilla arms?" Dagmar echoed.

She was scrunching up her face, squinting as I kept swinging on my vine. Not since I had made a surprise appearance in her master bedroom on the night of Swan Crest Farms' First Annual Masquerade Ball, had I ever known Dagmar to be at a loss for words. Back then, I had even given her the power to order my long hair cut short—and bleached! While I might've secretly loved my new look, I'd never admit it. Not to Dagmar. But if I were about to die—and I didn't care then if I did—I needed to change my karma. I had to insult her back.

"Yeah," I said. "Your hairy, gorilla arms need a good waxing!"

Jafford looked like his popcorn laugh wasn't sure to pop or not.

"*Arm* snob! That's what you are!" Dagmar said. "You judge people by their arms!"

"Well, you're an animal snob," I said. "You think animals are better than people!"

"What's the matter with you?" Dagmar asked. "Animals *are* better than people!"

"You only think so, because you have the arms of a gorilla!"

"I'd rather be an *animal* snob than an *arm* snob like *you*, "Dagmar said.

"Well, I'd rather be an *arm* snob than an *animal* snob like *you*."

"Arm snob!"

"Animal snob!"

"Snob!"

"Snob!"

"Snob!"

"Snob!"

We took turns calling each other "snob" until we seemed to be singing a duet. After a while, we sounded as if we were in agreement, singing in chorus. I needed to be one up on Dagmar. Maybe I lived with a champion athlete like Jafford long enough to have acquired a thirst to win. Or maybe it was time for my buried resentment to be finally be teased out. I knew I possessed one thing that Dagmar lacked. I was finally proud of my gene pool—whomever it came from—when I belted out:

"Snoooooooooooooooooooooob!"

Had my voice been any louder, it would've stopped the water from spilling out of Tannery Pond. But at least it was powerful enough to make Dagmar shut up. Unfortunately, her silence was temporary. My battle cry was apparently enough to unleash her inner fury.

"Freak!" Dagmar said. "They could've used that hellish scream as a siren on 9/11."

I don't know where Dagmar was on that tragic day, but I had a feeling the collapse of the World Trade Center's twin towers had made a lasting impression. Jafford had told me how she often declared herself to be a proud American and always displayed enormous flags all over Swan Crest on the Fourth of July. I guess she was the patriotic type.

"Not only are you a freak," Dagmar said, "you're superficial!"

"What?" I said, still dangling over the water. "Me? I'm not the one who's superficial!"

"Oh, yes you are, Valentina," Dagmar said, using my name. I suppose then my "sister" status had been suspended. "I bet you're not even registered to vote. You probably care more about your looks than who's running this country."

She was right.

"A superficial freak-snob!" she said. "Oh, you must wear your precious designer labels, now that you've hooked a rich, tennis celebrity like Jafford Ames and live at Willow Run." She was posing like a supermodel. "Ralph Lauren! Ralph Lauren! Ralph Lauren," she said, taunting me. "I suppose you're going to palm yourself off as a Republican now and claim that you're from Connecticut. Why don't you move there? That's where they wear Ralph Lauren. It's the state's uniform."

Connecticut? I pondered the thought of an entire state population dolled up in Ralph Lauren, while Dagmar was wound up. She was strutting around the knolls of the Far Hill as if she were demonstrating the signature walk of a supermodel. Only, with her meadow stompers and jerky movements, she looked like Herman Munster.

"And how many people do you know who wear make-up to collect eggs?" Dagmar asked me, now standing still long enough to strike a few poses. "Don't you like your face as it is?"

"I don't *know* anyone else who collects eggs," I said. "I'm not exactly a member of the Egg Collectors of America Union. But now that you mention make-up, Dagmar, you could use a little blush and lipstick."

A mist was spraying from the waterfall, causing my mascara to run. I must've looked more like a raccoon than a chimpanzee by then. My foundation cream and blush were dripping off my cheeks. But I wasn't exactly in a position to fix my make-up—nor was I accustomed to discussing cosmetics. They were simply part of my daily grooming. I no more talked about them, than I did about deodorant, hand cream, or corn starch to keep my feet from chafing inside my mud boots.

"And would it kill you, Dagmar," I went on, "to tweeze those thick brows of yours? You're not exactly Brooke Shields, you know, or Ali McGraw."

"Who?"

I was picking up as much momentum as my willow vine swing. I was proud to know a few things that Dagmar did not. I bet she never went to the movies or watched television, not when she had so many animals to care for all by herself at Swan Crest.

"Although, I must tell you, Dagmar," I called out, wanting to taunt her, "your brows do coordinate well with your hairy arms!"

Dagmar was cackling. For the first time ever, I realized that her deep, rich laugh matched her bank account. I wondered if you could figure out a person's wealth by vocal qualities alone, or by posture. Dagmar's was confident. She was standing with her feet firmly planted on the bank of the pond while shaking her head back and tossing her long hair over her shoulders. Just as I was thinking that maybe her gene pool outclassed my own, it was starting to occur to me that the stronger her armor on the outside, the more fearful she probably was on the inside. But I had no time to consider the theory further, not when my grip on the willow vines was slipping again.

"My animals don't care what I look like," Dagmar boasted. "They like me for who I am. Maybe if you were more genuine, you'd get along with them better."

"More genuine?" I cried. "Me?"

"Yes, you, missy!" Dagmar said. "You always had to get all gussied up at the crack of dawn. Who were you trying to impress in the hen house, my rooster?"

"Gussied up?" I echoed. "What are you talking about, Dagmar? I clumped around in mud boots all over Swan Crest."

But Dagmar wasn't listening to me as she started walking in circles. She was flapping her arms as if they were wings and jerking her head around as if she were a chicken. But I knew that she was impersonating me!

"*Oh, Mr. Rooster,*" she said in an unflattering, high voice. "*My name's Valentina. Do you like me? Don't you think I'm hot? Do you want to peck off my Ralph Lauren designer clothes then hump me like one of your chickens?*"

"Say something, Jafford," I yelled. "Stick up for me!"

"Could you hang on, Valentina?" he said. "I want to see if Dagmar lays an egg."

"Jaf-fooooooord!"

I heard the branch of the willow tree crack. I was losing altitude.

"Ahhhhhhhgha!"

I was still kicking the air, not the water, but that last scream was so loud, I was swinging dangerously over the falls. The willow branch seemed to be breaking …

"Valentina!" Jafford called.

"Sister!" Dagmar cried. She finally stopped clucking.

The willow branch snapped …

I took my last breath …

"Don't look down," Jafford said. "Not until I say jump. Just aim yourself toward me."

My newly acquired bravado quickly turned. I followed Jafford's suggestion. I looked up instead of down. Monkeys were squealing. I hadn't noticed that they had been watching us from the top of the willow. Now they were scrambling over one another out of the vines just as I was swinging back over the pond. Jafford caught me by the thighs.

"I've got you," he said, holding me steady.

"You're only a foot away from me," Dagmar said. She was actually so close, she could reach out and grab me. "Either take my hand, or take the plunge. Make a decision!"

And then she said something I never thought I'd hear from her big mouth.

"Please!"

I couldn't reach her, but I knew that I had won. I could die happy. Before I did, I was squirming around so much I must've yanked Jafford off balance. Or maybe the force of the water at the tip of the falls was strong enough for both of us—me still clinging to the vine and Jafford in the water—to be pulled dangerously close to the edge, unable to recover.

I could hear the *whoosh* of water rushing like Niagara Falls …

I could no longer see Jafford's head above the pond …

The willow branch was hanging lower and lower …

I was suspended in air over the falls …

One swing in the wrong direction and I could be mashed to pieces—along with Jafford. I hung onto the vines for dear life. I changed my mind. I wasn't ready to die …

"You win!" Dagmar shouted. "I do have hairy, gorilla arms! I'll let you slather them with hot wax and yank the hair out from the roots—

anything!" Dagmar continued. "Just don't die! I want my one and only sister alive. And in one piece."

I had no time to savor the view or my victory over Dagmar. My shoulders were hurting. I thought my arms were about to pop from their sockets—not to mention the branch from the tree.

"Don't you dare go over the falls!" Dagmar shouted. "Let go of that vine! I order you to jump into that pond! Now!"

"Ahhhhhhhgha!"

"Valentina!" Jafford yelled, reaching up further to secure me at the hips.

I could hear Dagmar splashing into the water. By the sound of her grumbling, it seemed she was holding onto Jafford, while he was latched onto me—and the three of us were still nearing the drop-off point of Tannery Falls. Geese were honking, ducks were quacking, and the familiar blue heron was soaring through the sky, while a giant turtle crawled out of the water and onto a boulder on the other side of the pond, seemingly watching our show.

"Ahhhhhhhgha!"

Finally, I had no choice. Ralph Lauren or not, I let go of my vine and slipped into the two feet of water near the edge of the waterfall at Tannery Pond—three feet, tops.

When I opened my eyes, Jafford was cradling me under the willow, kissing my forehead and smiling, while Dagmar was pulling leaves from her hair and leaning between the sun and my face.

"Okay, okay! I give in! I give up!" she said. "Go back to your cheesy honks. I never want to hear screams like *that* out of you *ever* again."

She was dripping wet, but her Rolex was glistening in the bright sun.

"Dagmar," I said. "Your watch!"

She looked at her Rolex and shrugged. Then she ripped that overpriced hunk of metal studded with flashy rocks off her wrist, and tossed it high into the air. It landed on the giant snapper who had been sunning himself on a boulder, and the two of them—the turtle and the watch—slid into the clear, cool water of Tannery Pond.

"I can buy ten new watches!" Dagmar said. "I'm rich. Or have you forgotten that fact?"

Honestly, I had. But I thought I had better hold off on making another confession.

"I can get another Rolex, but there's no telling if I'll ever find another sister. And one of you is about all I can handle. Two like you would cause me to go deaf."

I was learning how to translate Dagmar's verbal garbage and I was beginning to feel as precious as one of Dagmar's swans—and just as wet. I stretched out on the grassy bank and let the hot sun dry me off. Jafford pulled off his T-shirt then stretched out next to me.

"Besides," Dagmar continued. "I could use a maid of honor for my wedding."

"Wedding?" Jafford and I repeated at the same time, sitting straight up.

"Who are you marrying?" I asked.

I knew that Duncan was long gone. The rumor was that he and Bertha had run off to an island somewhere in the South Pacific, where the two of them put on hula dancing shows at the airport for the burgeoning Japanese tourist crowd. That left Dagmar single and living all alone at Swan Crest, isolated in a neighborhood that seemed populated by couples and a slew of children—or apparently *not*. While I had only been her sister for less than an hour, I wasn't privy to her dating patterns. Neither was Jafford.

"Couldn't be Peepers," Jafford said. "He's too short. That leaves your horse, although I heard he was confiscated along with the rest of your larger animals after your little safari went off-track. So give it up, Dagmar. Who's the lucky fellow? And has his arm recovered after you twisted it until he said 'yes?'"

I watched as the man I loved took off in a flash. His muscular legs were charging up the Far Hill, running through the tiered gardens near the remains of the old cottage. He darted through a hundred rows of iris that lined the way to the top.

Dagmar was close behind him.

I was tuckered out just watching the two of them loop around the purple flowers. I guess they were tuckered out, too, because they both rolled down the smooth side of the hill, and then took a flying leap back into the pond—one after the other.

Maybe Dagmar was right. It was fun being rich. I had never minded being poor before. But I had to admit that gazing at a private pond, while lingering under a towering willow tree and petting Cuban Pete who'd followed us over to Swan Crest Farms, was quite a treat. And I liked wearing spiffy new clothes, despite that they were now wet and grass-stained. I realized then that I never really knew the pleasures of having so much leisure—or laughing so freely with people I loved. I made a mental note to fine-tune my natural honk as Jafford and Dagmar had a splashing contest going on. A pair of butterflies fluttered overhead, while humming birds drew nectar from honeysuckles by the edge of the pond. I wiggled my toes, and the world never seemed quite as luxuriously relaxing before.

I just wished I could figure out what kind of man would marry … That is, would any guy be strong enough to handle … Who could possibly be a match for … I mean, was it possible that there was a man alive who was worthy of marrying my sister?

Someone needed to love Dagmar the way Jafford loved me.

Chapter 30

The Gang

The sound of the ancient gong echoed in the Bamboo Garden as Laughing Sun took his place at the podium. If the groom beside him was nervous, it never showed. But I couldn't help wondering if he was truly comfortable wearing a tux. Wedding jitters always hit at the last minute. They're natural and to be expected. Only Vanilla John would be stoic.

"My man's a hunk!" Dagmar said as the two of us peered through the wooden lace of the gazebo atop the Far Hill. "I hooked a big one this time," she said with more joy in her voice than I had ever heard before. "Six-three suits me fine. Finally, I got it right!"

I couldn't disagree. Jafford looked sharp in his tux, too. He said it was an honor to serve as Vanilla John's best man. But it was Dagmar who was glowing—only she didn't know it. I swear, that woman had no self-awareness. She never bothered with mirrors and had no idea that she actually possessed natural, rosy-cheeked good looks. With her fondness for the outdoors, she could have just as easily been wearing a T-shirt with jeans and mud boots, as she could an Austin Scarlet original bridal gown and veil. While she might've appeared vain that day on her horse when demanding that Jafford give up his spiffy black hat, well, I'm telling you, it was all just an act. Dagmar, despite all her lottery money, couldn't care less about the latest fashion trends. But she does care deeply for her animals just as she does her friends—and her sister.

What would be more fitting for Jafford and me to give the happy couple as a wedding gift, but a lifetime supply of bubble gum and pair of his-and-her sterling silver spittoons?

"What's the matter with you," Dagmar teased Jafford. "You couldn't shell out for gold?"

That's my sister. That's Dagmar. Someone needs to love her. She's one no-nonsense kind of woman, never afraid of speaking her mind. I think she'll tease Jafford about his spending habits for a long, long time. All he has to say to get her to shut up is, "I really love my new Bug, Dagmar. Drive it all the time!"

Dagmar bought him a nice, but very used and dented Volkswagen Beetle to replace the one that had been demolished in the Lincoln Tunnel. But officially, she had Vanilla John present it to Jafford. It was a best man gift. But Dagmar didn't stop there. She bought me a present, too: my very own waxing salon in town. She even named it, "Valentina's." She never again wants me to run away to New York—and needs a handy place to assure her brows are always trimmed and well shaped, and her arms stay smooth.

"I get a present?" I asked. "An entire salon? Of my very own? But you're the one who's getting married!"

"It's a bridal present, stupid," Dagmar said. "Great! I finally get a sister and she's dumb as dirt. I'll have to teach you *everything*. A bride always gives a gift to her maid of honor."

"*Matron* of honor," I corrected. She knew full well that Jafford and I had eloped. We didn't want a lot of hoopla or to have the media find out that *The Jaff* was finally getting hitched, so we quietly flew down to his home state of North Carolina where his family's from. And now mine, too!

Dagmar may have easily afforded to travel anytime and anywhere she wanted. She could even stay at the finest hotels around the world. But Dagmar would quickly get homesick for mucking out the horses' stalls or sitting on the dock, content to sip cheap white wine on the rocks and name all the swans as they blissfully glide by in Tannery Pond. With Vanilla John by her side and his two sons whom she adopted, she has everything she's ever wanted—and more. Sure, she's loaded. But it would never be enough had she not found true love.

"Swan Crest's our forever home," she said. "Why travel? We have what we need *here*."

But the truth really was that Dagmar wasn't allowed to travel. Long before she and I declared ourselves to be sisters, after spending sixty days in jail and assigned to community service for the next ten years, Dagmar actually had no choice but to stay home. Besides, it was the same time that she and Vanilla John were falling in love. He had started bringing her cans of *fiske bola*, or Dagmar would've starved to death in her cell.

"I'd rather eat from Swan Crest's hog trough," she had told the guard after being served the standard jail fare. "Remove this slop at once or I'll vomit in your face. Do you really want to be sued for making me sick? I refuse to eat anything else, but *fiske bola* for the remainder of my stay."

You have to admire Dagmar's fiery spirit. It's her imperfections that make her perfect, at least she seems that way to me. As her sister, I'm loyal. That's the way *family* ought to be.

Vanilla John had volunteered to take care of the animals while Dagmar was behind bars. Then he'd leave for the jailhouse on his scooter to keep Dagmar posted on the goings-on. He visited her every single night, and the two of them would dine together on their favorite meal. As the former fire chief of Burberry Hills, he had special privileges. I think that fact alone impressed Dagmar. She always bragged about how her man had been granted access that *ordinary* people would be denied, but I think the truth was that Vanilla John was about the only one in town who—I have to be honest—could stand all of Dagmar's animal chatter. But that—along with a fondness for *fiske bola*—was what the two of them had in common.

Oh yeah, that dumb duck, Peepers, pulled through. He's back to his old habits again. Only now he leaves me alone. I once saw him hopping out of his private little pool behind Tannery Falls. One look at me and he hopped back in again. Not even a quack. Maybe Cuban Pete gave him the snake eyes as he and I passed by. Ever since the fire burned down the cottage, my cat follows me around wherever I go. I guess he wants to make sure I don't high tail it back to the city without him again—or be locked up in a furnace room alone.

Dagmar had her fill of losing her freedom. She did try hard to get out of going to jail or at least have her sentence reduced. She might've hired the smartest attorneys money could buy, but she still paid dearly for her mistakes, ones that were not accidents, but faults. Dagmar *was* wrong. But she's since learned her lesson. She had caused quite a raucous riding her horse through bumper-to-bumper traffic on Route 80 East and the New Jersey Turnpike. But she was on a mission, she had said. She was bound and determined to chase her former *Jou Jou* all the way to the Mason Figg Fine Arts Gallery. She told the cops and the reporters that she knew where he lived. She had been the one who had discovered him, she had claimed. He had been a lowly artist who'd probably never amount to much had it not been for her. She blurted all that out as they stopped her wild ride before she could enter the Lincoln Tunnel. As they dragged her away in handcuffs and confiscated her horse, she was bemoaning how she had helped Mason with his sagging art career, but that after he'd incited a stampede and let out all her animals, she was going to finish him off.

"I'll tear him apart," she kept screaming to the cameras. "You can hide, Mason Figg! But I'll get you, you *Jou Jou*! I'll find you if it's the last thing I do!"

Officially, Dagmar's crimes were listed as "Reckless Driving," "Operating an Unregistered Vehicle" and "Endangering an Animal." It was that last count that really got to her, for if there's one crime that Dagmar regretted most, *that* was it. She even established a foundation for a Horse Rescue Society. It's her third charitable endeavor, the first one being a rescue mission for Mute Swans. The other is *The Laughing Sun Center for Right Living*.

"We never actually said that Laughing Sun was the Dalai Lama," Jafford told her when she learned the truth. "I'm sorry if we led you astray. That entire day was quite a mix-up. And you still owe me a game of tennis. That is, if you have the balls."

Between Laughing Sun's glowing smile and Jafford's sincere gesture of friendship, Dagmar conceded that she had been the one who goofed up. Knowing her now—as well as the way she used to be—I'm quite certain that taking part in the blame showed more guts than any other act of bravado she'd demonstrated in the past. I admire her for lowering her shield. I like her true self. Laughing Sun told her she has a kind heart.

Upon hearing that declaration from someone she perceived was an authentic spiritual leader, Dagmar made an offer to Laughing Sun that he just couldn't refuse. He hung up his Guacamole Man sombrero and Mexican blanket and moved to Swan Crest, where Dagmar had her architects design and build a tea garden and monastery for his monks. And now each morning at the crack of dawn, as I warm up milk bottles on one of Willow Run's stoves for the goats and head over to Dagmar and Vanilla John's place to search the hen houses for freshly laid eggs, I smile and bow at the sound of the gong. I think The CEO is used to the routine now —and to me, too.

Jafford said that Dagmar only had Laughing Sun and his monks move into a monastery at Swan Crest in an attempt to establish a new tax write-off. But he's always cracking jokes like that. He has a way of making me laugh. I told him that I thought Dagmar wanted to examine her soul, but Jafford said he wasn't sure if she really had one. The way she played tennis, he told me, she needed prayers.

And that's when I gave his long, braided ponytail, the one that lands him on the pages of the "Top Ten Trendsetters" in *Celebrity Faces* magazine every single year, a playful little tug.

But that's all I'm saying. I'm done with opening up the door. What's private should stay private. Jafford's life is public enough. He says he only lets people he trusts get close to him. I guess I knew then that he really did like Dagmar. I know he's nuts for Vanilla John and his—*their*—sons. The bunch of us, I'm sure, will always be neighbors and friends. Maybe that's why Jafford offered to fly them all on his new private jet for a honeymoon.

"I told you," Dagmar said and Vanilla John nodded. "We have no need to go anywhere. Why should we? We're happy right here. We have our routine. Every Sunday night we have *fiske bola*. Come on over and join us!"

It's nice to talk in terms of a "us," although Jafford and I seem to always have something planned for Sunday evenings. We may be married now, but some things about Jafford I still wonder about, like when we were leaving Dagmar and Vanilla John's reception at Swan

Crest. I asked him why he never bought a private jet sooner. I mean, I'd think it'd be more convenient and maybe cheaper in the long run. For all I knew, it'd be a tax write-off. So I asked him why he always used to fly in commercial airlines to his tennis tournaments. It couldn't just have been for the Podcasts. But Jafford shrugged.

"I used to be lonely, I guess."

Not anymore.

As Jafford and I were leaving for another tournament, right after Dagmar and Vanilla John's wedding, Hector was ready to drive us to the private airport where the new plane was awaiting our departure, waiting for us with a brand new Jeep. After the calamity in the Lincoln Tunnel, Jafford wanted to pull out of his Bentley endorsement and opted for a new sponsor.

Arnold slipped us a video that his crew had shot. It was just a rough cut, he told us, but he knew we'd enjoy previewing it on our long trip to Spain. He said that I could phone in my next performance and didn't have to worry about rushing to his new movie set location. With a promise to Dagmar that we'd bring her back a crate of blood oranges, we were off.

"It was a perfect day," I said to Jafford as we clicked our seatbelts for takeoff. "Dagmar never seemed happier. And Vanilla John actually spoke more than a few words at a time."

"You just have to hit the right subjects with him," Jafford said. "Mention ducks, and his eyes light up."

"It was nice to see Peepers in one piece."

"See what I mean?" Jafford said. "Who else could've persuaded a duck to be ring bearer? Only Vanilla John."

"And Dagmar!"

"I've got to see that again. Amazing!" Jafford said. "Hector, will you …"

"All ready, Mr. Jafford!" Hector said. "You tell when I should hit *play* button!"

And so the three of us sat back to watch the wedding video as the pilot took off. Arnold had opened with a wide shot of Swan Crest, then panned over to the swans dancing along the edge of Tannery Falls, then cut to sweeping views of the Great Lawn, past the tiered gardens, the Goat House, and Chicken Coops, up the cobblestone walkway that leads clear over to the Far Hill, then zoomed up to the Monkey House and the Bamboo Garden as the last of the wedding guests were escorted to their seats.

"Where's me?" Jafford said. But I shushed him.

After Laughing Sun took his place at the podium and Jafford was, at last, on screen, a close-up of Vanilla John revealed that he had actually cracked a faint grin. Mustache or not, stoic as he might have been, there was no denying it. Vanilla John was beaming.

"He must be looking at Peepers," Jafford said. But I shushed him again.

As a trio of harpists was strumming "Here Comes the Bride" and Peepers was waddling down the long, white carpet, I could hardly remember how he used to scare me. He looked so charming now in his little duck's tux, while tugging a little pillow behind him that held the wedding rings.

But then just as Dagmar and I made our entrance from out of the gazebo, and the cameras panned back for a wide-shot, Jafford and I couldn't help but notice that one of the monks standing solemnly in a line behind the wedding party looked familiar, the one who was banging the gong. Just like the other monks, he was dressed in a long, flowing crimson gown and his head had been shaved clean. But something about him seemed slightly different. It was the way his body was moving as he hit that gong with such aplomb and smooth, flowing strikes; he seemed to be—dare I say it? Could he be dancing beneath his long, flowing gown?

As Laughing Sun welcomed the wedding guests and the monks arose from their bow, the one by the gong looked directly at the camera. Then, with two luscious eyes popping out, he seemed to be moving while the other monks kept still and remained silent.

It was then that I finally understood the value of insurance. I hoped the policy Jafford had for his plane covered shattered margarita glasses. It was an accident; I didn't mean to cause them to break. I just couldn't help myself. Some sounds are just spontaneous and organic:

"Maaaa-soooon!"

Epilogue

The Kids

A yellow tennis ball was sailing through the blue sky. It was heading directly for my face. I didn't know what it was exactly, at least not at first. My eyes were too teary.

"Just saved us about twenty grand," Jafford said. "Plastic surgeons don't work cheap."

I liked being married to a professional athlete who could protect me from a wayward tennis ball, grabbing it in mid-air. I liked being married to Jafford. After five years of marriage, we seemed to have blended together well. Sometimes I thought we were two people who'd fused into one. Only our hairstyles had changed. While Jafford had his long braids cut off and he sported a crew cut, I let my short, blond locks grow out past my shoulders and revert to my natural, brown color. But no matter how short, long, dark, or light our hair was, we were starting to feel that something was missing from our lives.

Jafford was tossing the captured ball with one hand as he scanned the people at the party. Children were everywhere. So were prospective parents. Dagmar had rounded them up, promising that she'd hire only the finest chefs to cater the special adoption event she was hosting in the rose garden on top of the Far Hill.

"It'll be *the* social event of the year," she had claimed.

All the guests needed to do was take in a foster child or adopt one permanently. Or they could take in two or three—even *more* if they qualified. Adoption laws were very specific and strict, Dagmar had said. But while she strong-armed everyone in Burberry Hills to attend her party, she also knew how to sell them on the benefits of having children without conception. Leave it to Dagmar to be persuasive. She even got Vanilla John to grin once in awhile. She merely appealed to their natural instincts.

"Just think of it as shopping," Dagmar said. "Pick out the best ones!"

"Sort of like going to Macy's?" Jafford asked. "Where's the sale rack?"

"Not a chance, Mr. Big Shot," Dagmar said. "I've already selected yours. Strictly top shelf."

The party began so awkward for the children and the guests. It really did seem like we were at Macy's, where everyone was trying to find the right fit. We were all dressed up and smiling as the grown-ups sized up the kids, and the kids were busy playing as if they were in a live orphan display. I knew Jafford would never agree to take them all home, so I parked myself on a bench by my favorite coral-colored roses, unsure of how to choose. I was happy—and confused—and worried. Would any of them like me? Would we ever mesh? Would a child want to stay with Jafford and me forever? Or beg to move onto someone else's home?

"Try hitting this one back to me, Mr. Tennis Boy!"

A little girl with a freckled face and a pom-pom bun on her head was shouting at the top of her lungs. She sounded too familiar. I knew immediately that she not only had been personally selected by Dagmar, but also expertly coached. She was throwing a yellow tennis ball in the air. She smacked it with a tennis racket. It sailed beyond the Far Hill. A little boy with a *Dennis the Menace* cowlick who was holding a racket small enough for a gopher, chased after it, and he dissolved over the horizon.

"Not sure she's ready for Wimbledon," Jafford said, "but the Yankees may want her."

The other grown-ups were cringing at the little girl's shrill voice and bold commands, but I was lighting up. That little girl needed a mother to give her love. I was brimming with it. Jafford couldn't help but notice. Dagmar did, too.

"What's the matter with you?" the little girl shouted, cupping her hand to her mouth. Her voice was echoing across the Great Lawn loud enough to cause ice cubes to tremble in the punch bowl. "Hit it back to me! Are you blind or just stupid?"

But the little boy was no longer in sight.

Jafford sat down with me on the bench, holding my hand, drying my tears, and looping his arm around me. We watched as Dagmar and the little girl were huddling together, taking turns whispering in each other's ears. Before we could blink, the little girl was sprinting toward us on the bench.

"Hi, my name is Patty," she said. "Will you play tennis with me?"

Jafford was grinning. He exploded with his popcorn laugh. But I was holding back more tears. I wanted to cry out loud. Instead, I blew my nose.

"What's wrong with *her*?" Patty said.

"She's happy," Jafford told her.

"Then why is she crying?"

"That's what happens when you're really, *really* happy."

"Oh," Patty said. "I'd hate to think what she'd do if she were really, *really* sad."

"She was a foster child, too, when she was your age," Jafford explained. "That's why she—you can call her Valentina—wants you to come home with us. Would you like that?"

"You didn't tell me *your* name!"

"It's Jafford."

"That's a funny name," she said. "Maybe that's why you have a funny laugh."

Jafford was unleashed. He was howling. I wasn't sure when he was going to stop.

"Don't worry," I said to Patty, finally able to speak. "You'll get used to Jafford's laugh—and mine, too. You'll probably be laughing along with us in no time at all. That is, if you want to live at our house. Would you like that?

Patty was nodding her head *yes*. I could see Dagmar spying on all of us through the coral roses as I leaned down and explained to Patty how Jafford and I wanted her to stay with us as a foster child. If she liked us, then she could stay on. If not ...

"Don't say, *'If not,'*" Dagmar piped up. "It's all arranged. I've taken care of everything. It's a done deal. Patty's already packed up with her duffle bag. I even slipped some goodies in there for her. She's ready to move in. Now! Today! I picked her out myself!"

"No way," Patty told us. She was shaking her head and holding her hands on her hips. Then she was swaying all around in a way that made it abundantly clear that she was the one calling the shots. "If you take me, you have to take my little brother, too," she said. "We're a packaged deal."

Jafford looked at me, but I was still tearing up. I was nodding my head *yes* as the young boy with the sawed-off tennis racket was scampering back over the Far Hill, knocking a yellow ball around as if he were playing croquet. He shouldn't be left all alone. He, too, needed what every child of any age deserves: he needed to be loved.

"Hey, kid! Wanna play tennis?" Jafford asked him, but the little fellow kept on chasing the ball. "Wanna come over to our house and … You can come live with …" Jafford was actually stumbling for words.

"His name is Joe," Patty said, still stern. "You've got to call him by his name."

"Joe," Jafford began again and squatted to the ground. "Wanna play tennis?"

"Yeah!" Joe said. "Tennis!"

Jafford reached out to collect the stray ball that was rolling on the ground. Then he looked back to me. I was still nodding *yes*.

"Works for me," Jafford said. "Wrap him up. We'll take Joe, too."

Jafford hoisted Joe up on his shoulder while Patty stood with her hands on her hips.

"Lift me up," she demanded. Compared to Jafford, she was as small as a squirrel posed to climb a tree. "I want a ride on your shoulder!"

"We'll take turns," I said as the four of us were headed for the registration table.

"But he has *two* shoulders," Patty reasoned. "One for me and one for Joe. Fair's fair!"

"You can hold my hand," I said. "When one of you is riding on Jafford's shoulder, the other can hold my hand. That's fair. That'll be our rule."

And just like that, with one single hand-holding, shoulder-riding, *fair's fair* rule, I entered motherhood. Jafford became a father. Finally,

Dancing with Jou Jou

we were complete. Together with Patty and Joe, the four of us had found our forever home. Whether we had conceived or adopted them, the *truth* about kids is the same: you never know who you're going to get or even how many. Just when we thought we were set, we found one more.

She was in the rhododendrons, hiding from Peepers who was fluttering his wings and quacking. After Cuban Pete chased the dumb duck away, I could see two big brown eyes peering through the leaves. I parted the branches. Her tiny, pouting face suddenly brightened. She smiled and cooed. Then she held out her chubby arms and crawled toward me. I scooped her up and held her close, picking out leaves that had clung to her soft black curls. Jafford, Patty, and Joe were right beside me.

"Oh, no! Not her!" Patty cried, holding her hands on her hips and stomping her foot. "Just remember, *I* was number one and *Joe* was number two. That makes *Velveeta* number …"

"Velveeta?" I questioned. "Is that really her name?"

"Could've been worse," Jafford said. "She could've been called Limburger, Gouda, or Blue."

"Her name really is Velveeta. I'm not lying," Patty said. "She doesn't talk much yet, but she's still a little brat. So don't forget. *She's* number …"

"No numbers," I said firmly. "You each have a name."

Patty looked stunned. I didn't think she was expecting me to be so commanding.

"Then how will you know that *I* came first? And *she* came last?"

"It doesn't matter," I said. "You each have equal standing."

"Huh?"

"Let's just say that you're the oldest, Velveeta is the youngest, and Joe's in the middle."

"I like numbers better," Patty muttered as she kneeled down to pet Cuban Pete from his head to his tail, and our cat rolled over on his back, purring.

Three hours later when we were crossing River Bend Road, we heard Dagmar calling to us from the Far Hill as Peepers was quacking.

"Oh sure," she hollered. "Don't say *thank you* or anything. Just leave without saying good-bye."

"I'll be up to feed the goats in the morning, Dagmar," I said over my shoulder.

"How about those eggs, missy," she hollered back. "Give 'em a waxing salon, a husband, and the best *top shelf* children there are, and they think they rule the world. Ungrateful sister …"

Hector was rolling the garbage down the driveway. Patty and Joe hopped on the trolley for a ride as I held Velveeta on my hip. Jafford wrapped his arm around my shoulder and we watched the two older kids play. Swan Crest was in the distance. Willow Run was our home. But I knew we never needed a giant house. We only needed each other.

"Hey, Dagmar!" I shouted.

But my sister-for-life had already disappeared over the Far Hill. Peepers trailed behind, still quacking.

"Thanks!" I said.

Patty was now riding on Jafford's shoulder. Joe was holding my hand and Velveeta was holding his. We were walking to the threshold of our forever home when *truth* was reminding me what every orphan knows. It's not the gene pool that matters. It's not even the size of your tennis racket. The only thing that counts is sitting around the kitchen table for a shared meal. There's nothing that beats one of Hector's homemade taco dinners to fill up the empty spaces.

Yes, I have a healthy appetite now. And I have love—the kind that's mutual, unconditional, and shared with other people who grace our lives—the sort of bond that grows stronger over the years as it's passed through the generations—during this lifetime and the next.